MW01124015

The Militant Genome

Braxton DeGarmo

Christen Haus Publishing

COPYRIGHT

"The Militant Genome" – Copyright © 2012 by Braxton DeGarmo. All rights reserved under International and Pan-American Copyright Conventions. By payment of the required fees, you have been granted the non-exclusive, non-transferable right to access and read the text of this e-book on-screen. No part of this text may be reproduced, transmitted, down-loaded, decompiled, reverse engineered, or stored in or introduced into any information and retrieval system, in any form or by any means, whether electronic or mechanical, now known or hereinafter invented, without the express written permission of Braxton DeGarmo.

E-Book Edition Publication Date: July, 2012
Paperback Edition Publication Date: November, 2012

ISBN-13: 978-1481027991
ISBN-10: 1481027999

This is a work of fiction. The characters, incidents, and dialogues are products of the author's imagination and are not construed to be real. Any resemblance to actual events or persons, living or dead, is entirely coincidental.

Cover design by BookBaby

For more information:
www.amazon.com/-/e/B009H9T6E6

DEDICATION

For my mother, Barbara, whose longsuffering faith in my abilities kept encouraging me to write, and to my wife, Paula, who provided valuable feedback and proofreading.

TABLE OF CONTENTS

ACKNOWLEDGMENTS

First and foremost, I again want to acknowledge and thank my endearing wife, Paula, for putting up with my pursuit of writing, for graciously giving up time that we might have spent together, and for her proofreading skills. Without her help, this novel might never have seen "print" – e-ink or otherwise. (Note: any typos or errors are mine, made after she proofread the manuscript.)

I'd also like to thank Chief Thomas O'Connor, Police Chief of Maryland Heights, Missouri, for his valuable assistance in nailing down local police procedure and for the inspiration that led to Sergeant Seamus O'Connor. Likewise, I'm indebted to Sergeant Devaney of the St. Louis Airport Police Department for his help in detailing the organization of the department as well as airport emergency procedures.

I'd also like to thank three tireless readers, Lora, Kathy, and Patti – you know who you are – for their valuable feedback on my manuscript. Lora, in particular, put up with trying to read this chapter-by-chapter, as I wrote it, not an easy task. I promise never to inflict that pain on a reader again. Also, the three nurses in the E.D. – Kathy, Sandy, and Stephanie – are based on three friends of the same names. They're just as faithful to provide comic relief in our real-life E.D. as I hoped they offered in the story. Long live the float trip queens.

Finally, many thanks to my editor, Patrick LoBrutto. Pat, thanks for the encouragement, the guidance, and your valuable suggestions to hone this book into being ready for publishing.

CHAPTER 1

"Doctor Wade, a gang dispute in East St. Louis has spilled across the river into downtown St. Louis. We've got several victims moving into the trauma bays. This guy's been triaged to the top of the list."

Sarah Wade, M.D. had a reputation in the E.D. for her cool and collected manner. She gazed at the twenty-something black male lying on his right side on the table, a knife embedded in his left chest, and took a deep breath, thinking through the ABC's of advanced trauma life support: airway, breathing, and circulation.

"The scene wasn't totally secured by police but the paramedics managed to scoop and run with this guy. Didn't have time to deal with his airway or get I.V. access before hitting our doorstep."

"Vital signs?" she asked.

"Pulse, 144. Respirations, thirty, short and shallow. Blood pressure, eighty systolic."

"Get two large-bore lines started, normal saline …" She paused, remembering the Trauma Service's penchant for lactated Ringer's solution. "… make that LR and get blood for a CBC, chemistry panel, coags, and type and cross … six units of packed red cells to start."

She surveyed the man, who showed no signs of movement. Even his chest wall appeared not to change with breathing. She would check him more thoroughly after completing the ABCs, but she predicted a Glasgow Coma scale of between 3 and 5. Not good.

"Get me a 7 and a half ET tube, check the cuff, and give me the fiber-optic scope. Get respiratory in here with a ventilator."

Sarah's friends assured her that next year's Chief Resident's slot was hers for the taking. And she wanted it. But right now, she had this ATLS certification to pass and her self-assurance ebbed as she nodded to the man sitting before her, his arms crossed, eyes glaring at her. Her heart rate accelerated and her gut grumbled. She knew him by more than reputation.

Doctor Robert Rickelmann.   Internationally renowned trauma surgeon. "Roarin' Robert." The surgeon's surgeon to whom residents-in-training were lesser mortals. As a first-year resident, she had experienced his trial-by-fire methods of "teaching," the scorched scrubs and third degree burns he left behind on surgical rounds.

Doctor Rickelmann tapped his pen on the table, a look of impatience etched upon his face, and then waved his hand dismissively toward the bed. "Go ahead. Examine your patient. As you move from one system to the next I'll provide basic details. You need to ask questions for information you don't get from me."

She continued, "While they're getting venous access, I'll prepare to intubate and check his cardiovascular status. His airway is …?"

"Light pink froth is noted in his mouth."

As if on cue, crimson-tinged bubbles emerged from between the man's lips. *This guy's good*, she thought, continuing in clinical mode as if she was in the E.D. She pulled back the sheet, grazing the man's cold forearm with her fingers. The *moulage*, makeup and props used to simulate physical injury, appeared more realistic than any she had seen before. A large plastic knife protruded from his chest several centimeters to the left of the sternum. She directed her "exam" to his lungs, but stopped as a droplet of "blood" escaped the wound. *Can they make moulage do that?*

"Lungs?"

"Absent on the left, coarse sounds on the right," replied Rickelmann.

"I'll yell for a STAT portable chest X-ray and proceed to intubate him."

As if urged by an inner sense, she placed the diaphragm of the stethoscope to the man's chest and listened.

"You see the knife … what's the main thing you're <u>not</u> going to do, doctor?"

The question and its answer, you don't pull the knife until you're ready to control the consequences, preferably in the O.R., registered at the edge of her consciousness. What captured her attention was the man's <u>lack</u> of breath sounds. Sarah listened intently. How long could he hold his breath?

"Doctor? Your patient's going down the tubes while you hesitate. What do you do next, and what do you make sure you <u>do not</u> do?"

Sarah reached to the man's neck and tried to locate a carotid pulse. His skin here was also cool, with subtle mottling. Where was his pulse? Her hands rushed to the man's face, pulling back the upper eyelids so she could take a quick look at his pupils. He didn't flinch.

Roarin' Robert was on his feet, his face reddened.

"Doctor Wade, this is a trauma scenario, not some damned ophthalmology quiz! What the hell are you doing?"

Sarah looked up at him, her usual assertiveness regaining control, the gastric butterfly gone. "No, Doctor Rickelmann, this is a real stabbing victim. Look, he's not —"

"Nonsense. We were talking just an hour ago, before the lunch break. He was on call and worked all night. I told him he could sleep. Steven, wake up." He took two quick strides toward the body, reached for the prop, but stopped short. "He —"

Sarah saw a brief look of puzzlement on the surgeon's face, and did what no resident dared to do with Doctor Rickelmann; she interrupted. "Don't Doctor Rickelmann! We need to call 911 and get him to the E.D."

Sarah couldn't believe the surgeon's response. Did he think so little of her training that he ignored the obvious? All of his shouting would have awakened the dead much less any sleeper. This young man remained moribund.

He looked at her and frowned, shaking his head. "Crap, you work in the emergency department and can't tell a fake wound from the real thing? Watch!" He grabbed the knife and pulled just before her hand caught his arm in an attempt to stop him. Startled by the sucking noise of air rushing into the chest, his face registered an apparition of shock when something more than a fake knife handle and plastic wound peeled away from the body. As blood covered his bare hand, he stood speechless and dropped both the stage prop and the disposable scalpel hidden within.

CHAPTER 2

Sarah sat in the lobby of the Eric P. Newman Education Center, jean-clad knees pressed together, nestling a cup of coffee between her hands. Her eyes roamed from the escalator to the second floor, to the security guard at the revolving door, to the woman at the reception desk and back again. The large glass windows of the two-story atrium reminded Sarah of the lateness of the day as the main hospital towers now cast their shadows into the lobby. What was taking so long? She was there, made the 911 call. Shouldn't they have interviewed her first?

Her coffee was cold now, but sipping it had been one of the distracted actions she performed while waiting for her interview by the detectives. As in the E.D., she tried to compartmentalize her emotions and focus her mind on the victim and his family. Walter Johnson, from somewhere around Chicago. Was he, like her, the first in his family to go to college, much less make it into postgraduate studies? Was Walter the product of middle class suburbia, or had he grown up on the streets, avoided the gang influence, survived the drive-bys and the all-too-common black-on-black violence, only to be murdered while playacting as a trauma victim?

Once again, she put her lips to the cup, but stopped. Hot coffee or iced coffee, one or the other, but not room temperature. Even hot, this coffee was mediocre; now, the slop was awful.

She sighed and stretched her back, then stood and walked over to the security guard. "Any idea how much longer?" she asked.

His eyebrows arched up as he shook his head. "Sorry. Not a clue."

Sarah sighed and acknowledged a disquieted feeling inside. She had first thought it her usual impatience, tired of waiting on the police. This event was different, unsettling, too close to home. She struggled to place her feelings into the box where she wanted them to hide.

She walked over to the reception desk, poured a fresh cup of coffee, and headed back to her seat. Before she could sit down, she heard the rustle of movement from above.

Doctor Rickelmann, looking none too happy, hustled down the moving escalator at a pace that belied his annoyance. Sarah stepped toward him as he neared.

"Doctor Rickelmann, do you —"

The surgeon slowed his stride and glared at her. "Quiet. We're not supposed to discuss this. Don't make it worse." He resumed his speed and brushed past her.

"I was just going ..." He was nearly ten feet away now. She sighed and started back toward her seat.

Doctor Rickelmann continued to live up to his reputation. Earlier, he hadn't even known the student's name. The great Rickelmann had walked into the room, gathered his papers, and called her in for the test scenario without even talking with his "patient." Now, he blew her off, too.

She could only imagine what went through his mind as the scalpel emerged and blood covered his hand. Walter might never have made it to, or out of, the operating room. Maybe he was dead already. But by pulling the blade, the eminent Doctor Rickelmann had ensured the man's ticket to the morgue. He knew it, and he knew she knew it.

Rickelmann stopped abruptly and turned toward her, his face displaying anger. "What the hell did you say to the paramedics?" he asked.

Baffled, Sarah jerked back as if slapped. "What?"

The surgeon shook his head and waved her off with his hand. "Nevermind." With that, he turned and rushed out through the building's front doors.

Sarah shook her head. *What was that about?* she wondered. Before she could conjure up an explanation, she heard her name spoken above. She turned and saw one of the uniformed officers pointing toward her. *About time.* A moment later, a red-haired man started down the escalator.

She assumed him a homicide detective, but that role was less than obvious. A modest suit, expertly pressed, paired with running shoes. *Who dressed him?* she thought. He had the hint of a limp as he walked down the moving steps. She wondered why. With his short-cropped red hair, fair but freckled complexion, and trim figure, he looked no older than his mid-twenties. And baby-faced? His youth confounded her. How could he have worked his way into the ranks of homicide without at least a dozen years of experience? She scanned him head to toe and nothing screamed police detective. After three years in the trauma center and having worked dozens of fatal cases, she thought she knew every homicide detective in St. Louis.

Seamus O'Connor appreciated the escalator ride to the first floor. Fatigue claimed him. His left thigh ached, and he had been up and down between the floors of the building at least two dozen times in the past three hours. As he slid down to the main lobby, he scrutinized the young woman waiting near the bottom. She was about his height, maybe an inch shorter than his five-foot, ten-inch frame, but her skin commanded his interest. The patrolmen had described her as African-American, but her delicate features, flawless complexion, and light butternut coloring belied a racial mix that could confuse any census taker. She appeared slim and toned, and knowing the hours the emergency residents put in, he knew that either her parents had passed on "thin" genes or she worked rigorously to keep herself that way.

As he neared the bottom of the moving stairway, she approached. Once on solid ground, he extended his hand.

"Doctor Wade?" She nodded. "I'm Sergeant O'Connor, with the Homicide Division. Thanks for waiting around."

"Like I had much choice. Look, I ..." She stopped and examined him. "Let's just say this ATLS course has been stressful enough ... but to have something like this, I ... Obviously it's not been a great day and I'd really like to get home."

Her brusque manner did not deter Seamus. "Doctor, let's not forget that you are, in fact, getting to go home. Someone else wasn't so fortunate."

As Sarah glanced at her feet, Seamus thought he sensed a

slight tremble in her body. Seamus had already interviewed a dozen other participants in the trauma course, several who were openly belligerent, and knew it had been a stressful day for all, but he couldn't let that distort her perspective on what had happened. A young man was dead. Her reaction seemed to reflect that this fact was not lost on her.

He managed a half smile. "Let's find someplace to sit and talk and maybe we both can get out of here a bit sooner."

He pointed back to the escalator and a minute later, he ushered her into a small office off the second floor promenade. As he sat down, he rubbed his left thigh with his hand, while pointing to her coffee with his right. "Need a refill? My treat."

Sarah shook her head.

"Okay." He took out a small notebook from his jacket pocket. "I'm also going to record this conversation. Hope you don't mind."

She shook her head. "No choice there either, right?"

The doctor's attitude he could understand. She'd been kept waiting for hours. But her body language puzzled Seamus. So defensive. Legs crossed, sitting stiff and upright, her face tense, her hands clutching the coffee cup. Why? Even though she showed resistance, he believed compliance would arise out of her sense of duty if nothing else. But if there was compassion for the victim and his family, she seemed to be struggling with it. Again, why?

He produced a small recorder and held it up to her before inserting a new tape in the machine. "Yeah, um, right." He placed it on the table between them. "Makes my job so much easier." He pushed a button, sat back relaxed in his chair, and started. "This is Sergeant Seamus O'Connor interviewing Doctor Sarah Wade at 1638 hours on the twenty-first of May regarding the apparent homicide of Walter Johnson at the Newman Education Center on the Barnes-Jewish Hospital campus. Doctor Wade discovered the body."

Sarah raised her hand to shoulder level. "Umm, I didn't discover the body ... just the first one in the room observant enough to discover what had happened."

He smiled inwardly as he nodded. He'd already interviewed the pompous Doctor Rickelmann. Nothing more needed saying. "So noted. Okay, Doctor Wade, let's start earlier in the day. Begin at, say, eleven a.m. and tell me what you did until the time you discovered the crime."

She sipped her coffee before starting. "Okay. So you've already interviewed a bunch of people. Do you need a minute-by-minute replay from me, too?"

Seamus tensed, but tried consciously not to show it. He needed her to relax and open up, not get uptight because he added to the strain. What he didn't need was some ball buster interviewee. He couldn't predict which she'd be.

"Well, I know that the course is all about teaching a consistent approach to injured people. I got the general schedule. What I need to know is what you did from eleven a.m. on."

"Right. As usual, things ran late, so at eleven, we were still in a question and answer session. Our written test started twenty minutes later. I finished that, met a friend for lunch about twelve-fifteen at a small place on north Euclid, rushed through eating and made it back here about five 'til one for my first test scenario. Doctor Rickelmann was ten minutes late. I watched him go into the room and two minutes later, he called me in. As we started the scenario, that's when I discovered our pretend patient wasn't just, um, pretending."

Seamus nodded. "What are these test scenarios and why was the deceased there?"

"The scenarios are simulations. The tester makes up a story about what happened to the victim, and we have to pretend it's a real patient, describe our actions in assessing and treating the patient. The tester can make it as simple or complex as he wants. Sometimes we have real people acting as the victims because it adds a sense of reality, although they've come up with pretty realistic test dummies."

He noticed the doctor seeming to relax a bit.

"Okay, so this simulated victim has this fake wound, this *moulage* wound I believe it's called. Anything suspicious about it?"

"You mean other than it being lethal? I should have seen that right away." She sipped her coffee and stared at the wall behind Seamus. A moment passed before she continued. "To be honest, the knife wound looked good, a good make-up job … and, well, this is just a certification course so I wasn't expecting a real injury." She sighed. "Then I saw a drop of blood seep from the wound, and I wondered …" She shook her head.

Seamus also wondered how he might have felt, whether he'd be questioning his observation skills if he were in her shoes. Was this producing her defensiveness? He fidgeted in his chair, the fatigue of another long day wearing him down.

"Can you give me a detailed account of what happened, what was said? No detail is too small. Anything and everything you can remember."

"Then I can leave?"

Seamus offered no answer in his body language. "Your account, please."

Sarah looked irritated, but proceeded to give him an exhaustive replay of the events leading up to the call to 911. He made a few notes as she described Doctor Rickelmann's comments and response, and having interviewed him earlier, came to realize that no matter how good a surgeon the guy was, he would much prefer looking up from a hospital gurney and seeing her in charge, not him. He noticed how she squirmed as she told how Rickelmann pulled the knife. Her body language was being candid, even if she wasn't.

He knew a bit more about trauma than she probably suspected. He'd seen enough of it during four years on patrol and six more as a detective, the last three on homicide. Even Seamus knew better than to pull any deep, penetrating object from the body unless you were prepared to deal with deadly consequences.

"Was the deceased already dead before the blade was pulled out?"

She squirmed again, but didn't stiffen up, and sipped her coffee.

"I-I don't know. There should have been a pulse, but there wasn't and suddenly I'm trying to find any beat I could. My mind still wasn't fully registering the reality of it. I thought I felt a weak pulse, but I could have been sensing my own. It happens. Or maybe I was imagining a pulse because I figured there <u>had</u> to be one. I mean ... he was just acting, right? So, sure, there had to be a pulse. But there wasn't ... normal or otherwise. I do know his pupils were mid-sized and didn't appear to react to light."

"How do you know? Did you have a light?"

"Well, uh, no. It's just that when you force open the eyelid in a bright room, the light change will trigger a response even without a direct light source."

"So you had to force open his eyes?"

"Well, no, not in the sense of, you know, <u>forcing</u> them open, like against the patient's will. But now that you bring it up, he didn't flinch at all when I opened them, not like an alert person would, even someone acting a part."

"Tell me, Doctor Wade, you said there was a gap of a couple of minutes between when Doctor Rickelmann entered the room and when he called you. Could he have killed him during that time?"

She huffed a quick laugh. "Hardly. First, I'm sure we all would have heard a cry of pain if Mr. Johnson had been stabbed then. More importantly, though, is that he wouldn't have deteriorated so fast. I was there within minutes and —"

"That's okay. I don't think he did it either. Just had to ask." Seamus flipped back a page on his notepad and looked at her.

"Where do you think the scalpel came from? Would it have already been in the room?" Her legs were now uncrossed and she leaned a bit forward toward him. She was warming up to him, relaxing.

"Well, sure ... there were several on the table. It is a trauma course, with all kinds of medical equipment and techniques on display. I saw scalpels in several of the rooms during the practice sessions, in addition to some in that specific room."

"So, it could have been picked up from any of the test

rooms?"

"Uh, sure." She took a long drink from her coffee. "So, maybe a crime of passion?"

"What?" Her question threw Seamus off.

"You know, something personal. A crime of opportunity. Someone striking out with a weapon conveniently at the scene. Not something premeditated that required bringing the weapon with you."

Seamus furrowed his brow. "Let me guess, you're a murder mystery buff, or maybe a devotee of TV police shows."

"Get real, Sergeant. I'm an E.M. resident. I have no time for pleasure reading or TV. But I've had plenty of time in the E.D. talking with your homicide buddies about other cases."

"Well, statistics support that possibility. But who says the murderer didn't bring the scalpel here? Be easy enough to conceal something that small in a pant pocket or purse, between the pages of a book, in a sock. We have to look at all possibilities ... just like you have to consider a differential diagnosis."

She cocked her head, looked at him, and smirked.

"What?"

"You know what a differential is? I think you know more about medicine than I gave you credit for."

"Yeah, well, I've spent my share of time talking with doctors, too."

Seamus tried to read the look she gave him, but could not fathom its meaning. He did note, though, that she had relaxed. The self-protective pose had disappeared. "Look, we're almost done here. You'll be home for dinner. So, did you know the victim?"

"Not really. I learned who he was after he'd been pronounced in the E.D. and realized I'd seen him in the department a few times. Can't help but think about his family right now. My mother's so proud of my becoming a doctor. What does Walter's mother have in store for her now? She ..." Her voice cracked and she looked away. "Oh God, I should have been faster ... should have stopped Rickelmann from pulling that blade."

Seamus paused. Indeed, the facts of this young man's death had not been lost on Doctor Wade. He gave her a moment and brought her gently back on track with some routine questions, contact phone numbers, address, and the like. "Two final questions and we'll be done. Where'd you eat and what's your friend's name?" A sharp twinge ran from his hip to his knee, and by reflex he began to rub his thigh again.

"You should get that looked at."

"What?"

"Your thigh. I can give you some names."

"Don't change the subject. I'm being followed by one of the best orthopods in the city, by the way. Again, where'd you eat and who'd you eat with?"

She stiffened in her chair, her right leg swinging across her left knee. "Why do I ..." Her shoulders sagged just a bit in resignation. "Okay, okay. Look, we ate at Duff's. I had a cranberry walnut chicken salad and iced tea. You can confirm that through my credit card charge. We talked about boyfriends ... well, mostly the lack of qualified candidates ... and about this trauma course. Satisfied?"

He looked at her and smiled lightly. "Your friend's name?"

She crossed her arms and frowned. "Why do you need her name?" He was about to reply when she continued, "Nevermind. I guess you need to verify my story, right?"

Probably not necessary, he thought, but she'd made such a big deal of it that now he was just curious. He pursed his lips and nodded.

"I'll tell you, but please don't drag her into this. She gets enough bad press and ..." She set her coffee cup on the table and rubbed her hands together. "Oh, crap. Look, please promise me ... really, she had nothing to do with this. Okay?"

"Doctor Wade, if she wasn't involved, it won't happen. Simple as that. I might not have to contact her, but I still need to know."

Sarah hesitated, and then nodded. "Della Winston."

Seamus tried not to act surprised.

CHAPTER 3

Sarah, excused from the building and with her stomach growling, exited through the revolving door and pushed out onto the pedestrian concourse that made up the south end of Euclid Avenue. She took a deep breath and sought the warmth of the sun, now hidden behind the tall medical center buildings. Her mind drifted back to the interview and her inability to keep her emotions in check. Why? Why was this death different than the dozens she'd handled so professionally in the E.D.? She couldn't put her mental finger on the cause.

She glanced around, looking for any sunny spot. The remains of a splendid spring day still promised a delightful evening ahead, ideal for a meal outdoors at a quaint sidewalk café or for a jog through Forest Park. Earlier that morning while lamenting having to spend such a day indoors for a stressful certification course, Sarah had promised herself both. Under the circumstances, neither held any appeal.

Sarah walked toward a large cement planter still bathed in light, while watching medical center workers fill the avenue, presenting an array of dress from lab coats over jeans to expensive suits. They headed for their cars in one of the many parking garages in the hospital complex or to the nearby MetroLink light rail station, everyone eager to get home to family or friends for the evening. Surrounded by hundreds, yet she felt alone and isolated.

Sarah stopped next to the planter overflowing with spring flowers in full bloom and the scent of hyacinth, to which she paid scant attention. She pulled her BlackBerry from her brown leather Dooney & Bourke purse. Dinner with her friend Carolyn first came to mind, but she was on the evening shift. Her next thought: to forewarn Della.

"Hi. If you recognize my voice, you've reached the right number but I'm not available. You can fantasize and leave me a message. Just don't expect a call back. You know the drill. At the tone …" Beeeee...

Despite her frazzled emotions, Sarah couldn't help a brief

14

chortle. Della had a habit of quirky, often quite risqué, voicemail greetings, but this was tame and to the point. The woman never answered her phone directly. Never. Too many snoops, alleged "reporters," and paparazzi had caught her unaware over the years.

The 'beeeee...' fizzled before reaching the 'p.' *Damn*, she thought. *I forgot to charge my phone again. Why can't this thing be smart enough to charge itself?* Now, even if Della recognized the number and called right back, she couldn't answer.

Deflated, Sarah dropped the dead smartphone into the cell pocket of her purse, which she looped over her shoulder as she turned toward the North Parking Garage, took two strides, and stopped again. No way she could go home and be alone. She needed distraction. She checked her watch, did a one-eighty, and walked back toward the main hospital. With over seven hundred interns, residents, and fellows in training, surely someone she knew would be grabbing dinner in the main cafeteria. Among the top five rules of medical training: never miss a meal.

Fifteen minutes later, tray in hand, she walked toward the physician's dining room. As she reached its door, she turned and used her back to push it open.

"Hey, Sarah, come join us!"

"Over here."

Even before turning toward the voices, she recognized one as a fellow senior resident in the E.D. Ricardo Cristo de la Fuego Alvarez was as flamboyant as his name. When they'd first met, she had been fascinated with his Cuban heritage of well-to-do professionals who'd fled their home with Castro's ascent to power. She appreciated his sense of play, his ability to break the high tension of the E.D. with the most deliciously non-PC jokes. Yes, she envied his *joie de vivre*. He was unflappable, even in the middle of a major trauma code, just the person to get her mind off the afternoon's events.

Sarah approached the round laminate table and its well-worn wooden chairs as Ricky cleared a place next to him and beckoned her to the spot. As she neared, everyone stood up, put their hands over their heads and began bowing, murmuring, "Hail, oh

Great One! Hail!"

She stopped dead in her tracks and eyed them suspiciously, prompting Ricky to step forward and lead her by one elbow to her place. He took her tray, placed it on the table, pulled out her chair, and with a dramatic wave of the hand, encouraged her to sit down. He then placed one hand across his heart and continued.

"Ladies and gents, I introduce to you the one and only Doctor Sarah Wade, emergency physician exemplar, a saver of lives, a font of wit and sass ... and, I might add, the owner of one great –" She frowned. He stopped, but quickly resumed. "The model of house staff chutzpa, a friend to the friendless, sandwich maker to the homeless, and most of all, one great human being. But tonight ... tonight, we honor her and induct her into the Resident's Hall of Fame for a feat never before accomplished ... and likely never again to be repeated. Hear! Hear! To Doctor Sarah Wade!"

She recognized almost everyone around the table, and the woman she didn't know possessed an ID badge identifying her as a medical student. They picked up their glasses and raised them in a toast to Sarah.

"Okay, what the hell is this all about?"

With no answer forthcoming, she took a bite of food. She had attributed the turmoil in her gut to situational jitters but now recognized the grumbling of her empty stomach for what it was, basic hunger.

She took another couple of bites and turned to Ricky. "Well, Ricky?"

"It's all over the hospital, you know," he replied with his mouth full. He continued eating without offering any more information.

"Okay ... if you say so. What's all over the hospital?" Her exasperation surfaced. "C'mon, I don't need this right now. I've had one awful afternoon."

His brow furrowed in confusion. "Awful? You've made house staff history."

"I am not following you at all here, Ricky. Humor me. Spell

it out." She took another bite of institutional roast turkey and bland gravy.

"You're kidding, right? You don't know?"

She raised her eyebrows and shook her head.

"Damn, Sarah. It's all over campus. You're the first resident ever to put Roarin' Robert in his place, to kick his pedestal out from under him. They're singing your praises in every call room and operating suite in this place. Maintenance is rebuilding that pedestal ... for you ... as we speak."

Sarah found it difficult to swallow. Embarrassed, she glanced around the room. Several attending physicians sat nearby, casting furtive glances toward their table. A couple of them arose and left. To her surprise, tears welled up at the corners of her eyes. This was not the camaraderie or the diversion she sought. She plucked the napkin from her lap, dropped it onto her tray, and started to rise. Ricky placed his hand on her arm to stop her.

"Sarah, wait. Hey, look, we –"

"No, Ricky, you look." She glanced around the table. "What's wrong with you people? Has medicine hardened us so much something like this becomes a joke? I've had one hell of an afternoon. A young man is dead. You do know that part, don't you?" She looked and pointed at the med student. "One of your classmates, in fact." Tears flowed, but they failed to soften her concrete attitude. "This wasn't some north city drive-by. It's hard enough dealing with that stuff day in and day out, but to find one of your peers stabbed in the chest ... right here ..." She waved her arm in an arc around her. "... where we practically live. It's ... it's ..."

She took one additional look around the table to make sure it was sinking in.

"Believe me, there was no joy or satisfaction in my interaction with Doctor Rickelmann. None at all." Her shoulders sagged as she relaxed back into the chair. "I've spent all afternoon thinking about a mother who's lost her son. Wondering what he went through to make it to medical school here. This is just too close to home."

17

The table remained silent. There was no clinking of cutlery, no mandibles macerating.

"Please don't make light of it. We get too hardened to death as at is."

There were murmurs of apology from some of those at the table. The two junior surgical residents made brief comments and excused themselves from the table, followed shortly by the OB/GYN resident. Sarah took another bite, but her appetite was gone. She again removed her napkin from her lap and scooted her chair back to leave.

Ricky stood first. "No. Hey, look, I'm sorry. You're right. We were too cavalier. I guess I didn't really think about what you must have gone through. I've been an insensitive ass. Anything I can do to help?"

Sarah stood and handed him her dirty tray before marching from the room. In the main cafeteria, she noticed another fourth-year med student, Kendra Samuels, seated alone, isolated in a far corner of the hall. Kendra had worked with Sarah six months earlier and had applied to the Emergency Medicine Residency program. Sarah moved in her direction and, as she neared the table, could see from the condition of Kendra's mascara that she had been crying.

The woman appeared distraught and didn't notice Sarah. Sarah placed a hand softly on the woman's shoulder. "Kendra? You okay?"

Kendra jerked and looked up, startled. Then she pulled away and stood up. She put her fist to her mouth and it appeared she would vomit at any moment as she tried to control the heaves.

"Kendra?"

The student turned and rushed from the cafeteria.

CHAPTER 4

The Colonel sat at his grandfather's well-polished mahogany desk. That he used the desk in his office at the University's medical genomics lab honored the man whose influence had stoked the passions the Colonel held dearest. His favorite photo of the Grand Wizard and Grandmother remained safely displayed at home, along with his grandfather's white robe and conical hat. This office, however, showed only his public image with photos of his family adorning the office. His daughter Amanda, aged ten, playing soccer, diving from the springboard of their backyard pool, holding her Pomeranian, Boop. His wife, Sherry, holding Amanda, laughing. Another together at the piano. A third from their wedding portfolio. Photos of an earlier, happier time.

"Here you go, Sir. The papers you wanted."

Anticipation lifted the Colonel from his seat.

"Shut the door." With the door closed, he asked, "Did you look? Marcus, are they reporting success?"

"Just took a quick glance as they printed, but …" The tech broke out into a broad grin as he gave his superior the thumbs up.

"Yes!" The Colonel clenched his fist. "I knew it would. And we didn't even have to do the work. Such sweet irony."

He breezed through the papers from the National Cancer Institute at the NIH. There was something inherently sweet about letting the government fund and prove what he suspected would work all along. He had no university oversight, required no justification of budget, and faced no federal nitpicking to complete this phase of his plan.

"I'll read this later, but tell me, have they gotten the cure they wanted?"

"Almost. They still need a way to help the lymphocytes home in on their target cells."

The Colonel understood. "We won't have that problem. Is he sending us the promised samples?

The tech grinned. "Yes, Sir. Heinz and I should be able to

test them with our antigen before you get back from the conference."

"Great. Better than I hoped for." The Colonel picked up the papers and stuffed them into an inner pocket in his briefcase. The Colonel smiled. "Just think, Marcus. We're steps away from solving some of the world's biggest problems. There'll be food and water aplenty for everyone. Illiteracy will be halved, or better. No longer will the overextended needs of a burgeoning population rape our environment, threaten the rainforests, or contribute to global warming. We might even be praised as forward thinking heroes of the planet."

Marcus beamed. "Have a safe trip, Sir."

The Colonel acknowledged the comment and, with briefcase in hand, left the department. Fifteen minutes later, he stood in the office of the Curator of Rare Books. One might consider the office spacious if not for the overflowing floor-to-ceiling bookcases on every wall; tables and chairs filled with books, theses, and papers; and stacks of papers in piles on the floor. Even the few framed family photos sat on top of short piles of books. If clutter became a school of *feng shui*, Greg Whitlow, the curator, would be a master. Yet, the Colonel doubted that a *luopan* could find even a trace of good *qi* in this room.

Whitlow stood and welcomed the man who was one of the collection's generous benefactors. "I see you got my message. This is quite a find. Please have a seat." Whitlow pointed to the only open chair in his cramped office.

"I don't have a lot of time, Greg. I have a plane to catch. What's the verdict?"

Whitlow smiled. "Well, the 1883 first edition of Sir Francis Galton's 'Inquiries into Human Faculty and its Development' is in extraordinarily good condition, but the most exciting thing is that the signature appears authentic. How in the world did you acquire a signed first edition?"

The Colonel smiled. "All I can say is that I stumbled across it. The same goes for the other papers. They were together."

This, in fact, was true. Although his grandmother's mahogany, fall-front, George III secretary had graced his home since her death, he had been unaware of the hidden compartment accessible only from the back of the cabinet until he sought estimates in restoring the antique. *What a pair*, he thought of his grandparents. Kindred spirits. North meets south … Klan royalty wed to child of the Oneida Community. Grandmother's dedication to the field of eugenics needed no proof for him. She had taught him all of its finer points.

"Those are quite interesting as well. Much of Margaret Sanger's writings still exist in various collections, but I've never seen any that were so personal. This Mary Alice she writes to must have been a very close friend and supporter." He paused and held up one of the letters in its protective sleeve. "The thoughts expressed are quite scary really. To read first-hand that Sanger promoted legalized abortion as a primary means of eliminating the lower classes and inferior races so that mankind would improve on an evolutionary scale sure doesn't jive with Planned Parenthood's image of her. In this letter, she actually applauded Hitler's eugenics program and we know where that went."

The Colonel nodded. *If only they'd had the tools we now have*, he thought. "Yes, I thought so, too." The Colonel stood. "Can you do me a favor? Would you safeguard these until I return from my conference?"

The curator stood and answered, "I'd be more than happy to. Could I put them on display … until you claim them?"

The Colonel thought about that for a moment. With his current project so close to completion, having such inflammatory material publicly tied to his name in even the most benign way did not appeal to him. He wanted no one digging into the authenticity of the letters, much less how he came to own them, lest they uncover his family background and his personal history. He had too much invested in his philanthropic, altruistic image as a medical researcher.

"I, um, don't know. Sanger's letters might stir up a real hornet's nest of controversy. Don't you think?"

A look of concern dawned on the man's face. "Right. I hadn't thought about those implications. I'll keep them under lock and key until you request them."

"Thanks, Greg. Well, I have to run." He wondered what Grandmother would have thought of this curator. Was he an anomaly to the dysgenic deterioration of today's society or just the result of affirmative action? "Thanks for seeing me on short notice."

The curator smiled his no-problem-at-all smile. "Always a pleasure. Always."

The Colonel smiled back at the middle-aged black man with the graying, short-trimmed beard and thought, *Next time, maybe not.*

CHAPTER 5

Seamus arrived at the BOI - the Bureau of Criminal Investigations - thirty minutes late. His thigh ached and the limp seemed more pronounced when he was tired, but this morning upon waking he just wanted to cut it off, the pain was as intense as it had been those weeks after the injury. He cursed the scumbag who'd shot him eight months earlier while Seamus participated in a high profile drug bust. More than that, he cursed himself for having neglected protocol and putting himself in harm's way before backup arrived.

He stopped for a cup of the bureau's nuclear coffee, brewed by craftsmen so skilled that Mini-Thins, Red Bull and a dozen other energy drinks combined and distilled to high proof caffeine and ephedrine couldn't match it. Its aroma assaulted you upon entering the Bureau and alone could awaken normal people. Detectives just weren't normal, in any connotation of the word, and their long work hours required heavy, but legal, drugs.

With his cup of caffeine concentrate in hand, he walked into the bureau and headed for his desk. His partner, Richard Harris, so named because of his mother's love of the 1967 movie "Camelot," sat at his computer reviewing the security video from the previous day.

"Glad you could make it to work."

"Hey, Stick."

Harris' childhood nickname of Dick, with its phallic overtones, had long been replaced with "Stick," an appropriate moniker for someone six-foot-four and maybe one hundred and seventy pounds, in wet jeans and hunting boots.

"See anything? I kinda ran through the video last night, but I didn't have time to really scrutinize it."

"Last night? Shay, I thought I had you covered for a hot date with that Rams cheerleader."

"Yeah, well, don't start. It didn't happen. According to the message she left, she got called away for a modeling job ... somewhere in outer Mongolia ... for the next five years." That wasn't quite true, but Seamus wouldn't admit to his partner that

23

he'd been told in very definite terms that after four dates and twice as many cancellations on Seamus' part, she didn't want to see him anymore. She refused to become a mistress to his "wife," his job. In his mind, Seamus wasn't married to his work. He had sworn to a duty to serve and protect and he gave that duty priority, leaving little room in his life for a relationship and fun. Still, after several failed relationships, a glimmer of reality poked its way into his head. Maybe, just maybe, he had his priorities in the wrong order.

Still shaking his head, Stick turned back to the monitor.

"Hmm. So far, I've worked through the footage from the main door and one of the second floor walkways. Nothing unusual. No one in a hurry or obviously distraught. Pretty boring stuff."

"Well, best I could tell on fast forward, that doesn't change." Seamus sat at his desk and pulled a sheaf of phone messages from his "In" box. Nothing urgent in the pile. "You want me to look over your shoulder? Maybe two sets of eyes …"

"Nah. I'll index anything suspicious and get your opinion later. I've got time to review one more camera and then I have to get over to forensics. You still heading back to the med center?"

"Yeah. Appointment with Dean Moore at nine. Then I thought I'd ask around some of the departments where our vic worked recently. Maybe someone knows something."

"By the way, while you was getting your beauty sleep, I located the *moulage* artist this morning. She applied the makeup and props to all the "patients" during the morning, which prevented them from leaving, so lunch was provided. Best I can tell, the last time Walter Johnson was seen alive and well was right before the lunch break but after the *moulage* session. And that was by our notorious Doctor Rickelmann. Oh, and the prop knife hilt was definitely moved. The artist said she applied it to the left side, to the outer side of the nipple, not near the breast bone."

Seamus reflected on the previous day's interviews. Forewarned about the surgeon's arrogance and attitude, they had each interviewed Rickelmann with another officer present to safeguard their investigation and their personal reputations. Despite his ego, the man had cooperated and provided a clear picture of the events, including his own shortcomings. That he had left out nothing was obvious after the corroborating testimony of Doctor Wade.

"So that gives us a time window to focus on. That helps."

"Yeah, what doesn't help is that two of the cameras was out of commission."

Seamus approached the ambulance entrance of the McKnight Trauma Center following his brief meeting with the Associate Dean of Student Affairs, Doctor Irene Moore. The last time he'd seen these doors weren't good memories. Actually, they were more fleeting images than memories, as he'd been loaded up on morphine by the paramedics.

Doctor Moore had been most helpful in providing a brief personal history on the victim. Middle son of an upper middle-class family from outside Chicago. The father started with an east coast insurance business back when affirmative action was in vogue. Smart, advanced on merit, not skin color. Following a transfer to the Midwest, he ultimately started his own company and prospered. The mother, a Nigerian immigrant and schoolteacher. Full-time mom after she no longer had to help support the family. Devastated, heavily medicated. Seamus empathized, and thought back to Doctor Wade's concerns for the mother. No, he realized his reflection focused on the attractive doctor herself. *That would never work*, he thought.

The Dean had also provided him with the young man's schedule for the previous year. Seamus decided to focus first on the previous three months, which included rotations through Internal Medicine and Emergency Medicine. As luck would have it, two of the residents were on duty in the E.D. that morning.

Despite the congestion of his mild seasonal allergies, Seamus had no difficulty identifying the metallic perfume of blood as he approached the nurse's station of the trauma center. The two residents were supposed to be waiting there for him, but a quick glance around the department confirmed what his nose told him … he might be waiting a while. For a weekday morning, the place bustled with the kind of ordered chaos and frenetic energy found only in major, inner city emergency departments. The nurse's station appeared abandoned as staff ran between rooms. Yet, most of the activity centered on one of the trauma rooms. From a few glimpses beyond the bay's curtain, Seamus could see that this room was the source for the blood he smelled. A voice from behind interrupted his watchful curiosity.

"Help you?" Her "help" came out like "hep."

Seamus turned to see a harried-looking, middle-aged black woman holding a sheaf of papers between her crossed arms and chest. He held out his badge and introduced himself.

"Yeah. Been expectin' you. Them two residents you want is in there, with the trauma code." She pointed toward the action, center stage of that moment's drama in the E.D. "Doubt they'll be there too much longer. The old guy's not going to make it."

"What's going on?"

"Sorry, Sergeant. HIPAA and all that privacy foolishness. Like the government just want a monopoly on knowing everbody's bidness." She sounded out each syllable of the word 'monopoly' carefully as if concerned about its pronunciation.

Seamus knew HIPAA. The Health Information Portability and Accountability Act of 1996 was the federal government's way of guaranteeing easier access to personal health data by no one while denying access to those with a true need to know … all the while causing the deforestation of a medium-sized national forest to supply paper for the myriad of new forms and pamphlets that now-protected consumers would use to stuff burdened landfills across the country. Seamus knew all-too-well the burdens of HIPAA on law enforcement simply trying to do its job.

"Feel free to have a seat, if'n you wants to wait." She pointed to a chair behind the desk.

Seamus turned his curiosity first toward the trauma bay and after seeing no abatement in activity, moved toward the chair. He reflected on the melting pot of America as he watched staff from numerous ethnic and racial backgrounds parade through their choreographed steps of the code. His thoughts returned to Sarah Wade and again he dismissed the attraction. He was a white Irish Catholic, raised in an insulated white Irish family. His friends were Irish, his past girlfriends, Irish, and, by faith and begorrah, he was expected to keep the family Catholic, Irish, and white.

Before the seat warmed up, a sudden silence shrouded the trauma room. One by one, staff members emerged from the room, faces drawn and sullen, heads shaking back and forth. *Job security,* he thought. The callousness of his senior colleagues had claimed him long ago and he had discovered that E.D. gallows humor was much like that of the police. For both, it was a coping mechanism.

The clerk, who had been heading back to the room, caught the attention of one scrub-attired male who appeared to be of western European heritage and several years younger than Seamus. The man started to pull off his personal protective gear as the clerk spoke to him and pointed over her shoulder toward Seamus. After dumping his head and foot covers into a nearby biowaste receptacle and lathering his hands with alcohol foam, he walked toward the detective.

Seamus stood and greeted the man's extended hand with a firm shake.

"Detective, I'm Doctor Stowell, the E.D. resident."

"Sergeant Seamus O'Connor. Nice to meet you. Got a first name?"

"Yeah. James. And I'm in my second year here. I understand you want to talk about Walter Johnson. I was here yesterday when they brought him in."

"You were?"

"Yeah, not much to say. DBA."

"DBA?"

"Sorry, dead before arrival."

Seamus gave one nod of his head as acknowledgement. "Kinda like DRT?"

The resident smirked. "Yep, dead right there."

"So, is Doctor Isaacs around? We can do this together and save some time. If that's okay."

"Anything that saves time around here is appreciated, believe me. He'll be out in a couple of minutes. There's a consult room around the corner where we can get out of the way and talk." A nurse approached and handed a chart to the doctor. "Give me a minute to chart some things while we wait on Isaacs." He turned toward a nearby countertop and started scribbling on a medical record.

Seamus glanced back toward the room, looking for another young doctor to emerge, and was surprised to see several dark-suited men convene outside the curtains. *Feds?* he thought. Except for the undercover guys, they always stood out. *Why are they here?* His curiosity ratcheted up several notches as several more agents joined the assembly, along with three black African males in some sort of traditional garb. There was obviously more to the "old guy" in the room than implied by the clerk's offhand comment.

"Sergeant?"

Seamus turned to find Doctor Stowell and another white-coated young male who looked more like Howser, MD than "ER's" Doctor Doug Ross. Seamus had a glimmer of empathy for his mother's complaints that her doctors were too young.

"This is Nathan Isaacs. He's first-year Internal Medicine."

They shook hands.

"Lead the way," Seamus said.

The two physicians turned away from the trauma area and led the detective to a private room used to confer with families over decisions of life and death and to console those of the deceased. The room was typical institutional fare with blond wood furniture of average comfort and soothing off-white walls. The heating system vented the room well and Seamus could feel the air moving about him, but he found nothing consoling about the room.

Once seated, he led the interview with the basic questions. How did they meet Walter Johnson? At work, on the various rotations where he worked with them. How long had they known him? Only a couple of months. What kind of person was he? Easy going. Jovial. Hard working. Enjoyed an occasional practical joke. Did they ever socialize outside of work? No. Different social circles. Did he have any obvious enemies? Unsure. There was always the chance of upsetting a patient or family member. Seamus thought of Doctor Wade's comment about a crime of passion. Was he involved with anyone or recently break off a relationship? Not that they knew of. Their answers revealed no clear leads.

Doctor Isaacs looked pensive. Seamus knew he had something more to offer.

"Doctor Isaacs? Something to add?"

"I-I'm not sure. I saw Walter two, no, three days ago outside radiology. He seemed terribly distracted."

"Did he give any indication at all about what was bothering him?"

"Nothing. But we weren't that close, so I didn't expect him to tell me."

"Okay. Anything else either of you can think of?"

Both physicians shook their heads.

Seamus stood to signal he was finished. "Doctors, thank you. I know it doesn't seem like you provided any useful information, but every bit helps, believe me. And maybe you'll think of something later." He handed each man one of his business cards.

Doctor Isaacs opened the door for him and Seamus stepped into the hall. An adjacent room overflowed with dark-suited men and women in traditional African dress. The detective turned to the E.D. resident.

"What happened? Seamus nodded toward the crowd outside the nearby room.

The resident hesitated for a moment. "I'm not supposed to say, but I'm sure you'll hear about it soon enough. The Deputy Chief of Mission from the Nigerian Embassy in Washington was here for the International Student Festival. Some yahoo stabbed him outside a restaurant on Laclede's Landing. He didn't make it."

CHAPTER 6

Sarah felt spent. She had no idea how she would make it through her upcoming night shifts in the E.D. One more week, all night shifts, and then a break … a month's rotation in a research lab. No nights. No weekends. A chance at a normal social life.

She had returned to her apartment the previous night where the walls collaborated with her comfortably overstuffed furniture, some new, some family cast-offs, in creating a claustrophobic cocoon. Her appetite had returned, but she satisfied it with comfort food. After a full quart of Häagen-Dazs Mocha Almond Fudge ice cream, her gut rebelled and added to the restlessness that had prevented her from falling asleep until well after midnight. It was a sleep disturbed by every stray noise within, and outside, her bedroom. Gastronomic guilt enveloped her the next morning, despite a health-conscious breakfast, and she set off into a double set of her Pilates workout and a full hour of cardio.

Her exercises completed, Sarah turned off the treadmill, tossed her workout ball into the closet, and started toward her bedroom for a shower just as the noon news came on. The lead story revealed how quickly the medical center murder had become just more filler.

"Victor Aminu Oruwari, Deputy Chief of Mission Ambassador from Nigeria, was attacked and killed this morning as he emerged from a private breakfast gathering at a popular Laclede's Landing restaurant. His scheduled tour of the Jefferson Expansion Memorial and the Gateway Arch with a group of Nigerian students from local universities was violently cut short when an unknown assailant forced his way into the group and stabbed the deputy ambassador twice in the chest. The diplomat was rushed to Barnes Hospital where he died a short time later. Local authorities have promised full cooperation with the Nigerian Embassy and federal investigators."

"This is the second high profile murder in as many days and

already local black leaders are calling for St. Louis Police Chief Hartman to call in every possible form of assistance in finding the killer or killers. A spokesman for the department asked that we remind the public that a diplomatic murder such as this falls under federal jurisdiction, but that their department will assist in every way possible. However, as we speak, protests have started outside City Hall and Police Headquarters. For more on this story, we go to ..."

Sarah tried to remember which senior resident was on duty as she turned again toward her bedroom door. A video clip showing the diplomat as he emerged from the restaurant drew her attention back to TV. A cluster of students surrounded him and suddenly a shaved Caucasian head appeared amidst the pack and forced itself toward the diplomat. A scuffle ensued, the victim fell to the ground, and the white assailant pushed away and fled, his stocking mask fully evident. Only one person appeared to pursue the man, a black female. And Sarah needed only one quick glance to recognize the woman.

She winced as the attacker shoved the woman to the pavement and kicked her in the ribs. *Damn it girl, you could have taken him down*, she thought. The next moment, the woman grabbed the man's leg and toppled him. She ripped the man's stocking mask free of his shaven head but the camera angle missed his face as he pulled away and escaped the woman's grasp. As she picked herself up and turned back toward the group, Sarah applauded her effort. "At least you tried, Della," she spoke to the silent TV. "No one else did."

Sarah stepped out of the shower, wrapped herself in a towel, and rushed into the bedroom to answer the phone. She had left her answering machine off in hope that Della or Theresa might call. But it wasn't either one.

"Doctor Wade, this is Connie, at Doctor Hrabik's office."

This call was not expected. Residents typically did not get calls from their department heads. That task was usually left to the residency director, and even then only for scheduling emergencies and the like. Plus, she and Connie were on a first name basis. Connie's formal address sent a flare of warning through Sarah's mind.

"Um, hi, Connie. What's up?"

"You okay? We've all heard what happened."

Maybe this wasn't so bad. They were just concerned about her.

"Didn't sleep much, but I'm managing. Thanks for asking. I should be ready —"

"That's good. Look, Doctor Hrabik wants to see you right away. How soon can you get here?"

Oh crap, Sarah thought. *What now?*

"Um, half an hour, forty-five minutes at most. Why?"

"That'll work. Come in ASAP, okay?"

"Okay. But again, why?"

"Just a second." Pause. "He says he'll see you whenever you get here, so don't rush."

Sarah rubbed her temples and tried to think. Something else was going on, and from the tension in Connie's voice, that something else was not good.

CHAPTER 7

The old office and its well-worn wooden desks seemed smaller than usual as Seamus stormed in. The piles of paperwork covering his own desktop took on the proportions of the Rockies as seen when approaching from the eastern Great Plains. The off-white paint on its walls appeared drab and dirty. The black-speckled linoleum had lost the luster of a recent waxing. And his work, his alleged wife, became a tempestuous woman scorned. *Of all the nerve*, he thought.

"How'd it go at the medical center?" Stick asked as Seamus pulled his chair up to his desk and picked up his messages.

Seamus failed to respond.

"How'd it go?"

"What?" asked Seamus. "Oh, the med center. Yeah, fine. Everyone glad to help but not really helpful. Guy was liked by his peers. No known enemies or love interests. Eager to become a surgeon, maybe an urologist."

Stick winced. "Saw my plumber last week. Got a clean bill on my finger wave. Always the same old line – 'Okay, Richard, bend over and smile. You'll feel a little pressure.' And then it feels like he's grabbing your tonsils." He grinned at Seamus, but received a blank stare in return. "Okay, partner. What's up?"

Seamus thumbed through the stack of messages and glanced at the phone. "Isn't a gift supposed to be just that, a gift?" Seamus glared at his partner, who returned the expression with a questioning look.

"I don't know where this is going, but, yes, most of the time."

"I'm on my way back to the station, and Miss Cheerleader of the Year calls again. She wants the season tickets back, the ones she gave me for my birthday."

Stick stifled the laugh emerging from within, but not in time to avoid being observed.

"It's not funny."

Stick started to nod, then shook his head. "No? Just take a step back and ... oh what the hell, no comment. Hey, you seen the video coverage of that diplomat's stabbing down at the

Landing?" asked Stick.

"No, but I was in the E.D. while they tried to save him. The two residents I interviewed were in on the trauma code. Not a good scene."

"Yeah, well, the crap's really hitting the fan on this one. Not just any fan. More like one of them fans they use to fake storms in Hollywood. And now you and me are right in the middle of the shit storm," Stick continued, taking a deep breath and shaking his head.

"How's that? We aren't up for the case and we got enough on our plate with this med center case. Besides, the feds will take it."

"Yeah. But don't go saying anything to the Lieutenant 'cause he'll just say tough shit and get back to work. He'll also tell you to be on your best behavior and be helpful to our federal buddies ... 'cause we'll be working with them, too."

Seamus still didn't understand.

"What aren't you telling me, Stick?"

His partner sighed. "Remember our vic's background? Family's pretty well off - upper middle class. Well, they're also well connected ... yeah, definitely connected." He paused. "Seems our vic's mother is the Vice-Consul's cousin. You do the math."

Unlike past visits, Sarah hesitated in entering the department office suite. Pushing open the door, she walked into a waiting room full of eerie silence. *Oh, oh.* She would have preferred the normal hustle and bustle to calm her jangled nerves. At least she hadn't entered a noisy office only to have the voices fall silent at her entrance while strangers milled about making secretive glances toward her.

The small waiting area held comfortable, upholstered chairs set around a small oak coffee table, but even her favorite chair seemed to say, "no time to sit today." To the left were the receptionist's desk and the entrance to the back offices, where Connie's workplace sat adjacent to Doctor Hrabik's. It was not the position of a resident, except perhaps the Chief Resident, to walk casually back there. Yet, the receptionist's desk remained unmanned and this was no "casual" moment.

"Ellie? Connie?" She directed her voice toward the back offices.

No reply. She peeked down the hallway and saw no activity, only closed doors.

I'm not getting very far, very fast this way. Rather than sit and wait, she ventured toward the director's office. She glanced into Connie's office to find it empty. Just as she raised her hand to knock on Doctor Hrabik's door, it opened and a startled Connie appeared in the opening.

"Oh, Sarah, you surprised me!"

"The look on your ... anyway, um, I'm here. Ellie wasn't out front so I hope I'm not out of line coming –"

The administrative assistant cut her off and faced back into the room. "Doctor Wade is here, Sir."

So formal, Sarah thought. *Not good.*

A moment later Sarah's Department Chief stood at the door and Connie beat a hasty retreat to her office, seeming glad to be leaving the room. Sarah tried to gauge the mood of both people.

"Sarah, come in, come in." Doctor Hrabik ushered her to a chair across from his desk, and sat down next to her. That was her third signal that all was not right in the Land of Oz. Could she just tap her heels together and find herself back on her treadmill?

"So, how are you doing?"

He rested both elbows on the arms of his chair and steepled his fingertips together, his customary "I'm concerned about you" bedside manner. She had seen it many times in the E.D. Where was this leading?

"Doctor Hrabik, I'm doing just fine," she lied. She still hadn't pinpointed why this had affected her so much. Her self-prescribed cure consisted of immersing herself in work and exhausting herself on the treadmill. She had taken only one of those "pills" so far. "It's more or less just like any case in the E.D."

"Right. I've been told you didn't know this medical student."

"That's right, Sir. I've seen him in the department, but never worked with him."

"I see. And this isn't affecting you?"

Sarah shook her head.

"I heard something about an episode in the cafeteria last night. Are you –"

"Doctor Hrabik, that happened after a very long afternoon and I –"

The director took his turn to interrupt. "Sarah, you might want to take some time off. You only have a few shifts before your research rotation and under the circumstances, we could arrange coverage."

"Honestly, I'm doing okay. I just need to nap before my shift tonight and I'll be fine. This isn't upsetting my clinical judgment or emotional stamina or anything else that might affect my ability to work. Really!" Sarah wasn't sure who needed convincing.

Doctor Hrabik looked aside and gazed out the window overlooking Kingshighway. He became serious.

"Don't worry about tonight. We've already covered your shift."

"But Doctor Hrabik, that is <u>not</u> necessary."

"On the contrary, Sarah, it is. Until this all blows over, it is quite necessary."

Her puzzlement must have shown on her face.

"Sarah, I hate this, believe me, but you're relieved of your E.D. duties. This won't affect your research elective and we'll fix things before the month is over."

Sarah felt a heavy weight yoked to her shoulders. Why? Why did her superiors feel required to take such drastic action? She would weather this event as she had other emotional cases from the E.D. and be the stronger for it.

"I-I don't understand …" Sarah started to protest.

Her department chief glanced at the ceiling, sighed, and looked directly at her.

"Sarah, there is no one on our staff who questions your diagnostic ability, your dedication, or your technical skill. Please understand that this will not show up in your personnel record, nor will the time off be counted against you as vacation or sick leave. This is a purely political maneuver; one that I detest being forced to make." He sighed. "At least he's not making it a civil suit and has kept it inside the medical center."

Sarah's heavy yoke morphed into a sense of impending doom.

"Doctor Rickelmann filed a formal complaint that you've slandered him, in the dining hall and in comments to police and EMS personnel."

CHAPTER 8

Sarah stormed from Doctor Hrabik's office thirty minutes later, her dread having fissured with amoebic ease into a cell of anxiety and one of anger. Having explained in detail the events of the previous day, she learned that their dinner table discussion had been overheard and reported back to Doctor Rickelmann, although not in its entirety it appeared. Still, the formal complaint had been filed and she was stuck until the investigation was complete and a hearing of the staff disciplinary board convened. Doctor Hrabik promised to investigate the matter fully and quickly, and voiced his confidence in her.

Yet, like the amoeba, which could quickly spread to cause dysentery, the incident could progress beyond control and infect the whole department ... and beyond. Her mind rampantly produced vivid scenarios in which a vindictive man, with an eggshell ego, haunted the lives of her fellow residents, fired political cannonball after cannonball across the bow of the Emergency Department, and brought her career and others to a screeching halt. The specter of a civil slander lawsuit loomed in her mind, even though she saw no realistic chance of Roarin' Robert winning such a case. Her peers had regaled her for "taking down" Rickelmann, and now he wanted to reciprocate.

She saw herself relegated to Podunk places like Ironton and Pilot Knob, Missouri, where even second year residents were welcomed to work the small hospital ERs. With a little luck, they would banish one Ricardo Alvarez first, but that thought stimulated only a little pleasure. At least she'd had the presence of mind to recommend him for filling the rest of her shifts that week ... and under the circumstances, after a glance at the schedule, Doctor Hrabik had agreed.

Before her mental gymnastics ended and she returned to earth, she found herself outside, across Kingshighway and several hundred yards into Forest Park. She scanned the immediate area until she located a park bench, and walked straight to it. She sat down and pulled her knees up to her chest, her arms wrapped around them. The smell of lilac caught her attention and the coolness of the shade from surrounding oaks and maples brought a deepening sense of peace to her body. She took several deep breaths, trying to still the rush of thoughts encircling her mind. As she enforced the calm that was finally taking reign, the thought of having to "take the man down" recalled in her mind the televised account of Della Winston's tackle of the ambassador's killer. With a week of forced vacation, she had plenty of time. She knew her next move ... to track down Della.

Seamus sat at his desk, fidgeting, wanting to put his left foot up to ease the ache in his thigh, but frustrated at not having the room to do so. While the bullet he caught in a drug raid was long gone, he feared the results of its damage might never ease. He rubbed the thigh out of habit and focused again on the task at hand.

He reviewed his notes, speculating on the two cases. The feds would be handling the Deputy Chief of Mission's death, using his department's resources when needed. He saw his immediate task as one of finding the link, if any, between the two murders. How could he tie the student's death to that of his mother's cousin? Why, if this kid had so many contacts, was he playing "pretend patient" to get on the good side of Doctor Rickelmann? Was he a make-it-on-his-own kind of guy, or were the family connections not as influential as one might consider? His cousin, or second cousin, or whatever their formal relationship was, had come to St. Louis the morning before the young man's death. Where had the diplomat been at the time? Why hadn't the man canceled his breakfast plans to console his cousin and family? Why had it taken his murder to bring their relationship to light?

He gave in to the throbbing in his thigh, clearing a corner of the desk by making one large pile from two smaller ones, hoisting his foot onto the scratched surface, and sitting back in his well-worn wooden chair. The new position still wasn't comfortable but it helped. With the discomfort easing, he pursued connecting the two murders. He needed to arrive at his own deductions and act on them, not play fetch for the feds. They had different motives for solving the diplomat's murder and his case may or may not play into those reasons. And if it didn't, the feds weren't going to help him with his task, even though they expected his help with theirs.

He leafed through his notes one more time, and then through those his lieutenant had provided him about the Deputy Ambassador. Other than the family tie, he could see no commonality. In frustration, he set the notes on the desk and rubbed his thigh.

"Leg botherin' you again?"

Seamus looked up at Stick and nodded. His partner appeared to tower over him as he stood next to Seamus' desk.

"Too much stair work recently. All that up and down still aggravates it."

Stick held a computer disk out to Seamus. "Here. A copy of the televised videos of the ambassador's stabbing. Has two different angles from two different news cameras. I've already been through it a couple of times. Not much to go on but one disturbing thought comes to mind. After you review it, let's see if we both have the same idea. I'll be in the lieutenant's office."

As Stick left, Seamus placed the disk into his computer and waited for the appropriate software to load and start the replay. The first account showed the assault on the diplomat, graphically catching the writhing pain on his face as the knife penetrated his chest. The attacker's back was to the camera but one thing was apparent. Stocking mask or not, the man's head was either shaven or extremely light. *A towhead?* Seamus wondered.

The first clip did not show the murderer's escape so Seamus moved on to the second account. The angle was different, as Stick had noted, with less emphasis on the diplomat's face. This time, however, the attacker was closer to the camera. There was no doubt now. His head was shaven. *A skinhead?* Seamus almost asked it aloud. If that was Stick's concern, he could understand his partner's comment about something disturbing. Before Seamus' time on the force, Stick had been there when the militia movement caught its foothold in Missouri and quickly became dominated by the so-called Christian Identity groups. Seamus did recall the stink raised by National Alliance ads on the MetroLink only a couple of years earlier. Police units across the state had been on alert when that white supremacist group caught the headlines briefly following the ruckus, only to disappear from the radar again. Their resurgence would indeed be disturbing, particularly if one of these groups was involved in a diplomatic assassination.

This camera's angle allowed the cameraman to follow the assailant's escape. Seamus had heard something about a Good Samaritan in action but had been too busy with his own investigation to see the replays on TV. Now, he was surprised to see it was a woman who had tried to stop the fleeing perpetrator. He watched the stocking mask come off, confirming the man's shaven head. Then he sat in astonishment as the woman turned back toward the camera. It was none other than Doctor Wade's friend, the famous, or maybe infamous, Della Winston. Seamus knew that instant what his next move would be. He had to talk to Della Winston.

CHAPTER 9

The Colonel returned to his hotel room for his midday call home. He had spared no expense to care for his wife, Sherry. The icy road that had taken the life of his ten-year-old daughter four years earlier had put Sherry into a coma for three months. Three months of her doctors giving him hope. Three months of vigilant prayer for her recovery. When she opened her eyes one day at the beginning of month four, he spent hours each day reliving their memories together and telling her of both his daytime and afterhours work.

She, too, had been a "product" of the Oneida Community and its eugenic thinking. Perhaps more than he, she had yearned for that utopian world where intelligence ruled, where the lower classes no longer remained, and where illiteracy and hunger were issues of a dysgenic past. He told her of his efforts to make that utopia a reality. He promised her he would not give up on her, or their shared dream.

Within weeks of opening her eyes, the Colonel, and her doctors, realized no one was home. Neurology consultation and evaluation, along with functional MRI and PET scans, confirmed the worst, a brain functioning at the most basic level. A persistent vegetative state where all the autonomic functions kept her alive, but without cognition on any level. Doctors now held out no hope. Her vegetative state would be permanent according to every expert he consulted.

After a fruitless year in a rehab center, he moved Sherry to a private "hospital" room in their home, with twenty-four hour care. The Colonel called home three times a day, no matter where he was. He talked with her caregiver and made sure the caregiver let him talk to her. He promised himself he would never "pull the plug" until he could tell her face-to-face that he had succeeded.

As he prepared to return to the conference, a second, disposable, cell phone in his pocket rang.

"What?" He could feel his blood pressure rising and his face flush. "Give me that again."

He glanced at his watch. Almost noon on the West Coast made it nearly two o'clock in the afternoon in St. Louis.

"… this morning, Colonel, on Laclede's Landing —"

Before his subordinate could finish he interrupted, "Hang on." He resisted slamming the phone onto the bedside table but threw it onto the bed before crossing the room to retrieve the TV remote. As he returned to the phone, he clicked the television on and changed channels to the evening news. He caught the story just as the news anchor gave an update on the Deputy Ambassador of Nigeria's murder in St. Louis, complete with a video replay of the incident.

"Of all the idiotic …" He picked up the phone. "I just saw the replay. Is that shithead one of ours?"

"Yes, Sir. We think so. Two or three of the men were on an all-night binge on the Landing and we think it might have been one of them. I'm still trying to confirm. Nobody got a good look at him, so we might get luck —"

"Nobody?" the Colonel screamed into mouthpiece. "That black bitch who pulled off his mask got a look! She's probably with some damned police artist as we speak." He paced at the foot of the bed. "We really don't need this right now. We can't afford any attention. We're too close to our goal." He stood at the sliding glass door leading to a small balcony but remained oblivious to activities below him. "Damn," he muttered.

He put the phone back to his ear to confirm the connection still existed. Satisfied that it was, he walked back toward the bed and continued, "Look, confirm your suspicions and if he's one of ours, you let that, that … hell, he's expendable. Scope out wherever he lives, whomever he lives with. If there's anything, anything at all that could tie him to us, get rid of him. Nothing. I repeat, nothing must get in our way, or call unhealthy attention to us." He paused. "Look, I need to get downstairs for the presentation and my other meetings. I won't be back to this room until after supper. Call my cell and keep me abreast of the situation."

The Colonel walked back over to the sliding glass door and gazed across the water of San Diego Bay, its placid waters disturbed by the Marriott Water Taxi as it churned toward the Coronado Island Marriott Resort. The tropically lush resort afforded a beautiful view of the city, the Embarcadero waterfront, and Petco Park and provided the perfect setting for the advanced genetics conference where he and his fellow researchers were to present their findings on genetic factors for late-onset Alzheimer's disease. Their work involving chromosomes 9 and 10, and the formation of Abeta42, the main peptide involved in the senile plaque formation thought to be the key initiator of Alzheimer's disease, was groundbreaking work.

The past day had been idyllic. Colleagues from across the globe knew his lab had discovered a major breakthrough and there was an anticipatory rush leading to this afternoon's sessions. He basked in the glow of their compliments. Yes, the week would have been near perfect … until now.

Eric Deamus bounded down the two flights of stairs from his third floor room and made a beeline to the lunch reception provided by Jessup Genetics. Their newest drug targeted the Abeta42 peptide, but Eric's lab had derived both a new test on Alzheimer genetic markers in the blood and a new drug with the potential to reverse the plaque development of Abeta42, not just slow down its progression. The reception had started in the outdoor banquet area beneath his room and overlooking the bay, but he'd been delayed.

As he hit the ground floor landing he brushed his right hand up through his sandy short-cropped, gelled hair to get that spiky look which was still popular in the mid-west, but already passé in California. Exiting the stairwell, he found a large, ornate mirror on the opposite wall and double-checked his appearance. The suit was right on, and he liked his hair whether or not anyone else did. With his personal seal of approval on "his look," he took off with a confident stride toward the luncheon.

He heard the elevator door chime and open behind him as he passed by.

"Eric."

Eric stopped and turned. When the boss called, you didn't

ignore him.

"Hey, Mitch. You're not at the luncheon yet? I figured you'd be front and center with Jessup's big mucky-mucks."

Mitchell Hudson, M.D. had received his medical degree at Georgetown University, followed by a residency in Medical Genetics at the University of Washington, where he stayed for an additional five years. Then came a fellowship in Clinical Molecular Genetics at the Mayo Clinic, a move that put him on the "fast track" in genetics research. Next, he became a lead researcher with the National Human Genome Research Institute before Washington University lured him away to head its new medical genomics program. He often joked that his two-year stint at the Mayo Clinic was his rebellious phase; that he otherwise just bounced back and forth between Washingtons. And for that, he could never tell a lie.

Except maybe regarding his age. Nothing about him - his lean, athletic body; his full head of onyx hair, nor his face, line free and toned - gave away his age of forty-six or the fact that he'd had a stellar career for a man his age.

Mitchell smiled. "They haven't won the gold ring yet. After the presentation this afternoon, I'm sure they'll have some stiff competition. Jessup wouldn't be champing at the bit so hard if they hadn't had their 'inside man' in our lab."

Roger Coulter, their PhD medical geneticist, had been enticed to leave Jessup when it was still a highly speculative biotech start-up whose first drug failed to get FDA approval for Phase III trials. Now it was a major player in the pharmacogenomics field and Roger continued to groom his contacts with the company. A night of partying had led to loose lips and a revelation of their work to Dillon Watts, one of Jessup's vice-presidents. Mitchell learned of the incident and let Roger know, in language few in the lab thought possible of the boss, that such information was and would remain proprietary to the lab until such time that he and the medical center's board licensed it. The blow-up had strained their relationship and affected the entire lab. Mitchell's request that Eric watch Roger more closely for any indiscretions had caused more than a bit of tension between them as well.

"Speaking of Roger, I saw him upstairs right after I saw you bolt into the stairwell. He's on his way down, so why don't we wait up for him and make a grand entrance together." He smiled, but Eric read between the lines. Mitchell expected him to help contain Roger's contact with Jessup.

Moments later the second elevator's door chimed and both men watched their associate emerge from the opening doorway.

"There he is now," said Mitchell. "Roger, please join us."

Roger nodded as he approached. "Mitchell. Eric." He smiled. "Ready to talk some serious biochem? Jessup's top chemist wants to know more about the nuts and bolts of plaque regression and you're the go-to guy on that one."

Eric looked at their boss with questioning eyes.

"Roger, let's save that for later, okay?" Mitchell replied, getting Eric off the hook. "Let's all have a nice lunch, enjoy this beautiful spring day in southern California, and not give away any secrets just yet. Be on your best behavior. Please."

Mitchell again smiled, but Eric thought it a bit forced. He watched the others as the trio walked together. Both men seemed stressed. Was it the work of the conference or was there something else? He, too, felt pre-occupied, but he subjugated his worries and worked to look like the confident, genetics superstar that all three would become once Mitchell gave his keynote address on their breakthrough work.

That evening the Colonel found himself pacing the room once again. The presentation had been flawless, the accolades immediate, and newfound commercial interest from big pharmaceutica overwhelming. Their dinner at Azzura Point along the Silver Strand to Coronado had been celebratory. Yet, all these distractions had proven limited in taking his mind off the events at home. He had arrived back at his room and found no messages waiting. So, again he paced.

As the evening rolled closer to the top of the eleven o'clock hour, he grabbed the remote and flipped on one of the local stations to catch the beginning of the late night newscast. He was unsure whether the incident in St. Louis would warrant coverage by the local broadcast affiliates. After a lead story about a local politician, the news anchor answered his question.

"In follow-up to a story we brought you at noon, there's some new information in the murder of a Nigerian diplomat in St. Louis this morning. John Bradshaw has this report."

"Thank you, Greg. If you saw our earlier broadcast, you might recall the violent video of the stabbing of the Honorable Victor Oruwari of Nigeria. Although no new leads in the case have been revealed, new pieces of information have emerged from review of the video." The screen filled with a replay of the news video, while the reporter continued with a voice-over. "Watch as the assailant tries to escape. A young black woman appears to overtake and stop the man, but she gets attacked and fails to hold him. We have learned that the young woman is St. Louis celebrity, Della Winston …" The video switched to a head shot of Winston. "… known for her daytime talk show and social escapades in St. Louis. Some of you might also remember her well-publicized dalliance with the nationally known rapper, Alley K, and her appearance on the cover of his platinum selling album, Kewl Kat. Their romance ended with Alley K's conviction in the club shooting of a rival performer in Las Vegas."

The video returned to the screen with a still shot of the killer's head. The voice-over continued. "The other evidence that has come to light regarding this video comes from expert analysis of the footage. Video experts have computer-enhanced this still shot. Watch as we zoom in on the back of the killer's head. Even though we cannot see his face, a tattoo clearly emerges on the nape of his neck. What we show you now is an artist's re-creation of that tattoo — two daggers crossed to form an 'X' with a small Byzantine cross above and the letters 'W' to the left and 'S' to the right."

The reporter reappeared on the screen. "When asked about it, police and Secret Service sources in St. Louis said they are unaware of any significance to the tattoo. They have asked, however, that anyone familiar with such a tattoo should call their local police, the FBI, or the Secret Service with whatever information they can offer. They have issued a nationwide alert about any individual, or individuals, with such a tattoo, stating that they are concerned the killer may have already fled the St. Louis area. Other anonymous sources speculate that authorities are concerned about the killing being a political statement of a white supremacy group, a group whose members wear this tattoo. Back to you, Greg."

The Colonel restrained himself from throwing the remote control into the television. The tattoo was not a gang mark, as the newscast implied. But he knew that tattoo.

CHAPTER 10

The Colonel felt too wired to sleep. He needed to work out his anguish, but the room seemed too constrained for renewed pacing. He wanted to leave the room and walk along the bay, clear his head, and decide how best to play out this new revelation. Yet, a glance through the sliding glass doors revealed many others enjoying the balmy evening along the waterfront path, despite the late hour. He couldn't risk being overheard on his cell phone, not that he was ready to make the call. He regretted his anger earlier in the day, and the command he had given. His emotions roiled through his mind. His position of command required that he deal with the troublemaker ... deal with him definitively. Still ...

No, he wasn't ready to make a decision. He had much to think through first. But he needed to rescind the earlier order until he'd had time to consider all the ramifications. Hoping he wasn't too late, he picked up his cell phone and placed a call to his second-in-command.

"Evening, sir. We've found —"

"I know, Sayer, I know. I saw the news tonight."

There was a pause.

"I'm sorry, Colonel. I've been out all evening trying to track down certain people and haven't seen any recent news. But I believe I know who did it."

"Hell, Sayer, it was on the news here in San Diego. The tattoo. They know about the tattoo." The Colonel checked his rising frustration. Sayer was his Man Friday, his *consigliari*, his go-to guy. He was doing his job and couldn't be faulted for that. His voice softened. "It was Bobby and it's only a matter of time 'til they catch him."

"Yes, Sir. I believe so."

"You said you've been out all evening. Where are you right now?"

"At his apartment, like you ordered. No sign of him ... or his roommate. Word is that Chas was also part of the group on the Landing this morning. They've both gone to ground from what I can tell. Can't find their rucksacks or any other gear here. Edwards and I have gone through this apartment with a fine-tooth comb, nothing here to point to our group."

Sayer's mention of Edwards stopped the Colonel short. Edwards was remorseless and as cold-hearted as they came. His Special Forces training had served him well in Afghanistan. They were talents the Colonel had utilized before. The remains of Jimmy Hoffa would be found before those bodies. But there were extenuating circumstances in this case. Or were there? The Colonel needed time to think this through thoroughly. He could make no mistake on this one.

"Sayer, leave a signal in the apartment for him to check his dead drop. Something he'll know came from me or you … so he'll know we're looking for him. But nothing obvious … in case the police learn enough to search the place. Then take off so you don't make the neighbors suspicious. I have a feeling he might have headed for the lake compound. He knows how to arm the perimeter sensors and how to use the hidey-holes in an emergency. Send Edwards. If he's there, have Edwards sit on him until I decide what to do."

"Understood, Sir."

"And, Sayer, treat him well. He's in deep shit one way or the other. Keep me posted, but don't leave any voicemails."

"Yes, Sir. Never do."

The Colonel closed his cell phone with a snap of the wrist, and decided to take that walk. As he left the shelter of the hotel, he felt a cool breeze coming across the island from the ocean and took a deep breath of the salty, night air. The thought hit him that, despite the liberal mindsets of many coastal residents, it would be pleasant to live on either coast, east or left, after his work was completed.

First things first. For his plan to succeed, they had to continue unhindered. No distractions. No attention. No unforeseen obstacles. And that meant dealing with the potential crisis at hand. As he had told Sayer, the young man was in deep shit. If left to the authorities, he would end up on death row faster than those liberals could paint their picket signs. But his capture would threaten to bring his plans to light. He couldn't let that happen. Unfortunately, they'd never be able to hide him forever. A sudden and permanent disappearance might be the least painful way for all concerned because the Colonel's immediate dilemma was personal. Could he make this young man a sacrificial lamb? Could he order the death of his sister's only child?

CHAPTER 11

"No idea, huh? Look, if you see her or find out where she is, will you get word to her to call me STAT. She has all my numbers and I won't be working at all this week. Thanks, Walt."

Sarah hung up the phone. She'd hated to call Walter Hays, Della's producer, so late in the evening, but she'd tried everyone else she could think of who could help locate her friend. No one answered at Della's home, where her aunt, Beatrice Clay, doubled as her housekeeper. She'd left half a dozen messages in Della's voicemail. Della's driver and bodyguard, Antoine, hadn't answered his cell either and she'd left almost as many messages for him. She had also tried to contact Detective O'Connor only to learn that he was out of the office and presumed to be at the courthouse. By dinnertime, Sarah had pieced together the details of Della's day but hadn't talked with her.

Sarah sat on the cream leather couch in her apartment, staring absently at the muted images of some young actress she'd never seen before talking with Conan O'Brien. O'Brien was animated and his guest was blushing, but Sarah had no interest in why. Her thoughts were on her friend. She decided to try Della's home once more. Surely, someone would be there by now.

After ten rings, Sarah started to hang up when an out-of-breath voice said, "Hello?"

"Beatrice?"

"Yes?" Sarah could hear the older woman sniffling.

"Beatrice, are you okay? This is Sarah …" The woman didn't respond. "… Sarah Wade."

"Oh, child, it's terrible, something terrible. Haven't seen the likes of this since I was a girl in Mississippi. And I can't find Della. I was already worried to death about her after all that nasty stuff this morning. Now, I can't find her and I'm just sick. And the police … the firemen … they're all still here."

Sarah sensed the distress in the wavering voice.

"Police? Firemen? Aunt Beatrice, what's going on?" The woman's rambling comments jolted Sarah.

"A cross … burnin' in the front yard."

Chad Sayer was deep in thought as he drove toward the lake compound with Edwards. Without the interference of city lights, the clear night sky glittered with stars and a dazzling half moon. Yet, those heavenly lights did little to illuminate the twisting country roads he now traveled. Open farm fields offered full view of the spectacular night sky, while intermittent thick stands of oak and cedar created black arbors arching over the road that blocked the natural light almost completely.

But he paid little attention to the celestial display. He had a mission … and his mind focused on that assignment and all of its ramifications. He had a gut feeling that something terrible was in the wind, something that could jeopardize their entire plan … something that was moving beyond his or the Colonel's control.

Sayer didn't consider himself a wicked man, although he recognized that many would call him evil if they knew who, or maybe what, he was. A day before Sayer's fifth birthday, his father became the victim of a carjacking by two black youths looking for a joyride. The injury they inflicted on his dad had left him paralyzed from the waist down, and medical complications killed him a year later. They lost their home and his mother started a long downhill slide with depression that resulted in her suicide before he entered high school. He had been fortunate to land in a foster family who lifted him out of his own emotional morass and provided him with a stable home and an education that he used to become financially successful. But he never lost the desire for revenge against those two black youths.

Hate had left its penetrating dendrites in his soul and on the day the penal system released his father's attackers to resume their criminal activity, he made a vow to avenge his family's demise. The mechanics and logistics of his vengeance remained poorly formed in his mind, until he met the Colonel, a distinguished man of science with strong family roots in the Klu Klux Klan. The meeting had been happenstance, but its result focused his mental acumen on developing the Missouri White Alliance. Early on, recruiting had been slow, their paramilitary training nominal. September 11th, 2001 changed all that. A new enemy brought eager new recruits and their ranks swelled. The addition of Randy Edwards, fresh from Afghanistan, changed the tenor of their training … and the fulfillment of a long sought desire. His father's killers did not disappear painlessly.

Then another great change occurred. Breakthroughs in genetic and cancer research in 2005 demanded a new direction for the MWA and a higher level of obedience by its members. The Colonel devised a new plan and to fulfill it, they needed a strategic retreat into complete anonymity. They stopped recruiting new members, and eliminated firearms and other forms of military training in favor of learning stealth and biochemical dispersal techniques. The members did not understand the reasons behind the change. They had no need to know until the right time. After all, the fewer who knew it, the easier the secret was to keep. Had they expected too much from their cadre? Was the level of blind obedience too great to expect of anyone, particularly eager young hotheads like the Colonel's nephew, Bobby?

Yes, there was something terribly amiss. Sayer just knew it.

"Whoa, watch it!" barked Edwards.

The winding roads leading to their Ozark facility demanded Sayer's full attention. Turns came out of nowhere in the dark and he'd almost missed one, correcting his course just before hitting the gravel shoulder of the opposite lane.

CHAPTER 12

Her stomach turning, Sarah raced toward University City where Della lived on prestigious Westminster Place, a gated avenue of multi-million-dollar, historic mansions. If it weren't such a heinous symbol of racism, the idea of such an event occurring in this mostly white, upper-class enclave might seem curiously provocative. But in the twilight of the day's earlier events, this marked an evil twist in the tumultuous past of racial relations in the city. She knew this would add fuel to the protests and an outpouring of outrage from local and national levels. The Reverends Jackson and Sharpton were probably already winging their way to town.

Traffic was light and she managed to hit all the lights on Delmar Boulevard, but as her aging Jetta approached Skinker Boulevard, she found the entire street blocked off. Television news crews claimed prime positions for coverage, while the police had barricades blocking the street less than 100 feet from the intersection. She passed the turn and drove west for two blocks before turning onto a small back street that would enable her to come close to Della's street. She had no doubts that police barricades would be cordoning off all access to Westminster Place, but if she could find a place to park, she might be able to walk through and pull some strings to get into the crime scene, into the house with Aunt Beatrice.

She parked at the first open spot and jumped from the car. She wrapped her light jacket a little tighter against the night chill and rushed toward Della's. At the barricade on Center Street, a uniformed officer stopped her.

"Sorry, Miss. No one 'cept residents allowed past here right now."

"I understand officer. I'm Doctor Wade …" She flashed her hospital ID up for him to scrutinize. "… that's my Aunt Beatrice in the house where this happened. She phoned in the report on the cross. Anyway, she asked me to come over. She's not handling it very well."

The officer turned away and spoke into his shoulder mic. A

minute later, he returned and let her pass. As she neared Della's house she could see Aunt Beatrice at the front door, a bright yellow shawl sweater wrapped tightly around her and held even closer by her arms folded across her chest. She hadn't seen Sarah yet and another officer stopped her. This one had sergeant's stripes. She stopped to fish out her ID from her purse. The man held up one hand as if stopping her.

"Doctor Wade, right?" Sarah nodded. "I guess you've seen your aunt over there, but before you go to her, one of the detectives wants to talk to you. Would you come with me, please?"

He swept his hand down and pointed in the direction of the detective. He led her across the street and down two houses where several plain-clothed men stood together talking under a streetlamp, next to an unmarked police sedan with its emergency lights blinking. As she drew near, one man separated from the others and walked toward her. The man was tall, thin and had medium length light brown hair. He wore a shirt and sports coat but no tie. He looked vaguely familiar.

"Doctor Wade …" He held out his hand to her. "… I'm Sergeant Richard Harris … Seamus O'Connor's partner. Pleased to meet you. Seamus had good things to say about you."

The comment caught her a bit off-guard, but she returned his firm handshake, aware now where she had seen him before and finding it hard to believe that had been only one day ago. Her life had taken an S-curve at career threatening speed since then. She looked at him curiously, thinking, "*What's homicide doing here?*"

"He's supposed to be here shortly. He'll probably want to talk to you, too. He's been chasing down Della Winston all afternoon and keeps falling one step behind her."

Detective O'Connor hasn't seen her either, Sarah thought, worried. "But I thought she spent the afternoon at the Federal Courthouse and that he was there," she replied.

He shook his head. "So much for secrets. No one was supposed to know where she was. Maybe you're in the wrong calling there, doctor. You've just shown better detective skills than some of those guys leaning against that car over there." He nodded toward the sedan where he had been standing moments before.

"So, I hear you're related to Beatrice Clay." He used his thumb to point in the direction of the house.

Sarah was unsure whether to continue the charade, or come clean. Until she remembered Aunt Beatrice's own words that honesty was always the easiest route.

"Not really, but I might as well be. Della Winston and I grew up together and her aunt was like my own, treated me like part of the family. I've called her 'aunt' for as long as I can remember." She glanced toward the older woman. "I called earlier looking for Della, and Beatrice was so upset she didn't even seem to recognize who I was. I'm worried about her."

The detective smiled. "Not a problem. I think she needs some family right now. Go on over to her and I'll tell O'Connor where to find you."

She returned the smile and said, "Thanks."

Sarah walked slowly up the driveway, past the smoldering ruins of a wooden cross. It appeared to be roughly constructed of six-inch timbers, the kind used for landscaping. She guessed its charred remains to be about eight foot tall and wondered how someone could have securely planted it in the yard without detection until they set it on fire. She cringed. It was just a mass of burnt wood, yet it tore at her soul and distressed her in a way she couldn't understand, like some ancestral memory of a previous era passed on in her genes.

She watched Aunt Beatrice fingering her rosary in automatic motion, without ever looking at the beads. As Sarah climbed the two short steps from the drive to the front walk, the older woman turned toward her. She seemed confused at first, but then recognition ignited her face with a smile. She extended her hands toward Sarah.

"Sarah, child. Whatever are you doing here? Is Della with you?"

Sarah embraced the woman and held her close, concerned that she didn't recall their phone conversation. Was it simply the stress of the situation, or was this the first sign that Beatrice might not be living with Della much longer?

Sarah backed off, still holding the woman's hands in her own. "No, Aunt Beatrice, Della isn't with me. I thought she might be here."

"I thought it was her calling a little while ago, but it was some other nice woman who wanted to know how I was. I can't seem to remember who she said she was, though. Oh well … you're here now. Would you like some tea? I've got my own special additive, you know." She winked.

Yes, Sarah knew well the liquor Aunt Beatrice used to spike her tea.

"No, thank you. I don't think now is a good time for your favorite tea, Auntie."

The woman glanced away briefly and her eyes opened wide as if she noticed the front yard for the first time that night.

"Oh, my, where did that mess come from? And who are all those men? Did they do that?" She resumed fingering her rosary and developed a noticeable tremor.

"Come on, Auntie, let's go inside, and let those men clean things up for you."

Aunt Beatrice smiled and turned toward the open door. She turned back to Sarah.

"Would you like some tea, dear? I can fix it up special."

Sarah gently took Aunt Beatrice's elbow and directed her toward the house, closing the door behind them to block the view of the yard. Once inside, she guided the elderly woman to the kitchen. Beatrice immediately went to the sink, filled the teapot, and placed it on the stove.

"Don't look, dear."

Sarah played the game, and covered her eyes, sighing. Everyone in the family knew where Beatrice kept her "stash." But every time, Beatrice acted as if it were a secret. Sarah couldn't help but smile. It was a familiar routine, and it took Sarah's mind off the immediate circumstances … for a moment.

As the teapot began to whistle, the doorbell rang.

"I'll get it, Auntie," Sarah said.

"Thank you, dear. Would you like some tea?"

Sarah made a mental note to ask Social Services at the hospital for recommendations on the best assisted-living facilities, so she could pass them on to Della. Beatrice was in no condition to be left alone like this.

At the door, she found Detective Seamus O'Connor and a young woman in casual nursing attire.

"Doctor –"

"I'm sorry I'm late –"

They started together and Sarah glanced back and forth at them, unsure whom to address first. She faced Detective O'Connor and said, "C'mon in, Detective." She then addressed the young woman. "And you are?"

As Seamus stepped inside, the young woman stammered, "I-I'm Angie. Look, I just got the call thirty minutes ago. I-I came as fast as I could, but all these police and firemen. I couldn't get past them. The regular aide couldn't get her car started. She was s'posed to be here two hours ago. They musta worked down the list 'til they found someone who could come. And that's me. I've been here before. Is Beatrice … oh, there she is."

Sarah turned to find Aunt Beatrice behind her, cup of tea in hand. The elder woman was looking Seamus up and down.

"Would you like some tea, young man?" She took a generous sip from the cup in hand.

Sarah looked back at Angie. "She's all yours, Angie. I need to talk to the detective here."

Angie took Beatrice's free arm. "C'mon, Beatrice, we need to get you to bed. It's way late."

"But dear, there's a mess in the front yard …" Their voices faded as they walked down the hall toward the kitchen.

Relieved that Beatrice had a caretaker, Sarah led Seamus into the front room where they sat in antique Chippendale chairs opposite each other. Seamus glanced around the room at the array of antiques, both furniture and tapestries. Sarah could tell he was impressed … and surprised.

Seamus spoke first. "Must say I didn't expect this of Della Winston. The public portrayal of her speaks to more contemporary décor. So, Doctor …"

"So, Detective, here to validate my alibi?" She didn't smile. The issues at hand mandated a serious appraisal and somber discussion.

"Not necessary. I was hoping to find Ms. Winston at home."

"She's not ... and I have to say I'm a little worried. Her aunt hasn't heard from her in hours and I can't get hold of her by phone."

Seamus crossed his legs, then uncrossed them and rubbed his left thigh.

"That's the story of my day as well. I was supposed to catch up with her when they released her late this afternoon, but I missed her. Then I learned she managed to ditch the officers who were there to protect her."

That sounds like Della, Sarah thought, suddenly not as concerned about her friend. Della did what she liked, period. If anything had happened to her, her bodyguard-driver would have contacted police.

"So, what's homicide got to do with hate crimes, Detective? Why are you and your partner here?"

Seamus didn't answer right away. "I don't think I can answer that to your satisfaction, Doctor Wade. All I can say is that I was hoping the situation would have brought her home and I could find her here."

"You're right, Detective. That doesn't answer my question."

Sarah felt a need to try contacting Della by phone, and started to rise.

"Doctor, I'm curious as to how you know Della Winston so well."

Sarah fidgeted, tension filling her gut. She sat back into the chair, hoping the anxiety didn't show, and thought for a moment about how much to tell, how to best answer that query without breaking a promise made years ago. Della Winston was St. Louis' own "celebutante," a cross between Oprah Winfrey and Paris Hilton. Like a younger Oprah, she was a vibrant, talented black woman who had a successful talk show on local television and a developing media presence. But like the Hilton heiress, she was something of a free spirit, known for her social escapades, her sexual liberality, and her occasional wardrobe *faux pas*. She could be found at one of several clubs along Washington Avenue on almost any night of the week, Antoine hovering close by. It was her way of letting off steam, de-stressing. Unlike this public persona, her private life was much more complicated. But then, whose wasn't?

"Detective, there's a whole lot I could tell you about Della, and a whole lot more that I wouldn't tell you or anyone else." She paused and glanced out the window, alerted by the clarion of a fire truck backing up. "Della and I grew up together in Berkley. We were next-door neighbors on a small street off Frost. Her daddy drove a taxi; our mommas were thick as thieves together. Her daddy was real good with money and 'bout the time we started school he bought a coin-operated laundromat, figurin' everybody needed to wash their clothes and most folks in the neighborhood, black or white, couldn't afford washers and dryers. He kept the machines running right; gave people their money's worth and soon he had a second one and then a third. By the time he had opened his tenth, he hired my momma to manage some of them, and he branched out into car washes, knowing all his friends liked to keep their rides clean, too. He was the father I never had." She paused. "Della was the sister I never had."

She paused again.

"But that's a whole other story. Anyway, he had a major heart attack at the age of fifty-five; didn't make it out of the ER … which, I guess, is why I'm working there now. Della came back to start her career here; hoped to move to the big time in New York or Washington, but found a niche here and never left."

Sarah intuitively observed the man's body language and noted that he was leaning forward, elbows on his knees, listening. This wasn't just his job; he seemed truly interested in her story.

"How old were you when he passed away?"

"It was my third year in med school. I was about to turn twenty-five."

He nodded. "Must have been tough. Wanting to make him

proud. Looking forward to having him there when you graduated, became a doctor. My dad died a month before I graduated from police academy. He'd been a policeman, too, as was his father and grandfather." He rose from the chair and looked out the window. "Sometimes I wonder if it was worth carrying on the legacy." He turned back toward her. "We don't exactly see the best of society in either of our professions." He blushed. "Sorry, that was probably out of line. Been a rough two days."

He sat down and tried again to cross his legs. "So, where's your brother?"

"Korea. In the Army. And just itchin' to go to the Middle East for some fool reason."

"And what about Della's brother? You never mentioned him. Our state's first black Senator."

Sarah stiffened in her seat. "Let's not go there. DeWayne and I have nothing to say to each other and I don't want to talk about him." She stood.

"I need to check on Beatrice … see what Angie's supposed to do. And I really need to be getting home."

Seamus stood to face her. "Hey, sorry, I didn't mean –"

Sarah held up her hand to stop him. "I know. Look, it's obvious Della's not coming soon and as long as Beatrice has someone here with her, I really do need to get home."

The detective nodded. "I understand. Um … I can let myself out. Goodnight."

Sarah watched as he walked toward the front door. She knew she'd been too abrupt. He'd had no way of knowing about the bad blood between her and DeWayne. Or between Della and DeWayne, for that matter, because of what he'd done to Sarah. That secret, known only by the three of them, gave Della considerable power over her brother and his political ambitions. Sarah knew something neither of them did, but that secret gave her no power over either.

Seamus gazed out across the front yard as he emerged from the house into the bright lights that flooded the area to give the crime scene and arson investigators ample lighting to do their jobs. He noted that the charred cross had been removed and the fire trucks had left the scene. His fellow detectives were no doubt canvassing the street, interviewing neighbors who even at this late hour might have seen or heard something. He looked around for Stick but saw that his car was gone.

As he stepped down onto the driveway, he heard the house phone ring and stopped, wondering if Ms. Winston was finally checking in. After four rings, it stopped and he resumed his walk with a considerably slower step and noticeable limp while debating whether he should return to the house. As he reached the street, the front door burst open.

"Detective O'Connor, where –" The doctor stopped as she spotted him. She appeared frantic, close to tears. "Oh God, dear God. Quick … quick, you have to hear this. Oh God." Her chest heaved in frenzied respirations. She pulled him up the walk and pushed him through the front door. "I was upstairs talking with the aide and didn't answer the phone, expecting the recorder to pick up," she continued as she dragged him to the kitchen. "By the time I got to the phone, all I heard was Della scream and the phone clicked off. Listen." She hit the replay button on the answering machine.

"Aunt Beatrice, Sarah … someone pick up …"

CHAPTER 13

After a second near miss on a curve, Sayer remained focused on the road until he saw the sign for Pea Ridge. He turned to Edwards and said, "The turn-off is just a mile or so ahead."

"Yeah, but stop at the intersection first," replied Edwards.

A few minutes later, Sayer slowed down and pulled into a gravel turn-out just before the turn. Edwards jumped out of the car and slipped on a pair of night-vision goggles before sliding into the brush beside the road. Sayer was anxious; Edwards' absence seemed to stretch on and on but a glance at his watch showed only a ten minute lapse when the man re-opened his car door.

"Somebody's there already. The first sets of cameras have been turned on. We can go in the front door as long as we're prepared for the worst ... or we can swing to the southwest and use a backdoor approach I know about. The Colonel showed it to me a few months ago. We can slip in, scout out the compound, and leave if we have to ... or not."

Sayer's concern showed on his face. "A backdoor? I thought the compound was totally secured."

"Oh yeah, it is. There're monitors there, too, but you need a special access code for the system to turn them on."

That revelation disturbed Sayer. Was Edwards stating that the Colonel would be willing to leave the others behind and slip out unnoticed in an emergency? Did that include leaving him behind as well, after all that Sayer had done to finance and build their operation? Sayer wanted to know about this route in and out of the compound.

Della shifted around in her usual seat at The Monsoon, as it grew uncomfortably warm. She should have expected no less. After all, she had occupied it full-time after her arrival instead of monopolizing the dance floor, as was her custom. The day, with its torrent of interviews and a mind-numbing session with the police artist, had produced a pent up anxiety that resulted in Della's breaking her one-drink rule. The breaking newsflash crossed the screen of a nearby TV as she finished her fourth Cosmo. What she saw sobered her in a snap.

"Oh my God, OH MY GOD! That, that's my house!" she screamed as the startling image of a large cross burning in front of a century old mansion filled the flat panel display. She jumped up, knocking over the table. Empty glasses shattered on the floor. "Antoine!"

She glanced about for her driver. A moment later, he was at her side, whispering in her ear, "I'll get the car."

Della gathered her things and waved at the barkeep. He nodded in return. He would add the bill to her revolving tab. She pushed through the crowd and climbed the stairs leading out of the basement club to its entrance at the side of the building. Once outside, she retrieved her cell phone from her purse.

"Aunt Beatrice, Sarah … somebody pick up. Sarah, I saw you with Auntie on the evening news. It's horrible … my home … I … look, I'm at The Monsoon. Antoine's getting the car and I'll be home in minutes. Sarah, please don't leave yet. Here comes the car."

The club's sign on the front of the building flickered and movement reflected on a storefront's glass window caught her attention. She turned to look but the apparition had disappeared. She looked to the front of the building where the whine of her car's engine and an open car door greeted her. The smell of exhaust assailed her nose as the screeching of tires filled her ears. The flickering light revealed a rusting white van skidding to a halt behind her Mercedes. As if lit by a strobe, the side door opened and several men emerged wearing baggy sweats and ski masks. Two ran to her.

"Who … What the hell? Get your hands off me, asshole!"

She fought to break free and the second man moved in to assist the first. Gunshots rang out. She watched Antoine's fedora fly off his head before he crumpled to the ground next to her car.

"Oh shit, they just shot Antoine!" She screamed, hoping to find help.

The first man yanked the cell phone from her hand and

dropped it to the ground where he smashed it underfoot. The two men together lifted her from her feet and carried her to the awaiting van. As she landed on the cargo bay's floor, she felt a jab in her upper arm. Her scream withered to a whispered wail.

CHAPTER 14

Sayer made his decision.

"Okay, let's use the back approach and see what's going on in there."

Edwards gave him directions and ten minutes later they parked along a dirt and gravel path that Sayer estimated to be roughly a half-mile from the southwest corner of the facility. Edwards handed him a set of night-vision goggles and the duo struck off toward the buildings. The going was slow through the thick brush but they soon approached the fence line defending the perimeter of the training ground. Along the way, Edwards pointed out several motion sensors and two video feeds, none of which were active.

"We can only move about ten yards in either direction before we get picked up by sensors," Edwards whispered. "Let's move east. That'll give the best vantage point without actually going in."

Sayer followed the other man and soon they found a spot with a reasonably unobstructed view of the main buildings. They didn't need night-vision gear to see that something was going on. He counted at least twenty men unloading boxes from two trucks.

"Looks like they're unloading rations. Someone must be planning to be there a while," whispered Sayer.

Edwards nodded. "Bobby's down there with them."

"Then maybe this will be easy. If he's already planning to lay low here, we may not have to convince him to stay."

"Yeah, maybe. But there's a whole lot more coming off those trucks than a few guys are going to need. There's enough there to feed a company of soldiers for several months, and we don't know what they've already off-loaded."

Sayer thought about that for a moment. Edwards was right, again. And that tingling of suspicion crept through Sayer ... again.

"Let's get back to the car. I think I need to wake up the Colonel in California."

"The Monsoon" was still a relative unknown among the usual crowd that engulfed the club district of Washington Avenue nightly in downtown St. Louis. Occupying the basement of an old warehouse that the Winston family's development company had recently renovated into trendy lofts above, its entrance in the rear of the building was accessible only by a dimly lit alley. They maintained the poor illumination to keep casual partiers out, but security was tight and there had never been an assault, robbery, or any other crime against persons in the immediate area. Until now.

Seamus and Sarah pulled to the curb just outside the police cordon, the police lights of his unmarked car flashing in the front grill and rear window. Sarah gazed about the scene and felt she was chasing the television news crews around the city. Those who had left the house on Westminster Place had already positioned their satellite trucks along Washington Avenue and reporters performed their 'talking head' leads to the latest story. Della Winston had become a one-woman news item that promised to dominate both local and national airtime for days to come.

Anger bubbled up inside as Sarah overheard one reporter speculating about the Winston campaign capitalizing upon the morning's stabbing of the diplomat to stage the late night events for political publicity. Sarah prepared to stomp over to the brassy haired, surgically enhanced shill when the detective grabbed her elbow.

"C'mon, ignore her." He pointed her toward an ambulance parked next to a black Lexus that Sarah recognized as Della's. A second ambulance pulled away at the same time.

Sarah's mind slipped into "ER Doc" mode right away and she rushed toward the boxy vehicle. She'd worked on these rigs as a junior resident and knew them inside and out. Without hesitation, she jumped up through the rear door.

"I'm Doctor Wade, can I help?" She looked at the nearest paramedic and then the other, recognizing them both. "What've we …" she asked as she reached for latex gloves nearby. She stopped as she realized the gurney was empty and the two men were sipping coffee, biding their time.

"Sorry, Doc. Nothing you can do. Thirty-two year old black male. J-4 when we got here. He's still outside waiting for the investigator from the M.E.'s office."

Shaken and her sense of purpose deflated, she managed to mutter, "Where?"

The closest EMT-P pointed back through the door. "Right next to the driver's door. The Lexus there."

She eased out of the door and hesitated. She'd never faltered in a bad case before. Gunshot wounds, crispy critter burns, limbs mangled by power tools, "Beatle Baileys" with limbs pointing in all directions after major trauma – she'd worked them all and never wavered. A dead body was no big deal; she encountered more DBs in a year than most people would see in several lifetimes. But she didn't want to face this one.

As she glanced toward the Lexus, Detective O'Connor was already there talking to another detective. She approached but stopped short of where she could see the shrouded victim.

The two policemen turned to her.

Seamus spoke. "Doctor Wade, this is Detective Brian Carter. This is Doctor Sarah Wade."

"We've met before," Sarah answered.

"Hello, Doctor," Carter said in acknowledgement, a certain edge to his voice. "We think this is Della Winston's driver, but we've found no wallet or other ID. Did you know him?"

Sarah felt a pulse of bile rise into her throat. She nodded.

"Would you mind?" he asked as he reached down to pull back the sheet.

Sarah forced herself to look. For a brief moment, she saw the face of "Dad" Winston, but the visage quietly morphed into that of Antoine DeMoyne. Tears welled up into the corners of her eyes as she nodded confirmation. She had just started her clinical training when "Dad" had died. Now, with her training almost completed, she had been too late to save another family member. Like "Dad," Della took care of family first. Driver and bodyguard, yes. But first and foremost, Antoine was Della's cousin ... and Sarah's first big pre-teen crush. She felt as if life was tumbling down around her, as if she was in the midst of the crumbling World Trade Center and would never escape the mountain of rubble. On the verge of collapse, she felt someone take hold of her and lead her to the ambulance.

Refusing to lie down on the same gurney that might soon carry away Antoine's body, she sat on the back step of the rig. She accepted the paramedics' offer of a cup of coffee and sipped it slowly as she tried to compose her emotions.

Seamus returned to her side a few minutes later. "You okay, Doctor?"

She looked up at him and nodded. "Please ... call me Sarah. The formalities are getting cumbersome."

"Sure. My friends call me Shay."

"Have you learned any more about what happened?"

Seamus shook his head. "Actually, I gave Carter a better picture of what happened than he could give me. I told him about the phone call. One of the club's security guys was found at the entrance of the alley. He'd been Tasered. That's who the other ambulance toted away."

"Who the hell is in charge here?" boomed a deep bass voice full of belligerence.

"Oh shit," muttered Sarah.

Seamus looked in the direction of the voice and saw three black males entering the police cordon, one of average height and the other two distinctly taller and broader in the shoulders. He had the impression he wouldn't want to meet either of the two in a one-on-one match, whether it be a dark alley or well-lit ring.

Sarah suddenly found a new source of resolve and steeled her mind and emotions to what was about to happen. She knew that voice.

CHAPTER 15

The Colonel must have dozed off. He remembered reclining on top of the bed, his mind twisting and turning through the maze of options he faced, trying to develop a mental list of pros and cons. Now, the melodic tones of his cell phone, a ring tone assigned to only one person, awakened him. He had no idea how long it had been ringing, but he quickly rolled both feet off the bed, sat up, turned on the bedside lamp, and answered the call.

"Colonel, he's there alright, but we might have a problem," Sayer said.

"Oh?" 'Problem' was not the word he'd wanted to hear.

"Bobby's there with at least twenty other men and they're stockpiling supplies. We saw them off-loading food and stuff, but no munitions. We don't know if that's already there or yet to come. Edwards and I are just outside your backdoor to the compound. We haven't made contact with him yet."

The Colonel noted the subtle emphasis on the word 'backdoor.' He felt a slight annoyance at Edwards for using that route, but after a moment's thought, knew the man had made the right choice in going there. He didn't respond right away. He needed to add these new variables to his previous ponderings. The presence of so many men implied actions on his nephew's part that he had not considered. Bobby was aggressive and self-righteous. He had shown great impatience with the recent change in tactics. Was he also mutinous enough to go rogue?

The Colonel required no deep study of the situation or psychoanalysis of his nephew to answer that question. Bobby was, and he had.

"Sayer, I believe young Bobby has decided to branch out on his own. I don't like to think that's the case, but if you can confirm it, we need to capitalize on it. We can't afford any attention and he seems intent on bringing it our way, even if unintentionally."

"Yes, Sir. Should I go ahead and talk with him, let him know what's at stake?"

"No! No, don't even mention that my work is involved here. We have to get rid of the problem, not add to it. He brought this on himself, and whoever's following him. Here's what I want you to do …"

"I said, who's in charge here?" the voice boomed again.

The three black males neared the ambulance and Lexus, and Seamus watched as Carter stepped forward. Before Seamus could warn Carter, the other detective replied, "Who wants to know?

Seamus joined his peer and whispered, "That's Senator Winston. Watch your step."

The smallest of the three men stepped up to the detectives while the two hulks stayed back, their eyes constantly scanning the area. The man did not offer his hand and had an imperious air about him. In an instant, Seamus knew who was <u>not</u> getting his vote come November. His back was to the ambulance now and Seamus saw Sarah ease up and into the back of the rig, somewhat out of view.

"I'm DeWayne Winston. What happened here? That is my sister's car. Where is she?"

Carter extended his hand, but was not rewarded in kind. "I'm Detective Carter, Senator. To answer –"

"What's your rank? What division?"

"Sergeant Brian Carter, I'm with –"

"Where's your lieutenant? Or better yet, your captain."

"Let the man answer your questions, DeWayne." Seamus turned away from Carter and Winston and saw Sarah approaching them. She appeared angry and ready to whup someone. Seamus had a good idea who that someone would be and mentally prepared himself to arrest the two bodyguards if they tried to stop her.

Winston turned toward Sarah and glowered at her. "What are <u>you</u> doing here? Where's Della?"

"Maybe I should ask what you're doing here. Aren't you supposed to be somewhere kissing babies? Or is it just ass-kissing you do these days?"

The politician stiffened and raised his hand, summoning one of his men.

"Dupree, make sure the doctor here gets home safely. She's out after her curfew." One of the two men started to approach.

Seamus stepped in. "She's not going anywhere. She's part of this investigation and she's with me."

Winston raised an eyebrow and stared at Seamus, questioning.

"I'm Detective Sergeant Seamus O'Connor. We're both with homicide and you've entered a crime scene without authorization. I need for you to leave."

Winston glared at him as if saying, "I dare you to try."

Sarah placed her hand on Seamus' arm. Shaking her head, she said, "Don't you know not to mess with pit bulls?"

Seamus saw the look on her face. If he persisted, the man was going to sink his teeth into his flesh and career and never let go.

Sarah looked back at Winston. "You wanted to know what's going on? Well, under that sheet over there is your dear cousin, Antoine. Remember him? Maybe not. I remember it was Della who got him straightened out and gave him a job after you turned your back on him. He bought two rounds to the chest trying to protect Della. As for her, we have no idea where she is. There … that answer your questions?"

For the first time, Winston's arrogant veneer seemed to crack. "Damn. May I?" he asked, pointing toward the body.

Sarah stepped aside and let the man follow the detectives to Antoine. Carter pulled back the sheet to reveal the dead man's face. The honest wave of emotion evident on DeWayne's countenance surprised her. Antoine had idolized DeWayne. DeWayne the scholar; DeWayne the All-State athlete; DeWayne the lawyer. But it was DeWayne who had introduced Antoine to a young woman who proved to be his downfall. She introduced him to crack cocaine and when he had fallen to the nadir of his life, he had asked DeWayne for help. But DeWayne was too busy … always too busy going after what he wanted to help anyone, family or not, unless he received something in return.

What could a crack addict offer to an aspiring politico?

DeWayne stooped to touch Antoine's cheek, but Carter stopped him.

"Sorry, can't let you touch the body. The death investigator hasn't been here yet."

DeWayne seemed to soften. "What do we know?" he asked.

Carter proceeded to tell the man about the phone call. DeWayne glanced at Sarah as the detective detailed her role at the house. *Yeah, I was there for Auntie. Where were you?* she thought. From his response, she realized he did not know about the burning cross. Yet, knowing the man as she did, she had no doubt he would turn the situation to his favor. Somehow.

It didn't take long for the real DeWayne to re-emerge. "I want to talk to your captain. Now!" he commanded.

Sayer and Edwards drove slowly up to the entrance of the grounds. The closed gate appeared locked, but both men knew their approach had been watched. A young man, no older than twenty with close-cropped hair and wearing military BDUs, suddenly appeared at Sayer's window. Sayer lowered the glass.

"Fletcher."

"Uh, um, hey Major. No one expectin' you to be here." He nervously fingered the assault rifle slung over his shoulder.

"Where's Bobby? We need to talk to him."

"Bobby, um, the Colonel is at the main building."

"Colonel?"

"Yes, Sir. He says he got promoted and is taking over the company."

"I see. Let us in and inform him that we're coming up. We're not here to make trouble. His uncle needs some things he has stored out here."

"Um, sure. I mean, yes, Sir." The fellow moved to the gate, unlocked and opened it, and waved them through.

"I guess that answers our first question," Edwards said as they drove toward the main building. "I musta missed the memo 'bout promotions." He grinned.

The lake compound had started out as the small country

retreat of a St. Louis urologist. The two bedroom log home, five acre lake and forty wooded acres had been purchased from the doctor's estate and expanded over the past two years to include a dining hall, multiple bunkhouses, underground munitions storage, a large utility building with a wing that was to become a laboratory, a second utility building that served as a motor pool and housed several vehicles, and one small isolated bunkhouse that had been fortified for use as holding cells if necessary. Their firing range sat beside that building. Enclosing almost five acres, secure fencing, and a high tech surveillance system surrounded this main complex.

As they pulled up into the large gravel apron in the center of the complex, their quarry stood on the wide plank front porch of the old home, his arms folded across his chest. The two men emerged from the car and Sayer saw Bobby's right hand slide toward the sidearm on his belt. He sensed that Edwards saw it, too.

Sayer held up his right hand in greeting.

"No need, Bobby. Blood's thicker than water. We're just here to talk and pick up some equipment."

The young rebel nodded and waved them inside, to what had been his uncle's headquarters and office, but he never removed his hand from his handgun. As a sign of peace, Sayer and Edwards sat down in the circle of rustic chairs with stick frames but comfortable upholstery. Bobby remained standing.

Sayer started the discussion.

"Your uncle sends his greetings … and his concern."

"Yeah, sure. I'm not taking orders from him anymore. He's gotten soft."

"Look, Bobby, he might have a different game plan, but soft isn't the word I'd use. Give things some time, and see if you still think so. As far as your using the compound here, he says make yourself at home … just make sure you stay at home. You're a wanted man, Bobby."

"Says who? Nobody saw us, 'cept that one bitch and we're dealin' with that."

"Oh?" That revelation concerned Sayer. He knew any

additional actions by Bobby would further cement the Colonel's plans for his nephew, and again he felt a tinge of remorse. He knew the Colonel well enough to know the man would suffer the rest of his life with the secret that he was responsible for his nephew's death, whether directly or indirectly. In his mind, he could rationalize that Bobby had brought this on himself, but his heart would forever be tormented.

Edwards entered the conversation. "You do realize that by tomorrow, next day at the latest, the police will have your name, your home address. They'll be talking to your mom and neighbors. The TV cameras caught you escaping. Your tattoo's been on every major local and national newscast since six o'clock."

The young man shifted uneasily on his feet. His body language revealed that this was news to him.

"That's why your uncle wants you to lay low here. One trip to town, the gas station, a restaurant, any place, and you'll be targeted," Edwards continued.

"I know that. You think I'm stupid? We've stockpiled everything we need to sit this out."

"We?" asked Sayer. "Yeah, having a camp full of guys with rifles and wearing BDUs sure won't get noticed." He shook his head.

Bobby reddened, appeared angrier. "I know that, too. These guys are just here to help unload. Most of 'em will be gone before daybreak. There's only goin' to be four or five of us here at any one time."

"Why, Bobby?" Sayer held his hands out front, palms up, questioning. "Your uncle wants to know why you killed that diplomat."

Bobby rolled his head, massaging the tension in his neck with his right hand.

"Didn't know who he was at the time. Me and my friends were down there partyin' and we're getting ready to head home when this group of niggers comes toward us. Two of 'em, two big guys, just upped and pushed us aside. Ain't no darkie that's gonna get away with that. Guess I showed them how good a bodyguards they are." He grinned nervously.

"Yeah," Edwards said. "They'll still be crying in their beer when the executioner pokes you with that lethal injection."

Bobby tensed, his hand at his pistol again. Edwards glared at him, daring him to try. Sayer knew who would win that contest.

"Cool it, both of you," declared Sayer.

The young man turned to Sayer. "Fletcher said you're here to get some stuff for my uncle. Get it and get lost. I can take care of myself."

Sayer looked at him calmly and encouraged him. "I know you can, Bobby. I have every confidence in you." He paused, and then stood. "Look, what we need is in building three, but we're gonna need your guys to help load it into one of those trucks. We'll take care of it on the other end and leave the truck in the usual lot in Potosi … if that's okay with you?"

"Uh, sure. What is it?"

"Just some medical equipment, lab stuff your uncle stored out here. He was thinking about setting up a lab here, but we still have a lot to get to make that happen. Since you're taking over, he wants to get it out of your way. You might need the space."

Sayer kept stroking Bobby's ego, playing along. It was the best way to avoid any objections to removing the equipment and any links to the Colonel or their plan. He sensed an easing of tension in the young man.

"Sure. Sounds like a plan to me. What kind of stuff is it?"

"It's complicated to describe. Your uncle understands it. He tried to explain it to me three times and I'm still not sure what it does," Sayer lied.

They moved out into the compound and Bobby called together several men. They assembled in front of building three and Sayer unlocked the door. Inside were several large crates on pallets and a hydraulic pallet mover. One of the men backed an empty truck up to the door and with some effort they loaded the crates into the truck and hoisted the pallet mover in as well. Edwards double checked the tie-downs, closed the roll-top door to the truck and secured the latch.

Bobby eased back into the building, while Sayer followed.

"Never been in here before. Looks like clearing this out will give us a ton of new space." He looked around the room and pointed to a set of doors. "What's back there?"

"A small lab. Not sure what your uncle did in there," Sayer lied again. He knew exactly what was there, a decoy lab with enough anhydrous ammonia and pseudoephedrine to flood the St. Louis meth market for a month. There was also enough C4 explosive to take down the building and its immediate neighbors. The intent of the room was to throw off investigators should the facility be raided. Any attempt to force open the doors would set off the charges and the debris would point to little more than another rural Missouri meth lab.

"I'd show you in, but your uncle's the only one with the keys and combination to the alarm system. I wouldn't mess with it if I were you."

"Speaking of alarm systems," Edwards added, "there's a small gap in your perimeter guard in the southeast sector. We added new motion detectors and a video feed, but never got around to incorporating them into the computer system. Your uncle wanted me to secure that for you … if that's okay with you."

Bobby eyed him suspiciously, but Sayer backed up Edwards' by saying, "He's right, Bobby. It's a five-yard wide corridor from the southeast corner. Starts at that fence post with the blue paint on it. If you stay on a true southeast heading, you'll avoid detection by the system. Your uncle wanted a safe escape route should the feds come in and try to use our own system to track anyone trying to leave the area."

"I know that post," replied Bobby. "I always thought it just got sprayed accidentally."

Sayer smiled inwardly. The poor kid was taking the bait. If he let Edwards onto the computer system, they would open a backdoor into the computer system that would allow them to monitor the place remotely. But more importantly, it opened a phone line that would allow a single phone call to destroy the entire facility. Sayer wished there were some other way, but he knew that Bobby was too big a risk. If it came down to choosing Bobby or their plan, the Colonel would make that call. The

Colonel had no God complex, but he'd sacrifice his nephew for the good of the many.

"Okay, but make it quick. We still have things to do here," Bobby said.

Edwards followed the young man to the main building and to a security console manned by two men in their early twenties. They sported identical short cropped hair, forest BDU shirts, and frayed jeans. Edwards typed in a password and a security screen appeared.

"Hey, where'd that come from? We've never seen that screen," said one of the two.

Edwards ignored them and entered a username, followed by another password. Another small window appeared. He quickly typed in yet another password, and pressed the "OK" button. All of the small windows disappeared instantly.

"All done," Edwards said. He turned and walked out of the building, followed by Sayer and Bobby.

Edwards started off in the truck while Sayer said goodbye to Bobby and climbed into his own car. As Sayer turned the corner around the last building, a white Ford utility van passed him heading into the complex. But instead of turning toward the main buildings, it continued straight, heading for the detention building. That sparked Sayer's curiosity so he slowed to a crawl and watched the activity in his rear view mirror. The van parked and the doors burst open. The lighting was poor but he saw enough.

"Aw crap!" he exclaimed as he saw three men drag a blindfolded, black woman out of the truck and into the building.

CHAPTER 16

Sayer had become a successful businessman because he could instinctively see the value of a product and its place in the market. He knew what trends would become red hot, and which ones were about to die. He could also quickly assess things like cost-benefit ratios, time efficiency savings, and other pertinent factors that enabled him to sell the products and services he picked up at outstanding margins.

He could also read people well, and he didn't like what he read in Bobby, who he now saw as a brash, aggressive usurper. Sayer never claimed to be a strategist. Chess had never been his forte. He sometimes couldn't see ten, five, or even three moves ahead. No, strategy was the Colonel's strong suit, not his. And Bobby, like Sayer, did not share in his uncle's strategic abilities. He lived in the short term, while his uncle played out the long term.

Yet, even he could see that the kidnapping of Della Winston was a reckless move fated to result in a severe and devastating backlash. Unlike moving a pawn to protect the queen, this action held no promise of delay but instead threatened to expose their "queen," to attract attention to the Colonel and his plan. The Colonel did not want the scrutiny the violent death of Della Winston would precipitate. Even Sayer could foresee the checkmate move on this one.

Immersed in thought, Sayer tried to place himself in the Colonel's chair. Should he go back and try to discern Bobby's plan for the woman? Maybe he needed to be more direct, simply confront Bobby, and tell him outright the danger of what he was doing. He didn't want to disturb the Colonel yet one more time that night. Would the woman be safe through the night, so that he could get the Colonel to contact his nephew directly the next day?

The next curve in the road caught Sayer by surprise. He cursed himself for not paying closer attention to his driving. Route 185's twists and turns had almost snared them on the way to the camp. Now, alone on the way back, he found himself slipping along the gravel shoulder toward a steep drop off as he overcorrected his turn. Braking, he slowed the slide and almost made it back into his lane, but his back end continued its deliberate glide toward disaster until the sidewall of the back passenger tire hit a piece of discarded scrap metal and ruptured. The sudden flattening of the tire allowed the wheel's rim to gouge deep into the gravel. He came to an abrupt stop, perpendicular to the road.

He gently gassed the car, hoping to inch forward until he was fully on the road and facing the right direction, but the tires spun without traction. After placing the gear into park, he gingerly exited the car and walked toward the back to determine the extent of his problem. He found both rear wheels dangling over the edge of the hill and the frame of the car resting on the gravel and dirt.

Front-wheel drive, all-wheel drive, it didn't matter. He wasn't going anywhere until the car was winched, pulled, or lifted back onto the road and the spare tire put on. He could do the latter, but he was helpless in getting the car back on the road. He knew Edwards, with the truck, could do it.

He retrieved his cell phone from the car and flipped open the case. Pressing the speed dial for Edwards' cell phone, he placed the phone to his ear. Nothing. He glanced at the display. No service.

It was after 3 AM; it could be hours before another car came along that rural road. Should he wait at the car or start hoofing it to get help? Cursing under his breath, Sayer tried to think where he'd last seen a house or someplace with a phone. He knew he'd passed a barn maybe a mile back, but he recalled no house. With his thoughts focused on Bobby, he'd not been paying attention. He looked but saw no lights ahead.

After a moment of thought, he decided. There was no sense in staying with the car. He needed to seek help. He sat back in the car and glanced around. Nothing there of value, nothing incriminating. Just an older car, close to a junker, he used to blend in when driving in rural Missouri. He turned on the emergency flashers in hope that any driver coming along would see them in time to avoid hitting the nose of his car as it jutted into the lane. Then he exited the vehicle, locked it, and started walking north toward the small city of Sullivan. Although he could only guess at the distance, he felt it more likely to find help heading toward town than away from it.

The first five minutes involved an uphill climb and he started to lag, not out of a lack of fitness, but from fatigue. He hadn't slept in over thirty-six hours. He reached the crest of the hill and stopped. Was that the sound of a vehicle? Was he going to get lucky? Not a car. Something bigger, maybe a diesel engine. A truck. Then he heard the whistle. It was a train somewhere in the distance, from a direction he couldn't determine.

He resumed walking, wishing he had a light jacket. Jogging would expedite an end to the night's misadventure as well as him warm up. Yet, he resisted that desire, having no idea how long he would be walking and needing to pace himself. As it was, the exercise soon had his body at a comfortable temperature.

He rounded another curve and saw the lights. Headlights headed his way. Maybe the driver had a cell phone with service, or could give him a lift.

As the vehicle neared, Sayer could tell that it was a truck but nothing more in the glare of its lights. He stepped into the lane and waved his arms. The truck slowed down and pulled up next to him. *Of all the luck*, he thought. It was a tow truck with "Rick's Towing" and a phone number on the door. The window inched down in a series of jerks and the driver stuck his head out.

"Help ya?"

Sayer almost declined when he saw the driver, a slight but muscular black male. He didn't want the help of a Negro and he really did not want to get into the truck with one. But ... the boy had a tow truck. Did he want to free his car and get home, or keep plodding along until he reached Sullivan?

"Um, yeah," he answered. He explained the situation as tersely as he could.

"The Good Lord's smilin' on you tonight, yessir. I'm jus' what you need. Hop in."

Sayer circled around the truck and hesitated. He'd never sat next to a darkie before and didn't want to catch anything from him, but what choice did he have? He climbed in and sat as close to the door as possible.

The man smiled at Sayer. "Yessir, the Good Lord's smilin' on you tonight. I jus' finished another call and felt like God was tellin' me to take this back road home. Normal, I go another way, but I jus' felt like this was where I needed to be. How far'd you say?"

"Mile, mile and half. Hard to say at night."

The man smiled again, his white teeth appearing fluorescent against his dark skin.

"True enough in the daylight, too, with all these twists and turns. Kinda like the twists and turns of life, eh? Never know what's 'round the corner or what could knock you off the road. You a prayin' man, sir?"

Sayer didn't want to answer. It was bad enough to find himself relying on this boy for help. He didn't want to converse with him, too. Yet, he found himself shaking his head. God had never been much in his life.

The driver must have caught his head movement.

"Too bad, 'cause then you might had a good testimony to answered prayer."

Sayer saw the glimmer of flashing lights ahead. So did the driver.

"Looks like we're there." He turned on his emergency flashers and the scene was swathed in rotating yellow light. He pulled up next to the car and stopped. "Let's see what we got."

Sayer jumped from the truck before the driver could open his door and moved about ten feet away. The driver surveyed the situation and shook his head. "Mighty lucky … if'n you believe in luck. I'd say God was watching over you tonight, sir. He's got a plan for you. Yessir, I believe he does."

Sayer, ignoring the reference to God, watched the man climb into the truck, position it, and lower the winch cable. The man attached it to the front.

"Don't wanna damage your undercarriage or exhaust system, so I'm gonna take it real slow 'til those rear wheels catch and raise up the body."

Sayer had never thought of blacks as being competent in anything, but he watched and saw that the man was true to his word. He knew what he was doing. Despite the crunching of gravel and grinding noises that Sayer knew positively were the sounds of his muffler disintegrating, the car was soon on solid ground with the muffler intact, or appearing so by flashlight.

The driver walked over to the blown tire and inspected it.

"Well, sir, besides a blown tire, this rim is shot. You'll need a whole new wheel. Got a spare?"

Sayer groaned. He'd removed the small donut spare for more hauling space the previous week and had never replaced it. Now he was going to have to rely on this man to tow him to town, too.

"No. Took it out and forgot to put it back."

"Hmmm," the driver muttered. He pulled a small penlight from his shirt pocket and flashed it across the good tire up front. That glowing smile of his reappeared and he laughed. "Yessir, I keeps saying it. The Good Lord's watchin' over you tonight."

Sayer looked at him quizzically.

"That last run a mine … car was totaled, but he had two good wheels and practically new tires. Accepted 'em as part payment for the tow. Same size as yours."

Sayer sighed in relief. "Man, what a lucky coincidence."

The driver smiled again and answered, "Sir, I'm a Christian man. For us there's no such thing as luck or coincidence. God's got everything in the palm of His hand and He's there to help you sweat the small things as well as the big."

Sayer felt uncomfortable with the man's persistent references to God. Where was God for his father? Where was God for his family after his dad died?

The man stood, walked to the back of his truck, retrieved a wheel, and rolled it to the back of Sayer's car. Ten minutes later, he detached the winch and moved the truck away. Coming back to Sayer, he said, "Climb in and start 'er up. Let's see how she does."

Sayer obeyed and first noticed that the muffler was indeed

intact. He slipped the car into gear and started forward. Everything seemed okay, so he stopped, and rolled down the window.

"What do I owe you?"

The man laughed and his smile gleamed whiter than ever. "Well, sir, likes I told you. God told me to come this way, and He made sure I had a wheel for you. So, I guess this one's on Jesus."

Sayer shook his head, and said, "Seriously, how much?"

"I am serious, not a thing. God's got a plan for you."

Sayer didn't know what to say. He actually felt ashamed at some of his earlier thoughts … and that emotion surprised him.

The driver continued, "Yessir, I feel God's tellin' me to warn you. He's got a plan for you and you ain't gonna like it, but He's watchin' out for your eternal soul. Ever try to ponder eternity? Think about it. Like the proverbial bottomless well where nothing ever hits bottom. Well, have a good night."

He started back to his truck, then stopped and turned back. "Tell you what, I'll follow you for a bit, make sure your car's okay."

The man returned to his truck, and again, true to his word, pulled in behind Sayer as he drove up the hill he had walked only half an hour earlier. Sayer felt unsettled and couldn't pinpoint why. Was he letting the man's mumbo jumbo about God get to him? He glanced in his mirror. The truck's lights were still behind him. The car seemed undamaged. He noticed no strange noises or wobbling. As he entered a long straight stretch, he glanced again in the mirror and saw the truck's lights maybe a hundred yards back. He looked forward again and let go of the wheel. The car stayed true on its course, its alignment intact. He glanced once more into the mirror, but the lights were gone. He hadn't passed any turns, pullouts, or driveways. Where was the truck? He looked again. The road had been straight for almost a mile now. No truck. Sayer felt a cold shiver go down his spine.

CHAPTER 17

"I want to talk to your captain. Now!" Winston commanded.

Carter and Seamus looked at each other and a slight grin flashed across each mug.

Carter responded, "Sir, our lieutenant is on his way here, but you'll have to wait outside the police tape so we can keep this area clear for the ME's people and crime lab folks. We'll send him your way as soon as he gets here. So, please, wait over there." Carter pointed to a spot outside the tape, but as close as possible. "You can observe from there."

DeWayne glared at Sarah. "What about her?"

"We still have to finish taking her statement. Then we'll make sure she gets home," Seamus said.

Sarah was sure he was misrepresenting her role in the situation just to get DeWayne off their backs. She wasn't about to go home at this point.

"Doctor," Seamus continued, "if you'll come back to the car with me, we can finish up."

Sarah waited until DeWayne moved off before complying. She entered the front passenger seat of Seamus' car, as he climbed into the driver's seat.

"What was that?" she asked.

"What was what?"

"You know. You and Carter grinned when you mentioned your lieutenant."

"You caught that, huh?"

Sarah nodded. "I hope your lieutenant chews DeWayne up one side and down the other for interfering or something. The jerk is so full of himself, he'll probably play this whole thing for the sympathy vote."

Seamus paused. "Doubt it. The Senator's the one with all the clout. Lieutenant's been dogging us all for the past two weeks ... since he stopped smoking. Time for a little payback."

He grinned that grin again. Curiously, Sarah thought it cute.

"Yeah, sure, I see. Nothing like piling it on top and then waiting for the shit to roll downhill. Just where do you sit on that hill again?" The grin disappeared. "So, what now?" she asked.

"I get your statement and get you home. Like I told Senator Winston."

She crossed her arms. "I don't think so. No homey white boy's gonna take me home with all of this going on. I'm here to help find Della. That's final."

He didn't smile when he glanced at her. "Well, I really don't see that I need a formal statement from you since I've been with you for the past couple of hours. Give me a minute."

He exited the car and walked toward Carter's sedan. Sarah wasn't about to let him just walk away. She wanted a game plan. She was pumped, anxious to help find her best friend, her sister. She jumped out of the car and stormed after him. As he neared the car, he waved at a black, uniformed officer standing next to the car. Sarah caught up to him as the officer joined Seamus.

"Jenkins, please escort brown sugar here back to her car and then home." With that, he dismissed her and walked away.

"This way, Miss. Car's over here."

Sarah looked at the officer, then to Seamus as he walked away and back to the officer. She quickly rejected the thought of being accused of obstructing justice or failing to comply and ran after Seamus.

"C'mon, Shay ... I can still call you that, right?" He stopped and nodded. "Look, I really can help. I know her, how she thinks, what she might do. We've shared past experiences. I'm convinced I can help."

He scrutinized her from head to toe.

"Not my call. I'm not assigned to this case. Fact is, kidnappings go to the FBI, so I doubt I can help."

As they talked, Carter joined them, holding a VHS cassette and a plastic bag. "Looks like our suspicions were right on. Security video ... recorded the whole thing. Five guys, ski masks, in a rusting, white Ford utility van snatched her after shooting the driver. Didn't get the license." He held up the bag. "We also found this. Looks like someone stomped on it to break it." The plastic bag held a crushed cell phone.

Sarah nodded in recognition. "That looks like Della's."

"Must be what she called home on. The call probably broke off when it was destroyed," Seamus added.

"That's only her decoy phone."

"What?" both detectives said in unison.

Sarah smirked at Seamus. "Told you I could help. That's what she always called her decoy." She paused and both men looked impatient. "She was making a call on her cell one time … back during the Alley K debacle … and some asshole reporter ran up past Antoine and grabbed it from her hand. He published her phonebook on the Internet. What a major headache that was for her … and her friends. Ever since then she's carried a phone with no numbers in the phone book."

"Okay, but it would still show the last ten or fifteen calls made," Carter said.

"True, but with no names listed that's a whole lot less trouble than the dozens of private numbers that had to be changed last time."

Seamus shook his head. "Great. So what? Just how does this tidbit of Della Winston trivia help us?"

"Well, she carries a second one to use in the car or anywhere else private. Did you find another one in the car?"

"No," replied Carter.

"Her purse?"

"Spilled across the back seat. Money gone. No phone there."

Sarah heard the ME's investigator hailing Carter and the detective turned to leave.

"Then she probably has it hidden on her person … snuggled into the top of a boot or the cup of her bra. I've seen her do that before. We can trace it, right? What was she wearing in the video?"

Carter stopped and turned back a step. "Couldn't tell about the shoes, or boots, but her top was cut so she could easily slip something into her bra. Wouldn't that be really uncomfortable? I mean … a cell phone?"

Sarah rolled her eyes and replied, "Believe me, that girl's got enough there it's only a minor intrusion." She glanced back and forth between the detectives. "So we can trace it, right?" She looked hopeful.

Seamus answered, "Maybe. This isn't television. If she makes a call, we can narrow down the area pretty quickly. We can do better if the phone's equipped with a GPS locator. The one thing we <u>can't</u> do is try to contact her. That would alert the kidnappers that she has a phone … if they haven't found it already."

CHAPTER 18

Eric Deamus felt like he'd been running late all week and it was no different for the closing brunch. He entered the banquet room with its potted palms and tropical floral centerpieces to find it nearly filled and most tables with their seating complete. He'd wanted to sit near the front since both Mitch and Roger were addressing the group that morning, Roger with a brief discussion on governmental regulatory actions and Mitchell as the closing speaker. He also desperately needed a dose of "the hair of the dog" after celebrating too much the previous night.

With Vodka-fortified orange juice in hand, he wandered around the perimeter of the room and found a table with an open seat off-center to the head table on the opposite side of the room. Sitting there was an old classmate from Duke, as well as two ladies, geneticists from Princeton, whom he had met by the pool three days earlier.

As he neared the table, the previously animated conversation died to a few whispers between the women. John Easton, wearing a Blue Devil's basketball polo, welcomed him to the table.

"Eric, good morning. You're looking more chipper than I expected this morning," he said as he grinned. "We were at Azzura Point last night, too. You folks seemed to be partying hard. Gotta admit, though, you guys deserved to celebrate. That was quite an announcement yesterday. Good work."

"Thanks," Eric replied. "Sorry ... I didn't see you last night."

His friend waved him off. The two women were still whispering.

"Joanne, Barb, how are you today?" Eric asked.

"Fine," answered Barb.

Joanne nodded in agreement, and then asked, "You're from St. Louis, right?"

"Yeeeaaah," Eric replied, unsure where this leading.

"Have you been following that Nigerian ambassador's murder?"

"I'm aware of it. Why?"

"Just curious. Remember the video showing a woman going after the killer? The news this morning says she's now missing. Some local celebrity. Della somebody."

"Della Winston," added Barb.

Eric knew that name; but then, he'd have to live under a rock not to know it. She was arguably the best-known television news reporter in the city.

"And what about that tattoo?" Barb asked.

"Yeah. Your partner has one something like it," said Joanne.

Eric was puzzled. "My partner?"

"You know ... Roger," she continued. "The other day, at the pool, we noticed a tat peeking out from under his tank top, over his right scapula. We asked him about it and he showed it to us."

"Of course, he wanted us to come back to his room for a private showing," added Barb, giggling.

Joanne laughed. "Yeah, like that was going to happen. He had a cross just like the one that guy, the killer ... but with a single dagger sitting horizontally underneath the cross."

As Eric stabbed and cut his first sausage link in two, he noticed Roger taking the stage. Without notes, the man began to address the group.

"Ladies and gentlemen, good morning. I'll be brief. ..."

Roger was never brief and Eric tuned out to the message. He'd heard it many times from Roger, and others, and although he realized better than most the cost of the work they did, he still had reservations about their ability to patent something so intuitively in the public domain: nature. It wasn't like they created the gene sequences. Why should they be able to patent them?

Instead, he pondered the women's remarks about Roger's tattoo. He'd heard a few rumors about Roger making some very rude, very distinctly un-PC comments about minorities. He'd also heard that Roger had influence on Mitch's decisions about hiring and some of his friends speculated that Roger was the reason their lab was uniquely Caucasian. He knew of no other university-based lab where a wide diversity of racial and ethnic backgrounds was not the norm.

Roger had finished his spiel and now introduced their boss, "the distinguished Doctor Mitchell Hudson." Eric's eyes glazed over and he heard only bits and pieces of the talk as he devoured his Eggs Benedict; sausage, ham and bacon; dessert breads; and fresh fruit. "On the frontier of new medical miracles…" "…at the brink of a new understanding of the human body…" Eric returned to the buffet for more. "…extending the human lifespan…" "…eliminating the scourge of mankind…"

Eric stopped chewing to contemplate that last statement. He had seen or heard that phrase recently. Actually, he'd heard them all before, but this last one was different. War; malaria, leprosy and other infectious disease; obesity; even remote controls have all been listed among the scourges of mankind. But the reference that came to Eric's mind was a reprint from the May 7, 1945 "Time" magazine article entitled "The Betrayer." He'd recently read the article that detailed the rise and fall of Adolph Hitler and called him "the future scourge of mankind." But wasn't that label subjective? To the Nazis, the Jews, gypsies, blacks, homosexuals and non-Aryan peoples in general were the scourge. What could Hitler have done with today's genetic research? An all-Aryan nation? An all-Aryan world?

Della Winston awoke slowly, her head throbbing worse than any party-produced hangover she'd experienced. She'd had a terrible nightmare. Men wearing black ski masks had attacked her, shooting Antoine. It was the stuff of Hollywood or Columbian drug cartels. But she was no A-list celebrity, and her dalliances into recreational drugs other than alcohol were with no more than casual acquaintances, people of no interest to drug lords.

Her mind cloudy and confused, she tried to glance around the room to figure out on whose couch or floor she'd landed after the previous night's binge. She sensed something was wrong but could not figure out what it was. The room was dark and confining. She saw nothing and her hands and feet were stuck. A surge of dread raced through her. She felt the palpitations take control of her heart and she couldn't get enough air. She was suffocating. A small dark room ... unable to move hands or feet ... was she buried alive? She tried to scream but no sound emerged. Her anxiety spiraled downward, sucking her into a maelstrom of terror.

Although her hands and toes soon began to cramp, her head seemed to clear. She recognized she was hyperventilating and forced her breathing to slow. By focusing on slow, easy breaths, her heart rate decreased and the cramps diminished. The panic attack gradually subsided and she began to take stock of what had happened, was happening, to her. And that realization allowed fear to return.

She opened her eyes, but couldn't see. Blindfolded? She could not see around any edges and her head seemed encased in rough cloth, not simply a band of cloth around her eyes and head. A hood. If there was light in the room, she couldn't sense it. She had no concept of time. Had she been there minutes? Hours? Days? No, she reasoned, it couldn't have been more than a few hours. After an evening of drinking, she hadn't peed herself. Or had she been there so long she'd had time to dry out? Yes, her clothing felt dry. Clothing. *Oh, thank God*, she thought. She was still clothed. She didn't feel sore between her legs so maybe she hadn't been raped. She began to weep at the thought of being drugged and sexually violated.

She again tried to move her extremities. She had the ability to move. Rope or cord, something bound her extremities and her struggle against those bonds was brief and futile. At least she was lying down. It wasn't soft like a bed. She could feel the surface with her fingers, something coarse but tightly woven and taut. She deduced it to be a cot of some kind, like those she'd seen in a military field camp.

It hadn't been a nightmare. The news had reported a cross burning in her front yard. Someone had shot Antoine. Men in ski masks had abducted her. She had to fight for control of her mind, her breathing. She couldn't give in to panic.

She lifted both legs together and explored the size of her makeshift bed. True to the size of a military cot, she found the edges just inches to both sides of her. She swung both legs over one side and, unable to use her hands, struggled to sit up. She tried to stand but her leg muscles still felt flaccid, no strength.

That's when she sensed light all around her. A light had been turned on. She heard scuffling footsteps from somewhere to her right and a door opened. She could feel a rush of cool air swirl about her.

"Who's there? Where am I?" she squeaked. Her throat felt like parchment.

She heard something being carried into the room. It hit and scraped along the doorjamb, or maybe a wall, and produced a thud as it landed back on the floor.

Suddenly two sets of strong hands hoisted her roughly from the cot and held her tightly while another set of hands yanked her slacks and panties off in one swoop together.

Rape? She couldn't breathe again. "Please … please don't. Oh god … please don't," she pleaded.

CHAPTER 19

Sarah's second wind had been little more than a puff. Seamus had been correct. They both needed rest and she no longer resisted his taking her home around four-thirty. She collapsed on top of her bed fully clothed.

Now, the persistent buzzing of the door intercom insisted on waking her. She stirred on the bed until the cause of the noise registered in her mind. Groggy, she noticed she had somehow managed to shed her boots and jacket during the night. She inspected her appearance in the cheval floor mirror by her bedroom door. *No worse than after a night on call*, she thought as she stumbled to the kitchen and pressed the button on the intercom.

"Who is it?" she grumbled.

"Sarah, thank goodness, you're here. It's Ricky. Let me in."

She hesitated. Hadn't he caused her enough trouble in the past two days? She pressed the button that released the lock on the outside door and a moment later, there was a knock on the apartment door. She let her colleague in.

"Gawd … I must look awful. You woke me up."

She led him to the kitchen and proceeded to brew a pot of coffee.

Ricky smiled. "You look great. Knowing you're alive and well is, well … man, am I glad I found you. We were worried, all of us."

"C'mon, Ricky. I'm still half-asleep. Who's worried?"

Ricky made himself at home on a stool next to the counter and articulated with his hands as he spoke. "Me, Doctor Hrabik, the office, half of the department I think. Anyone who saw the news today. I was in Hrabik's office after doing my penance, your night shift…"

Sarah did not sense any annoyance on his part for having been stuck with the extra shift.

"I explained to him what happened in the staff dining room the other day and he seemed to think we could get this whole thing settled right away. He made some calls and expedited the disciplinary hearing. It's this afternoon at three. Then, we couldn't reach you and Connie came barging in to tell us she saw you on the news, the video from Della Winston's house last night and at the bodyguard's murder, and told us what had happened and we got concerned. That musta been awful."

Sarah had not been aware of being videoed at either scene and a flicker of concern over becoming another target for these people encroached her mind. She pushed that fear aside and focused on Ricky's statement.

"Three o'clock? What time is it?"

"It's almost one."

Sarah's mind flashed alert. *One o'clock? Della! I need to get hold of Shay. We need to find her!* "Oh, crap," she exclaimed. "I can't do it today. I need –"

"What do you mean, you can't do it? After the strings Hrabik pulled, you better be there." Ricky yawned and rested his head on the counter. "I'll be testifying ... he made it clear that if I didn't show I'd spend the rest of the year on night shift." He yawned and closed his eyes. In less than a minute he was out, a Glasgow coma scale 5.

Sarah cupped her face in her hands. Indecision had been whipped and bled out of her by her medical training, but now she questioned herself. Did she risk jeopardizing her career to help her friend? She had no doubt that Della had to come first, but how could she help? Despite all her bluster with the detectives earlier, and all that she knew about Della, she had no idea where to start. Not a clue. How could she help the police?

Sarah felt the previous day's emotional meltdown encroaching again, that sense of helplessness she abhorred. The thought of not being there for Della twisted and wrenched her gut. She couldn't let that vulnerability gain control.

She watched as the last of the coffee dripped into the carafe and then poured a cup to which she added a splash of milk and sugar. Her parched mouth welcomed the first sips, but her stomach rebelled in open turmoil. Somehow, she managed to contain the nausea and regain the vigor, the sense of direction she had felt at four A.M.

First things first.

She retrieved Shay's business card from her jacket and dialed the cell number he had written on the back. Voicemail. She left a message and then tried his office number. Another voice mailbox, another message. She redialed the precinct offices and asked for Detective Harris. He, too, had signed out to his voicemail. She left no message this time. Ditto with Detective Carter.

Pacing the floor, she had no options open but to wait on Seamus O'Connor … and to wait to clear her name.

Della's terror subsided quickly after her captors forcibly lifted her and sat her on something hard and cold. Her bare skin discerned the shape of her seat as a horseshoe. She felt her feet on the floor, but she wobbled at any attempt to stand so she elected to remain sitting rather than fall blindly. The seat warmed after a while but that added no comfort. Her bladder screamed for relief, the chill on her rear side adding to the pressure to void. She felt as though she'd been sitting there for an hour when she could withstand the pressure no more. If they, whoever they were, wanted a mess to clean, they were about to get it.

As she urinated, the sound of her water hitting metal registered in her mind. Instantly, she knew what she was sitting on … a portable commode! She sighed in great relief … both from the release of her bladder and in knowing that her captors were not so inhumane that they'd deny her such a basic accommodation as a toilet.

Now, if they'd also think about feeding her …

She continued to sit on the portable commode, the stench of her urine becoming irritating. Her stomach rumbled and growled.

Her sense of time remained incapacitated. She had no idea how long she'd been sitting when she sensed the light again. The opening door brought welcomed fresh air.

"Thank you," Della said. Her voice sounded as raspy and dry as her throat felt. "I … I need some water … please." She didn't want to come across as demanding and she knew instinctively not to rile whoever was in the room with her.

"Stand up!" The voice sounded oddly mechanical and seemed to resonate from overhead, not in the direction of the fresh air.

Della attempted to stand but with the bindings and her clothing wrapped about her ankles, she started to fall forward. She could not keep her balance.

A pair of powerful hands caught her and steadied her. Someone else roughly pulled her clothing up but did not zip or fasten them. Instead, they dragged her to the cot and pushed her down onto it. She felt them doing something at her feet. They were undoing the bindings. The tightness around her ankles eased.

"Thank you," she again whispered. "That feels better."

But the relief was short-lived. Suddenly a hard, cold ring clamped around her left ankle, followed by another on the right. She heard the clicks of each one lock into place. As the hands released her, she moved one leg and heard the rattle of a chain. *Shackles?* The demeaning symbolism of these new bindings assaulted her emotions. A slave? Never. A prisoner? Yes. But of whom?

Something then poked her lips. She didn't understand. It poked her again and she realized it was a straw coming through a small hole in the hood. Hesitantly, she sucked until a small amount of fluid entered her mouth. *Water. Just water,* she thought, relieved. She suckled the straw voraciously, getting as much water as possible before they took it away. She wanted to reach out and take hold of the cup, but her hands remained bound behind her.

"Are you hungry?" the odd voice asked.

Della nodded.

"Speak up, bitch!"

The tone of the voice and the slur insulted her, but the water had relieved the dryness of her throat and again she thought, *don't upset or offend them.* She found her voice. "Yes, please."

"Sit up!"

Della shifted her body on the cot. It was easier without the tight bindings on her ankles, but the fetters still made her movements clumsy. She finally found herself sitting on the cot, uncomfortably, with part of its frame digging into the backs of her thighs.

"Close your eyes!"

She didn't want to. She wanted to see who held her, where she was.

A hard slap struck her across the left cheek, the rough cloth chafing her skin.

"Close your eyes! Now!"

How could they know? she wondered, but she closed them tightly and whispered, "They're closed."

She felt a fidgeting around her neck and the hood lifted from her head, replaced by a wide blindfold secured at the back of her head. A moment later, her nose was assaulted by an awful smell and a moist substance pushed against her lips. She resisted, but the metal utensil – *a fork?... yes, it's a fork,* she thought – persisted, forcing the material into her mouth.

Dog food! she realized. Disgusted, she spit it out and worked to control the nausea sweeping over her.

"Eat it!" commanded the voice.

She shook her head.

"Eat it!"

"No!" she cried, anger replacing appeasement.

"Then play the game!"

She heard a whirring-clicking noise behind her head, followed by a louder single clack.

"One bullet, six chambers," the voice explained.

Fear devoured her as she felt cold metal forced against the back of her head, followed by a click that exploded into her ears.

CHAPTER 20

Sayer had been surprised by the Colonel's call and even more amazed by his proposal. The call had come just before the Colonel left the hotel for the airport and proved to Sayer that the man was staying well informed of the situation at home. He knew of the "crime" that occurred at Della Winston's home, and Sayer confirmed that Bobby was behind it. The burning cross was just the kind of first amendment political statement Bobby would express. No originality, but it had been effective. The uprising in St. Louis' black community over the incident and Della Winston's kidnapping had been the lead news items across the nation. Protests were already in progress in front of City Hall and civic leaders had called the police chief to task over his department's inadequate response to the crimes.

But through all of this, the Colonel had had an inspirational moment. His proposal was simple. Keep Della Winston alive to become a complacent and willing accomplice in his plan.

The idea of converting normal lymphocytes, a form of white blood cell, into antigen-charged destroyers of specific cancer cells had developed at the University of Chicago, Inserm in France, and a number of other cancer research centers around the world. Researchers took a cancer victim's lymphocytes from the body and infected them with a retrovirus that transferred to those cells the ability to recognize antigens from the cancer. Once transfused back into the body, these white cells sought out and attacked the cancer. The NCI report signaled success with melanoma. Melanoma. Melanin. To the Colonel the difference was subtle.

They needed a high profile test subject and Della Winston would be just the person to deliver it face-to-face to her brother. Although he had spared Bobby of the details, Bobby had agreed to keep the woman alive, and reasonably well.

Sayer had business to attend, and left the Sydney Street Café after a late working lunch to drive toward his warehouse office in the city. He passed rows of historic townhouses in varying states of rehabilitation and the Soulard Farmers Market, St. Louis' year-round produce market and the centerpiece of the Soulard neighborhood, until he reached his old warehouse in the shadow of the new Busch Stadium. The area had been marked for development to enhance the ballpark, so he'd sold the property at a healthy profit, which in turn he had used to obtain a larger, newer facility two miles south … and to develop a surprise for the Colonel.

Ensconced in his nearly empty office, he pulled out a disposable cell phone and called Bobby at the lake compound.

"Hello."

"Bobby, it's Sayer. Edwards there yet?"

"Oh yeah, he's here." There was a pause and Sayer could hear voices in the background. "He's just come back from visiting her." There was an air of delight in the young man's voice. "Want to talk with him?"

"Sure." Sayer could hear Bobby apprising Edwards of the call and handing off the phone. When he was certain the man was on the phone, he continued, "How's it going?"

"Piece of cake. This bitch is soft and moldable, like Play-Doh. Hasn't been here twenty-four hours and she doesn't know if it's day or night, how many days she's been gone, or anything. Bobby's really getting into the Russian roulette. We've only played three times and he's got her eating the Alpo® without throwing it back up. 'Course, after we told her how lucky she got in the second game, we slipped in a real bullet and fired it into the ceiling. She shit her pants that time." He laughed. "We'll need another case, by the way. The dog food. Your next trip here."

"Already in my car. She still handcuffed and manacled?"

"Oh sure. Don't trust her that far yet. How's the setup going?"

"As good as we can expect until the Colonel returns tonight. The rooms at the new place are finished and secured. I tested the place with infrared, ultrasound, and ground radar and couldn't find the hidden rooms. The crates we picked up are down there, unpacked, and the equipment positioned. The reagents and other stuff are mixed in with my boxes for the warehouse and should be there tomorrow morning. I'm bringing the Colonel over tomorrow to surprise him. All goes well, we'll be up and running in two days."

"He'll be glad to hear that. Thought yesterday was going to set us back by weeks."

Sayer agreed, signed off, picked up some paperwork, and returned to his car. Five minutes later, he entered the new warehouse and went to his new office. His office supply vendor had delivered and placed the new furniture that morning. His business files were due to be moved over that afternoon. By tomorrow, phone lines would be operational and he could resume business as usual there. He walked over to a nearby door. At first glance, it looked like any closet door, except for a digital keypad on the adjacent wall. He keyed in a security sequence and the 4-inch thick steel door opened with near silence. Inside, the room looked like the small bank vault that it was. Sayer's business sometimes included gemstones and rare documents, among the more mundane items he warehoused, and the city inspectors had already passed his vault for use, its fire suppression and ventilation systems functioning and safeguards in place so no one could get locked in accidentally.

What they didn't see was a demonstration of its other function. Sayer placed his thumb on an innocuous looking surface near the door and heard the audible click of a drawer unlocking. A drawer popped open and he extended it fully to reveal another security pad, one with a fingerprint biometric pad. After verifying the code, the door slid closed and the entire floor lowered slowly to a basement level that existed on no building plans in the city or county files. Lights turned on as the floor stopped and Sayer stepped off the conveyor.

He stood in the green room where anyone wishing to enter the lab had to don special suits that helped keep the laboratory free of contaminants and even simple dust. Through the large safety-glass windows, the new facility gleamed in white sterility. From that entry area, he could inspect three separate rooms for general lab work, genetic sequencing, and recombinant RNA development. A smaller, level-three virology lab lay beyond these, with another tier of security and safety measures. With tomorrow's delivery of general lab equipment, followed by the Colonel's personal delivery of samples from his university lab, at the time he felt it appropriate, this facility would become operational.

Sayer smiled. Alleles, base sequence analysis, recombinant clones, cloning vectors. He didn't understand all of the terms, but he had a vague visualization of the final result. The retrovirus would modify the body's white cells to attack the skin pigment, melanin. Dark-skinned people would find their immune systems overwhelmed, unable to resist the accompanying H5N1 flu virus. Not perfect, but doable. No speculative science required. Fulfilling this dream of the Colonel's for a new lab had become his greatest success. This lab would lead the way to a new and better world.

CHAPTER 21

Seamus' day revealed all the glory of working with the feds. While the Secret Service and FBI agents-in-charge held news conferences, conferred with city leaders, and met to give assurance to the city's black clergy coalition, Seamus, Stick, and another half dozen detectives pulled from other cases were beating the streets. He and Stick pulled the tattoo parlor duty and split not just the city but also the entire region in a 50-mile radius, into north and south sections with Olive Street as the dividing line. There were forty-nine legitimate businesses to canvas. Seamus defined legitimate as being licensed parlors, most of which also advertised in the Yellow Pages. They hoped those people might also lead them to individuals who worked alone or in other less-than-legitimate establishments. In addition, they needed to cover the tattoo removal businesses should their perp try to have his tattoo removed. This added at least seven more places to go.

Seamus spent the morning in Belleville and Fairview Heights, east of the Mississippi River, grabbed a bite, and then followed the outer beltway of I-270 to areas southwest of the city: High Ridge, Fenton, Valley Park, and Lemay.

The stories had been the same at each place. Only some of the artists were at work; others wouldn't be in until evening or the next day. All of the artists acknowledged the cross as Byzantine in style. Some thought the daggers were Byzantine as well, while others didn't. None recognized the combination. All said they'd ask around, but few sounded like they would follow through.

Seamus pulled away from his fourteenth tattoo parlor with a greater appreciation of the artistry but no new leads. He glanced at his watch ... almost five in the afternoon. Having worked all day on three hours sleep and eight coffees from as many Golden Arches, he needed a good meal and a full night's sleep.

As he entered the traffic lanes of eastbound I-44 heading into the city, he called his partner.

"Hey, Stick. I hope you've made more progress than me."

Stick laughed. "Guess that depends on your definition. If you mean watching four butts getting colored butterflies, one shoulder getting a full-color tiger, two winged fire-breathing dragons in different stages on different parts of the anatomy, and a mix of bored artists doing nothing in ten different storefronts as progress, then maybe. But no one's seen our tattoo of interest."

"Well, got you beat on the butterflies and bored artists anyway."

"I'm heading home. By the way, good news, bad news."

"Oh?" replied Seamus.

"Yeah. The high profile of these cases got us some priority FBI lab time. Don't have to wait on our own overworked people. They found us a good partial print on the scalpel used to kill our med student. Bad news is ... no matches to anyone."

Seamus perked up a bit. "Okaaay. Guess we need to find out if that scalpel was part of the teaching equipment, and if so, where it's been and who might've had access ... besides just grabbing it from a nearby table."

"I know ... needle in a haystack time, but we might get lucky and find they really do inventory and track that stuff."

"I won't hold my breath. Catch up with you in the office tomorrow."

Seamus disconnected and moved into the right lane to prepare to exit. His nearly ninety-year-old home sat one block away from Tower Grove Park and four blocks away from the Missouri Botanical Gardens. He had spent five years meticulously restoring the two-and-a-half story brick home as part of the early wave of rehabs in the neighborhood. It was a typical inner city area of modest brick homes on narrow lots, just enough room for one person to easily pass between houses, a small "yard" with two steps down to the sidewalk, and a cozy backyard pinned between six-foot high privacy fences. He could have found something with a bigger lot, but who needed that extra work. He loved that old house and its proximity to the parks, as well as to work.

As he turned onto Shaw Avenue and drove past the Botanical

Gardens, his phone rang. Fatigued and almost home, he didn't want to answer it. Late day calls always meant more work. He glanced at the caller ID and didn't recognize the number, other than being the same person who had called four or five times already that afternoon. He decided to ignore it again; he would check for messages after eating.

He eased down the alley behind the row of houses and parked in his spot behind the house. His mind wandered back to some of the comments made by his now ex-flame. Instead of turning off the car and getting out, he gazed across his neglected back yard to the house and thought about how empty the house seemed at times. No, he didn't want to spend all evening alone, staring at the walls.

He pulled out of the spot and maneuvered east down the alley, making a couple of jogs north and east to get to S. Grand Blvd. Maybe it was nothing more than a sleep-deprived auditory hallucination, but he could hear O'Malley's Irish Pub, not far from the Anheuser-Busch InBev Brewery, calling his name.

Heading down South Grand, he started to pass a store, CheapTrx, which was on his list for the following day, and found it still open. Seamus had been there a few times in the past, strictly on business, and always came away amused. A stalwart in the gay community, the store had been founded by two queens selling painted, faux finish furniture. They had branched out into an eclectic mix of gifts, furniture, and collectibles. The Cage, downstairs, sold a selection of fetish items and its clientele was as diverse as they came, and often outlandish. However, he wanted the upper floor, which held a state-of-the-art tattoo and piercing parlor.

Seamus found a place to park and walked back to the store. He ignored the admiring stares of the male customers and clerks, and found his way to the steps. Once upstairs a young, redheaded woman, with a lower lip piercing that could accommodate a horse's reins, greeted him.

"Hi, do you have an appointment?" she asked.

"No, sorry," he replied. He flashed his ID and told her the reason for his visit.

She smiled. "Yeah, we all wondered, like, when you guys would be calling on us. We saw that tat on the news and talked about it the next day. Wasn't done here."

"I see … um …" Seamus was too tired; his mind couldn't come up with a follow-up question.

"Think about it … what skinhead fascist is going to come to a gay store for a tat?"

She had a point.

"You're probably right. If you folks hear of anything, would you give me a call?"

Seamus took down her name and those of her fellow artists, and left his business card.

"Hey, there is one guy you might want to, like, check out. He applied for a job here, but, you know, his political views didn't mesh with the rest of us. Didn't last a week. John said he heard the guy set up shop in his house, probably not licensed. Give me a sec."

She disappeared downstairs and returned a few minutes later with a sheet of paper. "Here. The boss said it's okay to give you his name and address."

"Thanks," Seamus said. "Again, if you hear anything else, please let me know."

She nodded and added, "Hope you catch the bastard."

Seamus walked down the stairs and endured more stares and a couple of catcalls as he passed through the store. Politely, he deferred to two drag queens coming in the front door. "Ladies." He nodded his head as they passed, then shook his head and chuckled as he hit the sidewalk.

He looked at the name and address and groaned. The guy was located to the southwest – in territory he had already covered. And if the guy really was operating an unlicensed parlor in his home, Seamus would need local police support. He decided to call that jurisdiction the next morning and see if they could help and save him a repeat trip.

As he climbed into his car, his cell phone rang again. A glance at the caller ID revealed that same wrong number. He wavered. If he answered it now, he could straighten them out and stop the annoying calls. But if it wasn't a wrong number, it could mean more work before going home. Before he could flip open the phone to answer, his voice mail intercepted the call.

Seamus yawned and realized he was too tired for the good meal and couple of brews he thought he wanted. He drove back home and parked in his usual spot off the alley. Loaded down with paperwork and gear, he entered the kitchen at the rear of the house and dumped everything onto the table. He went to the front door, retrieved his mail, and turned to go back to the kitchen. His front bay window, one that he'd lavished with attention, restoring every detail in the fine molding, had been shattered. A brick, with a note tied to it, lay on the living room floor.

CHAPTER 22

Sarah's patience wore thin. An emergency surgery delayed Rickelmann and one of his "witnesses," and the hearing didn't start until after 4 p.m. Now, she sat outside the conference room while the hearing board discussed the matter. She was amazed that one man could hold that much sway over such a huge medical center. He had no case, except maybe one of injured pride, a trait he possessed in overabundance. In perspective, her alleged affront amounted to nothing more than a scratch.

Ricky's testimony accurately described the events in the dining room and countered the statements of the two staff surgeons who had left the dining room before the incident had played out completely. Doctor Rickelmann alleged that she had made comments to others as well, but could produce no such witnesses. She countered with a detailed account of her whereabouts after the ATLS course, and offered to bring in at least one police detective to attest to her veracity.

Why, if this was such a slam-dunk, as Doctor Hrabik believed, was it taking so long? She sat in the chair, fidgeting and tapping her toes on the floor, as first fifteen minutes and then thirty rolled past.

And, why, despite having his personal cell phone number, was it so hard to get hold of one certain detective? She had tried half-a-dozen times to reach Seamus O'Connor, without success.

She dropped her cell phone into her purse after yet another failed call and glanced toward the conference room door. The faint noise of people stirring drifted from the closed doorway. A moment later Doctor Hrabik emerged, frowning, and hurried to her.

"Sarah, I'm sorry. This should all be over, but that pompous …" He sighed. "Doctor Rickelmann refuses to back down. He insists on more time to check into these other alleged comments. I think someone has convinced him there's more to this than what it appears to be."

Sarah stood in anger. "What? Who? There aren't any other …"

"I know that. And I think the committee does, too. But they gave him twenty-four hours."

Sarah took a deep breath and controlled her building frustration. Doctor Hrabik's assurances had raised her hopes that this particular ordeal would be quickly put to rest. Now, she had to contend with another day of anxious waiting when she wanted, needed, to focus on helping find Della. And her annoyance increased with every unanswered phone call to Detective O'Connor.

"We won't be meeting again, but they promised me that if Rickelmann does produce any other witnesses, they will give you like time for rebuttal. I think we'll have this resolved in no time." He smiled and patted Sarah on the shoulder.

That's what you keep saying, she thought. But it's not over yet.

She thanked her department head and turned to leave the building, but stopped. She had nowhere to go but home, and that thought distressed her. She would go stir crazy at her apartment. She couldn't sit there waiting to hear from one or more overworked detectives, not knowing where Della was or if she was hurt. She needed a plan. Della needed her.

The more she thought about it, the more aggravated she became. Over the years, her instructors had taught her to develop thorough and careful treatment plans. She could assess acute trauma and major medical problems without hesitation and initiate life-saving measures in less time than it took to shock a heart back to life. Even if she found a comatose body in a remote area with no life saving equipment on hand, she could still assess some basic vital signs; evaluate the ABCs of airway, breathing, and circulation; determine likely injuries; and initiate first response measures that might save a life. But now she felt helpless. She had no data to act upon. And she didn't even know where to find the data without relying on some jerk policeman who wouldn't answer her calls.

Her tachycardic ire focused and fed itself on Seamus O'Connor's lack of response. He was her lifeline to Della. And how could she expect to find her friend if she didn't have the talent to even find him. Yes, that would be step one; she had to find him first.

Sarah didn't wait for the elevators. She bounded down the nearest fire well stairs to ground level. With some luck, the goal of her immediate search – a collection of business cards - was in her locker at the E.D.

As she turned a corner she bumped into another woman bearing an ID that marked her as a fourth year medical student. It took Sarah a moment, but she realized it was Kendra Samuels, who looked much better than their last encounter in the cafeteria.

"Kendra! You look great. I love the haircut."

Kendra smiled. "Thanks, Sarah. Decided it was time for a new look."

"Well, it certainly suits you. You're positively glowing."

The younger woman blushed, but then turned serious. "Hey, about the other day ... in the cafeteria. I want to apologize. I think the stress of this ICU rotation was getting to me. I've been having some nausea and not sleeping well."

Sarah scrutinized the woman. She didn't look stressed. She looked ... Sarah couldn't pinpoint it.

"For how long?"

"Like, since the rotation started. I'm really hoping it won't affect my evaluation."

"Have you been to student health? Maybe something else is going on."

The student glanced at her feet, sheepishly. "No ... well, I was going to go today, but I felt a whole lot better when I woke up this morning, so I, uh, put it off. Maybe it's just a viral thing."

Sarah frowned. "Don't make assumptions. If it doesn't get better, don't wait any longer."

"Okay, I won't. Look, I gotta run. Again, sorry about the other day."

"Not a problem. Bye."

Sarah watched as Kendra walked away. There was something about her. *Pregnant?* she wondered. *I bet she is.*

She smiled at the thought and continued on her way to the

E.D. As she passed through to the locker room, she glanced into an open door and saw Detective Salvatore Repazzo. He wasn't her first choice of contact but he might have the information she sought and they'd become friendly enough that he'd helped her a couple of times in the past. She just needed to approach him the right way. She straightened up, smiled, and poked her head in the door. She immediately noticed a dressing covering his left hand.

"Detective *amico*, did you miss me?"

Repazzo smiled. "Hi Sarah, excuse me, <u>Doctor</u> Wade. I thought I asked for the best doctor on-duty."

"And I'm sure you'll get him. His name's Ricky, by the way, and I know he'll think you're a cute one. He loves Italians. Just watch out if he asks you to turn your head and cough."

Repazzo looked uncertain, but held up his bandaged hand and replied, "Yeah, sure. It's my hand, not my … We was checking a car for drugs and someone shut the door on it."

"Well, Ricky won't mind. He's very thorough … with aallll his patients." Her smile broadened.

Repazzo laughed and shook his head. "You're somethin' else. I see you've been making the news a lot lately."

Sarah nodded. It was time to get serious. "Hasn't exactly been a fun-filled few days. Hey, Sal, look, I need a favor."

He smiled. "Another parking ticket?"

She frowned. "No, nothing like that. I've been working with Seamus O'Connor and I need to give him something STAT." *Yeah, a piece of my mind*, she thought. "It can't wait 'til tomorrow and I'm not getting any response on his cell phone. Do you know where he lives?"

His countenance turned solemn. "Ahhh, my young brown-sugared *cugina*, you know we're not s'posed to give out stuff like that."

"C'mon, Sal. It's not like I'm gonna pass it on to all the riff-raff comes through here." She gave him her most pleading look.

"Okay, okay. It's by the Botanical Gardens, on Shenandoah. I've heard him talkin' about all the rehabbin' he did on it." He took out a small notepad and scribbled the address on it, handing it to Sarah when he finished.

"Thanks, Sal. I owe you again." She turned to leave the room.

"Hey! What about my hand?"

She smiled. "Your doctor will be in shortly. Don't worry; he's almost as good as me."

As she exited the room, Ricky brushed into her. "Hey, what happened? You're exonerated, right?"

She explained what happened and of the additional time given to Rickelmann.

"Ah, shit. That's not right, the bastard." He shook his head. "So, what're you doing here?"

"I needed something from my locker and I saw a friend in room twelve, Sal Repazzo. He's here with a hand injury. Are you seeing him?"

"I was just heading that way."

"He's a good guy to know, another detective –"

Ricky interrupted, "He's the guy fixed your tickets, isn't he?"

Why is it they all remember that? she thought. "Yeah, he's the one. Look, no need to get formal with him. He likes using first names. Oh, and he's had a history of epididymitis, so you might want to ask him how his groin's been doing."

"Okay, thanks."

She waited until he entered the room and overheard Ricky introduce himself as "Doctor Ricky Alvarez." *Oh, to be a fly on the wall,* she thought, as she hustled down the hall.

Ten minutes later, Sarah drove south on Grand Avenue past Reservoir Park. She couldn't remember which street came first, Shenandoah or Botanical, and almost missed Shenandoah when she saw the street sign. She drove west toward the Botanical Gardens, and one block shy of the end of the street, she could see a police cruiser, its lights flashing. *What's that about?* she wondered.

She found a parking spot at the beginning of the block and stepped out of the car in time to see a young black officer approaching the cruiser. She ran toward the car, waving at him.

"Officer! Excuse me!"

He looked up and watched her approach, stopping her as she neared the house.

"Officer, hi. I'm looking for Detective O'Connor."

She watched, as he looked her up and down, questioning who she was. He didn't answer, but gazed over her shoulder, past her, toward the house he had just left.

"It's okay, Frank. I know her," said a voice from the front door.

Sarah turned to see Detective Harris at the front door.

"He's inside, Doctor Wade. C'mon in."

As she walked toward the door, she noticed the damaged front window and hurried her step? What had happened? Had she been too harsh to pre-judge why he hadn't returned her calls? Harris stepped aside as she entered the door. Inside, she found Seamus, his back to her, vacuuming broken glass in the front room. A piece of plywood sat in the hallway.

She gazed around the room and hall. It was beautiful. Although lacking artwork or other decoration, the tall walls were finished with wide, dark cherry baseboards at the floor, picture rail at the eight-foot level, and intricate dentil and crown molding along the ceiling. Someone had expertly plastered the ceiling with a seashell swirl and added elaborate medallions from which hung ornate brass light fixtures. The floor glistened with the natural honey color of refinished old growth fir. Sal had mentioned that Seamus had rehabbed the place. Had he personally done all the work? If so, she was impressed so far.

The vacuum's stopping brought her attention back to Seamus. He looked around and saw her, surprised.

"What are you doing here?" he asked.

"I-I needed to talk with you and you haven't answered my calls. Look, I can —"

Harris interrupted, "Shay, I need to go. The wife's getting a bit frantic and I'm not comfortable leaving her alone."

"Isn't there a local patrol car there?" Seamus replied.

"Yeah, but you know how it is. We'll catch up in the morning." He nodded to Sarah. "Doctor."

Sarah returned the gesture and looked back to Seamus. "Look, I can leave if ..."

"That might be best. I have lots to do, starting with boarding up my window."

"Need some help? I can help hold it, or something." She paused. "I used to help Dad Winston all the time with stuff around our house."

Seamus didn't say anything for a moment.

"Okay, you're on." He put on a carpenter's belt and handed her a short stepladder. "Need it out front if you can manage."

"If I can manage?" She huffed as she hoisted the ladder up and carried it out the door. He followed her with the plywood and moved to the window where he set the wood on edge on the sill.

"Now, can you set up the ladder and climb up and hold the top against the frame while I nail the bottom and work up?"

"Of course, I can. Do I look useless?"

She saw Seamus take a breath and sigh. "Look, I don't need —"

"Sorry. I ..." She complied and, as he started to nail, asked, "What happened?"

"Not outside. We can talk in the house," he replied and then wordlessly continued his task. After several more nails, he had her step down and then he used the ladder to secure the top of the plywood. When he finished, he folded up the ladder, pointed to the door and started inside. She followed, closing the door behind them.

"Have a seat. I'll be back in a minute." He took his tools and moved down the hall. She heard a door and what sounded like footfalls on stairs, and assumed he had taken his gear to a basement. A few minutes later, he reappeared.

"Can I offer you some coffee? Seems that's been my main food group today." He smiled.

"Sure," she replied, and she stood to follow him to the kitchen, which she discovered would be a gourmet cook's delight, the kind of kitchen she hoped to have some day. "Haven't you eaten?"

He shook his head. "Only a cheeseburger and fries around eleven, and more coffee than I care for."

"May I?" she asked, sweeping her arm toward the cooktop and refrigerator.

Seamus looked surprised and unsettled. "I, uh, I don't know. Ummm."

"Look, if you're expectin' corned beef, boiled cabbage, and potatoes, you're outta luck, Irish. But it won't be chitlins and okra either." She was surprised at her boldness. She started peeking into cabinets and the fridge.

"Um, okay, sure. I got plenty of antacids. Rather have a beer?"

"Why not." She discovered boxes of various pastas in one cabinet, extra virgin olive oil in another, and a variety of herbs and spices in a drawer. The refrigerator delivered some fresh garlic, lemon juice and a package of chicken tenders. Within minutes, she was ready with a cutting board, knife, and sauté pan, as well as a pot and colander for the pasta. *This is not the kitchen of a bachelor police detective,* she thought and wondered who normally did the cooking in the house.

He handed her a cold beer and said, "Sorry about not answering your calls. It's been a long day and I didn't have time to take calls from numbers I didn't recognize."

"What happened here?" she asked as she put a pot of water on the cooktop to boil.

"Just a sec," he answered. He left the room and returned a minute later with a clear plastic bag. "Came home tonight and found this on my living room floor. I think you can figure out how it got there." He held up the bag to show her a brick with a note tied to it. The note said, "do your job, whitey. protect and serve."

She stopped what she was doing and looked at him. She thought about all that had happened in the past days. Sure, she'd had her share of racial barbs thrown at her, but Dad Winston had protected them all from much of that. His Bahamian mother had never understood why American blacks continued to carry the baggage of slavery from a hundred and fifty years earlier. She had passed those ideas on to her children, and he to them. He had always told them to move past race, that to live as equals they had to show they were equal, and that hard work and accomplishment paid off no matter what color your skin. She had found that to be mostly true. Mostly. But then, because of him she lived in an economic stratum that many blacks would never know.

Still, here they were, black and white, sharing conversation and a meal. Why did others have to burn crosses and throw bricks?

"It's getting nasty out there. By the way, we have nothing new on your friend, no ransom demands, or leads on the truck. I talked with Carter about half an hour ago. He got home to find his car windows smashed in. And Stick's wife arrived home to find a swastika and the word 'lover' spray-painted on their garage door. Some of the other detectives received similar warnings."

So much for guarding these detectives' home addresses, she thought, feeling grieved and disheartened. And she feared where this was leading. She had seen newscasts of the escalating protests at City Hall, in which a mob burned the police chief in effigy. At one point, additional police were required to control the crowd. Sarah had never seen racial unrest of this level. And individual, targeted actions like these were not helpful. A tear eased from her eye and she reached up to wipe it away.

"Hey, stop. Look, I'm sorry some asshole burned a cross on your friend's lawn. We're doing our best to catch the idiots."

She finished cutting the chicken and dicing some garlic and started to sauté them in the oil. She added a selection of herbs and spices, and checked the pasta.

"How come you're not on the case then? What I heard on the street is that you're working the ambassador's murder."

He laughed. "I am gonna have to start checking out your sources, lady." He took another swig of beer and looked at her. "Okay, fair question, but what I say in this room stays in this room. Got it?"

"No problem," she replied as she turned down the heat on the chicken and added some lemon juice to the pan. She found some fresh parmesan in the fridge and grated some onto the meat as well.

"That smells great." He took another drink. "Anyway, we think the cases are all related. Do you know who the med student was, the one you found?"

"Well, yeah, sorta. Walter Johnson, a fourth year student. From around Chicago somewhere."

"True enough. So far, we've managed to keep this from the press, but he was also related to the ambassador through his mother. The FBI thinks there's something going on in Nigeria that made the man a target, but the whole skinhead thing doesn't jive with that, so everybody's still scratching their heads over it. We think your friend Della just got caught up in the whole thing because she saw the killer's face."

She finished draining the pasta and put some on two dishes, covering them with the improvised lemon-garlic sauce and chicken. Together they rose and moved to a nearby table. Seamus bowed his head silently for a moment, and then dug into the pasta *ansiosamente*, eagerly.

"Wow, this is delicious! And you just sorta threw that together, no recipe or anything. I'm impressed."

"Thanks. I love to cook. Just never seem to have time for it." She watched him consume the meal, wondering if the flavors had time to register on his taste buds. "So, why can't you be assigned to help find Della?"

"Not my call," he answered with a half-filled mouth. He finished chewing and swallowed before continuing, "The powers-that-be tell me do this, do that, and I jump. Do the best I know how. All I want is to solve the case and see some justice. Look, I can hook you up with Carter. He's a good detective." He took another forkful.

She shook her head vehemently. "No, that won't work. I want you on the case." *Yeah, like I have that kind of pull,* she thought.

"I don't see how …" He paused long enough to stare at her. "You already know Carter, why can't you give him your input, help him out?"

Again, she shook her head. She had no choice but to tell him the truth. "I can't work with Brian. We, uh … we have some history between us that would make it really difficult to work together. Besides, I've come to trust you. I want you on the case."

He put his fork down. "Sarah, I just don't see how that's gonna happen. The lieutenant would need a good reason to pull me from a dual murder and move me to a kidnapping where we have zero jurisdiction. Sorry, but telling him you want me on the case isn't gonna cut it."

Sarah felt a ripple of discomfort in her gut. She knew what she had to do. She hated the idea of it. She didn't want to do it. But, for Della's sake, she would swallow her pride to get Seamus on the case.

CHAPTER 23

The Colonel had caught a red-eye flight back home and fought for sleep on the plane. Too much on his mind. He found it curious that he had no trouble dealing out death to millions as a way to improve mankind, yet struggled with ordering the death of one. Perhaps blood truly was thicker than water.

He entered his wife's room and sat next to her, picking up her hand and stroking the back of it. He nodded at the nurse, Rebecca, who left to get some breakfast downstairs. Theirs was a familiar ritual.

"Dear, we've come so far in the past week. It will only be a brief time 'til we see our biggest dream fulfilled. If only my biggest dream could come with it. I wish you could wake up to share the moment with me."

He told her of their progress with the viral study, and of the conference he'd just attended. He knew she'd be proud of him and his accomplishments. When Rebecca returned, he kissed Sherry on the forehead, and left. Sayer had promised him a big surprise and he felt almost giddy in anticipation. Sayer's "gifts" were always excellent.

The Colonel and his aide watched the live newscast on a large-screen television in Sayer's new office. They watched footage as the mayor's car passed, the decibel levels of the throng's chants and jeers rose logarithmically to a level that muffled the reporter's voice to indistinguishable tones. He checked his watch. Only 8 a.m. and the crowd marching and chanting around City Hall numbered in the thousands. Some carried signs but, in the Colonel's view, most toted only bales of resentment. The camera zoomed in on an improvised podium near the steps to the main doors where a series of black leaders took turns addressing the crowd. Police, their numbers reported to be increasing as the mass grew, stood off to the side as a visible but subtle reminder for the leaders to maintain control.

The Colonel glanced at Sayer, who perused the morning

paper. The link between the Nigerian ambassador and his medical student second cousin shared the morning headlines with criticisms of the police and their admission of having no new leads in the kidnapping of Della Winston. The newscast made it obvious that the previous evening's assurances by Police Chief Allen to allocate more resources to the hunt and to direct the BOI to assist the FBI had done little to quell the anger of the African-American populace.

The Colonel smiled. "With a little luck, they'll start a riot," he said. "And <u>that</u> would be good TV."

Sayer smiled as well. "Yes, Sir. Not to mention being good for the cause."

All three of them had witnessed first-hand the power of a common enemy. The government had capitalized upon 9/11 and the subsequent rise of terrorism in the public eye to promote its own policies, not anticipating a secondary result – an upsurge of support for groups like theirs. After years of decreasing membership and decentralization of authority, the Klu Klux Klan, Aryan Nations, National Alliance, and groups allied to Christian Identity theology had grown significantly in number and political influence. The Colonel himself had used that emergent sentiment to develop the MWA.

The Colonel turned from the TV toward his aides and focused on Sayer. "Chad, I like the new warehouse, but I'm waiting for the surprise you promised me. Anytime you're ready."

Sayer grinned as he ushered the Colonel to the vault. He opened the door after validating the digital code, stepped aside, and with a sweep of his arm, urged the two men to enter.

The Colonel looked curious, but eyed the vault with caution. He deferred to his aide. "After you."

Once inside, Sayer challenged the two men. "Okay, see if you can find anything unusual about this room." He stood in the doorway as the others hesitated, but then began to inspect the walls and attempt to pull out drawers, which were either locked or empty. They inspected the interior security pad that could unlock and open the vault door from the inside. After ten minutes, they gave up.

"Nice vault, Sayer, but I know you too well. Where's the surprise?" asked the Colonel.

"Yes, Sir. Watch where I do this because the system's programmed for both of you as well." Sayer placed his right thumb on the special panel. "This small panel is electrostatic as well as pressure sensitive." A drawer lock clicked open, and he pulled out one drawer to reveal a biometric pad. "Go ahead, Sir, place your right thumb on the pad."

The Colonel did so and stepped back in surprise as the door closed automatically and the floor began to descend. A look of awe materialized on both faces as the floor stopped, the door opened, and the lights of the underground lab rose to a soft glow.

Speechless, the men emerged into the green room. Sayer followed the Colonel from room to room as he examined the equipment, scrutinized the layout, and checked cabinets to see what they contained. As they came to the final room, the Colonel let loose a soft whistle as he gazed through the window to the virology lab beyond. He placed his thumb on the entry lock's biometric pad, but nothing happened.

"Sorry, can't go in yet. That room has been sterilized and will require proper suits for admission. They should be here today."

The Colonel stepped back and turned to take it all in once again. He then turned to Sayer and clapped his hand on Sayer's shoulder.

"Chad, I-I don't know what to say. How … when … this is truly amazing. It's beyond anything I had imagined for our proposed lab at the lake facility. How did you manage this? When?"

Sayer gave his mentor an abbreviated accounting of where he'd come up with the plans and the list of supplies, of how he'd financed the project, and of the means by which the work had been done in secret.

"What about the contractors? How can we keep this a secret?"

"Well, the rough work, the excavating and concrete, was

done by a couple of our guys. They think it's for hiding weapons and supplies. The electrical work, likewise. Done by a sympathetic electrician. They last saw it when stairs could access the room. The rest of it, ventilation system, hydraulic floor ..." He paused and swept his hand in an arc around the facility. "... all of this, well, only the three of us know at this point. Edwards guaranteed that without even asking why ... and I didn't ask how." He paused. "At this point, it's up to you, Sir, to bring in what you need and staff it as you see fit. We could be operational in days."

The Colonel rubbed his hands eagerly. He turned from Sayer and addressed the other man. "This afternoon, get everyone organized to bring over our samples, test notes, and anything else you see that we'll need. Tell Marcus and Heinz we'll be moving from the university and to remove all traces of our work from the lab. Let's get this place working."

He turned to Sayer and continued, "I have meetings all day so I'm out of commission until this evening. If you can, go to the lake compound and see how our project is going there. Suggest to Edwards that we might want to move her, confuse her."

Sayer nodded and ushered the Colonel and the other man to the lift and escorted them out of the warehouse. He returned to his office with a four-wheeled dolly on which he stacked several boxes that he personally unpacked in the green room. He deferred their placement within their respective rooms, knowing that the Colonel's technicians would deal with them without complaint when they arrived.

Back in his office, he checked his schedule for the rest of the day. Although they were in the middle of the move from the old facility to the new one, that process was more or less on autopilot and would not require his personal attention. Now was the best time to drive to the lake and check with Edwards.

Sayer signed out to his warehouse manager, walked out to the parking lot, and noticed a crew installing new signage on a billboard adjacent to the building. The message stopped Sayer in his tracks. His pulse and breathing accelerated as a sense of panic hit him. He ran for the car, fumbled the keys in the ignition, and finally, motor revving, screeched from the lot.

Della sat up on the edge of the cot. She had learned to manage the leg-irons and found that despite their cumbersome weight, they allowed her greater mobility than her initial bindings. She stood and steadied herself, finding balance a challenge without visual cues or free arms. She took a step and retested the limits of the irons. This was her third attempt to explore the room. She had fallen the two previous times and, unable to get up, her captors had roughly handled her back onto the cot and tested her with the game of Russian roulette. She did not want to experience that again. The thought of her luck running out nearly crippled her with fear.

Still, she wondered why they had not killed her outright. She had no doubt that her life was nearing an end. They would eventually kill her. They had said as much without saying it explicitly. But why prolong it? She had nothing to give them. Her money was tied into trusts she didn't control. Her brother's political handlers couldn't be trusted to help, and if her death at the hands of these bigots provided the political capital to propel DeWayne out of "freshman senator" status in record time, they'd feed her to the lions of racism above his objections.

Della found her confidence and shuffled one step forward. She had no idea where walls or furniture were located and had no clue about the size of the room. That was her first task, to determine those boundaries. She took another step, moving her foot forward cautiously. With the sixth step, her toe ran into an obstruction. She tried to lean forward, deducing that if it was a wall her forehead would hit it as well. Her face touched a solid surface and the cloth of the hood seemed to drag as she moved it. *Rough wood?* she wondered. It seemed to smell of wood. She turned her face from side to side, but could sense no light. *No windows on this wall?*

She slowly took six steps backward, but misjudged the size of those steps and tumbled backward onto the cot. She managed to avoid falling backward over the cot and upon regaining her balance, sat upright. She sat still and calmed her anxious breathing, listening for approaching footsteps. When she heard none, she relaxed and decided to venture in a different direction.

Again, she stood and when confident of her equilibrium she turned ninety degrees to her right. She brushed her right leg against the cot with her first step, and then brought her left foot up equal to the right before stepping again with the right. At the end of the cot, she eased forward with cautious steps until she came to an obstacle. This too proved to be a wall. She then stepped to the left until she hit another wall. Retracing her steps, she successfully found her way back to the cot and laid down, exhausted.

Sayer paced the small room in the compound's main building. The security monitor showed Della Winston exploring her room, but thoughts about the billboard outside his warehouse diverted his attention. "Eternity! Are You Prepared? Destiny Church" was all it proclaimed but after his encounter with the tow truck owner, its words ate away at him. What was eternity? He couldn't wrap his mind around the idea of time never ending. It was like the concept of a bottomless pit. How could someone fall and fall and keep falling without ever hitting bottom?

"She's a persistent one, that's for sure," said Edwards. His comment dragged Sayer away from his thoughts.

"From what I see, she's becoming more and more self-assured," Sayer answered.

Edwards smirked. "Yeah, we'll let her figure it all out, if she can. Then we'll rearrange the room on her, confuse her."

"That reminds me. The Colonel suggested you should move her to a new location, so she doesn't pick up too many clues about where she might be."

Edwards shrugged. "Can't imagine she could figure out where she is, but not a problem. We can move her between two or three places ... while she's sedated. That'd confuse her even more. Yeah, I like that. In fact, I know the perfect place."

They watched as Della stood to renew her exploration.

"Cliff, get over there. Let's catch her in the act. Time to play the game again. Then have six or eight of the guys take some target practice in back, behind the building." As the man left, Edwards turned to Sayer. "Want to go with me?"

Sayer shrugged, and replied, "Sure."

Edwards tossed him a black jacket and ski mask. "Just in case. I'm going to take off her cuffs and if she rebels and rips off her hood and blindfold, I don't want her seeing any faces or identifiable clothing. We'll let her eat by herself today. Gotta start showing some kindness if we want her to take up our cause." He turned to another man. "Blake, grab a plate of good food from the mess and bring it over ... with utensils." He started toward the door. "Okay, let's go."

By the time they reached the building, the game was over and Della Winston was a quivering, whimpering mass on the cot.

Della sobbed as she trembled on the cot. Her rapid heart rate and breathing began to ease as she realized she had once again beaten "the game." The click of the revolver's hammer still echoed in her mind, a psyche haunted by the dread that something other than that click, something explosive, would be the last thing she ever heard. She tried to control her breathing, to slow it, manage it.

She jumped at the first crack of gunfire from someplace outside the room. The repeated volleys caused her to shrink into a fetal position on the cot. So absorbing was the offensive noise that she didn't hear the footsteps or opening of the door.

"Ms. Winston –"

Della screeched in surprise at the sound of a voice, the trembling and fast respirations regaining their hold on her.

"... I must say you are quite the lucky woman. To be honest with you, I never wanted them to play that game with you, but I wasn't here to stop them. Now I am. We won't be playing that anymore ... unless, of course, you get rebellious. Then I might not be able to prevent it."

The galloping heartbeat audible in her ears began to subside. *Did I hear that right?* she wondered. A flood of relief surged through her.

Something else registered in her brain, the voice was

different. It no longer had that tinny quality that seemed to come from a speaker in the ceiling. No, this voice belonged to someone in the room standing next to her. Also, the guns had stopped.

"Who ... who a-are you?" she asked, her voice a shaky whisper.

"That's unimportant. But let me say that there are a lot of us and some of them would prefer just shooting you and burying your body where it would never be found. Even if I convince them to let you go, they'll be watching you closely. One wrong move and the last thing you'll feel is the bullet coming from nowhere tearing you apart."

"You're g-going to let me go?" For the first time since her kidnapping, she felt a tinge of hope. Maybe these people, whoever they were, weren't as bad as she'd imagined.

"I'm going to try to make that happen, if you cooperate."

She didn't want to die. She could cooperate.

"W-what do you want from me?"

"In due time. First, show us some cooperation. Close your eyes for the blindfold." The voice paused. "Closed?"

She nodded vigorously, and then kept her eyes tightly closed as the transfer was made.

"Very good. Thank you. Now, I'm going to release your hands to let you eat on your own. Any attempt to loosen the blindfold will show us your unwillingness to cooperate. Do you understand?"

Again she nodded. "Yes," she whispered. She felt someone take the handcuffs and heard the soft click of their release. Her hands were free. *Oh, that feels so good.* "Thank you," she whispered, her voice a bit stronger. She rubbed one wrist and then the other.

She startled at the strong hand that took her left wrist. The grip wasn't rough, but it was firm.

"Now, stand up and I'll lead you to a chair."

She followed and a moment later found herself sitting in what felt to be a straight-backed wooden chair. She could feel a table in front of her and the smell of food tantalized her. Real food, not dog food. This new man was taking care of her.

"Go ahead and eat. It might be a bit sloppy, blindfolded, but that's the best I can do right now."

She heard the shuffling of feet.

"I'll be back in a little while, but someone will be watching you, so don't do anything stupid."

She didn't answer. Her hands quickly moved to the surface of the table in front of her. She felt a paper napkin on one side of what felt like a plastic plate, and a knife and fork on the other. The knife would be too difficult to use. She carefully used her left index finger to touch the food, to determine what it might be and how best to attack it. There was a warm, round slab of meat, like a hamburger, covered with a warm sauce. She licked her finger. *Beef gravy.* To the left was something soft, warm, and mushy. She scooped it with her finger and brought that to her lips. *Mashed potatoes. Instant mashed potatoes.* She laughed inside at her thought. *What difference does it make if they're instant? This isn't the time to be a food critic.* She followed the plate around clockwise and found something cold and soft. A taste revealed applesauce.

She grabbed the fork in her right hand and with her left hand guiding, stabbed the meat. She picked up the whole thing and took a bite. *Not hamburger, more like a minute steak. No, Salisbury steak, that's what it is.* She took a few more bites and put it down. She then used her left finger to push potatoes onto the fork. After several bites, she repeated the process until both meat and potatoes were gone. Then she attacked the applesauce and devoured it.

She was thirsty and realized she hadn't explored any further than the plate and adjacent utensils. She gingerly felt around the plate and found a waxed paper cup. She picked it up and cautiously took a sip. Sweet tea, southern style, her favorite. She guzzled it down and was saddened when it was gone. She should have savored it.

Her nose began to itch and she started to reach up to rub it. She stopped before her hand reached her mouth. Whoever was watching might interpret her move as one to loosen the blindfold. She instead wiggled her nose and managed to ease the tickle.

With her hunger and thirst eased, and her mind hopeful of going home, she took notice of other things. Like her underwear being all twisted from when whoever-it-was pulled them back up for her. She stood at the table and pulled at her panties through her slacks. That was a little better. She'd rather lower her pants and do it right, but someone was watching and she wasn't going to bare all when she had the choice not to.

She also noticed her bra strap had ridden up in back. Only now with her mind at a tenuous peace did she notice how uncomfortable her bra had become. She reached behind and pulled down the strap. There was something hard in the strap near the cup of her left breast. *Omigod*, she thought. Her cell phone. She'd forgotten about it. Not that she could have used it. Now, it had partially slipped from the cup into the strap under her armpit. Sweat beaded up on her forehead and her heart began to flutter. She didn't know what to do. Any move to retrieve it would lead to its discovery … and maybe her immediate death. Besides, she couldn't call anyone. She had no idea where she was. Part of her wanted to give it up to her captors as a sign of good faith and cooperation. But she couldn't give it up. Not yet. She might need it. And she couldn't show that something was amiss. *I have to act like nothing is wrong.*

She sat down. Her mind raced. *What to do, what to do?* She had to decide. Footsteps were coming toward the door.

CHAPTER 24

Eric felt fatigue overwhelming him. The past week had been one of too many adult beverages and too many late nights with an intriguing young medical geneticist from Baltimore. She had returned his interest and her promise to keep in touch had already been validated by two phone calls. He had napped on the flight, almost fell asleep driving home, and slept soundly, as only the comfort of one's own bed can provide, for a full eight hours before waking for work.

After a day consumed by meetings, follow-up phone calls, and impromptu discussions with various technicians in the lab, he still had not had time to do any of his own work. They needed to finalize what looked to be the most expedient process for synthesizing their new Alzheimer's drug. Mitchell wanted this work done before they entered into licensing discussions with the several pharmaceutical suitors who had expressed interest. And before their next project.

Now, as the day ended for most people, he slowly worked his way through the drive-thru line of a nearby Del Taco, picked up a sack of his favorite fish tacos and a soda, and returned with dinner to his office in the lab. He glanced around the lab. No one was there.

"Anyone here?"

It was best that no one was there. He had serious work to do. Without distractions. But first, dinner …

Eric jerked awake, startled to find himself in the dark at his desk, his neck and shoulders stiff from being crunched forward on the metal desktop. He glanced at his watch and sighed. The digital readout showed the time at nearly midnight. He pondered his next step. The work needed to be done; Mitchell expected it, and the sooner the better, but he was still tired and felt his concentration flagging.

Eric thought a brief walk might stir him into a second wind, so he rose from his desk and walked toward the door. Footsteps and a voice in another part of the lab stopped him.

"I need to get this stuff out of here tonight. Everything's getting moved out."

Roger's voice was clear.

"Yes ... I understand ... I'll get this to you ASAP."

On his cell phone? Eric wondered. He heard a door open and the shuffling of feet, followed by silence. Eric had suspected that Roger continued to leak information to his old employer. Was he now sending clandestine samples and involved in outright industrial espionage and the theft of proprietary information?

Unsure if Roger was gone, he crept from his office and eased toward the location where he thought Roger had been. No one else seemed to be around. On a lab table, he found a heavy cardboard file carton, filled with lab notebooks, computer printouts and handwritten notes. He slipped off its lid and rummaged through the materials, noting that most were official university supplies. That made it clear that the information inside should be considered proprietary by the medical center.

But what to do about it? How could he obtain proof?

He hurried back to his office and grabbed a small digital camera from his desk. After returning to the box, he took photos of it, inside and out, suppressing the flash so that the bright light wouldn't give him away. He pulled a couple of the notebooks from the first box and took pictures of the first few pages of each. The handwriting appeared to be Roger's. Another notebook revealed a different hand, not familiar enough to identify. Tucked into one end of the box was a large sealed manila envelope. He began to lift it from the box, but stopped.

He heard footsteps in the hall and quickly replaced all of the materials in the box except for one set of computer printouts. Grabbing the camera, he scurried back to his office and eased the door closed. He sat at his desk pondering his discovery. Handwritten lab notebooks? Duplicates of secure computerized records? Or something else. A handwritten record would avoid university scrutiny and could easily be hidden within a cluttered lab.

He heard the door open and more footsteps. He imagined Roger lifting the box and leaving the lab. As if on cue from his imagination, the door opened again and after the click of a lock, silence returned.

What is Roger up to?

Sayer's day had started before sun-up and now appeared it would end at sun-up as well. The euphoria of seeing his project leaving its gestational stages and coming to term propelled him far better than never-ending java and a case of Snickers™. He needed no epidural to ease the birth of this baby.

The wall clock in his office had struck midnight a short while back and he sat at his desk, feet up, sipping on a vintage Chardonnay from the small wine cooler under the bar across the room. Only the hum of the cooler and a hint of smooth jazz from his MP3 player breached the silence of the night. And he reveled in the near silence because it belied the din of heavier equipment operating only one story below him.

Sayer's attention turned to a silent alarm on the security panel adjacent to the vault door. Someone had entered the main warehouse through the side door adjacent to the main loading dock. He expected Marcus and Heinz to be bringing materials from the university lab. His mood lightened by the wine, he decided to have some fun with the techs. With the press of a button on security panel, a selection of security work lights blazed.

He spoke into a microphone on the security panel, "Follow the main aisle to the end, take a left and you'll see the light from my office. Bring everything here." He then stood and went to his office door, opening it and allowing the light to spill out into the warehouse.

A moment later, the two workers trudged through his door, pulling their wares - cardboard file containers and two large trunks - on dollies. Sayer had seen these trunks before. Foam inserts filled one trunk, with cutouts for various containers and glassware. The other also held padding, but this foam protected two small thermos-like containers cooled by liquid nitrogen. A larger, similar freezer sat in one of the labs below, waiting for the transfer of these samples.

The two men grimaced.

"I'm getting a bit old for all-nighters," replied Heinz. The other man nodded in agreement.

"C'mon, let's get the rest of it and get it unpacked. I guess we have to set up a whole lab tonight, right?" Marcus asked, looking squarely at Sayer.

Sayer grinned. He couldn't wait for the reactions of these two when they saw their new worksite. "That's what the Colonel wants."

A few minutes later they returned, each carrying a cardboard file case. As they entered the office, Sayer directed them to the vault, which he had opened in their absence. He had also moved the trunks into the vault. He stepped back as the two preceded him and stood in front of the security panel. Once the men were inside, he pressed a combination of buttons and the door closed.

He laughed as their protests emerged through the speaker.

"Hey, Sayer, this isn't funny. Open up and let us outta here!"

"Shit, I don't like tight spaces. Open up, Sayer. I'm gonna get sick."

He let the whining continue for a minute and then pressed another combination of buttons to activate the lift … and listened.

"What the …"

"Hey, cool. It's like we're headin' to the Bat Cave or somethin'."

As the descent finished, he heard them step off the lift and knew that the automatic lights would be clicking on.

"Awesome!"

"Oh, wow. What a setup! Marcus, look in here."

Sayer spoke into the microphone. "Surprise! Unload the lift into the anteroom there and I'll come down to join you. Don't enter any of the labs yet."

Fifteen minutes later, he finished the abbreviated tour for the two technicians. He watched as they suited up to enter the lab and then began the careful process of unpacking. He doubted they would require the entire night to complete the task, but wondered if they would spend the night working anyway.

Back in his office, he picked up his cell phone and re-keyed a number he could dial in his sleep.

"Edwards," the voice on the other end replied.

"How's it going?"

"Piece of cake. We drugged her tea at dinner and she's sleeping like Little Black Sambo. 'Cept she's not gonna outwit us and eat our pancakes."

"What? Pancakes?"

"The story ... Sambo outwits the tigers, finds his way home, and eats 169 pancakes as a reward."

"What the hell do tigers and pancakes have to do with –"

"Just a story, Sayer. She was acting kinda squirrelly and I think she thought she was going to outwit us."

"Oh?"

"Yeah. When we were moving her to the van to take her to the safe house, something fell out of her clothing. The guys missed it on their initial search. She had a cell phone in her bra."

CHAPTER 25

The sun blazed through the partially drawn window shades and a warm spring breeze scented with lavender infiltrated her bedroom through the slightly opened sash, but the day failed to beckon Sarah from bed. She hadn't slept in over 36 hours, and sleep continued to elude her. If worry about Della wasn't causing her turmoil, the dread of what she had to do this morning clawed at her instead. And adding to her anxiety was the fact that Doctor Rickelmann's twenty-four hours had come and gone and she'd not yet heard anything from Doctor Hrabik.

Sarah had long ago learned to accommodate stress. She lived with it every day. Life and death decisions, although not taken glibly, had become second nature. The adrenaline charge of a major trauma case crashing through the E.D.'s ambulance doors produced a good kind of rush. And she wasn't a stranger to confrontation. She didn't shrink back from addressing belligerent drunks and addicts, demanding drug-seekers, or even the occasional doctor who tried to blame his own inadequacies on her. She had learned to stand firm with many of the overly testosteroned attending physicians, both male and female.

Still, today was going to be harder than any day in the E.D.

Convinced that slumber would remain a stranger until she eliminated the day's major stressor, she dragged her limp body from bed and into the bathroom. Her typical ten-minute shower crawled to fifteen minutes, then twenty, but produced a clinically insignificant amount of invigoration. It did even less for her stagnant level of enthusiasm, but she dressed, in a very complimentary skirted suit and heels, and walked to the corner Starbuck's for a cup of motivation grande.

After consuming enough caffeine to help a teenage girl lose ten pounds in the three days before prom, she rediscovered her car and climbed in. The eight year-old Jetta slowly cranked to life, echoing her mood. She pulled away from the curb with a jerk and made a U-turn at the first intersection. Della's house was just six minutes away; twelve, if she caught all red lights, which she hoped were all malfunctioning with detours to Illinois and back. Well, maybe not back.

As Sarah pulled up in front of Della's, she noted the pristine appearance of the yard. There was no trace of the event that had occurred only three nights earlier. She wondered who was responsible for that in Della's absence. She had no doubt there were those in DeWayne Winston's political camp who would have argued for keeping the damage intact as a reminder to the voters about the evils of racism. In fact, she had no doubt that some of those strategists would debate burning their own cross on her yard for a series of campaign ads. Would DeWayne sink to that level? She wasn't sure.

At the front door, she pressed the doorbell button and waited … and waited.

Where's Beatrice … or her aide? she wondered. She had expected an answer at the door.

As she stood there debating what her next move should be, she heard a car pull into the driveway and turned to see DeWayne's silver Mercedes ease to a stop. She glanced at her watch. He was uncharacteristically early, and without his bodyguard. But he was here now and there was no turning back. She felt her anxiety rise up inside.

As he approached, she asked, "Where's Aunt Beatrice?"

He didn't smile or frown but flatly replied, "Good morning to you, too, Sarah."

Sarah didn't respond but felt anger begin to blend with the angst. This was a combination of emotions she felt all too often when forced to be around DeWayne.

He stood in front of her and scrutinized her from head to toe. "Nice suit, but you look like shit. Sorry … 'feces' is the correct medical term, I believe."

Annoyed, Sarah started to respond but realized he was probably right and he didn't look much better. "You don't look so hot yourself."

"True. Believe it or not, but I haven't slept since Della's abduction."

Sarah didn't want to believe it but his appearance attested to his statement's truth.

"I think we should go inside for this discussion," he said as he pulled out a key ring and opened the front door. He directed her to the front room where she sat in the same Chippendale chair she had occupied while talking with Seamus O'Connor. DeWayne took the opposing chair.

"To answer your question, Aunt Beatrice is in an assisted living center and –"

"But why? This was her home and she had –"

DeWayne returned the interruption. "Think about it, Sarah. Della's missing. Her search, as well as my work, consume all of my time. The aides were only part-time. This was the best decision for her. She's having tea with new friends." A sly smile flashed across his face, but his sternness returned just as quickly. He took a deep breath and sighed. "Sarah, you asked for this meeting. What do you want?"

"A favor."

"A favor?" He huffed. "From me? A man you disdain and won't even show the courtesy of a polite greeting?" He eyed her carefully. "Why should I do you a favor?"

Sarah paused. She needed to word this carefully. "I want you to use your influence to get Detective O'Connor assigned to help the FBI on Della's kidnapping ...because you owe me ... and Della."

His scrutiny intensified.

"And how exactly do you figure that?"

"For keeping your secret for so long, and especially now, with your campaign."

He shook his head and sighed. "Sarah, Sarah ... don't you think my family and I have paid enough for this secret?"

Sarah's anger began to resurface. "Paid enough? You raped me when –"

He lowered his head and replied, "Yes, Sarah, I've admitted that ... and I've asked your forgiveness on a hundred occasions, but your pride keeps that unpleasant event hanging around your neck like some talisman aimed at controlling me, warding off some unseen evil spirit you associate with me." He paused and folded his hands. "The really sad thing about all of this ... is that once upon a time you were a faithful church attendee and I was the wayward youth. That event brought me to my knees and into the church while your bitterness has taken you away. Oh, you might say it's the demands of medicine on your life that prevent you from attending, but I know better and for that I am truly, truly sorry."

"Oh? And what about Della? She's kept your secret, too."

DeWayne sighed and his gaze seemed to penetrate right through her. He put his hands behind his head and stretched while pinching his lips. He appeared unsure. After another moment, his hands back in his lap, he said, "I think it's time to get this record straight. Della never kept your secret."

Sarah felt a punch to her solar plexus. "No way! She told me … You're trying to twist things to your liking, just like you've always done."

He rose to continue. "No, Sarah!" he exclaimed. In a softer tone, he continued, "I don't want to speak ill of the dead, especially my father, but –"

Sarah stood to confront him. "How dare you bring Dad Winston into this? He was the most honorable man I ever knew. I went into medicine because of him." Her indignation rose to a height she'd never experienced before. Of all the things DeWayne had done to her, trying to point blame to Della and his dead father was among the lowest.

His eyes revealed sadness and it caught her off-guard.

"Honorable? Yes, mostly. An inspiration to you? Most definitely. But he never deserved as high a pedestal as you put him on."

He sat down again, but Sarah remained standing, liking the position of dominance over him.

"I don't want to talk about this because I love my sister, and I loved and admired my father, but he was a much more pragmatic man than you ever knew. He …"

He paused again; his hesitancy evident and out of character for the man Sarah saw projected to the public.

"You have manufactured memories of a father figure you never had, Sarah. The perfect dad. But he was far from perfect.

You just didn't have to live with that part of him. As for my comment about my family paying for my error, well, your little secret wasn't so secret. Della spilled the beans long ago. Ask your mother, if you're brave enough. Your private education was the price they negotiated to keep the whole affair quiet and to keep me out of juvie. Della will confirm that … when we find her."

Sarah's eyes flared open in mixed emotions – astonishment, betrayal, rage. She didn't know how to respond. DeWayne knew too well that she could confirm his statement with a call to her mother, so he wouldn't take the risk of lying about it. All of these years, she had kept it from her mother when she really wanted to confide in her, to release the emotions the ugly event had birthed in her. But Della? The thought that Della had betrayed her raised gall in her throat.

"That's not why Dad Winston paid for my education!" she blurted out, stopping short of revealing what she knew as the real reason.

"Sorry. I know it must hurt to burst a bubble inflated by sixteen years of relived memories, but Dad wasn't perfect … and if it helps, he had no regrets giving you that education. He was as proud of you as he was of us when you went off to college on scholarship and then to med school." He strained to search her eyes. "As for me, I'd like to once again ask your forgiveness … but I don't expect an answer right now because I know you can't give one."

Within her mind's eye, Sarah saw in an instant that DeWayne was right in much of what he'd said. Maybe pride and bitterness had kept the incident hanging around her neck like rotting garlic fending off a vampire in her imagination. But as tears ebbed from the corners of her eyes and down her cheeks, rage filled her. She would come to terms with DeWayne, but Della had betrayed her, lied to her. She had let Sarah live with the unresolved anger and resentment all these years. *Well, Ms. Della Winston, you're on your own.* Sarah turned and left the house.

An emotional fog clouded Sarah's drive home as she fought

to digest the informational fodder DeWayne had fed her. Her mind told her that no man could be perfect and that her memory of Dad Winston most likely had been built and rebuilt over the years into what she envisioned now. But her heart held on to that perfect father image she had constructed. As for the fact that her silence had been bought and paid for, with her mother as chief negotiator, she felt her anger build. Anger at Dad Winston for protecting his son ... at her expense. Anger at her mother for sixteen years of silence. Anger at Della for being the instigator and accomplice. She felt belittled and patronized, yet for the first time those feelings weren't caused by DeWayne but by everyone else of significance in her life.

She drove a block past her apartment before realizing she had missed it. Her car's clock showed her it wasn't yet 10 am, but her desire for comfort food ignored the time. She drove another two blocks to a nearby convenience store, parked, and entered the store. They had a limited selection of Häagen-Dazs, so she settled for a quart of Prairie Farms Original Moose Tracks® -- and a wooden sample spoon, which she wasted no time using upon returning to her car. With a quarter of the container emptied, she left the lot and headed toward home.

Less than half a block from home, she was blessed with an open parking slot and she flipped on her blinker to prepare for parallel parking. She pulled up next to the car in front of the spot and was backing into the space when her cell phone erupted and broke her concentration. Her rear bumper tapped the car behind her, setting off that car's alarm. Flustered and only halfway into the parking spot, she threw the gear into park and grabbed her phone.

"Doctor Wade? This is Connie. Doctor Hrabik is on his way into the office and wants to talk with you ASAP. Can you come in?"

"I, uh ... sure. Be there in fifteen minutes, more or less. What's up?"

"I honestly don't know for sure, but he didn't sound happy. I'll let him know ..."

Her cell battery died. "Damn!" Sarah threw her

Blackberry™ onto the passenger seat. She didn't need this. Not this morning. Why couldn't this particular issue just go away? Why couldn't her smart phone stay charged? She wanted to crawl into bed in a cabin on a lake or at some beach, somewhere far away, and hide from the world … with a month's supply of Häagen-Dazs, or Ben & Jerry's, or whatever Denali® flavored premium ice cream she could stash there.

Twenty minutes later, her department chief closed the door behind her and directed her to a chair across from his desk. Sarah noted that he looked as unhappy as Connie said he'd sounded. And that didn't bode well for her situation.

"Coffee? Tea? I can have Connie get you something," Doctor Hrabik said.

Oh crap, he's starting with small talk, Sarah thought as she shook her head. Her ice cream was melting in a trash receptacle in the parking garage and no hot drink would replace it.

"Okay. Well, let me get right to the point. I just had a meeting with the Vice President of Medical Affairs to protest this whole mess, but he doesn't want to get into the middle of it. Rickelmann's alleged witness is conveniently out of town for a week, and now Doctor Riley, from Surgery, is recusing himself. He'd never admit it, but I'm positive he knows this whole thing is a sham but he's afraid to vote against Rickelmann. Anyway, this leaves an opening on the board and a theoretical tie vote. Even if the vote would be unanimous, which it should be in your case, the by-laws state that an odd number of members must hear and vote on any case, so now no one wants to bring this to a vote until a new member can hear the facts and join the vote." He sighed and his shoulders slumped forward in defeat.

"I'm sorry, Sarah, that this is dragging on and on. Politics. I just can't believe these people and their, their pettiness."

Sarah sat there calmly, trying to pinpoint how she felt about this turn of events. She'd experienced enough medical center politics that none of this surprised her. An earlier thought zigzagged through her mind … she didn't need this, not today. Yet, strangely, she felt empowered, not frustrated.

She tuned out Doctor Hrabik as he blathered about the trivial interdepartmental squabbles he'd battled since assuming his position as department head. But his comment about filing her own grievance caught her attention. She'd had enough and she knew what she had to do. If Rickelmann wanted to play power games, well, she'd give him a slice of his own surgery.

"Thank you, Doctor Hrabik, for all you've done," she said, interrupting his ramblings. She rose from her chair, rolling both hands into fists and gathering her resolve. *Play ball,* she thought.

She left the department offices and headed straight for the Department of Surgery. From her rotation on trauma, she remembered that Rickelmann always had the first time slot in the O.R. and typically finished surgery by mid-morning. He then gave his residents a reprieve, allowing them to round on patients and perform post-op care before taxing them with attending rounds in the afternoon. In all likelihood, he would be in his office dealing with departmental matters. At least, she hoped he'd be there where she could deal with him in private before her resolve dissolved.

She walked into the department suite and past the receptionist before the woman could protest. It took her a moment to identify Doctor Rickelmann's office but when she did, she found the door closed. She prepared to knock when a woman in her mid-thirties stopped her.

"I'm sorry, Doctor Rickelmann isn't to be disturbed right now. Can I tell him who you are and what you want to see him about, and then we can set up an appointment?"

Sarah's resolve flagged for a moment. What she was about to do could end her career. It was a make or break move. She turned to address the secretary and watched as the woman examined her nametag, became wide-eyed, and uttered a subtle, "Oh my."

That was enough for Sarah. She turned back to the door, opened it, and marched in. Doctor Rickelmann stood at the window, looking out over the medical campus. As she slammed the door closed, he turned, retaining his calm demeanor.

"Doctor Wade, has no one ever taught you the courtesy of –"

"Yes, Doctor Rickelmann, and courtesy is shown where

courtesy is due. I'm here to tell you that I've had enough of this charade. I don't know what you think you are gaining by continuing this grievance against me, but you and I and everyone at that hearing knows that I never did anything to offend you, slander you, or in any way affect your reputation. I'm not asking you to drop this, I'm demanding it." She paused. "Or I will play this game your way and file a counter grievance against you. How do sexual harassment charges sound? Wouldn't that just tickle your testosterone-charged fantasies? And talk about a reputation buster."

She gazed at his face. The initial scowl had flattened to the perfect poker face. She couldn't read him at all.

"You wanted twenty-four hours. Well, you've got another day. Drop this charge against me by noon tomorrow or be prepared for the next round."

At that, she turned around and marched back out the door, hyperventilating, and her hands shaking.

CHAPTER 26

Della awoke with a headache and an inner awareness of a new fear. If she hadn't known better, she would have thought she was waking up after an all-night bender. But there had been nothing fun about the previous evening and she wasn't lying on some friend's couch. Oh that she were.

But what was she lying on? This didn't feel like the cot. It wasn't exactly a bed, but it was larger and softer than the cot she'd become accustomed to. Something else was different. The smell, or more accurately, the smells. Spices, fabric softener, diesel exhaust. She could detect all of these, with each odor dominating the others in a random rotation. The sounds differed, too. She easily identified traffic noise and a siren wailed in the distance.

She focused again on the surface holding her. The fabric softener emanated from a sheet covering the makeshift bed. She lifted and dropped her head carefully on it and recognized the sensation as one of bouncing an air-filled ball. That was it, an air mattress. They had moved her to a more comfortable room with an inflatable bed. She tried to spread her legs across the plane to determine its size but the shackles still restrained her. Moving both legs together, she found the closest edge and rolled in that direction.

That's when she noticed the other difference, one that filled her with terror. Her body moved too freely in one aspect. Her breasts moved without restraint. She could feel no tightness of elastic in her groin. Her underwear was gone. This also meant they had discovered the cell phone. She trembled in fear of playing the game, or worse, of summary execution. She knew she should have been forthcoming once she discovered it on her body. She had been unable to act nonchalant. She had given away her hand. Now she would pay for that indiscretion.

She rolled off the mattress and hit the floor with a dull thud. After several attempts, she managed to kneel on the floor.

"That's probably an appropriate position for you to maintain right now."

She yelped at the voice. There had been no footsteps, no opening door. He had been there all along. Had he done more than strip away her intimate clothing? She felt no discomfort anywhere. She realized that the hangover affect was drug induced. Had they also given her something to mask any pain a gang rape might produce? She could no longer control her trembling.

"Don't worry. I didn't let them do anything except to remove any hiding places. You should have given me the phone. That might have convinced them you really mean to cooperate. Now, well, they don't believe you."

He paused and the silence exaggerated her anxiety.

"I had you moved to a new location … to keep them from hurting you. If you don't convince me that you're sincere about cooperating, well, I'll be forced to take you back and leave you with them."

The last comment had a noticeable effect on the woman. Amidst the shaking, a wet stain spread from between her legs across the front of her pants. Sayer knew then that Edwards had broken her. She would cooperate.

Sayer looked around. The men who had helped Edwards with the move had done their job to perfection. Old mattresses filled the rooms along with enough fast food debris to make it appear a group of four or five had holed up there since the abduction. Della Winton's lingerie lay on one mattress, along with enough hair for positive DNA matching. They scattered newspapers through the rooms, as if they had been following the abduction in the news. As Sayer watched, they now sanitized the rooms, wiping down all surfaces anyone might have touched before they'd gloved up. One man was in the far end of the building, setting up a device that would ignite a fire after a fifteen to twenty minute delay.

Sayer liked the way Edwards thought. They would move again, maybe tonight, maybe tomorrow night, but not without a little drama. Her cell phone would start the entertainment … when the time was right.

CHAPTER 27

His stomach grumbling for dinner, Seamus sat at his desk leafing through messages he'd received while out, reviewing calls and making notes on the businesses he'd visited over the previous two days. The public furor over the cases had eased after DeWayne Winston urged other Afro-American leaders to call for peace, but that hadn't allayed the private pressure sliding downhill from the Governor to the Mayor to the Police Chief to the Patrol Division Deputy Chiefs to the rank and file. He had swapped out the standard issue hip waders for chest waders, the muck had piled so deep.

Seamus resumed his review, jotting down names and impressions. A few interviewees seemed squirrelly enough to call for a second look, but most he judged reliable. As he breezed through the folder, he found the job application the redhead at CheapTrx had given him. Blake Howard. He lived in a small rental house in St. Clair, MO, about forty-five minutes southwest of the city. He had contacted that police department and asked for assistance, only to receive a non-committal answer. He had no reason to dissect this guy other than an instinctive sense to look closely at him. He mulled over reasons to justify a trip to St. Clair for what his lieutenant would no doubt consider a long shot.

"Hey, Shay."

Seamus looked up to find his partner standing at the edge of his desk, the aroma of French vanilla latte drifting from the cup extended toward him. He took it without hesitation.

"Thanks, Stick. Have a seat." Seamus pointed to his only empty chair.

"Thought you might want to celebrate."

Seamus took a sip, savored the blend of tastes, and replied, "Celebrate what?"

Stick shook his head. "I don't know how they expect you to get any real work done. First, you're working a local 9th District homicide. Then, two days later, they reassign you to a homicide with international ramifications. Now this."

Seamus knew his partner well enough to know when he was baiting him. He could play along.

"Oh that. I just figured it was a matter of time. They know real talent when they see it."

He caught his partner biting his lip trying to contain himself. An eccentric grin flared across his face.

"I couldn't have said it any better." He pointed over Shay's shoulder toward the growing sound of several people walking into the BOI. "Guess that's why they got you a new partner, one with real talent." He smirked, but quickly became serious and sat up, ramrod straight.

Seamus knew he'd walked right into something. But what? Would he now require a boat to replace the chest waders? He set down his latte and swiveled 180° in his chair. No one was there. He turned back to Stick, who nodded again in their superior's direction. Seamus again pivoted in his chair and a moment later saw the lieutenant's office door open. Leaving the office was Senator Winston, the Mayor, Police Chief Allen, and their captain. All of them looked at Seamus as the Senator nodded his way, as if saying, "That one. I want that one." Two seconds later, the lieutenant emerged with a familiar face, Doctor Sarah Wade.

His gut churned. His face flushed. He knew what was coming and he didn't want any part of it. No way. Civilians should not be riding with police. And he certainly did not need to babysit a kidnappee's worried best friend. The political and critical time pressures were too great for such a distraction. The physical dangers were too real.

He stood as they approached his desk and nodded to Sarah. The lieutenant was cordial but didn't appear all too happy.

"O'Connor, I understand you two already know each other." He pulled O'Connor a little to the side. "On orders direct from the Mayor, the Chief, the FBI S-A-C, and anyone else trying to put my ass in their fire, you're now assigned to the Della Winston kidnapping as our liaison to the FBI … and Doctor Wade here is officially endorsed as a ride-along with you on behalf of our dear Senator. Here's a list of the FBI contacts and others working the case. They're expecting to hear from you tomorrow morning at the latest." He leaned forward and growled into Seamus' ear, "Keep her happy, O'Connor. I don't want more shit flowing downhill to my office. Understand?"

Seamus grumbled, "Yes, Sir." What had he done to deserve this? What specific thing did he do to impress this lady doctor so much that she'd go this far to make his life miserable? He needed to avoid it in the future if this was the result.

The obvious source of this crap cascade had walked out of the office before her, but Shay knew that, somehow, the dear doctor herself had started the dung ball rolling. And that thought stirred him to copy his superior's attitude. On the positive side, the ambassador's murder and the Winston kidnapping appeared related so the work he'd done wouldn't be too far removed from this new assignment.

The lieutenant turned without any further word and walked back to his office. Sarah stood there, frowning, hands clenched at the hem of the knit top overhanging her cotton twill slacks.

"Look," said Seamus. "I really appreciated your stopping by the other night, but I really don't think you should –"

"I want to go home, if you would please take me," she said with a tuft of frost in her voice. "Your lieutenant wouldn't."

Seamus didn't answer, confused. He sat on the edge of his desk, knocking over a picture frame holding a photo of his ex-flame so that it lay face down. The noise of it hitting the desktop caught his attention and he wondered whether there was some subconscious motivation to this action, but he didn't move to right it. He took a deep breath and pondered his next step in light of his order to "keep her happy."

"What? I don't get it. You said you wanted me on the case and you obviously got the Senator involved to make it happen. Do you or don't you want to be part of this? Frankly, civilians have no place tagging along on a police investigation, and this one in particular has higher risks than most. I don't want to offend you, but you should stay out of it."

"I did. I mean, I do. I just don't think I want to be here right now, at this moment. Winston's two thugs came to my apartment and insisted I come with them. So, here I am." She frowned and cocked her hips to the left as she crossed her arms. She looked a bit petulant, but she didn't say anything further. In fact, her silence was more annoying.

"Okay. Lieutenant said to keep you happy, so home it is. But first, it's late in the day and I still have to sign over my current case materials to Stick. Then I need to touch base with the feds in charge, and I'd really like a good dinner and my first full night's sleep this week. I can arrange for a ride for you."

"I can wait." She shifted her stance to her other hip.

"For what?"

"For you to finish here. Then I can cook you dinner again. No problem."

Seamus caught the flare of Stick's eyebrows at her stating 'again' and its implications. *Yeah, big problem*, he thought. *And a bigger disruption.*

Sarah plopped down in the chair vacated by Stick, crossed her legs and refolded her arms. Maybe petulant was an understatement.

"C'mon, Doctor Wade." He caught her look at being formally addressed. "This isn't a good time to …" His voice trailed off as he looked into her eyes. She was in no mood for being passed off. He knew what kind of week she'd had, but there was something more. His gut told him something had happened today, and he was inheriting the fallout.

"Look, it's kinda like physician-patient confidentiality. I have to pass this material off to my partner and you aren't privileged to hear it." She didn't respond. He tried a different analogy. "Kinda like HIPAA, or need to know, that kind of stuff." She didn't budge.

"Okay. Look, if you'll move over there and have a seat, I'll make this quick and grab you as I leave. We'll get a bite to eat at a pub I know."

She uncrossed her legs and shifted her weight in the chair. Then, she finally nodded, arose, and moved across the room.

Stick chuckled. "Yep, that's real talent all righty. She wrapped you around her finger like bacon around a filet. I even see the little stick poking outta your back. Oops, sorry. That's the Senator's knife. My bad."

Seamus wasn't amused.

CHAPTER 28

At eight am the following morning, Seamus hobbled into the office after another near sleepless night. He had excelled in criminal psychology in college. His peers knew him as a superb interviewer able to coax coercion-free confessions from rocks. But nowhere in those courses did they focus on the female psyche. Dinner at O'Malley's had started out tamely enough … until he made the mistake of asking how her day had gone. When he asked why in the world she had confronted that pompous Rickelmann, in a tone that might have been just a wee bit patronizing, she became physical.

But the night might have produced one positive result. She might still be mad enough at him to stay home and let him work in peace. He crossed his fingers as he entered the division headquarters.

So much for crossed fingers, he thought as he rounded the corner toward his desk. Clothed in casual twill slacks and a three-quarter sleeve top, Sarah sat in the same chair she had tried to commandeer the previous evening. She stood when she saw him, and grimaced when she saw the limp.

"Still sore?"

He shrugged.

"I let you off easy. You deserved getting kicked in <u>both</u> shins," she added.

"I shoulda booked you for assaulting a police officer with a deadly weapon," he replied. "Been here long?"

"A few minutes."

Another detective, sitting behind her at a nearby desk, shook his head and gestured 3 – 0 with his fingers. Seamus smiled.

"Sleep okay?"

She took her turn to shrug. "So-so. It was a bad day."

"So I learned. Well, we have a long one ahead of us. Are you up to it?"

"Have you ever worked a twelve-hour shift at the Trauma Center?"

She's up for it. Damn it, thought Seamus.

"Give me a minute to make a couple of calls, and we'll take off."

She nodded and sat down, trying to look nonchalant. Seamus was about to point to the chair across the room but decided against it. He needed his other leg. Instead, he walked over to his lieutenant's office, peeked in, saw that it was empty, and made his calls from there. Five minutes later, he was ready to go.

As they climbed into his car, she asked, "So, what do we do now?"

He knew what <u>not</u> to answer.

"My first task is to follow-up on a lead I have on a tattoo artist. This means a trip to St. Clair. You get to ride along, but I expect you to remain in the car, stay quiet, and let me do my job."

She sat looking at the scenery as it passed by. Fifteen minutes later, they left the city limits in complete silence. He wondered what was going on in her head, but knew better than to ask. By the time they passed the Six Flags Amusement Park, the quiet had become like a vacuum pulling at him.

"What's on your mind?" he asked.

"You said you expected me to be quiet. Just complying with a police order."

Yes, it was going to be a long day.

"Okay, what do you want to talk about?"

"Nothing." She resumed staring out the window.

Seamus now felt obligated to keep up some light banter. This wasn't the Sarah he had come to know a few nights earlier. Something ate at her, but he wouldn't presume to intrude. He tried the traditional St. Louis conversation starter, "Okay, so … where'd you go to high school?"

Sarah glanced periodically at Seamus as he talked and drove. He had a smooth, confident manner as he spoke and she found his family background refreshingly different. Growing up she'd never known her dad, but Seamus had not only an active father but also grandfathers and multiple uncles who performed as surrogates when his real father was absent. And although they had Catholicism in common, the Irish culture brought a level of emphasis to the reverence of saints she'd never experienced. They invoked the names of saints she'd never even heard of.

Too bad he was white, redheaded, baby-faced, and Irish.

As they pulled off the Interstate and waited to turn toward town, Seamus grabbed a piece of paper from the back seat.

"MapQuest," he stated. He glanced at the map and resumed driving. Fifteen minutes later, they pulled onto a gravel road to nowhere. He drove up the road until it ended at a river, turned around and drove back. He repeated the drive.

"It's supposed to be here, but I don't see any houses at all. Do you?" he asked.

Sarah shook her head. "You sure it's a house? I saw some mobile homes sitting back off the road about a half mile after we turned."

He nodded. "Saw those, too. Nothing else here, so I guess we can stop and check there."

Sarah started to get out of the car with Seamus.

"No way! Stay in the car."

Sarah hesitated, but complied, and watched from the car as Seamus walked past the rusting hulk of an old tractor, a weed encased mound of worn tires and a trash burn pile to the closest trailer and knocked on a door that appeared ready to collapse with a mere push. No answer. The second trailer looked even worse for wear, its small porch missing its wooden rails, tattered curtains fluttering in open windows where screens bore large holes mirroring their counterparts in the curtains. She could see no rust on the ancient Airstream™ carcass that appeared repellant of paint. An old man tottered at the doorway as Seamus made his inquiries. Seamus walked to a third, equally disheveled mobile home and knocked there as well. A younger woman with an infant on her hip answered the door, but quickly shook her head and closed the door as he held up his shield to identify himself.

As he climbed back into his seat she said, "Guess you struck out here."

"More like retired the inning," he replied. "They never even heard of the street, Blake Howard, or Della Winston. So, it's back to town."

The mentioning of Della's name for the first time that day evoked painful emotion in Sarah's gut. All night she had wrestled not only with her stupid confrontation of Rickelmann but also with her resentment toward Della. What would Dad Winston have thought about such feelings toward Della? What would he have advised Sarah to do? It need not be said that he'd want her to keep searching for Della. Sarah's unresolved issues with Della, and DeWayne, gave her no other choice really. That's why she'd shown up at the BOI that morning to help Seamus. That's why she soldiered on.

After another fifteen minutes, Seamus pulled into the parking lot at the St. Clair Police Department, parked, and hopped out.

"This should only take a minute. Just wait here."

Sarah didn't hesitate. She'd been sitting in one place longer than she was used to and needed to stretch her legs. As she entered the station a step behind him, he stopped and turned to her. He took her elbow and tried to lead her back to the parking lot.

"Look, I really need you to stay in the car."

She pulled away and walked back into the lobby of the station.

"No. I'm tired of sitting, and I want to hear what's said. You know, so I can pass it on to DeWayne Winston firsthand." She gave Seamus a look that said, "Keep me happy, Officer."

Shay started to say something, but stopped, counted to ten, and simply shook his head. Together, they walked up to the reception window. Seamus identified himself, and her, and they were buzzed through a locked door into the front office, and asked to wait.

"Wait here by the door." With some effort, he added, "Please." He stepped further into the room and briefly turned to make sure Sarah remained by the door.

A burly, no-necked man in his mid-forties wearing a rumpled, ill-fitting suit ambled around a corner and greeted Seamus, giving but a quick glance at Sarah.

"Detective, I'm Joe Rankin, the closest thing to a real detective you're gonna find here." He laughed. "Kind of an inside joke around here. Anyway, I got your request and the fax you sent. Hope you haven't spend a bunch of time looking for that rental house, 'cause it don't exist. No such road either … despite what them Internet maps say," he added as Seamus started to show him the map printout in his hand.

"I did get some time to ask around, though. Meant to get out there as soon as I could, but … well, you know how time can get away from you." He handed Seamus a typed piece of paper. "Take Route 30 south outta town and pick up County K to the right. Follow K until it passes over the river. You'll pass a few roads, but the house you want is near the intersection of K and Oklahoma School Road. A few neighbors there you might want to talk with also." He handed Seamus a second paper. "And here's where he works part-time. I know some of the guys there. Decent folk. Hard working and patriotic. A few rowdies come and go there. The impression I got was he's one of them."

Sarah eased forward and looked over Seamus' shoulder. The company was a hardware store but not one of the national chains that she'd heard of.

Seamus nodded. "Thanks. Any other information on the guy? Licenses for tattooing? Anything?"

"Can't help you there, but you can check with the state folks. There's an Office of Tattooing, Body Piercing, and Branding from what I understand. They should know whether this guy is licensed or not."

"What about any activity by white supremacist groups in this area?" Sarah asked.

Seamus, face reddened, frowned at Sarah and nudged her, hoping the local detective wouldn't see. The man's eyes widened, as he looked her up and down. "And who might you be?"

Seamus broke in. "Sorry. This is Doctor Sarah Wade. She's riding along with me as an observer today. " Detective Rankin's brow rose for a subtle instant. "On behalf of Senator Winston."

Detective Rankin nodded and sighed, as if sharing a fellow officer's pain. "Okay. Sure. I place you now. Seen you on some of the TV news coverage." He rubbed his chin with one hand as he placed the other hand on his hip.

Seamus stopped him. "That's okay. You don't have to answer."

"Don't mind. Her question has me curious 'cause there have been rumors of some kind of militia group having a training camp somewhere southwest of here. Very secluded area. And there have been vague references to that group having ties to other white supremacy factions. Now, I have nothing concrete on any of that, mind you. And don't quote me 'cause it's all just rumor."

"Thanks. Hey, we need to get going if there's nothing else," Seamus stated.

"I got nothing else," the detective replied. "Good luck … on all counts."

Seamus grabbed Sarah's elbow and hurried her out of the building. Once in the car, he looked at her sternly.

"What'd I do?" she asked in response to his glare.

"Let me ask the questions," he answered. "You have no official capacity here and I can't let you accidentally give out any information we don't want released."

"Were you going to ask about any of those groups?"

"No, because –"

"See, somebody had to, if you weren't going to," she retorted, folding her arms across her chest. "I thought you were supposed to keep me happy. To do that, you need to ask better questions."

"Okay, smarty pants. How do you know he doesn't have any ties to one of these groups?"

Sarah slid down in her seat a bit, relaxing her arms.

"Just because he's a policeman doesn't mean anything. He could be on the phone right now warning the group leaders that someone is looking for them."

She slid down further, regretting her question and fearing that she'd just blown it for Della. Seamus was right. She didn't know whom to trust, except him. She had wanted him on the case. Now she had to let go and allow him to do his job.

He looked over at her and his voice softened. "That said, he probably isn't. If he was part of a group, he most likely would have just flat out denied there was any such activity around the area. But I think you catch my drift."

Sarah sat upright, her arms relaxed. Maybe she hadn't blown it … and wouldn't, if she could keep her mouth closed.

"Besides, we're still not sure a white supremacy group is behind the ambassador's killing or Della's kidnapping. That's all speculation based on one vague tattoo. Could be the guy's initials are WS." Seamus glanced at her. "So, you ever been to this part of the state?

Sarah shook her head. "Maybe. A group of us spent a week at some kind of Christian camp at the end of sixth grade. It was rural like this, but we were so busy talking on the bus, I honestly don't know where we went."

"That so. Did you enjoy it?"

"Sure. I was with friends. We were away from home for the first time. We got to swim and hike and stuff. Even did a high ropes course. That was a little scary the first time. Can't say I enjoyed rounding up the cattle but we only did that once. It was some kind of working farm as well as camp."

"What was the name of the place?"

"Heritage Crossing."

"Never heard of it."

"Last I heard it wasn't operating anymore. Don't know why."

Seamus followed the twisty curves of County K as it wound toward the river bottoms. Scrub oak and cedar lined the road, sometimes hiding the trailers, homes in various states of disrepair, barns, and mélange of vehicles, working and not, that dotted the landscape. Sarah found the display of poverty despairing and was happy a few minutes later when the road opened onto a broad flood plain and curved toward a cement bridge spanning the Meramec River.

"You know, this looks kind of familiar. We took a canoe trip for a day and it ended at a bridge and sand bar like this. I wonder …"

A few minutes later, they passed a road to the right with a fading sign for Heritage Crossing. Seamus laughed.

"Guess you have been in this part of Missouri after all."

Sarah's thoughts turned to that summer when she turned twelve. That was certainly a different time with its own pace, free of adult worries, yet full of discovery for two black city girls whose most advanced wilderness experience to that point had been the state's Powder Valley Conservation Nature Center in the city's southwest suburbs. It had also been a time of learning to trust God. The incident involving DeWayne occurred three months after they'd returned home from camp and that trust had been shattered. DeWayne's words about returning to God perseverated in her mind.

By the time her mind returned to the present, Seamus slowed the car and started looking for house numbers. She glanced to the right and saw Oklahoma School Road as it intersected with the road they were traveling.

"Bingo!" Seamus exclaimed. "Over there."

He pointed to a small, dilapidated frame house sided in faded white shingles that appeared no larger than Sarah's apartment. To her, a bulldozer seemed the most appropriate home improvement tool. She found it hard to believe someone lived there, much less paid rent for that "privilege." Seamus drove by slowly and scanned the layout. A half mile later, he turned around and returned to the house, pulling into the drive. There were no cars present and the building looked uninhabited.

He left the car running as he opened the door. Turning to Sarah, he said, "This guy might be a problem so I want you to stay here. You might even need to hightail it out of here for help, so I'm leaving the car running."

Sarah didn't like that implication, but after a moment of thought agreed that if this guy was connected to the group that kidnapped Della, he could be trouble. She debated whether she should move into the driver's seat and be prepared to drive, but recognized the melodrama her imagination could conjure.

She watched Seamus as he walked to the front door and knocked. After a second round of knocking with no answer, he cautiously moved around the house, not spending time near windows. She couldn't see him behind the house, but moments later, he returned to the car.

"Just like it looks, no one home." He scanned the neighboring structures for signs of life. "Did you see any signs of life at any of the nearby homes?"

Sarah shook her head. "No, they all look deserted, except for a couple of cars at a place across the road and a little ways back toward town." She pointed in the direction of the vehicles.

Seamus climbed back into the car. "Might as well check it out."

This home, although larger, appeared as ramshackle. The vehicles in front were late models, but the house needed serious scraping and painting, plus some roof repairs. Seamus didn't want to think about the work the inside might need.

Sarah started to exit the car, but Seamus grabbed her elbow again and stopped her.

"Stay here."

Sarah frowned and reached for the door handle.

He held on to her arm. "Do I have to put you in the back seat?"

Sarah gave him a "don't mess with me look." He had no doubt that she knew there were locks on the back doors that only the driver could release.

"Seriously. This is rural Missouri. You might be light skinned, but the first thing some folks are going to notice is that you're black, not that you're a doctor. We don't know who lives here, or if they'll shoot first and ask for your medical license later."

"You don't have to be flippant. I'll be okay if I stay close to you. Right?"

The lieutenant's words again echoed in his mind and his gut churned.

A minute later, they were engaged in conversation with a

small woman with short white hair and a wiry frame. Her skin was coarse and wrinkled, half way between weathered and Chinese Shar-Pei. He noted nicotine stains on the women's left fingertips, and guessed she was much younger than she appeared, the victim of too many pack-years of smoking or a possible meth addiction. Her "meth mouth" smile pointed to both. Either way she looked as if she had been ridden hard and put away wet, like many of the female addicts he'd encountered in the wide array of drug busts he'd participated in before joining homicide.

"Saw you across the way," she said after Seamus had identified himself and Sarah. "Bastard's been gone for at least four, maybe five days, him and his devil pit bull. Can't say as anyone around here misses him. Hope he stays wherever he is."

"You sure about the timing?" Seamus asked. If he'd been home four days ago, it might be difficult to tie him to any of the activities of the past several days.

"Yeah. I seen his killer dog chained outside five days ago. Everyone 'round here takes note of that beast and keeps a wary eye out when it's outside. Kilt one neighbor's two cats and got my Jack Russell six months ago. He denied it. Claimed it must have been coyotes, but no one 'round here seen any coyotes. The bastard. Anyway, pickup was there, too. Then I noticed him goin' in and out the house. Pickup was gone later that afternoon but I thought I heard the dog. No sign of either last four days. Positive 'bout it. Been nice an' quiet for a change."

"How well did you know him?"

"Only as well as you might get to know someone you're going 'round and 'round with about his dog killin' yours. Sure didn't drink no beer with him or his buddies."

"Buddies?"

"Sure. They come around more often than not. Just a handful, come and go. Rowdy group best I could see. Lots of drinkin' and shootin' off guns on the Fourth of July and New Year's Eve. That kind of stuff."

"So, you really didn't know him at all."

She shook her head. "Not enough worth tellin'. Sure would like to see him gone, though. I miss my Jack."

Seamus believed her and read between the lines. The guy sounded like the type who could cause trouble and get tangled up with racist groups.

"Ever hear anything about his doing tattoos?"

"Now you mention it, yeah. Nothing good, though. Heard he got in some trouble 'bout it. Something 'bout re-using needles and givin' some folks hepatitis C."

Seamus noticed Sarah scrutinizing the woman as she spoke.

"You know about hepatitis C?" Sarah asked, phrasing the question to be impersonal.

Seamus cringed and the woman, who seemed taken aback by her question, glanced at Sarah with squinty eyes. A frown crossed her face.

"Maybe, but that's none a yer business," she replied.

Seamus grabbed Sarah's arm and squeezed, but Sarah persisted. "Do you know about interferon treatments? They can help."

The woman abruptly straightened up and rolled her head, neck, and shoulders as if working out some kink in her neck. "Well, that's all I know 'bout the guy. You folks have a good day." She turned around in her doorway, entered the house, and closed the door on Seamus and Sarah.

Seamus gave Sarah a withering look, shook his head, and pulled her to the car. He unlocked a back door and sat her down on the seat like a criminal, holding her head to prevent injury on the doorframe.

"I swear. Keep it up and I'm gonna lock you in the back until we're back at my office."

"What?"

"Didn't I ask you to let me do the questioning? I might have gotten something more out of her if you hadn't attacked her personally."

"Attacked her personally? It was obvious she has Hep C and I just wanted to make sure she knew of all the options."

"Maybe so, but we weren't there to inquire about her. Most people start getting defensive when the questions get personal like that. Besides, how many folks you know have insurance that will cover interferon treatments? Do you think she could afford those treatments out-of-pocket? Does this place look like Town and Country? We're out here to learn more about Blake Howard. Let's keep it to that … and I'll ask the questions."

Like his mood, the skies had become heavily overcast and drops of rain spit randomly from the heavens, like Sarah's actions. She gazed past him, poker-faced. He couldn't read her, and at the moment, he didn't care if the Senator's fury raining down through the Chief to his lieutenant would engulf him like a California mudslide.

Sarah stared toward the house, feeling abashed again. Maybe she should just stay in the car. But if she acceded to that thought, what was the point of riding along with Seamus? She couldn't stand the thought of staying home, idle, worrying about Della. And she realized she _was_ worried about her, despite DeWayne's revelations. No, she needed to stick with Seamus, to keep her mind occupied and positive, to be available to help in any way she could.

"Okay. I'll admit I'm out of my element here. What can I do, that will actually help you?

"That's it? No apology. Diagnosis made. Move on to the next case."

"I don't apologize when I've done nothing wrong."

Seamus shook his head. "So, when was the last time you apologized for something?"

"Too long ago to remember. So, again, how can I help you?"

Seamus huffed. "You're something else. Okay. Like I said, let me do the questioning. If you have questions, pose them to me first, preferably while we're in the car. And when we're alone, give me your impressions about the people we talk to. You have good intuition, Sarah. I value that."

"Okay. What next?"

"What would you do next?" Seamus asked.

She thought for a moment. "Well, seems to me that folks here don't like Blake Howard much and probably can't offer much more than we just heard. So, I'd head back to town and check into where he worked."

"See? Like I said, you have good judgment and good intuition. Let's roll."

He let her move to the front passenger seat as he started for the driver's door. No sooner had he sat down, he got out again.

"Be right back."

Sarah stayed in the car as Seamus returned to the front door. Sally Rae's wrinkled visage reappeared in the opening and Sarah watched as he handed her a card and talked with her. She nodded and Seamus bounded back to the car as the spitting devolved into a light shower.

Inside the car, he wiped the water from his face. "She'd love to help nail the bastard, to use her own words. And I think she means it. She misses her Jack." He smiled. "She'll be on him like ... well, use your own metaphor."

Edwards looked at the weather reports and decided the time had come to move their charge again. She favored sweet tea; so once again, he had it laced with a fast acting sedative. With some luck, they'd have her moved to a new safe house before the storms arrived.

Thirty minutes later, with Della Winston in her drug-induced snooze and secured in a van outside, he gave the word to clean the place one final time. As they left, he took Della's cell phone and scanned her contact list. There it was, Sarah Wade. The young doctor from the newscast was his choice to call. With her number on the screen, he taped the phone to the back of the front door. He then pressed a button on a small electronic trigger. Within twenty minutes the other side of the building would be ablaze. On his way out, he pressed the 'talk' button to make the call, and shut the door behind him.

CHAPTER 29

Back in St. Clair, the rain had stopped. Seamus and Sarah stopped for a fast food lunch and then tracked down the home and farm store where Blake Howard worked part-time. They found the manager out back supervising a delivery. Sarah tagged along but stood back, observing. The wind had picked up with a slight chill to it and that distinctive smell of an impending thunderstorm. She glanced at the western sky and noted the approaching front promised by the local weathercasts. Would they be driving back to the city in a deluge?

"Mr. Hardy, I'm Sergeant Seamus O'Connor with the St. Louis Police Department. Wondered if Blake Howard was working today."

The manager stopped and grabbed a rag to wipe off his hands before shaking Seamus' hand. "St. Louis, huh." He frowned. "Besides St. Clair's finest, over the last few years I've talked with police from Union, Potosi, Sullivan, and Cuba about Blake, but never St. Louis. Guess he's spreading his troublemaking around."

Seamus appeared ready to respond when Mr. Hardy continued. "Not that anything was serious or nothing. Mostly the kind of mischief teenagers and young men get into from time to time."

"Is he here now?"

"No, Sir. He only works every other weekend here, so I don't expect to see him until a week from Saturday. What'd he do now?"

"Nothing. We're just following a lead on a case and his name came up. Wanted to ask him some questions."

"Well, if he's not at that shack he rents, I can't help you."

"How well do you know him?"

The man huffed and shook his head. "Not sure anymore. I've known him all his life. Comes from good people, but ever since high school he's just kinda drifted. Tried the trades for a while but kept showing up late and he'd get fired. Worked a few of the fast food places, but some health issues came up and word got out so they won't hire him anymore. I can only use him part-time but I try to help him as a favor to his dad."

"Hepatitis?"

The man gave Seamus a curious look and nodded. "Guess you already been talking to some folks."

Seamus played it straight-faced. "How'd he get it? Do you know?"

The man nodded again. "Tattoo needle."

"Does he still do tattooing?"

"Not that I know of … or he'd admit. Got into a bit of trouble in Union for that. But I know him well enough to know he would learn from the mistake. If he's doing anything on the side, he's doing it straight up now. New needles and such."

"What do you know about his friends?"

"Bunch of riff-raff. I think they're what's steerin' him wrong. All that pseudo-Biblical stuff they spout when they're with him. I was over at his folks' house one night when they all came by. Started talking all that trash and Ben, his dad, threw 'em all out."

Sarah eased forward and stood next to Seamus.

"What kind of stuff?"

"Oh, that lost tribe of Israel garbage what ends up justifying a bunch of racial crap. Not the kind of true Bible teaching like we have at the First Baptist. Ben's a deacon there and it makes him sick to hear his son talking up that trash. Ben's prodigal son. That's what we often call Blake."

Sarah leaned in to whisper in Seamus' ear, but he subtly nudged her away.

"Are these guys part of any larger group that you know of?"

Mr. Hardy pulled off his ball cap and scratched his head. "You know, I never really thought about that … but now that you ask, well, I'd have to say I think maybe so. Oh, not that Blake's said anything outright, but little comments here and there sorta add up to that conclusion. Things like coming in to pick up his check in surplus army BDUs and saying something off the cuff about heading out for training. I don't think he'd say that if he was just heading out to hang with some friends." A worried look came across his face. "Shoot. Seems you've given Ben and me something new to pray about."

"Sir, please don't say anything about this to anyone. Not yet. If there is a group, we can't afford the risk of alerting them."

"But, it's Ben's son we're talking about. I don't know that I can just stay quiet about that, not with my best friend."

"Sir, please. I can't force you to be quiet, but this could be bigger than either of us might believe. It's important to keep a lid on it."

Mr. Hardy nodded. "I'll pray about that, too."

"Do you have a picture of Blake? Or know about any of his hangouts, any place where we might be able to track him down?"

"A picture I can give you. Got that in his employee file. But about his hangouts, don't know what to say. I can ask around, though."

"Could you please? He seems to be the best lead I've got in a case I'm working."

"Can I ask what you're working on?"

Seamus shook his head. "Sorry, can't say any more. Here's my card. Please call me, collect if you need to, if you find out anything."

The manager took the card and inspected it before pocketing it.

"Let me get that photo for you," he said before he turned and entered the building.

Seamus turned to Sarah. "So? What do you think?"

"I think he's being up front with us. He's concerned about his friend's son and willing to help, but he doesn't know anything more. He also seems law abiding and true to his Christian beliefs, so he won't step over the line and compromise those ideals to help Howard."

Seamus nodded. Sarah smiled inwardly. This approach certainly seemed to work better. They had gotten more useful information this time.

Mr. Hardy returned and handed it to Seamus.

"Sir, I also need to talk to Mr. and Mrs. Howard. Could you give me their address and phone number?"

"Well, Delores died a few years ago, so it's just Ben now. He lives a good half hour out of town, down Route 30, almost to Cedar Hill." He took the photo of Blake Howard and wrote down the father's name, address, and phone number on the back. Then he took his cell phone and dialed a number. After a minute, he flipped it closed. "Like I thought, he's not home. Can't say when you might catch him. Just bein' him, he's out and about as he pleases ... except on Sundays. Pretty much always home after church."

"Thanks for checking. If you talk with him, ask him to please call me if he's in contact with his son." Seamus handed the man a second business card. "Thanks for all your help."

"Glad to be of service. Time to get these pallets offloaded, before the storm hits." He turned and walked back to the loading dock.

By the time they returned to Interstate 44, heading northeast toward the city, the gray clouds had yielded to pregnant black clouds, their waters about to burst as they promised the birth of new thunderheads amidst the laborious clamor of thunder and lightning. Bursts of high wind coerced semi-trailers to sway in and out of their designated lanes as their drivers fought for control of the rigs. The radio broadcasted tornado alerts in counties only thirty miles south of their present course.

Seamus tried to use his Bluetooth headset to call in to his unit leader but his need to concentrate on driving as well as the deteriorating cell phone signal made him abandon the attempt. He fought to control his car as wind gusts caught them and threatened to lift them off to Oz. Despite his windshield wipers operating at their fastest speed, he could barely determine the lanes on the highway and slowed to what seemed like a crawl on the Interstate system.

Sarah's cell phone chattered with the theme song from the daytime soap opera, "The Bold and Beautiful."

"Oh my God, oh my god," Sarah stuttered as she retrieved the phone from her purse and fumbled it to the floor.

"What's wrong?" Seamus asked as he fought another wind gust.

"It's Della! That's her distinctive ring tone!" She managed to corral her phone and open it. The Caller ID glowed as witness to her proclamation – "Della"

"Della? Hello? Where are you, girl? Hello? There's no one there." She started to close the phone.

"Don't lose the connection. Keep it open!" Seamus stated as he retrieved his Bluetooth device and tried to connect with his own phone.

His call went through on his second attempt and he hurriedly explained the situation.

"Quick, put a trace on … what's your cell number?"

He repeated Sarah's number to the agent on the other end of the call.

"Got it? Great. Let me know where. We're on our way back to the city …"

Before he could complete the call, a wind gust shoved the car sideways and the headset tumbled from its precarious perch on his ear. He took his eyes off the road in reaction to the falling earpiece, but was too late to catch it in freefall. His attention returned to the road in time to see an eighteen-wheeler in the distance tossed onto its side by a sudden wind shear. As it slid across and down both lanes of the highway, a car in front of them slid into the overturned trailer. Seamus yelled "Hang on," switched lanes and hit the brakes. The skid on soaked pavement aquaplaned them off the road and down an embankment into the trees.

CHAPTER 30

The Colonel watched from the lab's anteroom as Heinz and Marcus prepared to run their first sample through the new gene sequencer. He delayed joining them, waiting for a phone call. Despite being in an underground bunker, the building's signal repeater gave them clear cell phone service. Marcus gave him a thumbs up. The sequencer apparently was working without a glitch.

The new lab cut their original timeline in half. The modified H5N1 flu strain was in production. The retrovirus to be used in modifying the body's lymphocytes neared readiness. He wanted to run a few more DNA samples for additional confirmation, but otherwise, his retroviral delivery agent was ready for replication and a test of the dispersal system. If that work fell in line with what they had already learned, they could be ready for their test subject within days. And with that success, retroviral production would begin.

After all of the week's turmoil and protests, and endless diatribe on racial politics, he couldn't think of a better candidate for their landmark test. Missouri didn't need a black Senator any more than upstate New York needed ten more feet of snow last winter. Once upon a time one man died to save many. But the Colonel had no messianic ideations. This time, one man would die as the first of many.

His thoughts were interrupted by the chime of his phone.

"Yes?" he answered.

"Good afternoon, Sir," Sayer replied. "I'm on my way back. Need anything? I can stop and get food for everyone."

"Thanks. That would work. The usual lab sustenance -- pizza, subs, anything quick and easy. How'd things go?"

"Edwards is a master; that's all I can say. We moved her to the safe house between Desloge and Potosi. The windows and doors have all been blacked out and the women have been coached on how to treat her. Winston will still have her leg irons, but she'll have complete freedom indoors otherwise. He's even had the ladies take off the hood and handcuffs, but he won't personally see her again until you give him a date for the test."

"I have a thought on that but I can't confirm it until after tonight."

"Are Marcus and Heinz working all night again?"

"Probably not. I've arranged for them to take time off from the university, so they'll be able to work here full-time for the next week. I hope to have the test sample done in short order. How's Edwards holding out? He hasn't had much sleep."

"Are you kidding? The guy's having too much fun to sleep. I think he's living on pure adrenaline right now. Did he tell you about using Winston's cell phone?"

"Yes, something about using it as decoy."

"More like rubbing salt in the authorities' wounds."

The Colonel listened as Sayer described the scenario. He contemplated its repercussions and felt uneasy. Yet, he had foot soldiers to rely upon for the success of his own plan and a little action against the State would motivate them. Besides, he was too late to call off the plot. Edwards had already made the call. He hoped that decision would not be one to regret later.

Sayer finished by saying, "Yes, Sir, keep your eye on the news. It's going to be everyone's lead story for sure."

"How far away are you?" the Colonel asked.

"I'm just passed the Pevely exit on I-55. I –"

The Colonel heard a loud boom, like an artillery shell, followed by a crackling noise. He heard Sayer yell "Oh shit!" before the connection went dead.

Della welcomed the freedom of her new abode. The home was small but pleasant, decorated in a simple country style that showed a woman's touch with a sense of frugality. The place also displayed an appreciation for cleanliness. The rooms were tidy and dust-free. The only disconcerting aspect of the building was the inability to gaze outdoors. It was as if the hood had been removed from her head only to be stretched to cover the entire house. In that sense, it was more of a prison than some of the minimum-security facilities where Della had interviewed inmates. She longed to see the outside world, to sense the sun on her face and to feel the coolness of a breeze on her skin.

Della could openly roam through the house, albeit slowly in the shackles, and Carly had shown her the bedroom where she'd be sleeping. Although no larger than some of her closets at home, the room held a relatively new twin bed, a comfortable recliner, and a small wardrobe holding new utilitarian cotton underwear as well as three changes of navy blue cotton scrubs, similar to those worn by Carly. Her own expensive lingerie was nowhere to be found.

Carly was the middle-aged woman who had removed her hood and cuffs. She appeared Hispanic and there seemed to be a slight accent in her voice, but Della wouldn't place a bet on that impression. The woman's jet-black hair showed signs of graying and fine lines engraved an otherwise clear skin. She offered a friendly smile and had massaged Della's wrists with a soothing cream after removing the handcuffs. The blue scrubs hid a drooping figure but not her ebullient spirit. At first, Della had been suspicious of the woman who would be her guard, but that distrust ebbed away as the woman made a point of being friendly and hinted that the two shared a common bondage.

Della lay on the twin bed contemplating this ugly, unexpected turn in her life. The man had offered a hope of freedom, but this was not what Della had envisioned. With not even a glimpse of the outdoors, she had no idea where she might be. She did know that this place was different from the others. The smells were different. The few sounds that penetrated the house walls were different. Della listened intently. The sound of strong winds impressed her mind but she couldn't be sure of that. Then the noise of a shutter or door slapping against a wall confirmed that impression. A clap of thunder reverberated around and through the house, followed by the dull percussion of heavy rain on the roof. Della loved the smell of country air refreshed by the cleansing action of a cool rain, but that was beyond the bounds set for her.

As Della lay there, lulled by the drumming of the rain on the roof, she counted her blessings. She was alive. She was relatively comfortable. Maybe, in time, the shackles could come off completely and she would be allowed outdoors. *This is my new life*, she now accepted. She would do whatever they required … if that's what it took to stay alive … and comfortable.

A series of loud jolts startled Della. More thunder! The pacifying beat of the rain had put her to sleep, but for how long? That was another oddity of this house. There was no way to tell time. No clocks, no radios, or television. Even the clocks on the stove and microwave appeared broken. Was it day or night? And what day was it? Had she been captive a day, a week, a month?

As her head cleared, Della became aware of a wonderful smell in the house. Fried chicken. Not take-home from some fast food fryer but real, home fried chicken … like her momma used to cook.

She arose from the bed and wandered to the kitchen. There was another woman there with Carly. She was younger, maybe late twenties with curly blond hair and the rough complexion that results from bad teen acne. But she had pleasant features, laughter in her eyes and a smile on her face. She, too, wore blue scrubs.

She was doing the cooking. Real chicken, breaded in flour and crumbled corn flakes, slowly frying in an inch of hot Crisco. And a pot of fresh green beans simmered next to the frying pan. Just like when Della was a girl. Another aroma caught her attention - bread baking in the oven. She hadn't enjoyed homemade bread since she'd put together a piece on the Amish of central Illinois years ago. Della's stomach growled in hunger. Suddenly it didn't matter how long it had been since she last ate.

"Hi, you must be Della. I'm Sue. Hope you're hungry. Should be ready in ten, fifteen minutes."

"Coffee? Tea?" asked Carly.

Della sat at the kitchen table. "Thanks. Coffee, please. Black."

Sue walked from behind the small kitchen island and over to the refrigerator. Della stared at the woman's ankles. She too wore leg-irons.

Carly must have caught her gaze. "I used to have to wear them, too. But my arthritis is such, they don't consider me an escape risk anymore."

"They?"

The two women looked at each other, and Carly shook her head subtly at Sue who was about to answer.

"We better let one of them answer those kinds of questions."

"Actually," Sue said, "I was goin' to say they could just go ahead and take 'em off. I enjoy it here. The work's not hard and they keep us well fed and comfortable. That's a lot better than where I come from."

Della's brow furrowed at the mention of work.

"Nothing hard. Some light housekeeping. Cleaning up sometimes, after some of the men get a little too rowdy. Cooking, which I love. And they let us keep a good garden, which I also love doing. You'll get used to it and probably like it, too … if they let you stay." She paused and glanced furtively at the back door. Then she whispered, "I overheard the big guy, the one they call Major, say he had a special job for you."

"What if I don't want to do it?" Della asked.

"Oh, don't ever let them hear you say that," Carly answered with urgency in her voice. "Oh no, girl, not never. There's some of these guys would kill you in a heartbeat and you'd never see it coming. Oh no, you don't ever, ever want to cross these guys."

Della sat back in her chair and sipped the coffee. It was really good. Through the blur of expensive cappuccinos and fancy lattés, she had forgotten how good plain black coffee tasted.

Carly had just confirmed what Della had already determined. Cooperation and friendliness equaled life. Besides, maybe it was time for a simpler lifestyle. She could admit it. The club scene and constant partying had taken its toll on her. Like someone who just learned she had a life-terminating illness, Della saw life from a new perspective now.

The storm front advanced on the St. Louis metropolitan area much faster than the meteorologists had anticipated, and its ferocity followed a disturbing trend in storms across the globe.

Sayer and Edwards had left the house outside Desloge as Della Winston began to rouse from her drug-induced sedation. She was in good hands. Rebecca and Marie, aka Sue and Carly, could rival any liberal, bleeding-heart Oscar winner. They knew what to do and what Edwards expected of them.

As Sayer left U.S. 67 and merged onto I-55 north toward the city, he beheld an unrivaled display of lightening on the horizon to the northwest. Flash after flash lit up the distance, backlighting the hills in eerie contrast. The fact that he was driving toward the worst of the storm was lost on him as he concentrated on calling the Colonel. He expected to outrace the storm and reach the warehouse ahead of the front. The radio newscasters were already calling this storm "deadly" with at least five deaths reported southwest of the city, three from a chain reaction accident involving an overturned eighteen-wheeler and a dozen cars on I-44 east.

The storm cell and Sayer converged on the same hillcrest north of Pevely as he talked to the Colonel.

"How far away are you?" the Colonel asked.

"I'm just passed the Pevely exit on I-55. I –"

A deafening boom shook the car as a bolt of lightning struck the shoulder of the highway to the left just ahead of Sayer. The flash blinded Sayer for a second and his skin and hair tingled with static as his car drove through the shower of sparks that erupted from the gravel like a fireworks fountain. He emerged from on the other side, his vision returning, and his car apparently unscathed.

"Oh shit!"

He pulled over to the right shoulder and worked to control his rapid breathing and slow his heart. He laid his head on the steering wheel until a semblance of calm returned. He picked up his cell phone but it appeared fried. He looked out the windshield at the pouring sheets of rain. Above him, the lights of a billboard flickered back to life. "Eternity! Are You Prepared? Destiny Church"

CHAPTER 31

Seamus awoke, groggy, and more from reflex than conscious effort, tried to push away the heavy material collapsed in his lap. Rain pelted him in the face and his neck and shoulders ached. His thigh felt as if he'd been shot again. He stared straight ahead into a grove of small trees illuminated by a single headlight, a mist of steam rising from the hot engine. The windshield on his side of the car had caved onto the dash, while the right side of the glass appeared starred.

His mind cleared and he recalled the wind blowing over the semi in front of him and the skid that took him over the hill. But it wasn't just him; it was "them." Sarah was with him. He turned to the passenger side to find the seat empty and the door missing. The worst nightmare of a civilian ride-along -- the life entrusted to your care, gone.

Where's Sarah? He again saw the starred windshield. She must have hit the windshield. He looked to the floor and saw her crumpled airbag laying there, crippled by an obvious gash in its fabric. What had happened? In her seat, he found remnants of her seatbelt, a ragged cut where it had been sheared in two. Had something cut both the airbag and the seatbelt?

Frantic, he tried to move, but his legs were pinned under the collapsed steering column. He turned his torso to look out the side window. They were at least a hundred feet from the road in dense brush and small trees. He could not see the road, so could he expect emergency personnel to see them? The rain eased up but that mattered little. He had to get out, find Sarah, and get help.

He struggled to free himself to no avail. He could feel his toes and move his feet and legs. His thighs were pinned, and the pain far surpassed the accustomed ache of the healing bullet wound in his left thigh. He tried the police band radio but it no longer had power. He looked around for his cell phone but could not locate it. He twisted at the waist to look into the back seat. A metal fence post! *It must have come through the windshield and cut the seatbelt*, he thought. It stuck partly through the back window. Miraculously, it hadn't impaled either of them. He had to reach it.

He squirmed in his seat and twisted again, but his arms would never bend in any fashion close to approaching the stake. He raised his right shoulder and moved his arm down and backward. He was close. He brushed it with one fingertip. If only he could knock it down a bit. He grabbed the remnant of seatbelt and swung it backward. *Missed.* He tried again and on the third attempt, he hit the post. *I think I moved it.* He shifted again in his seat and reached backward. His fingers hit the post but he still couldn't grab hold of it. He stretched as far as he could and managed to knock the post down a few more inches. This time he was able to pinch it between two fingers and his thumb and pull. Slowly, he worked the post until he freed it. He swung it around through the open window, placed it between his legs, and wedged it between his seat and the steering wheel.

He took a deep breath and pushed. Nothing. The pain in his thigh intensified.

Lord, I need all the help I can get, he thought. Using the leverage, he was able to nudge the bent column, but not enough to get free. He bent down and grabbed the seat release, pulling with all he had to disengage the seat. He tried the metal post once again and this time the seat moved half an inch back at the same time as the wheel eased away. The release sent a wave of heat surging through his thigh. But rather than pain, the surge surprised him by bringing relief. The pain was gone, not just eased by the release of pressure, but totally gone.

Unpinned, he moved up into the seat and inched across to the passenger seat and out the doorway. Stumbling, his legs unsteady, he looked around the car. No Sarah.

"Sarah!" He paused, hoping to hear a response. "Sarah! Can you hear me? Where are you?"

He looked up toward the road. Emergency lights flashed like beacons warning sailors away from the reefs. Did anyone up there see them? He saw no one working down the hill toward his car. He staggered along the direction the car had taken and ten feet away, hidden by brush, he found her.

He knelt beside her and assessed her breathing. It was shallow, but she breathed easily. The pulse in her wrist felt strong. He noted a large bruise and swelling on her forehead but no bleeding or weird angulation of any limbs. *Concussion?* he wondered. He couldn't tell; she was the ER doctor, not him. He knew better than to move her, but he felt a sudden urge to cradle her head in his lap and caress her brow.

He had to get help, but was reluctant to leave her. Stronger and determined, he rushed back to the car. He realized that if his headlights still had power so should his emergency flasher and siren. He used the metal fence post to clear the remaining glass in the rear window and to pry loose the rear flashing lights. He yanked out the flasher and stuck it as high up on the roof as the cable would allow. He then flipped the switch to initiate the beacon and immediately the light and siren signaled their position. He returned to Sarah. No change. Several minutes later he heard yelling and then the crunching of brush under foot.

"Over here! We're over here! We need paramedics!"

Minutes later emergency personnel surrounded him, carrying backboards and other medical equipment. Seamus brushed them away.

"I'm fine, take care of her."

The nightmare of every emergency room nurse and doctor was to wake up in her own emergency room, clothes cut off, and tubes in every orifice. Sarah's first conscious recognition was her monster headache. And she urgently had to pee. She had never had such a headache and she didn't want to open her eyes, afraid she would aggravate the pain. But why did she have a headache? And why did she have such a desperate urge to urinate? She lay there thinking, trying to remember. The last thing she could recall was driving on I-44 with Seamus. He yelled something and they started to skid. Now she had a headache and a full bladder. She reached up to her forehead and grimaced at the tenderness of the tennis ball-sized hematoma on her forehead. That explained the headache, partly. She reached down to her groin and gently pushed. Her bladder wasn't full so that didn't explain the urgency. What had happened? And more importantly, where was she?

As she became more alert, she ventured to open her eyes and doing so caused her heart to accelerate. The room was as familiar as her bedroom, but there was a difference. She expected to wake up in the supine position in her bedroom. She never imagined waking up in a trauma room at the McKnight Emergency and Trauma Center.

"Oh, thank God. Sarah?"

There were sighs of relief echoing around her. She slowly turned her head from side to side, acutely aware of the increased cephalgia. Kendra Samuels sat on a stool nearby, her mascara blurred from crying. The three bourbon-slush, float trip queens of the department - Kathy, Stephanie and Sandy - hovered nearby, looks of relief replacing those of grave concern. Kathy, whose never-ending quest to lose weight had begun to show some success, slid off the stool, turned to the other two, and held out her upturned palm.

"Okay, girls, pay up. I won. Told you she was too hardheaded to stay out for long."

Stephanie, the redheaded aficionado of Victoria's Secret who did a better job of keeping that secret by wearing scrubs a size too big for her, impulsively proclaimed, "Nothing personal, Sarah. The ER pool was not if you'd gain consciousness, but when. We both said after the CT, she said before."

Sarah gazed at her, mouth agape. Steph continually proved the adage that redheads were just blonds without impulse control.

Sarah glanced at Sandy, a blond who fought the urge to act like a redhead, and said, "I have to pee."

Sandy smiled sweetly back at her and replied, "It's okay; it's just the Foley. You're fine."

Sarah's eyes widened at the realization that she wore nothing more than a hospital gown and a catheter.

Sandy's sweet smile twisted into a wicked grin as she continued, "Doctor Alvarez wanted to do the Foley, but he lost on the short straw. We did let him cut off part of your clothes, though. You'll just never know which part."

Kendra approached Sarah's head. "Don't listen to her. Ricky isn't even on duty yet. But he did stop by to see how you were. Half the department has."

"How, how did I get here?"

"A.R.C.H."

"But the weather ..."

"Yeah, it's been nasty, but there was a brief window of opportunity and when the flight crew heard it was you, they took that chance. Air Evac wanted to go, too, but their smaller helicopters couldn't handle the wind."

Sarah's eyes welled up at the recognition of the risk that crew took to help her.

"I ... the car ... a detective was driving. How is ... is he ..."

"Sergeant O'Connor is fine. A few scrapes and bruises. He'll be back shortly."

Kendra grasped her lower abdomen and winced. She turned pale.

"Kendra? You okay?"

The pain on the student's face intensified and blood stains spread across the crotch of her tan slacks.

"Kathy, get her to a room and get the nearest resident on-duty. Now."

Stephanie assisted Kathy, but not before rolling her eyes and saying, "Looks like she's back to her bossy self already. Next thing she'll be ordering labs on this girl."

The situation didn't help Sarah's headache, and she slumped back onto the gurney and closed her eyes. A moment later the stretcher began to move and she opened her eyes to find herself on the way to the CT room. Her head began to spin and a wave of nausea rolled through her gut. Fifteen minutes later, the spiral computed tomography scan of her head completed, someone rolled her back to her room.

Kathy met her in the room upon her return.

"How is she?"

"Looks like she's miscarrying. Did you know she was

pregnant?"

"I had my suspicions … from talking to her a couple of days ago."

Kathy nodded. "I think she knew it, too, but ..." Kathy turned at a knock on the door.

Another resident, whom Sarah had met only once before, came into the room, ignored Kathy, started asking Sarah questions and examined her. She resisted grading his technique, but gave him a low score on bedside manner. *Typical of a surgeon*, she thought.

Then it hit her. Surgeon? She knew where she'd met this guy before. He was a senior surgical resident. For Sarah the nightmare that became reality just got worse. Per protocol, she was about to be admitted to the Trauma Service, Dr. Rickelmann attending.

CHAPTER 32

Seamus stood inside the police perimeter watching the firemen reel in their hoses. He had flown back to the city with Sarah, and then caught a patrol car ride to the scene. The old house looked like so many abandoned properties in the inner city except that the once dignified brick two-story was now a half-burnt hull doomed for some landfill. *This can't be the right place,* he thought. But if it was, he feared they would find the body of a young black female inside, charred remains requiring dental records for identification.

He looked around the area once again, puddles of water had merged into small pools, and mud covered what the water didn't. Steam arose from the small ell of the building that had collapsed into a charred heap atop a slab foundation. The smell of doused embers combined with those of diesel and burnt rubber. The on-lookers beyond the police tape began to scatter but there was no sign of Bill Delaney, the FBI agent-in-charge of the kidnapping investigation. Seamus walked to the other end of the perimeter and still found no one from the FBI or BOI assigned to the case. A patrolman from his division stood at the cordon.

"Hey, Mac."

The uniformed officer nodded. "Shay. Heard you had a rough afternoon."

"Could have been a lot worse. Hey, have you seen any feds or BOI folks?"

"Nope. Maybe they're waitin' for clearance from the fire inspector. Also, something was said at roll call about reporters following them around, lookin' for anything new on these cases." He grinned. "Like in the movies, maybe they're trying to shake loose a tail."

Seamus thought about that a little. Although the first statement made more sense, the circumstances of this fire in light of all the political and public pressure on these cases made the latter comment more plausible than the officer probably knew. If word got out that a call from Della Winston's cell phone had been traced to this area, and most likely this building, the news trucks would fill the local streets. And if a body, her body, lay inside, well, hell would seem air-conditioned compared to the heat the police and FBI would feel.

He sauntered toward the closest pumper and tapped one of the firemen on the shoulder. The man slipped off his helmet and stashed away his breathing apparatus on the truck before turning to look at Seamus.

"Who's the investigator tonight?" asked Seamus.

The man pointed to a man at the western edge of the building. "Got two tonight. There's one. The other's Hank Grafton. He's inside."

"Still hot?"

"Don't know of any hot spots, but you know the drill. Clear it with Hank."

Seamus nodded and walked first toward the investigator whose job was to determine the origin and cause of the fire. Seamus watched the man photograph the scene and jot something down in his notebook. As the man turned toward him, Seamus recognized him, Martin Jamison. They'd worked together before.

"Hey, Marty. What's cookin'?"

"Not much, fortunately. Just this part of the building. The other side's pretty much intact."

"Any casualties?"

"No bodies, if that's what you mean." He scrutinized Seamus as if trying to read his mind. "So, what brings you to this bonfire? I thought I'd heard you were … Wait a minute, are you here on that case?"

"Not a word, Marty. Not a word. Can I go in?"

The investigator shrugged his shoulders and nodded. "Yeah, if it was up to me. I'm only helping out. But only on the other side, through the front door. Hank's in there. Just get his okay … he's already raggin' on about piddlely crap."

Seamus walked around the charred remains of the western addition of the old house and found the main door near the northeast corner. He stepped inside the open doorway and called out, "Hank? Seamus O'Connor. Can I come in?"

A bespectacled man in his mid-forties, also wearing a blue jumpsuit with STLFD emblazoned across the back, poked his head through an inner doorway.

"O'Connor. Come on in here. I want your take on this, and I think you're gonna want to see it."

Seamus was careful where he walked, as with any crime scene. He joined the fire investigator in a room that might have served as a dining area in the home's grander days. He saw three mattresses occupying three corners of the room surrounded by the litter of wrappers from at least four different fast food emporiums. He leaned over scattered copies of the St. Louis Post-Dispatch and noted dates covering the previous four days. Two of the papers were folded to make obvious the coverage of the Winston kidnapping. Otherwise, he saw no other signs of habitation. No clothing. No personal articles. The place looked like a temporary camp.

"You'll want to check this room, too," Hank said, leading Seamus toward a small room off a central hallway, across from the room they stood in.

In this smaller room, a single mattress lay positioned where it could easily be seen through the doorway. This time he saw no fast food debris, but on the makeshift bed lay a rumpled woman's royal blue silk tunic and black silk capris, along with expensive looking lace lingerie. The surveillance video of Della Winston's kidnapping showed her in such an outfit, which in a black and white video certainly could have been blue and black.

"Have you seen a cell phone anywhere in here?" Seamus asked. "An Ericsson. Top of the line."

The fire inspector shook his head. Seamus visually searched the room but saw nothing. He had one other option, a long shot requiring at least some charge in the phone's battery. He had located and retrieved Sarah's cell phone from his car before climbing back to the highway to meet the helicopter. He pulled this phone from his coat pocket, checked the received calls list, and redialed the number of Della's phone.

As the phone connected, he heard footsteps from the front room. Bill Delaney and two other detectives approached the doorway to the small room.

"Whadda we have?" Delaney asked.

"Shhhh," replied Seamus.

"What?"

"Quiet. Do you hear anything?"

Seamus left the room and re-entered the improvised dorm room. There seemed to be a faint buzz somewhere. He turned his head right and left, listening. The front room. He walked into the entry room, the others following. The sound was more distinct. A cell phone vibrating against a solid surface.

"Hear it? A cell phone vibrating. Where?"

The five men spread out across the room, checking in and under broken furniture, the floor, anyplace a phone might have been stashed in hiding from the kidnappers. Hank Grafton found it, duct taped to the back of the front door, hidden from easy viewing because the door had been left open.

"Those sons of bitches," Seamus uttered. "Now they're taunting us." There was no doubt Della had been there, maybe since her actual kidnapping. It appeared the kidnappers had found her cell phone and placed the call themselves before leaving. But what really rankled Seamus was that the partially burned building on Mills Street was but one block away from the Central Division Police Headquarters. Just one block away from his old office.

CHAPTER 33

Sayer knocked the covers of his bed into complete disarray as he fought a losing battle for sleep. Convinced that his recent lack of sleep contributed to his increasing level of stress, he battled for unconsciousness. Yet, the more he struggled, the more evasive slumber became. Throughout the night, every time he felt ready to doze off, a sense of falling overcame him and he would jolt back awake. Eternity. Falling forever, without end. He was losing it.

Dawn crept over the hillside behind his home. He eased out of bed and went to his wood deck balcony overlooking Wild Horse Creek. Even his fifty-two hundred square-foot home in posh Wildwood possessed the quiet, dull hollowness of a bottomless pit. His life and his soul seemed to follow suit. He had all the toys. He had wealth many could only dream about. He had a purpose, a goal that he felt passionate about even though he recognized most would call that objective evil. But he was as empty and hollow as his house. Even the hatred that once propelled him felt dulled.

Sayer watched a small herd of white-tailed deer grazing in a distant pasture. They looked so peaceful, shrouded by the thinning morning mist as the sun ascended and shone directly onto their small patch of turf. Yet, he knew they were constantly alert for predators. A slight movement in the nearby brush. A random unfamiliar noise. The wrong scent on the wind. Anything could alert them and cause them to bolt into the adjacent woods.

Were they telling him something? Should he be on the alert for a predator? Or was this all the result of being on the go 24/7 for the past week?

His mind still echoed … eternity. Falling forever, without end. He was losing it. He needed a day, or two, maybe three, off.

Sarah sat in the room's only chair gazing out the window across I-64 toward the St. Louis Science Center. She was fortunate that the other bed in the room remained unoccupied, its sheets stretched taut across the mattress, the bedrails at parade rest awaiting a new charge to protect. A scattering of flowers had arrived overnight and her mom had been by for a visit. That she had made it from the nursing home was a wonder in itself, but the fact that DeWayne Winston had arranged for her visit was more surprising.

The headache began subsiding hours earlier, but sleep had been impossible, thanks to the every-two-hour neuro checks forced upon her by the nursing staff. Megawatt flashlights checking her pupils. Repeated hand grips until she felt as if she was a milkmaid. Counting backwards from ten like some perverse Sesame Street audition. And just what are the capitols of all fifty states? At least that nurse had a sense of humor. Was this someone's idea of payback for all the borderline cases she had admitted to the Trauma Service over the years? Or was it Rickelmann? There was a remote chance he didn't yet know she was there. *Yeah, about as remote as the neighborhood Starbucks*, she thought.

"Hey, you're supposed to be in bed," said the dayshift nurse as she made her initial rounds.

"I'm fine," Sarah replied to the window.

"Maybe so, but the residents are rounding and we don't need some snitch telling Rickelmann you were up and about against orders. We like it as peaceful as possible around here."

Sarah turned and looked at her. She appeared sincere and the last thing she desired was to make the nurses' day miserable. She slowly arose and ambled to the bed.

"Think they're gonna let me go home?"

The nurse shrugged her shoulders.

"So which one do you like best? This one?" She cocked her head to the right, crossed her eyes, and stuck her tongue out to the right while flexing her left elbow and wrist. "Or this one?" She arched her head forward and flexed both arms and legs into a decorticate position.

The nurse smiled, and answered, "Oh, definitely the first one. Guaranteed to get you a nursing home transfer." She shook her head and chuckled. "You're right. You're fine."

Sarah sighed and lay back in the bed, waiting for the resident team so she could convince the fellow to discharge her, before afternoon attending rounds. As the nurse left the room, she heard her say, "She's definitely ready for discharge" to someone in the hall.

A second later the trauma team engulfed the room, fellow, resident, intern, and medical students alike looking like sleep-deprived zombies. *Maybe they needed neuro checks all night, too*, she thought.

Sarah said nothing as the resident quizzed the students and prepped them for questions Rickelmann would likely ask later in the day. Through the process, she learned she had a moderate cerebral contusion of the frontal lobes on CT but had an excellent chance of full recovery. *Like, duh*, she thought. *Already there*. She tolerated another brief neurological exam and finally was asked by the examining intern, "How do you feel?"

She resisted the urge to say, "With my hands," and instead replied, "Just fine. Ready to go home." Actually, she was ready to chase after a certain detective who had abandoned her to the vagaries of her own medical system.

"I think that can be arranged," said a familiar voice from the back of the crowd. The team parted to let Doctor Rickelmann through.

The resident spoke up. "Doctor Rickelmann, we didn't expect you for –"

"That's okay, Alex. Continue with your rounds. I need to talk with Doctor Wade privately."

Sarah felt a nervous twinge snake up her spine and she couldn't blame a Foley catheter for the sudden pressure in her bladder. Her hope had been that the resident would discharge her before Rickelmann made his formal afternoon rounds. She had not expected his presence this early in the day.

Sarah watched the team leave and close the door behind them. For a moment, she thought she saw the bedside intercom flash on as if someone was listening, but the light flashed off just as quickly.

"Doctor Rickelmann, I –"

"Doctor Wade," he interrupted. "I certainly didn't expect to find you on my patient roster this morning. How are you doing? And give me an honest answer."

Sarah hesitated. "Neurologically, I'm one hundred percent. I still have a headache, but on a scale of ten, I'd give it a two."

"I see. Have you seen your scan?"

She shook her head.

"Well, the contusion is obvious, but not severe. I bring this up because you need to take it easy for a while." He paused. "And I mean that. Take it easy. I know you're starting a lab elective day after tomorrow, but I'm arranging for you to get the next few days off."

"I don't think I need –"

The trauma surgeon interrupted again. "It's not what you think. It's what I'm ordering … after consultation with the chief of neurology, by the way."

Sarah looked him squarely in the eyes and realized he was serious about her well-being. That surprised her.

"Doctor Wade, I want you to know that in my many years as an attending, only three other residents have stood up to me as you have. One is now Chief of Surgery at the Mayo, one became Surgeon General of the Army, and the first one attended to President Reagan when John Hinckley shot him in 1981. All three with illustrious careers. If that track record is any indication, you'll go far."

He turned toward the door, paused, and turned back. "By the way, the person who informed me about your alleged slander proved to be a complete suck-up with no facts to support him. He won't go far. The charges have been dropped, Doctor Wade. Now, go home and get some rest. And if you ever want to switch to surgery, let me know."

Della awoke to the smell of cooking bacon, an aroma synonymous with heaven, although the combination of her cholesterol levels and indulgence in that porcine treat might conspire to help her get there faster. For the first time she felt fully rested, not hung-over from a drug-induced sleep.

Was it truly morning? She had to assume the other women worked on a normal daily schedule and that she would be as well. She wouldn't protest anything they assigned to her. Their satisfaction was definitively better than the alternative.

She arose and walked to the kitchen for her first real, home-cooked meal in what? Days? Weeks? It didn't matter any further.

Not normally one who would nose his way into other's activities, Eric remained alert to Roger's actions as well as others in the lab. Roger seemed more distant and pre-occupied, had made a few mistakes he would not normally make, and seemed sleep deprived. He was up to something.

Eric had read and reread the computer printout taken from that box of notes. Two of the technicians were clearly implicated. He wished he had had the time to peruse more of what was in the box. To the educated reader it would be clear that the data there didn't involve the new Alzheimer's drug, but something far more sinister. All of the experts in the human genome agreed that no master gene for race existed. Yet, the printout questioned that belief, implied that the discovery of the slc24a5 gene governing skin color might be only a stepping-stone to something bigger. Alarmed by what he saw, he knew he had to stop Roger.

Eric arose from his desk and walked into the lab, meandering from one section to another. No sign of Roger. He wandered over to the secretary's office.

"Lisa, is Roger in today?"

"Not at the moment, but he should be here soon. He and Doctor Hudson have another meeting about licensing the new drug."

Eric made straight for the director's office down the hall.

"Good morning, Mitch. Any closer to a license deal yet?"

Mitchell smiled and waved Eric into his office. Eric closed the door behind him and sat down.

"Between you and me, looks like Jessup is going to be outbid by Eagle BioPharm. Not going to make Roger happy, is it?"

Eric shook his head in response, but he appreciated the segue.

"Speaking of Roger, I've been watching him like you asked. I think he's onto something besides working on Jessup's behalf."

Concern spread across Mitchell's face. "Oh?"

He handed the computer printout and copies of the photos to Mitchell and leaned forward in his chair, his elbows on his knees. "I, uh, I picked this up in the lab the night after we got back from the conference. Roger was removing a large box of written notes and other materials from the lab. You can read through it and make your own conclusions, Sir."

Mitchell started to leaf through the printout, his brow furrowed and a deepening frown on his lips. After a few pages, he glanced at his watch. "Eric, he could be here at any moment. I'll need to take some time with this and digest it. Thank you for bringing this to my attention."

Mitchell Hudson leaned back in his chair and watched as Eric left the office. He took the computer printout and glanced at the pages again. Marcus and Heinz were clearly involved and Eric had observed Roger removing the materials firsthand. He had been right in asking his aide to pay extra attention to Roger. His next move, as much as he disdained it, was clear.

He picked up the phone and dialed a number he long ago had memorized.

"I think we have a problem. Coulter has somehow stumbled onto our extracurricular activity."

Edwards replied, "What can I do, Colonel?"

CHAPTER 34

After suffering through a four hour, politically inspired ass chewing of everyone involved in the Winston kidnapping, Seamus picked up a new car from the motor pool and drove directly to Barnes Hospital where he grabbed a police-only parking spot outside the Emergency Department. The bright sun and light breeze were the antithesis of the previous day's vicious weather. Unlike the weather, however, his mood had not improved.

Nor had his concern for Sarah abated. Yes, he hated having a civilian rider, but that was a generic objection, not one aimed at Sarah Wade. In hindsight, he found her engaging … and attractive, two factors that made him all the more concerned that she should be riding with him.

He rushed into the E.D. and walked up to the clerk's desk where he drummed his fingers on the counter, waiting for her to get off the phone. When she failed to look his way, he cleared his throat. She turned toward him, but his actions earned him little except her evil eye.

"Doctor Wade. What room?"

She continued her phone conversation while shaking her head. He displayed his police identification and her eyes widened in recognition. She nodded and fingered several keystrokes onto her computer's keyboard. Still talking, she waved him around to her side of the counter and pointed to the screen.

"Thanks," Seamus responded, before bolting to the main corridor where he made a beeline for the elevators across from the chapel.

After stops at every floor, he finally emerged from the elevator and scurried past the Nurses' Station toward Sarah's room. As he reached the door, he noted the room was empty and did an about-face to return to the Nurses' Station. This ward clerk was also on the phone, but seemed to be on hold.

"Can I help you?" she asked, as she cupped the mouthpiece of the phone with one hand.

"I'm looking for Doctor Sarah Wade, but she's not in her room. Can you tell –"

The clerk resumed talking on the phone while holding up one finger toward Seamus. He sighed in exasperation. She turned away and leafed through some papers, placed them on a patient chart, and initialed a sheet on the cover. As she hung up the phone, she turned back to Seamus.

"I'm sorry. Doctor Wade was discharged about fifteen minutes ago. Her nurse … well, there she is now."

She pointed to the elevator bank where another elevator had opened and a nurse emerged pushing an empty wheelchair.

"Ginny, this gentleman is looking for Doctor Wade. Did she leave the hospital?"

The nurse moved next to Seamus with the wheelchair on her other side.

"Actually, I took her to the Emergency Department. She said she had clothes in her locker there, and could probably find a ride home from someone there."

Seamus didn't hesitate. "Thanks," he said as he rushed to catch a descending elevator that had opened behind them.

After stopping at every floor yet one more time, he headed to the E.D. where he had to wait at the controlled-access doorway until someone let him in. He found the same clerk, still on the phone, but this time she saw him coming, stood up and pointed down another hallway. He walked toward where she was pointing and found no one. Then he heard a familiar voice coming from a nearby room.

"Yeah, it's a really weird feeling. I remember being in the car, and the storm getting worse. I vaguely remember the truck ahead of us turning over, and then … nothing. Next thing I know I'm waking up here. I don't even remember the helicopter. All I can say is that's weird … to have all this stuff happen to me and not remember any of it."

Seamus knocked at the door and stood there, gazing at Sarah who was lightly made up and dressed in tight jeans, a Wash U tee shirt, and running shoes, and sitting on a rolling stool. She turned to see who was knocking. A smile flit across her mouth but quickly morphed into something less pleasant. Seamus, thinking she'd be glad to see him, wasn't sure what this reaction meant.

"Man, I'm glad to see you up and about. You had me scared."

She pointed her finger at him. "<u>You</u> just left me here. You let them cut off my clothes and you just left."

He flinched at the show of anger, but he was never one to be browbeaten. And he was too tired to absorb any further harangue.

"Whoa, wait a minute. <u>I</u> wasn't allowed into the room. Your co-workers guarded you like a hen over a chick and told me they'd call as soon as you woke up. I left my cell number and never heard from them. I've been having my ass chewed off for the past four hours because of this case and now you want to finish where the Mayor, Chief of Police, BOI Commander, and FBI Agent-in-charge left off. Don't think so, sista."

With that, he turned and stalked down the hall toward the exit. He didn't need, or deserve, any grief from her. *If the lieutenant wants her kept happy, he can drive her around,* he thought. He almost reached the doors when he heard her speak up from the hall behind him.

"Wait, Shay. Please. I'm sorry."

He stopped and whirled around to confront her, but she did something totally unexpected. She reached her arms around his neck, hugged him, and hung on, quietly sobbing in his ear. "I'm sorry. You didn't deserve that. You saved my life."

Seamus stood there, his arms flaccid at his side, completely baffled and unsure of what he should do next. Was it the head injury or just a female thing? Slowly, he countered her clutch and placed his arms around her. He wasn't sure how long they stood there that way, but as she eased her arms away, he responded in kind and took her hands in his.

"Wait a minute. What'd you say? Did I hear the word 'sorry' not just once, but twice?" She nodded but gave no explanation. "It must be the head injury."

Her next action caught him off-guard. She kissed him softly

on the lips.

Seamus realized they were smack-dab in the middle of the E.D. and the blush on his fair complexion illuminated the hallway. He half stumbled - half backed away from her and tripped over a mayo stand, landing on his rump. She grabbed his arm, pulled him up, and led him to the same, private conference room where he'd interviewed the two young doctors about Walter Johnson. He marveled at how much had happened over the past few days and that the medical student's murder now seemed so distant.

He also recalled the fear he'd felt at the thought of Sarah's dying in the accident. He gazed at her now, still feeling the warmth of her kiss. Too bad she was African-American, and ... and ... so what if she was. She was beautiful, intelligent, hard working, and more. Did skin color really matter?

Once seated in the room, Sarah made a request. "Please tell me what happened. Everything. What few things I do recall all seem sketchy and you're the only one who was there through it all."

Seamus went into detail about her being ejected, his being trapped and how he got free to find her, about how he alerted the emergency workers to their position and about how they got lucky with a window in the weather that allowed A.R.C.H. to fly to the scene. He also told her of the unfortunate lives lost in the chain reaction accident he had managed to avoid.

"Thank you ... for saving our lives." She paused. "I vaguely remember something about cell phones and a phone call."

"It was a phone call from Della, remember? We were trying to put a trace on the call when the accident occurred."

Sarah got excited. "I remember now. What happened? Did the trace work?" Did they find her?"

Seamus then informed her of the evening's events and how, in his opinion, they'd been set up and mocked. He told her about the briefing he'd endured as a result. She reached out and took his hand, tears in her eyes. He could sense the pain she felt that Della had not been found.

She sniffed back the tears, blinked a few times and

straightened up in her chair.

"I'd like to see the house, the place where the call came from."

Seamus shook his head. "I was told that you're to go home and take it easy per orders of Doctor Rickelmann."

"He dropped the charges," she replied.

Seamus smiled. "That should help. One less thing to worry about."

Sarah nodded. "I want to see the house."

"I'll take you home … and if anything develops, I'll call." He could practically see her backbone stiffening as he said the words.

"I _want_ to see the house."

Seamus stood up and addressed her. "Sarah, why? There's nothing there. What wasn't burned up has been taken to the crime lab for processing. There's nothing there but a partially burnt shell of a building."

He looked at her again. What had he been thinking a moment ago? Beautiful? Yes. African-American? Who cared? He'd forgotten the petulant, stubborn, and overtly aggressive parts.

Sarah stood up to counter the physical "challenge" in his body language.

"I still want to see it."

"Again, why? Expecting some psychic link or something?" As soon as he said it, he knew he was in trouble and he prepared for the backlash, but she surprised him yet again.

"Not funny. Look, I just want to be able to help Della through this once we find her. Knowing where she was and how they treated her will help me understand just what she went through."

How could he argue against that? There would be no harm in letting her see the place and it had been released by both the police and fire departments. He acquiesced.

"Okay, but not right now. I have to get back to the office and check in with my BOI bosses. I'll take you home and you can do whatever it is you do when a doctor tells you to rest. I'll pick you up this afternoon and we'll go over there. I'll call as I'm coming."

She smiled and stepped up to him. "Thank you." She then kissed him on the cheek, then demurely on the lips.

It must be the head injury, he thought. But whose head was rattled. Hers? Or his?

Seamus had no trouble finding his desk at the Bureau. Obviously, a small dump truck had buried it in paperwork. He'd half expected at least one of the practical jokers he worked with to have littered his desk with city maps or MapQuest printouts with detailed directions to the house just blocks away or the address circled in red with big letters stating "Victim stashed here!" But under the circumstances, this was not a topic of humor. No one liked it when the bad guys taunted the good guys. That was like a glove slapped across the cheek, dueling pistols at twenty paces. The challenge only made the good guys work harder. It was a testosterone mandate.

He worked on clearing the debris from his desk's scarred wooden surface for about an hour before Stick appeared. He seemed upbeat, with a slight bounce in his step.

"Hey, glad to see you could find your way to your desk. It's been obstructing the view through the window for a couple of days now," said Stick. "Anything new?"

"I was about to ask you the same thing," Seamus replied.

"As a matter of fact, yes. I've been working the med student case and while canvassing the eateries near his apartment, I found someone who recognized him as a regular customer. Seems he had a couple of lady friends he often met there, one more than the other. Most of the meetings were a bit more than friendly, but the last one was memorable for the arguing ... to the point that other patrons complained. He didn't know any names but said he might recognize their faces if he saw them."

"Sounds like a solid lead, but where're you going to get a bunch of civilian mug shots for him to look at?"

"Well, since he's from out of state, I figure his most likely source of girlfriends will be current classmates. Figured I'd start with the photo roster from the Associate Dean of Student Affairs office. After that, it's a crap shoot."

"Who knows, maybe you'll get lucky. Let me know if I can help."

"You kidding? From what I see, you got two full plates and they're both overflowing. Speaking of which, how's the lovely doctor doing?"

"Fully recovered and as obstreperous as ever."

Stick chuckled. "As ob- what?"

"Obstreperous. Defiant. Quarrelsome. Argumentative."

"Ahhhh. Is that why there's lipstick on your cheek? Let me guess who won that argument."

Seamus felt the blush rise to his cheeks again and rubbed the cheek where Sarah had kissed him and inspected his fingers. He saw no color there.

Stick laughed. "No guessing needed."

"She just thanked me for saving her life."

"Hmmm, that might be promising …"

"You're kidding, right? I mean, the cultural and racial differences and all. I already see the handwriting on the wall 'bout this one."

"Menĕ, menĕ, tĕckel, upharsin," responded Stick.

"Huh?"

"The original handwriting on the wall, from the Book of Daniel in the Bible. Only in your case, it probably means the days of your relationship are numbered because you have been found deficient."

Seamus didn't know what to say. He had just wanted to know what was new in the Johnson case, not a pep talk from "Dear Prudence."

Seamus spent the next several hours clearing his desk, filing his reports, and talking with his peers and superiors at the BOI. He planned to follow-up on his leads on Blake Howard, particularly the man's father, but he first had to fulfill his promise to Sarah. He called her as he drove the ten minutes from his office to her apartment, and found her waiting on the curb.

"New ride, huh?" she said, stating the obvious as she slid into the passenger seat. "So, what do we do now?"

"We go take a look at the house, like you requested," he replied as he placed the car in gear and started toward the house.

Seamus parked on Mills Street at the east side of the damaged building. Sarah gazed out the car window at the charred shell of the western half of the abandoned dwelling and sat there as if mesmerized. Seamus opened his door, but she made no move to get out.

"You okay?" he asked.

She didn't react right away but finally turned and answered, "Um, yeah, I'm fine. What a dump! I was just trying to imagine Della's reaction to the place. She'd never step foot in such a hole, not even for a story."

"Well, odds are, she never set eyes on it."

She cocked her head and looked at him quizzically.

"Yeah, I'm not sure she was ever there, but the crime lab folks will give us that answer. But more to the point, we found a blindfold in with the clothing we discovered. She was probably blindfolded the entire time, so she can't identify any of the men who took her."

Sarah nodded.

"I didn't think about that possibility." She opened the door and climbed out, joining Seamus at the front of the car. "What else do you think she's been going through? You know, so I can help her work this through later."

As they moved across a soggy front walk, Sarah stopped and looked at Seamus.

"Hey, you're not limping anymore."

"Was it that noticeable before?" He paused. "Strangest thing happened after our accident." He related how he felt a wave of heat from his hip to his ankle while trying to free himself from the wrecked car. "Since then, no pain. How do you explain that, doctor?"

Sarah shrugged and preceded him to the front door, which Seamus opened to allow her into the front room.

"Here's where we found her cell phone, duct taped to the

back of the door."

He showed her the other rooms where they'd found the mattresses, and described what they'd found. The place was empty now, but Sarah cringed at the thought of her friend imprisoned in the small room by men with no scruples. Had they done more than keep her locked up? She looked up at Seamus again.

"What else? What do you think they've done to her?"

He didn't reply to her question. "Seen enough?"

"Seen? Yes. Heard? No. Tell me, Shay, what do you think she's been through? Have they raped her? Tortured her? You didn't mention any blood here. What?"

He stared at the front of the house for a moment, and then turned to her.

"No one can honestly say, Sarah. If she's been raped, it wasn't done here. No semen traces on any of the mattresses. No trace blood, either."

"What do we know?"

"Not much, I'm afraid ... and this information is confidential. This place was wiped clean of fingerprints. Everything appeared staged ... at least to me, anyway. Not all of my colleagues agree with that assessment. We've confirmed the clothing is hers and we found some hair with DNA that I suspect will match hers. Still, that could have been pulled out anywhere and planted here."

"What about the owner of this place? Any possible leads there?"

Seamus winced. "Not a one." He didn't want to admit that not only was the building only one block from his old office, it was one of the many abandoned buildings owned by the city, claimed in lieu of back taxes.

"What else, Shay? Forget the facts; give me your best speculation."

"Well, we, er, I'm assuming she was snatched by the same guy that killed the ambassador. If so, and assuming they know who she is, which has to be the case with her name and pictures all over the news, then they might want to keep her alive, use her as a bargaining chip. If it was me, I'd brainwash her to falsely testify about who she saw. Think about it. If she's dead and the body's never found, the prosecution can use her police drawing and the tattoo to ID the guy, and play up her disappearance to add weight to the sketch she helped make, make the jury mentally link her abduction to her ability to identify the guy. If the body's found, we might be able to develop the evidence to charge them with her death as well. But if she's alive, and testifies that she was never really kidnapped, and worse, testifies that the guy we catch wasn't the killer, the defense is going to have more than reasonable doubt to help them win. If it was me, I'd keep her alive and brainwash her."

Tears came to Sarah's eyes. Seamus regretted his being so blunt about the possibility that Della Winston was dead, but he knew Sarah would have hounded him if he'd sugar-coated his assessment.

He put his hand on her shoulder to comfort her and she took that lead to melt into his body, laying her head on his shoulder. He could feel her heartbeat against his chest and lifted his hand to caress the back of her head. She pulled her head away and looked into his eyes. Despite the hard shell she projected of a ready-for-anything emergency physician, he could see a vulnerability in her eyes that stirred a desire in him for more than the professional relationship they had been forced into. Still, it came as a surprise to him when she moved her face toward his and covered his lips with hers.

The kiss lingered until Seamus pulled away so slightly. Something didn't feel right despite the longing he perceived rising within. Was it a professional sense of decorum that inhibited him? He had known of peers whose jobs suffered when they became emotionally involved with one another and of one detective who had been critically injured in a careless act that arose from his personal feelings for another officer. Yet, she wasn't a co-worker and their working relationship was temporary.

She put her hand behind his head and pulled him back toward her. Seamus reacted in kind but with his mind in confusion. He saw the vulnerability in her eyes. He didn't want to bruise her self-esteem by pulling away, yet going with the flow might wrongfully lead her on. Part of him wanted Sarah, but the specter of family approval hovered about him.

He was about to break off the kiss when the staccato tones of his cell phone broke the mood. He stepped back from Sarah and flipped open the phone as he retrieved it from his pocket.

"Hello."

"Is this that St. Louis detective I talked with yesterday? O'Connor?"

The gravelly voice of nicotine abuse was not one to be easily forgotten. "Sally Rae? Yes, this is O'Connor."

"Hey, how'd you know it were me? … Nevermind. Look, you said to call if that SOB neighbor of mine came home. Well, he did. Him and a bunch of his redneck ruffians, all wearin' them camouflage hunting clothes."

Seamus signaled with his hands for Sarah to head to the car and together they hurried from the building, Seamus stopping long enough to pull the door closed behind them.

"Is he still there?"

"Well, no. Got here 'bout an hour ago and left ten, fifteen minutes ago."

Seamus stopped at the front of his car, perplexed and irritated. He could have had the county deputies there before they'd left. Now, they'd lost him again.

"Why did you wait so long to call?"

"Damn cell phone was still chargin'. But don't you worry none; I got 'em covered. Saw 'em packin' up, so I grabbed my purse and ever so nonchalant walked to my car. Been following the white van they come in. All the way down Highway K to where it runs into Highway 185. We're heading south on 185 right now."

"White van? I thought you said he had a pickup."

"He does. This ain't his wheels. We already passed through what used to be called Pea Ridge. Oops, blinked and missed the town." He heard her sonorous chuckle on the other end.

"Sally Rae, these guys are dangerous. Don't let them know

you're following them."

"Kinda figured that out for myself. The one guy's totin' an assault weapon. M-16 to be precise. Spent five years as a BAM, you know. I can dismantle, clean and reassemble that rifle in my sleep."

"A bam?"

"Yeah, broad-assed Marine. That's what they called us women in the Corps. Qualified at Marksman level, so, hell, I'm probably a better shot than any of 'em anyways."

Seamus closed his eyes and shook his head, trying to rid his mind of the image of Sally Rae in Marine Corps battle dress, cigarette dangling from her lower lip, homing in on a target with an M-16.

"Can you get the plate number of the van?"

"Oh sure. Already wrote it down. KTL …" She stopped. "Hey, they just turned off onto a small, gravel side road, to the left 'bout two and a half mile south of L'il Indian Creek and the railroad tracks. I'm driving past the turn now. Highway N's just ahead."

Seamus raised his fist in the air and pumped it down with a vigorous "Yes!" He didn't need the rest of the plate number to know they'd found the van involved in the kidnapping.

"Bless you, bless you, bless you. Sally Rae, I could kiss you," he said, forgetting the line was still open to the woman.

"Might jus' hold you to that, Detective."

CHAPTER 35

The kudos and high-fives were quick to come as Seamus reported the new development to his superiors at the Bureau. However, the sighting of an M-16 by someone deemed reliable in identifying the weapon altered the course of action and transformed the investigation into a turf war between the ATF and FBI. To the average man on the street, the potential of an arsenal of automatic weapons possessed by a previously unknown militia group that appeared involved in a murder and kidnapping should call for interagency cooperation of the highest degree. Instead, Seamus, who accompanied the FBI S-A-C, witnessed a clash of egos akin to the internecine squabbles of siblings contesting each other over the will of a wealthy uncle.

In the meantime, aerial reconnaissance was quickly arranged and provided details of some kind of camp with multiple buildings, a perimeter fence, and dense forest surrounding it all. FBI spotters moved into position to identify vehicles coming and going from the dead-end road. Both the FBI Hostage Rescue Team and an ATF SWAT team assembled to prepare possible scenarios and to rehearse their entries into said encampment. Finally, a Federal judge forced their cooperation, gave the lead to the FBI HRT since a hostage was involved, and issued warrants to search for Della Winston as well as weapons caches.

One way or another, Seamus would join the strike force slated to enter the compound, although not as a member of the lead group. Not surprisingly, the same judge authorized Sarah Wade to join the force as a member of the accompanying EMS personnel. Seamus knew better than to ask how she'd finagled that one, yet was glad that she'd be with them. If there was a turn for the worse, he felt far better knowing a competent Emergency Medicine physician was available.

The team converged on the gymnasium of a high school less than thirty minutes away from their target. Once all of the members had assembled, the HRT squad leader stepped to the front.

"Quiet down, folks. Let's get started."

Seamus listened as over the course of the next hour, the HRT presented detailed aerial photographs for review and discussed options. In the post-Waco era, they could no longer mount a full frontal assault unless they had no other alternative. In this light, they outlined those options and documented the scenarios for which a military assault would become necessary. There could be no grey areas in their plans, as the judge who issued the warrants had reminded them.

"Tonight, we're deploying three two-man teams with night vision and infra-red capabilities to approach the compound, here, here, and here." On a detailed drawing of the facility, he pointed to the north, east, and south edges of a fence line, which appeared to be tall chain-link topped by barbed wire on the photographs presented earlier. "They are to get as much last-minute intel for us as possible before withdrawing before dawn, at which time they will return to our staging area, here, and join the main force."

"They will be replaced by fresh two-man teams, who will act as support if we meet resistance when we present the warrants. And we believe there's a better than 50-50 chance we'll meet such resistance. Any questions?"

An ATF agent raised his hand. "Looks like we've got the layout of the land down pat. What about body counts? Are we expecting three guys or a whole platoon? Hand guns or assault weapons?"

"That's not clear yet. We know there were five men in the van when it was spotted coming here. Our aerial cameras have not given us an accurate count, but we count at least eight vehicles on the premises and we know that no one else has entered the area since we set up our spotters. We hope to get that information tonight. Anyone else?"

Seamus watched the assembly as men shook their heads and talked among themselves. He already knew that three vans would approach the complex's gate at full light. He would be in a fourth van, which would enter the compound only if the main force entered peacefully. All EMS personnel, who were attending their own briefing in a nearby classroom, were to remain at the staging area unless called for.

The HRT leader put his fingers to his mouth and whistled for attention.

"Okay, folks. There's food in the first room on your left outside those doors. Cots are available here in the gym. Grab a bite to eat, get your gear ready, and get some rest. We'll be up at dawn."

At that, the group dispersed, some heading straight for the food while others grabbed cots and claimed their personal space within the gym. Seamus noticed Sarah and a half dozen paramedics enter through the main doors. She spotted him, waved, and walked straight toward him.

"Hi. I, uh … have you ever been involved in something like this before?" she asked.

He shook his head. "Not this big. It's been an eye-opener. I've always heard about turf wars among the different federal agencies. Now I've seen it first-hand. What a bunch of egos." He looked around to make sure he hadn't been overheard. "But you didn't hear me say that."

She smiled. "Well, from my end, I'm impressed. These guys sure are prepared for any medical contingency. I've been through a ton of mass-cal drills before, but they're always just that, drills. I'm a little nervous 'cause this time I get the feeling it won't be a drill."

She pointed to several men setting up cots. "I guess you all are bunking down here, huh?"

Seamus nodded.

"Too bad. The EMS folks are all staying at the various county EMS facilities as well as those at the hospital in Sullivan. Real beds, showers, hot food. But I'll be thinking about you roughin' it here." She grinned.

A paramedic walked up to them. "C'mon, Doc. We gotta get the rigs packed before the steaks are done grillin'." He winked.

"Bye, Shay. Pleasant dreams."

Seamus laughed as she turned with the medic and left the gym, but the laughter was short-lived. Seamus felt a subtle shiver rise up his spine. She had confirmed his own suspicions.

Tomorrow was not going to be a walk in the woods looking for morels. The last thing he wanted was a gut heavy with food, hot or otherwise.

Sayer had joined Edwards at the lake compound earlier that morning. He needed a break and knew that the solitude of the wooded complex, along with some recreational target practice and maybe a little squirrel hunting or fishing in the lake, would serve him well. And it had. The quiet of the lake and action of the fish had been the diversion he needed, until the solitude was broken with the arrival of Blake Howard and his cohort, followed by a dozen others. Bobby had called his company in for drills, which Sayer knew as code for a night of poker and drinking. So much for the militia training Bobby always harped on. So much for the natural thrum of crickets lulling Sayer to sleep.

Sayer knew when to give in. Although not in the mood for drinking, he enjoyed a lively table of poker and was no stranger at previous "drills" at the compound. Tonight would be no different and by staying sober, he had a better than even chance of finishing the night a winner. He joined Edwards at a table of five playing Texas Hold'Em. He'd played with this crew before and found them all to be serious players. As expected, he found the stakes at this table surpassed those of several other tables combined.

He took his seat to the left of Edwards as Edwards took a turn as dealer. Sayer put up the first blind to get the pot started. The man next to him matched his blind and Edwards dealt each player two cards down. The first round of bets revealed a heady show of confidence in the players, but from experience, Sayer knew that at least two of the men would quickly fold. Their sitting positions had already given them away.

Next came the flop, with three public cards dealt face up. One of the two men Sayer suspected would fold, did. The other became more alert and sat upright. Obviously, the flop had helped his hand and his confidence. Edwards sat there stone faced and unflinching. He was always the hardest to read. Sayer studied all the players as the betting moved around the table and tried to gauge who would fold next. By the end of the betting, his estimate proved correct.

By the time the "fifth street" or final, face-up card was dealt, the bettors had dwindled to Sayer, Edwards and the man two players to Edwards' right. Sayer had little chance of winning, but he held three tens so he played the hand through. Edwards won the hand with a flush of hearts.

The games continued into the late evening hours and both Edwards and Sayer were ahead. The deal came to Sayer and as he started to shuffle, a young man rushed into the room and ran straight toward Edwards.

"Sir, there's an intrusion to the north. Looks like two men coming toward the compound."

Game night or not, Edwards never let his guard down and Bobby knew better than to cross Edwards. There were too many arms and munitions on site to get lax, even though they'd never had an intrusion into their perimeter security before.

"I'll be back," Edwards said as he rose to accompany the young man to the security center.

Sayer, poised to deal, decided he'd be better off to follow Edwards, so he handed the deck to the man on his left.

"Count me out this hand, too."

He joined Edwards in the command office.

"What's up?"

"I don't like the looks of this. Two men outside the fence line to our north appear to be setting up a recon position." As he pointed out their position on the computer screen, another warning icon flashed. "Crap, look, two more coming into our southern perimeter." He turned to the young man who had alerted him to the problem and said, "Jimmy, go get Bobby and have the guys hit the floor until I get the infrared lamps on. Tell everyone to keep a low profile. We don't want these guys to know how many people are here."

Sayer looked at Edwards as Jimmy left the room. "Infrared?"

"Yeah. If these guys are trying to find out how many people are here, they'll use infrared sensors to look for and count the heat signatures. We scattered heat lamps all over the camp to confuse this type of surveillance. Got your cell phone?"

Sayer nodded and pulled it from his back pocket.

"See if you get a signal."

Sayer flicked open the phone. "No signal."

"Damn, they're jamming."

As he said this, another warning blip appeared on the security monitor.

"Shit, we're under big time surveillance. Two people just entered the eastern perimeter. Since our access road heads west, they probably got that covered and now they're looking to gain control of other escape routes."

Edwards kneeled down and crawled toward an electric circuit box on a nearby wall. He flipped a switch and the glow of heat lamps brightened throughout the command building. He hit a series of breakers, which Sayer assumed triggered a similar illumination throughout the compound. Edwards turned off another breaker and the hum of the air conditioner died. Only the command building and mothballed lab had cooling units because of the computers and other equipment.

"Gonna get a bit warm in here, but I don't want them to discover our computer system. Need to let the whole building warm up to help hide it."

"What about night vision?" asked Sayer.

"That's next," replied Edwards. He flipped yet another breaker and floodlights lit up the perimeter, aimed into the woods. "That should effectively blind them, but it also tells them we know they're there and they're gonna wonder how."

"And signal that we're worried about them."

"True. But then, they wouldn't be there if they didn't already have some idea what was here. Which leads me to the next question. How in the hell did they find out about us? Somebody here screwed up big time ... but it's too late to change that. Gotta keep looking forward." He walked to the computer and entered a series of commands. "I've disabled the sensors along that southwest escape path. If the going gets dicey, it'll be every man for himself and you might want to hightail it out that way.

Once you make it to that ravine I showed you, you should be able to pass by our intruders. Just belly crawl to get there."

Sayer nodded, but wondered what he'd do. His car was there in the compound. Even if he escaped, they'd trace the car and eventually find him.

"What's wrong?" Edwards asked. "You got a funny look on your face."

"My car's parked here. Over by the lab building."

"Oh." Edwards sat there silently for a minute. "Okay, I'll take care of that … but you're gonna lose the car. Sorry."

"That's not a problem. Getting caught's the problem."

Bobby rushed into the room. "What's up? Jimmy says we got big trouble."

Edwards pointed to the monitor. "We're under surveillance. Three two-man positions … here, here, and here. I've activated the heat lamps and floods. That'll confuse 'em, but it also tells 'em we're on alert. They'll show up at first light with warrants and we need to be prepared."

Sayer looked at Edwards, confused. "How do you know that?"

"Feds can't just barge in. They need warrants. With a place this size, they'll want as much daylight time as they can get. But we need to prepare for more. After Waco, they won't attack the compound but the consequences won't be pleasant. Most likely, they'd lay siege, cut the power, and wait for food and water to run out."

Bobby grinned. "That'd be a mighty long wait. Got rations and gasoline for the generators to last a month or better."

"Well, don't get too cocky, Bobby. They'll do whatever it takes."

"Hell, so will we," replied Bobby.

"What's that mean?" asked Sayer.

Bobby didn't answer. Instead, he walked out of the building and returned to his men in the mess hall.

Sayer turned to Edwards. "I don't like the sound of that. That boy's been itchin' for a fight and I, for one, don't want to get caught in the middle."

Edwards nodded. "Like I said, every man for himself. I'm gonna go take care of your car and then I think we need to hightail it outta here."

"Sounds like a plan. I'll follow you."

Edwards shook his head. "No, we need to leave separately. Harder to spot if we go one at a time."

Sayer didn't like the idea of going it alone. He was a businessman, not a trained soldier or accomplished outdoorsman. But he didn't want to get caught and he didn't trust Edwards to help him if it became a 'him or me' situation. So he would indeed be on his own.

"If I were you, I'd give it some time and move out in the early morning hours. Those guys will be less attentive after a few hours out there. They might even pack it in and leave when they realize they're not getting the information they're hoping to get. Try to get an hour or two of sleep. You'll need all the rest you can get."

Sleep? How could he talk of sleep? Sayer knew he needed the rest, but the idea of napping under the circumstances was beyond his comprehension.

"When are you leaving?" he asked Edwards.

"Right after I destroy the VIN and plates on your car ... and wipe it clean of any possible prints. The Colonel has a job for me and I need to get clear of here ASAP. I can deal with those yahoos in the woods ... if it comes to that. But you need to stay in stealth mode all the way. Can you do that?"

Sayer hesitated. Could he? He'd have to. He nodded.

"You'll need clean clothes so you don't raise suspicion if you're picked up out by the road?"

Sayer nodded again.

"Good. Get me a set and I'll leave them for you at the place where we parked the other day. That way you won't have to deal with them."

"Thanks."

Sayer watched as Edwards headed out the door toward the lab building, thankful they had moved the Colonel's equipment out of the building. The decoy lab with its anhydrous ammonia and pseudoephedrine would throw off any investigation. But then Sayer remembered the C4 charges and anxiety filled him. He now knew what Edwards meant by losing his car. The man was setting it to blow with the lab.

After giving Edwards a small pack of clothing, as well as his poker winnings, Sayer watched the man ease to the southwest corner of the compound where he would work his way into a camouflaged conduit leading under the fence unseen. From that point on, Sayer knew he would remain out of sight. Sayer tried to let that image imprint on his mind so he could duplicate the movement for his own escape.

He returned to the command building and found Bobby, clad in body armor, an M-16 close at hand, focused on the computer monitor. "Something strange going on out there. Can't figure it out. Watch."

Sayer turned his attention to the monitor. The original intrusion team had remained in place to the north, with occasional movement as the two men changed places watching their equipment. The southern intruders remained in place, when suddenly a third image darted in and out of the sensor's field. A few seconds later, it happened again, but this time one of the two men arose and crept toward the phantom image. An instant later, the man jerked violently and crumbled to the ground. The other man instantly jumped up, took one step toward his fallen comrade, and collapsed. Neither image moved after that.

"Now what was that?" Bobby asked.

Sayer knew, but refused to voice his belief. Edwards had just added two more notches on his gun's handle. Sayer knew it was his time to leave and that his window of opportunity would be brief. As soon as the team failed to check in, the place would be swarming with agents. Sayer shuddered at the thought of Edwards' cold heartedness. While guaranteeing that Sayer's personal escape would be easier, the man had assured the capture and possible demise of every other man in the compound. And knowing Bobby's ego as he did, he knew the latter was the more likely scenario. *Each man is expendable, even me,* Sayer thought.

Bobby glanced at Sayer, who shrugged his shoulders in mock confusion. "Hey, you better get a vest. They're in the mess hall."

Sayer didn't hesitate to take the opening to leave the command building, but instead of heading to the mess hall, he ran from building to building until he was as close to the southwest corridor as possible. Then he crawled toward the fence, trying to remember where the tunnel lay hidden. A sense of panic filled him. What was Edwards up to? Was this the job the Colonel had laid on him? To eliminate all potential witnesses? Even him? The terror rose as he crawled search for the grate covering the opening to the cement culvert.

Finally, his hands hit something metal - the grate, camouflaged with leaves and sticks. He started to slide it to the side but the noise level scared him. He slowed down and eased the lid away. Should he take time to replace it? Or just keep going? He decided he had the time to conceal his escape, but once in the tunnel found it hard to replace the grate exactly as it had been. His lips and hands began to tingle. He had to slow his breathing. He had to gain control over the fear.

After a few minutes, he felt the pins and needles subside and he began to inch his body through the pipe toward the other end. Halfway through, he froze as he heard and felt the rumble simultaneously. He knew only one thing could produce that kind of shock wave. The lab and his car had just exploded.

CHAPTER 36

"Okay people! Up and at 'em! Get your gear! It's show time!"

Seamus, half asleep and lying on his cot fully dressed, jumped up and scrambled to don his vest, buckle his gun belt, and load up the rest of his gear. Men all around him rushed to get ready from various stages of dress and preparation. Yet, within minutes, all were assembled in front of the gym's bleachers where the task force leader had climbed to the third row to brief the group.

"We've had a major development at the target site. We've lost touch with Hutchins and McCrery on the south perimeter. The east team reports no movement in that direction and no communications with the team, so we have to assume the worst. In addition, six minutes ago there was a massive explosion within the compound. Our on-site teams report the smell of ammonia and casualties on the grounds. Our men there are going in and EMS and county hazmat resources have been mobilized. Get to your designated vans and let's roll!"

Seamus queued up with his squad and ran from the building to the fourth van. The driver hit the gas before the final man had fully closed the side door and raced behind the other units with full lights and sirens. They had no need for stealth under the circumstances.

The twists and turns of Route 185 proved gut wrenching for those riding in the back of the van. Seamus had never been prone to motion sickness before, yet he, too, felt queasy. Or maybe it wasn't motion sickness. He was going into the closest thing to a battle zone he had ever experienced. This made the drug bust where he'd taken a slug in the thigh seem like prom. And besides firearms, they now had to deal with toxic gas.

Despite their speed, the drive took fifteen minutes and when they arrived, they found the small road leading to the compound choked with emergency vehicles. The van screeched to a halt and the side door flew open.

"Everybody out! We hoof it from here."

The vans with units one and two had proceeded up the gravel road, while the third and fourth units were now going in on foot. Seamus glanced around but did not see Sarah. As he passed the nearest ambulance, a man in full hazmat gear handed him a gas mask. The man did not attempt to guarantee each person's familiarity with the mask and Seamus took it with reluctance. Yes, he'd had the training … over a year ago. His mind raced to recall that teaching. The rest of his squad were already masked and moving out in double time while Seamus struggled to tighten his mask, spurred on by the increasing smell of the spreading ammonia cloud. With another cinch of the top strap, the odor disappeared. He inhaled deeply and, satisfied by the mask's protection, he ran to catch up with his peers, a feat hindered by the mask's airflow restrictions limiting his breathing … and the pain in his thigh.

They approached the front gates of the compound and dropped to their bellies with the report of gunfire. The gate remained closed and appeared chained. Seamus noticed a large burr oak to his left and rolled over the moist leafy ground to reach the base of the tree. With its protection, he first kneeled and then stood behind it. Although the mask limited his visual field, he eased around the trunk and looked ahead into the fenced area. Another gunshot echoed out and splintered shreds of bark showered his head, forcing him to pull back.

One of his team members rolled along the ground past him, heading for cover to Seamus' left. The man suddenly yowled and grabbed his right thigh in response to yet another shot from inside the compound. Seamus grabbed the man's vest and yanked him behind the protection of the tree. They flinched and ducked together at the loud retort from behind them. Seamus recovered and peeked around the tree in time to see a camouflage-clad body topple from a nearby roof. He looked down at the wounded man below him.

"Friendlies behind us. Looks like our sharpshooters are in place to provide some covering fire."

He glanced to the right and saw two men from the first unit belly crawl to the gate. One man gave a hand signal and several rifles answered with shots into the camp. The two men jumped up, placed a charge on the gate's lock, and dove for cover behind their bullet-ridden van. Pre-occupied with finding cover, Seamus hadn't noticed the van's condition. He now imagined the reception given the initial responders. He wondered how many wounded men were in the hands of the EMS personnel at this point.

He crouched down to assist the injured man at his feet, fully aware of the sympathy pains from his own thigh. The wound did not appear serious, as direct pressure had already stemmed the active bleeding.

Again, a cacophony of repeated shots from behind him rang out. Seamus ducked reflexively when the charge on the gate demolished the lock. He could hear the first van rev into gear and burst through the gate. He looked out from behind the tree in time to see the van swerve to the right while the second van, following on its bumper, veered to the left. The first and second teams took cover behind their respective vans and a volley of exchanged gunshots echoed through the woods for the next five minutes.

Sayer lay immobilized by panic inside the culvert. The tingling in his lips and hands had returned and his fingers began to cramp and flex involuntarily. How long had he been there? He couldn't think clearly, but he knew he had to escape that culvert. He could smell the ammonia as it spread around the camp and he had the presence of mind to recall that ammonia was heavier than air and would settle into the culvert quickly. He had to slow his breathing and control the dread that filled him or he would become a victim of the toxic gas. Although the ammonia now stung his eyes, he found he could still take slow deep breaths without much discomfort. He focused on those breaths. Focused on slow easy respirations. Focused.

Soon the cramps in his hands lightened. The ammonia level remained low and he was thankful for the carefully woven, leafy camouflage that had hidden the grate from discovery and impeded the flow of gas into the conduit.

He listened to the sporadic gunfire at the other end of the compound and realized this was the diversion he needed to make his getaway. He felt more in control, but never had he felt such terror. He had to act. Now. He resumed squirming through the pipe away from the camp. He estimated that he was roughly under the fence and would find the end of his escape route in short order.

With increasing command of his body, he moved faster. He couldn't gauge how long it took, but he soon found himself at the other end of the culvert and easily pushed that grate free. He squiggled out of the concrete tube and rolled over on the leafy forest floor. The ammonia was more intense there and he knew he had to run, but he wanted the diversion of gunfire to resume.

He pulled his shirt over his nose and mouth, which provided some filtering of the gas. He slowly moved into a crouch, eyeing the compound first and then scanning the forest for his bearings to the southwest. A moment later, he heard a run of extended rifle fire, followed by an explosion from the direction of the main gate. This was his chance. A quick glance back revealed Bobby running toward the back fence line. Sayer jumped up and bolted for the tree line. Suddenly, the retort of a rifle from close range rang out and Sayer felt the searing pain of a bullet ripping through his right thigh. The force of the impact twisted and toppled him to the ground, unable to hold his weight on that leg. A second shot caught him in the right upper chest and took his breath away in an instant. Now facing the fence, the last thing he saw was Bobby lowering his M-16, grinning. Did he know who he'd just shot? Had he confused Sayer with an agent outside the fence? As consciousness started to fade, he saw the young man's grin change to a grimace and then a look of horror as he clutched his bloody throat and fell to the ground.

Seamus and his team advanced into the compound under the protective cover of gunfire from the first two units. Then, in turn, they provided cover to those units as they advanced upon the first of the buildings. Return gunfire was sporadic and dwindling. For each shot from the compound, the strike force answered with several shots from many angles. As they moved into the main grounds, Seamus saw a man near the southern fence line firing at someone outside the fence. The only men known to be outside the fence were federal agents. Seamus, noting that the man wore body armor, aimed carefully for a head shot and fired. With his second shot, the man collapsed.

A shout from his left caught his attention. Unit Two pronounced the first building clear. Seamus watched as agents entered building after building, sweeping through, and exiting, announcing each as being clear of any threat. Seamus helped his team inspect vehicles parked along the buildings and found no one inside. As agents proclaimed the last structure free of threat, Seamus took the time to scan his surroundings. At least two dozen men, some wearing forest camouflage, others in jeans and tees; some with assault weapons, others with handguns, lay unmoving on the ground. He joined the others in checking the bodies. A building near the periphery of the camp lay in ruin, obvious ground zero of the explosion. Many of the bodies nearest the debris field appeared uninjured and Seamus assumed the toxic ammonia had claimed their lives. As they moved closer and closer to the main gate, the casualties were those of gunfire. At least eight men appeared dead from bullet wounds to either chest or head.

Flashing lights caught his attention. Two ambulances had entered the compound and their occupants emerged in hazmat gear. Despite the mask and protective suit, Seamus recognized Sarah. He waved for her to join him.

"Follow me," he said as she walked up to him. He started toward the southern fence line, but she grabbed his shoulder and stopped him.

"Any sign of Della?"

Seamus shook his head. "Not here."

He continued toward the fence and found the young man he'd shot earlier. The man couldn't have been older than his mid-twenties.

Sarah knelt down and checked him briefly for vital signs. She stood, shaking her head. "He's dead. Shot through the throat.

Looks like it took out his spinal cord as well as one of the carotid arteries."

She rolled him over and suddenly dropped her hands and withdrew from the body. Seamus saw the cause of her reaction. On the back of the man's head, he saw the tattoo. He had killed the killer and kidnapper. A sense of wonder struck him. Had his shot followed his aim, he might have destroyed the one marking that identified the man they had been hunting. But was this a mixed blessing? Had he also eliminated their chance at finding Della Winston? He lowered himself and searched the man's clothing but found no ID. He stood and scanned the area outside the fence. He saw nothing.

"I shot this guy as he was shooting something or someone outside the fence. Do you see anything?"

They moved close to the fence and walked along it, searching the area outside. Sarah pointed first.

"There! Looks like someone on the ground."

Sayer saw a bright light, but it didn't appear like any light he had seen before. Its intensity was far greater than anything he'd ever experienced. But as he watched, the light began to move away. He felt himself falling and as each second passed he moved faster and faster. The light was soon the size of a pinhole, yet somehow he knew he wanted to be moving toward that light, not away from it.

The darkness that engulfed him was near total. No, in a flash of time, it became total. He could see nothing, yet he sensed many things. All of his senses seemed heightened. He reached for his arms and although he could not feel them, his skin felt a burning heat like that of being tossed into a cauldron of lava. The heat scorched what he sensed was his body, but not his body. He felt confused. The idea of phantom limb pain flittered through his mind. He had no body, at least not in a form he recognized, yet all of the senses of that body remained active. In addition to the heat, the strong smell of burning sulfur seared his "throat and lungs" as if he was in the process of one perpetual inhalation. He couldn't breathe out and remove the irritation or odor. It was ever present.

In the instant that his mind asked the question, "What is this place?" he had the answer. Hell. He'd never believed in heaven and hell, but now knew the folly of that failed conviction. Terror, anguish, and despair filled his mind and soul in logarithmic proportions.

He wanted out. He wanted another chance. He wanted relief. But as he thought those things, too, the answers came instantly. No way out. No second chance. No relief. This was his plight for all of eternity. Eternity! He had been warned.

The seemingly never-ending fall finally slowed and he found himself surrounded by torment and sorrow. Screams and moaning filled his "ears." The heat, the stench, the despair of his future assaulted him. Despite the utter darkness, he sensed another being. A creature with flaming yellow eyes, scaly skin covered with slime in a permanent state of rot, and breath so foul Sayer could not begin to describe it, approached. It spoke into his mind. "You're mine for all of time."

He wanted to run, to escape, but his "feet" had planted in place. He sensed something else approaching and felt worm-like things begin to burrow into his "legs." The pain -- burning, itching, and tearing all at once – was unimaginable as the worms worked their way up into his "body."

Memories of a physical life on a temporal plane of existence did not fade. Details he had long ago forgotten came to mind. The memories of pleasures in that life intensified the agony he now suffered. Acknowledging what he had lost became an unbearable burden. What he now faced for eternity forced on him a desolate gloom he could never have imagined. His thirst would never be quenched. His hunger never sated. Never again would he experience human touch. The reality of eternity no longer hid from his consciousness.

CHAPTER 37

Seamus ran along the fence. No opening. Razor wire at the top. He considered the distance and time required to run to the main gate and along the perimeter to return to the spot. As he ran back toward Sarah, he tripped over something. Looking to the ground, he saw diamond-shaped grillwork of rusty metal with branches and leaves woven into it. He tugged at the grate and pulled it aside.

Looking down into the hole, he realized he had found a culvert leading under the fence. Had some of the militant force escaped? If so, why would they have bothered to replace the grate?

Without hesitation, he shimmied into the cement pipe and wormed his way to the other side. Exiting the pipe, he glanced around and twenty feet ahead and to his right, he saw the body. He ran to the lifeless form and knelt beside it, placing his fingers against the carotid artery.

"There's a faint pulse! It's weak, but I'm sure it's there!" he yelled back to Sarah. She went running toward the compound. Moments later, EMS personnel converged on the area inside the fence. Sarah was not with them.

"There's a cement culvert over there. You can get through that way," he yelled, pointing the medics in the direction he had come.

But before they reached the pipe, Seamus heard a car engine come to life and rev into high gear. Unexpectedly, a rusty Ford pickup emerged from between two buildings and raced toward the fence, breaking through the chain link no more than ten feet away from Seamus. He flinched and prepared to jump away, but the truck's driver veered right, slammed on the brakes and skidded into a group of small trees that brought it to a sudden halt. The door popped open and out jumped Sarah.

In seconds, she and several paramedics surrounded Seamus and the downed man. There was no hesitation in her actions as she assessed the injuries. Seamus grimaced, though, as she ripped off the gas mask.

"Can't work in this damn thing." She raised her head and took a deep breath. "It's okay, the ammonia's dissipated," she said. The medics also tossed their masks and began to work.

"Two large bore IVs. Squeeze some Ringers ... two, three liters ... into this guy. Someone immobilize that thigh and get some pressure on it. Pneumatic trousers if you got 'em. Air splint if you don't. Get me an ET tube, size seven, and a straight blade on the scope. He's probably got a hemo-pneumo from this chest wound. Get a flutter valve ready."

Seamus stepped back and watched. Like a well-choreographed dance, each person performed his part and kept the beat. Two EMT-Ps established intravenous access and began literally squeezing the bags of solution into the veins. A third medic dealt with the injured thigh, while a fourth assisted Sarah, immobilizing the head and neck while Sarah made orotracheal intubation look easy. Seamus had been on trauma scenes where nothing went right. This time, it seemed that God's hand guided each player, and everything went right.

Seamus closed his eyes and said a quiet prayer to save this man's life. He was their only key to Della Winston.

Sayer? Yes, his name was Sayer. The fading memories seemed stronger. He heard the demon scream, "Noooooo! He's mine!" Yet the beast seemed more distant and he no longer felt the worm-like things. In that instant Sayer found himself hovering over his earthly body, watching people he'd never seen before working on it as in some surreal medical TV show. Curiously, the things they were doing looked like they'd hurt but he felt no pain. He watched as a young man began to pump air into the tube in his mouth, and he didn't flinch as a young woman stabbed his chest with a needle-looking thing. Yet, at that moment he felt his lungs fill with air – cool, clean country air – and he re-entered that battered body.

Sarah amazed herself with the successful intubation. The man's airway was full of blood from the chest wound and she could not see his vocal cords or other anatomical landmarks.

But, for one brief second, the cords miraculously cleared and she was able to slide the tube between them before they disappeared again. The medic took over from there, securing the tube in place and beginning the ongoing process of bagging the man, pumping air into the lungs with a plastic Ambu® bag. She listened to the chest but heard no breath sounds on the right side.

Tension hemo-pneumo ... she thought. She grabbed the package with the flutter valve, which once inserted into the chest would let pressure out and allow the lung to re-inflate if not too badly damaged. She palpated the ribs and located the space between the second and third ribs, above the nipple, and jammed the valve's needle through the muscle into the chest cavity. The hiss of pressure release rewarded that action. She listened again and heard faint breath sounds on the right side. *That should hold until we can get a chest tube in him.*

She watched his face as she listened to his chest and saw a quick flutter of the eyelids as he opened and then closed them just once. *It's not your time*, she thought. Two years earlier, another patient had taught her the truth about one's time on Earth. That man, age forty-two, had come to the ED complaining of chest pain and within minutes of his arrival collapsed in full cardiopulmonary arrest, his heart going into the deadly rhythm of ventricular fibrillation. She had tried every defibrillator in the ED in an attempt to shock him back into a life-sustaining rhythm. All twelve had failed to deliver their electrical shock to the man; yet the whole dozen tested normally when checked by the bioengineering techs an hour later. That man had come to his appointed time and nothing could have been done to avert it.

"We have a blood pressure," announced one of the medics. "Eighty over forty."

"Good enough. Get him packaged and let's get to a landing zone. Call in A.R.C.H. I want to fly with this guy," responded Sarah.

"They're already in the air. They'll meet us at the LZ."

Seamus watched quietly, shaking his head. Had it really been only thirty-six hours since Sarah's last flight with A.R.C.H.? The one where she was the patient "packaged" and lying on the stretcher.

"Sergeant O'Connor!"

Seamus turned to the voice behind him. One of the ATF agents from Unit One was waving his arm, beckoning Seamus to follow him back into the compound. There was nothing more Seamus could do for or about the wounded man; he was in Sarah's care now. He turned and jogged back to the agent, who led him to a small building at the end of the camp.

"Knew you'd want to see this," he said as he led Seamus through the door.

The building appeared to be a barracks of some kind with four small rooms coming off a common hall along the length of the building. It wasn't until Seamus entered one of the rooms that he realized these were more like jail cells than dorm rooms. The door locked from the outside, and the sole window was small and located high on the wall, large enough to allow some light into the room but not big enough for a man to squeeze through. He saw a military surplus cot against one wall and a hospital bedside commode in one corner.

Two items laying on the canvas surface of the cot caught Seamus' attention. He stared at the heavy leg irons and handcuffs, as well as the rough burlap hood with leather bootlaces woven into the opening as a drawstring. Then he noticed the paper stapled onto the wooden wall above the bed – standard letter-sized computer paper with a picture and its caption: "DW slept here." The photo showed a hooded and manacled Della Winston lying on the cot.

CHAPTER 38

Della tried her hand at baking, following closely the instructions provided by Sue. Such domesticity was foreign to her. As a young child, her family's only baked goods came from the Wonder Bread Hostess Thrift Store. By the time she'd graduated college, she had refined her tastes to only the finest cuisine. Now, she had even squelched her aunt's love of cooking by hiring someone to relieve Aunt Beatrice of that responsibility. That seemed reasonable. After all, her aunt could barely manage the housekeeping, which she insisted on doing. And it kept her out of the kitchen and away from her "tea."

This was her third attempt at making bread and, surprisingly, she enjoyed it. The homey smell of yeast as the bread rose. The tactile pleasure in kneading and shaping the dough. The aroma of its baking, and, finally, the delicious taste of fresh bread warm from the oven. She was sorry she had stopped Aunt Bea from indulging in her culinary arts. She now had a taste of what she had missed.

Yet, despite this newfound pleasure, something was amiss. The angst emanating from her two "housemates" was undeniable.

Sue walked into the kitchen while Della cleaned her utensils and the bread baked.

"Smells wonderful."

"Thank you," replied Della.

"Carly's almost done with her room. She'll leave the cleaning supplies in your room."

The one aspect of domestic life that Della would never miss was cleaning. She found no simple pleasure in cleaning the house, yet she saw its necessity. The other two women had spent all day cleaning, even though the place appeared spotless to Della. Carly and Sue vacuumed and scrubbed, wiped down all the counters and woodwork. They washed, dried, and folded their own meager wardrobes. They worked with a frenzy Della had not witnessed in them before. By the time they finished, it appeared as if Della was the only person living there. The kitchen and her bedroom were the only places they'd left untouched because those were Della's responsibility.

Yes, there was an underlying tension spurring them on, and Della could not figure out what it was. She had caught Sue crying at one point, but the woman quickly stiffened her lip and bucked up to complete the task she had undertaken. Carly, too, was misty eyed at times. Neither wanted to talk. Both seemed in a hurry to finish their work, as if under threat by the men Della never saw, but who held control of their lives. She never questioned their existence, or the fact that they would kill her if ever she became uncooperative.

She looked at Sue. Her reddened eyes betrayed her crying again. Something bad had happened, Della was sure. But what?

"I don't know what's happened, but I'm willing to listen if you want," Della said.

Tears bubbled up in Sue's eyes again, but she shook her head. "Nothin' you or any of us could do. So what's the use?" She walked over to the oven and peered through the window. "You're a quick study. I-I'm sure it will be delicious ... but Carly and I have to leave. They want us to work at their other place tonight. Takes two to feed the crew there. Probably won't be back 'til morning. You be okay?"

Della nodded. "Sure." But she wasn't sure. They'd never both left at the same time. Did this mean the men had come to trust her? Maybe they'd take the shackles off her legs. Maybe they'd grant her the freedom to walk outside sometime soon.

"Jus' be careful. Don't get any fool notions about leavin'. And don't answer the door if anyone comes knocking. I'd hate to see something awful happen to you."

Just then, Carly hurried into the room. "All done. Left the cleaning stuff by your room, Della." She glanced at Sue. "Did you tell her?"

Sue nodded.

"Okay, they're waiting. We gotta go." She walked over to Della and gave her a hug. "Take care of yourself."

Della felt tears in her own eyes. Sue had said they'd be back, but her intuition told her she'd never see these two women again.

225

She waved timidly as the women eased out the back door. Suddenly she felt more vulnerable and fearful than at any time since her abduction. The buzz of the oven timer caught her off-guard. She rushed to the oven, pulled out the loaf, and placed it on a cooling rack before turning off the oven. She glanced around the kitchen and listened intently. Silence. The loneliness brought back the horrible memories of being hooded and shackled. Did she dare to venture outside? She wandered from room to room, turning off lights and checking locks. She started to crawl into her bed but instead sat down in a corner of the room and drew her knees up to her chest. She could hold back the emotional strain no longer and heavy sobs shook her.

While their John Doe underwent surgical debridement and repair of his wounds, Sarah paced inside the ED staff lounge watched the TV intermittently. The gun battle at the militant's camp seemed tame compared to the firestorm of its aftermath. National and international news agencies camped outside the Market Street building of the FBI Field offices, as well as City Hall. News helicopters dodged each other over the site of the raid. The comparisons with Waco were inevitable but the venomous attacks from the far left gun control crowd were more toxic than the ammonia cloud that had actually killed most of the militants. And the cries of government suppression and harassment from the far right gun lobby matched the level of liberal hubris. Nowhere was the ever-increasing polarization of the country more evident; no one was happy. Everyone, pundits to man-on-the-street, had his own 20-20 hindsight, fantasy version of the event. They should have done this. They shouldn't have done that. Yet not one mention that Della was still a hostage ... somewhere.

Sarah found the newscasts as despairing as the lack of news on Della. None of these people had been there. They had no right to criticize. The initial EMS call had been one for possibly wounded federal agents. That quickly changed to one of responding to a hazmat situation. The fact that EMS personnel met armed resistance that required the early mobilization of the federal strike force seemed lost in the muck being stirred by a myriad of people with their own agendas.

A picture of Della flashed onto the screen and Sarah grabbed the remote and pushed up the sound.

"We now have unofficial reports that local television personality, Della Winston, who has been the subject of an intense manhunt since her abduction …" Sarah edged forward in her chair, hopeful. "… may have been held hostage in the compound that federal agents raided this morning. An anonymous informant tells News 5 that evidence found in one of the buildings confirms her presence there recently. However, she remains missing and her condition is unknown."

Sarah grabbed her cell phone and dialed Seamus.

"Sergeant O'Connor."

"Is it true?" Sarah asked.

"Doctor, thanks for calling. How's our fellow doing?"

"Is it true? Was Della there?"

"I see, Doctor. He's still in surgery and no news yet. Will you keep me posted? I should be able to get free in thirty minutes or so and I can meet you at the hospital."

Sarah wanted to strangle the man. "C'mon, answer me! Was she there?" Hearing voices in the background talking to Shay, she sighed. "Okay. I get it now. You can't talk freely. Just answer yes or no. Was Della held there and do you have any new clues to where she is?"

"Yes, that is an interesting insight, but no, that's not the information we have. Thank you, Doctor. Give me half an hour."

Exasperated, Sarah closed her phone and threw it against a nearby couch.

Several residents came and went as she waited for Seamus, but no one talked with her except Ricky. He found her wearing the vinyl floor thin and plopped down onto the couch, shaking his head.

"Good news, bad news," he said as he stretched out.

Sarah glared at him. He didn't respond. She finally gave in, taking a deep breath before replying, "Okay, good news first."

"Sarah, I don't know what it is with you and Rickelmann. I heard he dropped the complaint, but now you go and get involved in this mess. Rumor mill is spinning away like the millrace is in flood stage. He's heard you were on that raid, the one on the news, and he's not happy. Something about you being on sick leave or some such. The talk is he's not going to make any formal complaint about it, but you'll probably be hearing from him."

Yeah, thought Sarah, he's going to double his efforts to talk me into switching specialties. "So, any word on the guy I brought in?"

"Aren't you even worried 'bout Rickelmann?"

She shook her head and waved her hand in a show of indifference.

Ricky's eyes widened. "Mannn, what you got on him? Something we all could use?"

She furrowed her brow and looked crossly at him.

He held up his hands. "Okay, okay. 'Bout your guy. Word is he died once on the table but they got him back. They got the chest wound repaired and are working on the femur and thigh wound now. He's very critical and chief resident's giving him ten to twenty percent chance of making it. It'll be a miracle if he comes out of this with any brain function."

Sarah collapsed into the closest chair. "You call that good news, bad news?" Her mind raced with the implications of their John Doe coming out alive and brain damaged. He might as well be dead. Without him, how would they find Della? Provided he even knew where to look. Still, he was their one best chance. 'What ifs' filled her thoughts.

Ricky screwed up his face and bent his head to one side. "Well, maybe not... but whoever comes in saying bad news, worse news? I coulda just —"

There was a knock at the doorway and a nurse poked her head inside. "Ricky, they need you at the nurse's station, pronto."

Ricky jumped up and headed for the door. "Hey, Kendra Samuels was asking to see you. I guess you heard she was pregnant and miscarried. There were some complications, so she's still on the floor ... if you get a chance. See ya."

Sarah sat alone in the lounge, fighting back the tears prompted by her thoughts of never finding Della. She debated going to see Kendra and glanced at her watch. Only ten of Seamus' thirty minutes had elapsed. She had time. She walked over to the couch looking for her phone and found it wedged behind the cushion where Ricky had been sitting moments earlier.

Five minutes later, she was on the GYN floor and walking toward Kendra's room.

She stood at the doorway and knocked hesitantly. When there was no answer, she turned and took a step away from the door. But she couldn't walk away. She had first befriended Kendra as a med student in her ER rotation and had reached out to her when she saw her crying in the cafeteria only days earlier. The day she found Walter Johnson dead in the ATLS test room. The day that turned her life upside down.

Suddenly she realized the source of her apprehension. Kendra had to have been far enough along to suspect, maybe even know she was pregnant. Was Kendra's emotional distress that day a response to the news about Walter's death? Had she been involved with him? Had he been the father of the miscarried baby?

She turned back to the door and knocked more forcefully. Without waiting for a response, she opened the door and entered the room. Kendra lay on the bed, pale and withdrawn. A unit of red blood cells flowed through the IV line into her arm. She looked up at Sarah and barely acknowledged her presence. Sarah approached the woman and reached out to stroke her head. Kendra shrunk back, avoiding Sarah's touch, and tears began to flow.

"I-I'm so sorry," she sobbed. "I know you've tr-tried to h-help."

Sarah sat down next to the bed.

"I d-did something awful. I can't live with myself anymore."

Sarah wondered if Kendra had induced her own abortion.

She reached toward the young woman, but she flinched back again, unwilling to let Sarah comfort her. Kendra sniffed and blinked away her tears and straightened up in the bed.

"I f-found out I was pregnant a month ago. I knew it would really set back my education, but I figured the baby's father and I could work that out. When I told him, he went crazy. Insisted I get an abortion. He said it would ruin both our lives and he wanted nothing to do with the baby … or me." She started to cry again.

Sarah scrutinized the woman and Kendra's eyes met hers.

"Was Walter Johnson the father?"

Kendra's eyes widened and she went limp in the bed.

"How … how do …"

"Just a guess. What happened?"

Kendra turned away from Sarah, but continued. "I w-went to talk to him a couple more times and he kept pushing me away. That day … I knew he was helping at the ATLS course, and I went one more time to let him know I couldn't abort … that I wouldn't kill the baby inside me. H-he got angry and hit me."

She pealed back one shoulder of her hospital gown to reveal a large, healing bruise. Sarah noted the color pattern was consistent with the stated time of the injury.

"I stepped away from him as he tried to hit me again and grabbed a scalpel from the table. I only meant to threaten him, make him stop. I thought it still had the plastic guard on the blade. But just as I pointed it toward him, he lunged at me and … Oh, God … I am so sorry. I can't …" She buried her face in the pillow and cried.

Sarah sat back in the chair, stunned. She had not expected this.

"Kendra, I'm sorry." She reached out and put her hand on the woman's shoulder and this time she didn't resist. "I am so, so sorry."

At that moment, Sarah became aware of another presence in the room and turned toward the door. She was surprised to see Seamus' partner standing there. He nodded in recognition. Sarah stood slowly and walked over to him. He was holding a photo roster of the medical school class with Kendra's face circled.

"I was just coming to question her. I heard what she told you. A friend?"

Sarah shrugged and nodded subtly.

"Sorry."

She left the room, leaving Kendra and Detective Harris alone. She walked to a window overlooking Forest Park and stared into the distance. She tried to imagine what Kendra was feeling, to put the whole episode into perspective. To go from the elite in one of the best medical schools in the world to the possibility of jail on manslaughter in a fleeting moment was difficult to comprehend. As hard to understand was Kendra's decision to cover up the incident and flee. If only she had called for help at the time, she might have salvaged her life, her future.

Slowly, Sarah walked back to the elevators and returned to the ground floor where she returned to the ED as if drawn there magnetically, against her will. For the first time that week, she wanted nothing more than to go home, back to the cocoon of her apartment. Alone.

A clinical aide approached her as she entered the department.

"Doctor Wade, there's a police officer out by the nurse's station looking for you."

Sarah glanced at the woman, and replied, "Thanks."

She forced herself to compartmentalize Kendra's situation and resume focus on Della. A minute later, she found Seamus standing next to the nurses' station, talking on his cell phone. He flipped it closed as she neared and smiled, looking upbeat.

"Hi. That was my partner. Tells me you got a confession for us. What can't you do?"

Sarah frowned and continued walking toward the nearest exit. He followed.

"Sorry. Guess I just put my foot in my mouth, huh. You know her, I take it."

Once outside, she turned on him. "Yes, I know her. And what I can't do right now is find Della. Which, evidently, is something you guys can't seem to do either?"

She stood there glaring at him, arms crossed and her legs in an aggressive stance.

Seamus held up his hands. "Okay. And being a bitch doesn't help either. But actually, that's why I'm here. My car's over there. Let's go."

"Go? Go where?"

"We have a lead. We think we know where she is."

CHAPTER 39

Mitchell didn't like meetings in his home, but the circumstances gave him little option. He could not afford someone following him to the clandestine lab. He had only to look out his front window to know the media had tied him to the death of one of the militants. His nephew, it appeared, was a leader of the group killed early that morning in rural Missouri and various news teams had wasted no time camping in front of his office building and home, as well as his sister's home. His sister was a hurdle he had yet to jump. He had tried to contact her, only to find a continuously busy phone signal. She had always suspected his ties to the White Supremacy movement and blamed him for her son's involvement. Would she lead more than the media to his doorstep? Was she implicating him at that very moment to the authorities?

Edwards sat in the burgundy leather chair across from him, sipping a 30 year-old malt, on the rocks, in the Colonel's private study. His refuge, a room filled with leather and English antiques, its walls finely attired in rich Damask wallpaper. A room that clearly expressed his rise in scientific and social strata. Picture after picture on the walls showed him with a "Who's Who" of the scientific elite and political leaders. There were even a few shots with movie stars and rock idols. But those same pictures told another story. Not one face was black, Hispanic or Asian.

Mitchell took a sip of his own Scotch and contemplated the story Edwards had just related to him.

"So, there wasn't any other way? We couldn't have spared Bobby and the others?"

Edwards shook his head. "Sorry, Colonel. We discussed the hazards of the meth lab ruse before. I honestly didn't expect so many casualties from the ammonia, but they'd all been drinking and I doubt they understood the danger as they ran out into the cloud. As for Bobby, he was one of the last to die from what I've been able to learn. He was a hothead and too eager to do battle. I figured he might try to fight it out, but no one could have predicted his response with certainty. He posed too high a risk for the long-range plan ... as well as finger pointing to you. As it is, you can deny culpability now without risk of exposure."

Mitchell sat there silently. Edwards was right, no matter how much it hurt to learn of Bobby's fate. Nothing could tie him to the property or its contents. Sayer had arranged for its ownership through a series of dummy corporations with non-existent officers, useless mail drops, and phony streets for addresses. Investigating the land's ownership would be a maze of dead-ends that would consume hours and hours of manpower to run down. While he felt an unusual pleasure in taunting the authorities, he wondered if they had taken things too far.

"The news accounts have reported two federal agents as dead. What do you know about that?"

"Wasn't my doing. My guess is they got shot in the firefight. I took down the two agents outside the camp with Tasers® ... to give Sayer an edge in escaping. He wasn't real confident about it."

Mitchell nodded. So, not only had Bobby resisted, he and his band had killed two agents. Mitchell was lucky his nephew no longer posed a threat.

"That brings me to two loose ends that need clipping."

"Yes, Sir. I'm already working on the first one. I do have a 'go' on that, right?"

"Yes, his work at the university is basically done. About Sayer, I want it quick and as painless as possible. He's responsible for our being where we are, and I ..."

"I understand. That'll be easy, under the circumstances."

"Good. But look, don't make any moves you don't have to. I'm hearing rumors around the medical center that he's as good as brain dead. We can't afford for you to risk exposure unnecessarily."

"Yes, Sir." Edwards smiled and took another sip of his drink.

"And you have the details on the other problem, right?"

"Yes, Sir."

"He's a good man and a good scientist. I hate to have to do this, but ..."

"I understand, Colonel. He will go quickly as well."

Mitchell nodded solemnly. He didn't know what the man savored more, the premium Scotch or the tasks ahead of him.

Sarah sat in the passenger seat watching Seamus as he drove with lights and siren to clear the city roads between him and I-55 south. Once he hit the interstate, the siren stopped but his speed picked up.

"Okay, so what's this hot lead? And where are we headed?"

His eyes remained on the road, focused as he sped past yielding traffic at close to ninety miles per hour.

"We've been trying to find out who our John Doe is. So far, no hits on his fingerprints and no leads from his picture on the news. It's like he doesn't exist, at least on paper. The other curious thing is that he was wearing jeans and a polo, while the others were all decked out like soldier wanna-bes in the field. Makes us wonder if this guy was just in the wrong place at the wrong time. After all, he was <u>outside</u> the fence."

He glanced her way.

"Eyes back on the road," she said with insistence. "I've seen too much road kill in my short years in the ED."

"So, with no leads on him, we took a look at the property. Our first check found the land registered to a phony corporation with a bunch of fake names as officers. One name, however, came up on another property. We ran it and found another bogus company, so that got us thinking. If Della had been at the one camp, maybe she's at the other place now."

He turned toward her and smiled. She pointed back to the road, noticing they were already well into the next county.

"To answer question two, the property is just west of Desloge and there's a modest ranch home there, situated well off the road in the middle of a secluded ten acre plot. A perfect spot to hold someone."

Sarah watched the countryside as a blur passing by. She didn't want to get her hope up, to race to this house only to find it empty. Yet, if Della was there … if she was injured … time would be critical.

"Can't you go any faster?" she asked.

Seamus shook his head. "I could but I won't. This is fast enough."

At their current speed, they would reach Desloge in less than fifteen minutes. Sarah sat back in her seat but couldn't ignore the anticipation.

CHAPTER 40

After leaving the city limits of Desloge, heading west on State Route 8, Seamus turned off the lights and eased back to the speed limit. He picked up his cell phone, pressed the redial key, and simply said, "We're here." A mile later, two other cars filed in behind him, and a half-mile after that, two black vans pulled out in front and led the procession.

"FBI hostage rescue, the A-I-C, and county sheriff ... in case you're wondering who all these cars hold. The place is off Germania Road, so once we turn onto it, we'll pick up speed and storm the property."

Sarah furrowed her brow and cocked her head in concern. She noticed Seamus looking at her.

"And no, we don't think we're putting Della or anyone else at risk."

"Why not?" she replied. "Don't you think a show of force like that might result in their killing her? Look how they reacted at the other place."

"Exactly. We think they were all there. We moved a spotter onto the property an hour ago, and there's no activity there."

"Empty?"

"Well, maybe, but probably not. The FBI thinks if she's there, she's by herself, probably shackled."

The cars made their turn onto Germania Road and increased speed. Two minutes later, they turned onto a private drive and flooded onto the land, surrounding the small ranch home. There were no cars. Shutters enclosed all the windows, but a small air conditioning compressor hummed with use.

Men spilled from the vehicles and used them as shields. HRT members set their sights on designated targets – doors and windows where weapons could be used against them.

Sarah thought it appeared like a scene from a movie, but she was in the middle of it ... and unsure what to do. The typical movie scene would have Seamus telling her to stay low and then someone with a bullhorn would address the building. It seemed corny at the thought of it.

Seamus glanced at her. "Get out quickly and get behind the car … and stay low." He opened his door and knelt behind it, facing and watching the building through the glass. She did as told, but raised her head high enough to peer over the trunk of the sedan. She saw no sign of activity, nothing to indicate resistance.

The FBI agent-in-charge raised a bullhorn and announced their presence.

"This is the FBI. You have two minutes to open the door and come out with your hands where we can see them."

For Sarah the wait seemed interminable. Yet, nothing happened. There seemed to be no one home.

Again, the A-I-C raised his bullhorn and said, "This is the FBI. Open the door and come out or we're coming in."

After a brief interval, he nodded and the HRT squad cautiously advanced on the house. As they neared the front door, the door lock suddenly clicked and half a dozen guns aimed toward the slowly opening entry. A moment later, an elderly woman, in her mid-eighties by Sarah's estimate, appeared in the doorway, her hands on an aluminum walker outfitted with tennis balls on the front legs and a basket adorned with festive ribbons attached to the main frame.

"Oh my!" she gasped, her eyes flaring open. Sarah worried she would have an acute MI or stroke on the spot. The old lady's trembling was evident by the rattling of the beribboned basket. For a moment, she seemed about to collapse but remained standing and began to fumble with her right ear. *A hearing aid*, thought Sarah. *No wonder it took so long.*

The men lowered their weapons but remained alert. The A-I-C stepped forward.

"Ma'am, can you hear me okay?"

The woman fumbled with her left ear and then said, "Okay, I can hear you now." Her countenance turned angry and flushed. "What do you SOBs want, comin' onto ma property like storm troopers, scaring the wits outta me. Now, get off'n my land!" She raised her fist and shook it at them all.

"Ma'am, sorry to have scared you, but we have a warrant to

search this property. Is there anyone else in the house?"

"Naw, jus' me. Now get!" She slowly turned to go back inside.

The A-I-C cautiously approached the door.

"Ma'am, I'm sorry, but we need to check the house." He held out the warrant toward her.

She said nothing but kept inching forward, waving her hand above her head and leaving the door open. Several men nudged the door open and entered the building. The others remained outside while Seamus, Sarah and the deputies relaxed by their cars.

Seamus looked at Sarah and frowned. "Great. I can see the news now. First, we gun down a bunch of white supremacists without mercy, and now we raid little old ladies' homes." He shook his head.

The SWAT members emerged from the house and proclaimed it clear.

Sarah leaned against the car, deflated. She had known better than to get overconfident, but she couldn't avoid hoping that Della was there, alive and well. "What next?" she asked Seamus.

He holstered his gun and leaned back next to her.

"They'll question the old lady and inspect the house for any evidence that Della might have been here. If all that's a bust, then our lead is nothing more than a dead end and we keep plugging away."

Sarah stared at the gravel of the drive and kicked a stone. She didn't want this to be a dead end. She wanted to find her best friend, end this week of torture, and file it away as something to tell the grandkids about in her golden years.

She stood up and walked a short distance away from the cars. She turned back toward Seamus, but he was already in a discussion with the FBI agents. She felt superfluous, a non-speaking extra on the movie set. Quietly, she wandered along the gravel back toward the main road. *The place certainly is secluded,* she thought, *just as Seamus described.* About a hundred yards away from the house, she noticed what looked like three or four discarded Christmas trees piled next to the driveway. They seemed out of order, as there were no other brush piles and the rest of the surrounding space appeared clean and maintained. And they appeared as if illuminated by a single ray of light reaching through the trees. *Strange*, she thought.

She wandered over to the pile and noted gravel underneath. She walked around the trees and saw that a branch of the driveway passed beyond the pile and it looked as if some of the gravel had been overturned recently, as if a car or truck had used the path since the last rain. Curious, she started walking down the lane until she realized she could no longer see the main drive or the house. A dense stand of scrub cedars filled the understory of the oak trees. Off to her right she saw power lines extending through the woods in the direction she walked.

Sarah stopped, uncertain about continuing alone. If she encountered anyone, she was unarmed. And worse, as Shay had reminded her, she was a black woman alone in an area known for its racial prejudices. She took a few steps back in the direction of Seamus and the rescue team, but stopped. She didn't want to drag them there on another wild goose chase. She decided to check out the area and run like a greyhound if anyone showed up.

A short distance ahead, the drive curved to the left and the cedars crowded its berm, making it hard to see beyond. She approached carefully, her senses alert to potential trouble. She could hear the hum of an air conditioner, but could not determine if that was up ahead or from the house the agents were already searching. Then she got the faint whiff of a pleasant smell. *Baking bread?* she wondered. As she gazed beyond the cedar barrier, she saw another small house, almost a duplicate of the house she'd just left. She crept along and through the cedars as they skirted around the building, using them to conceal her presence, taking care as to where she stepped.

She could see no vehicles and there was only one small outbuilding large enough to hold one. Its door was far enough open, however, for her to see that it was empty. Like at the other home, there was no sign of activity here.

She edged up to the side of the house and tried to catch a furtive glance inside the nearest window. The glass was painted black on the outside. She resisted the urge to scratch away some of the paint, afraid even the slightest noise would call attention to her presence. She moved to the next window to find that it, too, was painted. She couldn't see in, but then, no one could look out to see her either. She approached the rear door and the smell of bread became more prominent.

Without considering the consequences, she took a deep breath, exhaled sharply and knocked boldly on the door. Quickly, she stepped to one side and waited for a response. Nothing. She knocked again. "Anyone home?" she shouted. Nothing.

She fiddled with the doorknob and found the door unlocked. She turned the knob, but stopped. *What in the world am I doing?* she questioned. *I'm about to get shot.* But that bit of logic evaporated as fast as it entered her mind and she opened the door.

"Anyone home?"

No answer.

She entered the house and found herself in a small but functional kitchen. Fresh bread sat on a cooling rack on the counter. She walked to the oven; the door still felt warm. She half expected to find three bowls of porridge on the table, but realized with a brief mental chuckle that she would never fit the description of Goldilocks. With assurance that she was alone, she decided to explore the house for evidence of Della. If Seamus' lead was a good one, maybe they just had the wrong house.

Off the kitchen was a small eating area. Not large enough to call it a room, it formed part of an el with the living room. She edged to the corner between the two living spaces and peered around it into the larger portion of the living room, which was also empty; its lights turned off save one small lamp that compensated for the blackened windows. Sarah sneaked into the hallway and moved slowly from door to door, making sure she didn't touch anything with her hands. A small bath, lit only by a plug-in nightlight, held a woman's toiletries on its counters and shelves. The next room, a small bedroom, was dark but she could see the outline of a single twin bed and an undersized chest. She wished she had a penlight in her pocket. A second room appeared modestly furnished like the first bedroom, but the chest next to the doorway held a stack of neatly folded clothes. Sarah felt the material and inched closer to look at them in the wane light from the bath. *Cotton scrubs.*

Just beyond this door, the hall jutted left and a subdued light emerged from the room at the end of the hall. Sarah could see a small mirror on the wall, and in it, she saw only the reflection of another twin bed. Nearing the door, she heard a faint whimpering.

Her nerves on edge and her heart pounding, she gathered the courage to enter the room and eased through the doorway. A shriek erupted from the corner behind the bed and she jerked toward the scream, prepared to fend off an attacker. Instead, she found Della huddled into the corner, shaking uncontrollably, her arms covering her head. She rushed to her friend's side and, sitting down, pulled Della's head and shoulders onto her lap, stroking her hair.

"Della, baby. We found you. You're safe now. You're safe."

CHAPTER 41

Seamus paced along the plaza outside the television station waiting for Sarah. He'd been surprised when informed that Della, after medical clearance by her doctor, had returned to work after just one week at home. He had not been surprised to hear that she'd gone into a tirade to insist on returning and had threatened leaving the station if they did not allow her to return. He could sympathize. Being laid up following his gunshot wound to the thigh had been torture. Focusing his mind on work would have been a blessing then.

He gazed into the large picture windows that separated the outdoor space from the main studio and watched the current production being televised inside. He often watched the early morning news show that made repeated use of the plaza as an outdoor stage, but the day's broadcast had ended several hours earlier and the current project appeared to be that of a show for airing later in the day. A clock in the window displayed 10:15 in large numbers.

He walked up to the main door and approached the security guard, pulling out his credentials.

"Good morning. I'm Sergeant O'Connor of the –"

The guard, a black man in his mid-forties with lightly graying short-cropped hair and bushy dark mustache that accentuated his large smile, interrupted, "Yes, Sir. Recognized you soon as you stepped into view. An honor to meet you, Sir. Thank you for bringing Mizz Della back to us." He held out his hand.

Seamus returned the smile and the handshake. "Thanks. I'm supposed to meet a Doctor Sarah Wade here and together we're supposed to see Ms. Winston. I haven't seen Doctor Wade yet, but is Ms. Winston available?"

"I know Doctor Sarah. Wonderful girl. Even took the time to show my oldest girl, Latecia, 'round the medical center when she expressed interest in the medical field. Let's see ..." He moved the mouse on his computer, checked the monitor, and looked up at Seamus. "She signed in around nine-thirty and ..." He looked at the screen again. "They checked out together a few minutes before ten. Umm, there's a note here you might show up and they'd contact you by cell phone."

"Does it say where they went?" Seamus was a bit perturbed at wasting his time on the plaza without getting a call.

"No, Sir. But a production crew went with them, so it must be something for Ms. Winston's show."

"Thanks for your help," replied Seamus. He turned and left the building, hurrying off the plaza onto 11th Street toward his car parked at the Bureau. He retrieved his cell phone from his pocket and sheepishly discovered he'd neglected to turn it on as he rushed out of the house earlier. There was a message in his voice mail.

"Shay, it's Sarah. Sorry we couldn't wait for you, but Della has a tight schedule this morning. We're heading for the medical center. She's interviewing Doctor Mitchell Hudson about his genetics research and a recent breakthrough drug for Alzheimer's. His lab is …"

Seamus absorbed the directions on the run and ten minutes later, he parked near the medical school and rushed toward the building at 660 South Euclid. He was to go to the Department of Molecular Biology and Pharmacology and ask for Doctor Hudson's office. Yet, as he emerged from the elevator onto the right floor, there was no need to ask. A crowd of people filled the far end of the hall and Sarah stood among them.

He walked up behind her and said, "Hi, got your message."

She turned and looked at him with a pained face. "Shay, I need to apologize for my –"

"Wow. Another apology. They keep stacking up." He grinned. She furrowed her brow. "Okay. For what? For running off like that? For not waiting for me?" He waved his hand in dismissal. "I gotta admit you scared me half to death. One moment you were next to me, the next you were gone and I thought you'd somehow been snatched, too … right in front of us. When you called on your cell phone to say you'd found Della, I didn't know which made me happier, that you were okay or that you'd found her. Of course, a lot of the HRT guys were mighty chagrined that you'd showed them up … again."

She shook her head. "No, that's not what I mean. I ... The other day in the ED, after I'd been discharged, I ..."

He gave her a sly grin. "Oh that. Hey, head injuries can do all kinds of things to a person, right? I just figured ... well, that's all it was, right? The head injury?"

Sarah smiled. "Thanks ... for letting me off so easily."

Seamus gave her a subtle nod. Nothing more needed saying. It could never have worked anyway. White Irish and Afro-American.

Sarah turned and nodded her head toward an office. "Della's inside with Doctor Hudson doing an interview. His lab has just finished development of a major breakthrough in treating Alzheimer's disease. She has a special interest in this, you know, with Aunt Beatrice being diagnosed with it recently."

Seamus leaned around Sarah and a solidly built, young black male he surmised was Della's new bodyguard. The camera crew had to record from the doorway due to the cramped office space, and blocked most of his view. Still, he garnered a glimpse of both Della and the doctor. She seemed more subdued than he remembered from the handful of her shows he had actually seen. Was it the solemnity of the current situation, the seriousness of Alzheimer's and its consequences on both the patient and the family? Or had her ordeal etched its effect on her personality?

Doctor Hudson was speaking. "... of course, no one person can claim credit for this breakthrough. It has always been and remains a team effort. My main assistant, Roger Coulter, our medical geneticist, has been indispensable and if it weren't for our biochemist, Eric Deamus, who headed up the drug's development, we wouldn't have anything to announce."

"Might we talk with these two men?" asked Della.

"I'm sorry, Roger is away from the lab right now, and Eric is off on a much deserved week's vacation. We don't expect to hear from him until his return."

Seamus felt a tug on his shirt and turned to find Sarah trying to pull him away from the group. He followed a short distance down the hall, out of earshot of the crowd.

"Hey, have you heard anything about our guy from the raid?

I tried to check on him earlier, but couldn't get anywhere near his room. I know he survived the surgery. What's the deal?" she asked.

"Feds have him under tight wraps … in case he wakes up. Last I heard, the trauma docs think he's gonna end up on garden row, a permanent veggie."

Sarah frowned at his comment. "That's 'persistent vegetative state' not a permanent veggie."

Seamus shook his head. "Whatever. The guy doesn't deserve sanitizing by the politically correct crowd. If he had anything to do with the activities of that militia group, he's no better than manure for the garden."

"And if he didn't? What if he was just at the wrong place at the wrong time?"

Seamus rolled his eyes. "C'mon, Sarah. Out there in the middle of nothing? What're the odds of that? He's got to be one of the guilty ones."

Sarah looked sternly at him. "But we don't know –"

A commotion from the doctor's office interrupted her comment. The cameraman had backed into the hallway and videoed Della and the doctor leaving his office. After several steps, he stopped recording and backed away to let them through. They approached Sarah and Seamus.

Doctor Hudson stopped as they reached them, scrutinized Seamus, and then smiled. He held out his hand. "I've already had the pleasure of meeting Doctor Wade here. You must be the detective. I'm Mitchell Hudson."

Seamus returned the man's firm handshake. "Yes, Sir. Sergeant Seamus O'Connor. Pleased to meet you."

"I've been watching the news. Sounds like you two have been on quite an adventure this past week. Murders, kidnappings, terrorists. Never a dull moment, eh?"

Seamus nodded and glanced at Sarah.

"Oh." Her gaze bounced between him, Doctor Hudson and Della. "Della, this is Seamus. Now I think everybody has been properly introduced."

Della reached past Doctor Hudson and hugged Seamus.

"Thank you ... for everything you did to help me." Tears welled up in her eyes.

Doctor Hudson smiled and laughed gently. "I take it this is an overdue greeting. I'm honored to be witness to the occasion."

To the doctor, Seamus replied, "Everything happened so fast the other day, we never actually met." To Della, he said, "Ms. Winston, you're welcome."

"Please, just Della. All my friends ... and rescuers ... call me Della." She wiped at the tears on her cheeks.

Doctor Hudson cleared his throat. "We were just about to take a quick tour of the lab. Please join us."

Seamus and Sarah fell in step behind the doctor and Della, listening as the researcher spoke about their work and the upcoming clinical trials of the new drug. He was not as forthcoming with information on who was being awarded the license for the drug but shook off that question with a witty reply that made Seamus comfortable with the man. He was in no way pretentious and Seamus saw a man of integrity whose desire was to help society cope with a disease that would increase in prevalence as the aging 'Baby Boomer' generation advanced in years. By the time the tour was over, he had decided he liked the man.

As they gathered near the entrance to the lab and exchanged 'thank yous' and 'good-byes,' the doctor shifted to a different topic.

"Ms. Winston, I understand your brother is having a black tie fundraiser this evening at the Ritz Carlton. Will you be attending?"

"I will be there. And you?"

"In all honesty, I was not invited." As Della began to protest, he raised his hand and stopped her. "Please, I'm not that politically motivated, so I don't feel at all snubbed. I do, however, want to make a contribution." He reached into his jacket's inner pocket and pulled out an envelope. "Please give this to him this evening ... a small donation to his race." He handed her the envelope. "And if he's curious about the card itself, it was handmade by an artist in Clarksville whom I admire. Besides the exquisite artwork, the scents he uses are unique and quite pleasant as well."

Della tucked the envelope in her bag. "On my brother's behalf, I thank you."

After the elevator door closed, Mitchell heard a laugh behind him and turned to greet Edwards as he emerged from the lab. Without a word, they walked to Mitchell's office and closed the door.

"A small donation to his race. That was rich," Edwards stated. "Do you think he'll take the bait and sniff the card?"

Mitchell leaned back in his chair and folded his hands together. "I have no doubt. The scent will be unmistakable when he opens the envelope. But whether he does or not isn't important. Even though inhalation would be the fastest route, the viral particles will get all over his hands and eventually into his body. And if he opens it at the dinner tonight, he'll pass those particles to everyone who shakes his hand afterwards. This isn't quite how I had first envisioned using Ms. Winston, but under the circumstances, let Plan B and our little clinical trial begin."

CHAPTER 42

Sarah pulled Seamus aside as they exited the elevator on the ground floor. She watched as Della gave instructions to her crew and waited by the front doors. Assured that Della was waiting for her, she eased up next to Seamus.

"I bet you look great in a tux. Want to come to the dinner tonight? Della's invited us both as her guests."

Seamus looked at her with a quizzical look. "Is this the head injury talking, or something else?"

Sarah hesitated, unsure of her real motive. She had, after all, kinda sorta invited herself to the dinner. Della had extended the invitation to Seamus, with DeWayne's blessing. Della hinted that her brother wanted to honor publicly those who had successfully recovered his sister. Sarah didn't know which would scare Seamus off faster: being honored publicly or her coming on to him again. But here she was coming on to him again.

"It's one of the many ways Della wants to thank you. Regardless of what the news is reporting, the FBI didn't find her, you did. Your footwork found the ambassador's killer and opened the door for the FBI to raid that compound and then find the other house. Don't think for one minute that Della and DeWayne give credit to the feds."

"Sounds like you've made amends with DeWayne. Still hate him?"

Sarah's opinions of DeWayne Winston had altered since their talk. She recognized the change, but it would take time to heal those old wounds. Still, Seamus' asking the question perturbed her.

"Don't change the subject. Do you want to come or not?" Her voice sounded cross.

"I don't do tuxes."

"Chicken."

"Seriously. I don't own one and I can't rent one by tonight."

She reached into her bag, pulled out a business card, and handed it to Seamus. "Donatello's Formal Wear. Della's already made arrangements and they can have everything ready by five if you stop by for sizing before two."

"I've got to check in with the Bureau. We've got debriefings slated for the afternoon. I don't know –"

"Chicken." She crossed her arms and cocked one hip to the side. "You know … I can arrange for a phone call that could postpone those meetings a day."

Seamus sighed and his shoulders sagged. She knew he was close to giving in.

"Besides, you've never seen me in formal evening attire. Might make the head injury take a back seat."

Why did she just say that? She wanted to slap the back of her head, but instead found herself slipping in closer to him. He didn't back off … but he didn't answer right away either.

"Okay. If I can make it, I'll be there. What time at the Ritz?"

"Drinks start at six-thirty. Dinner at seven-thirty."

"Okay, like I said. I'll be there if I can. I've got to check in with the lieutenant first. And I've got a bunch of phone calls to make, a report to write. My job doesn't stop for parties."

She smiled and kissed him on the cheek. "See you at the Ritz."

Seamus returned to his office to find his desk buried. Requests for interviews, phone messages, folders on open cases, a note to call the lieutenant ASAP about meeting with the mayor. Leafing through the pile, he attempted to prioritize the calls. Obviously, those calls from his superiors had top billing.

He glanced at his watch and noted the time. He hustled to clear his desk. He scrutinized a large manila envelope addressed to him and marked "Urgent," decided he didn't have time to deal with a new problem, and cleared it and the other mail to a pile at one corner of the desk, to be dealt with later. He decided to tackle the phone messages first, and started by calling the lieutenant. With a little concentrated effort, he could get to Donatello's by two.

Mitchell felt uneasy. He sat in his office reviewing a new twist in the negotiations for licensing their drug. A new suitor with money and good FDA contacts, but a start-up venture with no track record. Did they have what it takes to move their drug through the clinical trials and into the market?

Yet, his unease was more deep-rooted than his uncertainty about a company's ability to launch a drug. He'd lost two good men, one from each side of his double life. One lay in the hospital, reportedly brain damaged and unlikely ever to function productively again. The other lay at home waiting for someone to discover his deteriorating body. His role in the latter situation gnawed at him. He had been an affable co-worker, a superb scientist, a man who would have been able to greatly contribute to society. But self-preservation was stronger than the regrets he felt at ending that life.

Mitchell stood up from his desk and began to pace. He didn't want to be responsible for ordering the death of another friend. He didn't want Edwards to place himself at needless risk, but he didn't have enough contacts in the clinical world of Barnes Hospital to get the straight scoop on Chad, who apparently was under close guard. Edwards had insisted on penetrating that guard and learning the truth about Chad. And that persistence worried Mitchell.

At ten 'til five Seamus walked out of Donatello's Formal Wear with his tux and all of the accessories. By five forty-five, he had returned home, squelched his hunger with an apple, shaved, and showered. By six ten, he scrutinized his reflection in the mirror and saw that he did indeed cut one fine figure in a tux. He couldn't resist a few James Bond-like moves in front of the mirror as his confidence level rose. And he knew who his "Bond girl" would be this night. Halle Berry had nothing over Sarah Wade.

Unlike the secret agent, however, he had no idea where to hide his service weapon. His usual belt holster wouldn't work. He had an old shoulder holster, but the bulge of the piece was much too evident - and uncomfortable - in the well-fitted jacket. As much as he disliked the idea, he decided to go weaponless and locked his gun away in his bedroom.

Feeling jaunty, he sauntered out the front door of his house and walked toward his car. As he crossed the curb into the street, his cell phone rang.

"O'Connor? Delaney. They took the breathing tube out of our John Doe an hour ago. Looks like he's waking up. How fast can you get here?"

"Ten minutes," Seamus replied without hesitation. Only after he hung up did he think twice about showing up at the hospital dressed as he was. But duty called, and if all went well, he could still get to the Ritz before dinner.

Fifteen minutes later, he emerged from the elevator and headed for John Doe's room. Nurses and aids scurried about the nurses' station but at the end of the hall, Seamus noted the guard was gone. A lone janitor worked the hallway with his dust broom. He hurried to the room, upset at the absence of the guard and hoping the man was inside the room. As he passed the housekeeper, the man's appearance registered subtly as being out of character for the job. Not that Seamus held some strict stereotype for such workers. Their job was a vital one in the hospital. But this guy appeared too military, too well educated for the job.

Seamus brushed aside that fleeting impression and entered the room. Delaney, the FBI A-I-C, was there encouraging John Doe to talk. He turned to acknowledge Seamus with a nod.

"He seems to be aware of his surroundings, but he's not talking yet."

"Where's the uniform?" asked Seamus, referring to the police guard.

"Told him he could grab something to eat while I was here."

Seamus walked over to the man lying in the bed. He looked much improved from Seamus' first encounter with him at the compound. Seamus caught Delaney staring at him. The agent grinned.

"I see you came casual. What's with the maître d' getup?"

"Formal fundraising dinner," Seamus replied, trying to pass off the question.

"Wait a minute. You didn't get conned into going to that

thing the Winston campaign is throwing tonight, did you?"

Seamus blushed, but buckled at the comment about getting conned. There were reasons he and tuxedos didn't mix. Had Sarah lured him into something he'd rather avoid?

"Yeah, that's it. I turned down that invite soon as I heard he was going to use the event to promote some bogus honors on all of us. Just a campaign ploy in my opinion."

Seamus was about to respond when John Doe opened his eyes. He looked first at the FBI agent, but quickly fixed his stare on Seamus. After a moment, he moved his lips but nothing audible came out.

"I think he recognizes you," Delaney said.

"How? He was only conscious for a moment at the compound."

"Talk to him."

Seamus took a deep breath, unsure where to start.

"I'm Sergeant O'Connor. Do you recognize me?"

The man blinked and moved his lips again, but no words emerged.

"He's still heavily sedated. I'm gonna go see if the doctor can give him something to help him wake up." Delaney turned and left the room.

Seamus bent down closer to the man and enunciated his words carefully. "I was at the compound and found you outside the fence …" He continued to relate what had happened to the semi-conscious man.

He heard the door open behind him and, expecting Delaney, turned to say something. He was greeted by the major league swing of a broom handle striking the side of his head. He reeled from the blow and sank to his knees, confused and fighting to remain conscious. He glanced up to see the janitor wheeling a crash cart to John Doe's bedside. The man grabbed the defibrillator paddles and pressed the 'Charge' button. Seamus knew that a full charge delivered to John Doe would likely flat-line his heart. He instinctively reached for his gun, only to remember he'd left it at home. He struggled to his knees but the whirling worsened. As the man moved the paddles toward John

Doe's chest, Seamus pushed through the dizziness and rose to his feet, lunging at the man. He caught the man as he pressed the discharge button and one paddle hit the nearby bedrail. A shower of sparks flashed up from the bed and the assailant jumped back from the electrical shock.

Seamus grabbed him from behind and tried to take him to the floor, but the man was stronger than Seamus and threw him off faster than Seamus could think of a follow-up move. The man edged behind him and put him into a chokehold. Seamus began pounding at the man's rib cage with his elbow, but the man barely flinched with each blow. He remembered a self-defense move from the academy and raised his right foot toward his butt. With all his might, he kicked down on the man's kneecap and the man yelled in pain as he released his hold on Seamus. He backed away from the man, but not before receiving a solid punch to his left ribs.

Seamus mentally regrouped and worked to recall his basic martial arts training, skills he'd never used since graduating from the academy. He faced the man, who grinned as he moved toward Seamus in a traditional boxing stance. The man threw a right jab that caught Seamus above the left eye. Seamus managed to parry the next jab, but his own punch was ineffective. His opponent pummeled him in the abdomen with a series of jabs that felt like repeated violent Heimlich maneuvers and Seamus staggered backward until he hit the wall. He felt the nurse call-button cable behind his hand and yanked it free from the wall, knowing that would trigger a call at the nurses' station.

The man caught Seamus against the wall and landed another strong jab in his left ribs. Seamus felt a sharp, tearing pain in his side. Fighting to protect his rib cage, he took the offensive and pushed off the wall toward the man, head butting the man in the nose and jaw. Blood gushed from the man's nostrils, but he simply wiped at it with the back of his hand and charged Seamus, who managed to side step the attack and elude the man. The man spun and launched another kick that knocked Seamus to the ground.

The man turned his attention to John Doe, again picking up

the paddles to deliver a fatal shock. Seamus felt a moment of reprieve when the machine failed to work. Had the earlier contact with the bed shorted out the defibrillator?

As Seamus struggled to his feet, the man picked up a pillow and forced it onto John Doe's face. He stumbled toward the man who simply turned and shoved Seamus backward onto the floor, before resuming his attempt to suffocate John Doe. Seamus needed an advantage and saw it on floor next to him. As he regained his footing, he picked up the broom and swung it as hard as he could, aiming not at the man's head but at his throat. He caught the man in the larynx and heard the crunch of wood hitting weaker bone. The man released his hold on the pillow and clutched at his throat. Seamus stood between the man and door, prepared to swing again, when the man produced a gun.

"Seamus! Duck!"

Without hesitation, Seamus dropped to the floor. A shot rang out behind him and the man crumpled to the floor in front of Seamus. The man made one last attempt to aim the gun, but a second shot rang out and the man moved no more.

A young doctor rushed into the room ahead of Delaney and pulled the pillow from John Doe's face. He took his stethoscope and listened to his chest. A sigh of relief escaped his lips. "He's still breathing. Lungs sound okay." He then moved to the man on floor. After a quick check for any vital sign of life, he stood, glanced at the policemen and said, "He's gone."

Delaney nodded as the doctor rejoined him at John Doe's bedside. "Can we wake him up some? He was trying to talk earlier."

"I don't know if that'd be wise. We need –"

"Doc, this guy knows something that was worth the risk of killing him here in the hospital. If there are other lives at stake, we need to know now, not later."

Seamus, still breathing heavily, watched the young doctor nod at a nurse who had followed them into the room. She administered a medication through a port in the IV line. Seamus slowly rose to his feet, stepped over the killer's body, and approached the foot of the bed. Within a minute, John Doe appeared more alert. He focused on Seamus and moved his lips. A hoarse whisper emerged.

Seamus moved to the other side of the bed and bent over the rail, wincing at the pain in his side. The man's gaze followed him.

"Don't … let me … go back." He took a breath. "Destiny Church … need pastor."

"Go back where?" Seamus asked.

The man subtly shook his head. "Don't … let me …" He faded briefly, and then seemed to regain strength.

"Why did this man try to kill you?"

John Doe looked confused. Delaney repeated the question.

"Bio … logical … weapon." He took another breath. "Virus … to kill … dark skinned …" He paused and his eyes glazed over. Seamus nudged him gently and after another deep breath, he continued. "Test phase … Winston … senator."

Delaney moved closer. "How?"

John Doe shook his head.

"Who?" Seamus asked.

"Hudson," John Doe replied.

The reality of the situation surged through Seamus along with the adrenaline that brought new strength to his battered body. He raced from the room, Delaney following him into the hall.

"What is it?" Delaney yelled after Seamus as he raced down the hall.

CHAPTER 43

Seamus took no time to wait on an elevator and bolted down the nearest stairwell, each step and jump producing a jabbing pain in his side. His body cried out to stop for a breather but he pushed through the pain and made it to the ground floor where he had to regroup for directions. Once he had his bearings, he ran through the Emergency Department toward his car parked outside the ambulance entry. Curious onlookers stared at the formally attired but battered man who dodged gurneys and staff like a madman trying to escape a 96-hour involuntary commitment. As he emerged from the E.D., an ambulance screeched to a stop to avoid hitting him. He jumped back and slapped the front end of the rig as he passed it. He pressed the unlock button on his key and pulled the door open. A minute later, he pulled into traffic with lights flashing and siren screaming.

On a good day, the drive between the Barnes-Jewish Hospital complex and Clayton, the county seat, took five or six minutes if you got lucky with the lights. But the after-work traffic was heavy and vehicles yielded slowly, as each driver was able, to his emergent wail. He glanced at the clock on the dash, his anxiety mounting as each minute flashed. Stuck behind vehicles at a light, he pounded on his horn, adding to the cacophony of noise emanating from his car.

Moving nowhere quickly, he retrieved his cell phone from his inner jacket pocket and fumbled with it until Sarah's number displayed on the screen. He pressed the "talk" button and waited, but her voice mail answered immediately. It was off or, as he had learned with her, the battery was dead. He flipped the phone closed and laid on the horn again.

As the light turned green, the cars in front of him moved through the intersection and veered to the right to clear his way. With an open field, Seamus gunned the accelerator and launched forward. Traffic ahead of him finally thinned out as he passed Washington University and opened a path for him. He rocketed along Forest Park Parkway and just past the Ritz-Carlton he veered right onto the Carondelet exit and into the circle in front of the hotel. He pulled into the drive at the front of the building and screeched to a halt. Jumping from the car, its lights still flashing, he could hear additional sirens approaching from several directions.

Seamus ran into the lobby and grabbed a bellman.

"The Winston dinner, where is it?"

"Uh, the Ballroom." He pointed toward the meeting room wing of the hotel. "This floor, down that hall and to the right."

"I don't have time. Show me!"

A manager rushed up, concern all over his face. "Sir, please. Calm down. We –"

Seamus interrupted. "Police. Call EMS to the ballroom and clear your staff as quickly as you can from there. The Winston's are in danger." He again collared the young bellman. "Now run. Lead me to the ballroom."

Out of the corner of his eye, Seamus saw the lights of a second and then a third police car through the lobby doors. The manager, now aware of the increasing police presence, ran to the front desk and picked up the phone. Seamus took no time to eavesdrop on the call, and pushed the bellman into motion, running toward the ballroom.

A large crowd of people mingled in the ballroom lobby and a pre-function area strewn with tables for drinks and appetizers. He scanned the room but could not see the Winstons or Sarah. One of the politician's security men approached, the stern look on his face one of being prepared to throw out the rowdy interloper in the damaged tux.

Seamus flashed his badge. "Clear this area! Now!"

"Wait a minute. You can't come barging in here and –"

Seamus neared the man and lowered his voice to avoid others overhearing. "Senator Winston is the target of a terrorist plot, here, tonight. Start clearing this area. Where is he?"

The security man pointed toward the ballroom. "They've already moved into the main room to be seated for dinner."

Seamus ran into the main ballroom and searched out the head table. DeWayne Winston stood at the center of the raised platform, behind the head table and just to the right of a podium. Della and Sarah were at the end of the platform and walking toward the Senator.

"Sarah! Della! Stop! Don't ..."

The hum of hundreds of voices drowned out his cry. He hurried toward the dais dodging guests and flashing his badge repeatedly. Before he could reach the stage, Winston had given Della a brotherly kiss and she handed him an envelope.

"Senator! Don't open –"

He was too late. By the time he jumped onto the platform, the Senator had opened the envelope, smiled at the check he had pulled from inside the card, and took a deep whiff of the card's interior. Della took the card and held it to her nose. Seamus ran along, behind the main table and grabbed Sarah around the waist, pulling her away from the group to DeWayne Winston's startled, then angry look. Standing between the Winstons and Sarah, he put out his arms, as if breaking up a fight, to keep them apart. In unison, they started to voice their objections, but a growing commotion near the room's entrance caught their attention and their protests dwindled.

Seamus faced the women and held up his hand to stop them. "Stay back. Sarah, did you handle the envelope at any point?" A puzzled look covered her face as she shook her head. "Then get off the platform as fast as you can. I'll explain later."

He then turned toward DeWayne Winston, who appeared to be fighting for control over his anger.

"Sir, please sit down and try to relax." Seamus held a hand out toward the man and pumped it gently in the air, motioning for him to sit down. "You both have just been exposed to a biological agent. We have to isolate you, get you to the hospital, and quarantine you until the threat can be assessed. Your sister as well."

The man's expression turned from anger to disbelief. He looked at the envelope and card and started to toss it away, onto the table.

"No Sir. Please just hold it until we can put it into a protective container."

Four people in bright orange protective suits entered the room with a plastic shrouded gurney trailing behind them. They approached the main table and one of the individuals joined Seamus and the Winstons on the stage. He held out a large plastic envelope.

"Please drop the card and envelope into this bag."

As soon as the paper was inside, he sealed the plastic bag and tucked it under one arm. He produced a can of alcohol foam.

"Hold out your hands."

He sprayed a large dollop of foam onto the politician's palms.

"Wash your hands with it. Here, you two as well." He pointed to Seamus and Della and repeated the process with both.

A second person placed three sets of large, footed coveralls on the table. The first medic picked them up and handed one to each of the three people.

"Put these on over your clothes. We'll be taking you to a decontamination center that's being set up outside. These coveralls will reduce the chance of spreading anything as you walk from here to there."

Seamus hadn't even considered that he had put himself in harm's way, again. He looked across the room and saw Sarah. She looked ravishing in a form-fitting, rose silk evening gown with spaghetti straps. So much for Bond getting the girl tonight in the typical Hollywood fantasy. In reality, this good guy was facing at least a week in quarantine.

Mitchell left his wife's bedroom where the steady drone and beat of the mechanical ventilator and the beep of the IVAC infusion pump no longer kept time together. The eerie stillness seemed foreign to the Colonel, and brought back the painful memories of the night of the auto accident, a night when he returned home to stark silence. With tears streaming down his cheeks, he told Sherry of their success and said goodbye.

His cheeks still moist, he paced the antique Persian rug in front of the desk in his study at home. Edwards had failed to call in on schedule. The local news stations had interrupted their regular programming to report on a thwarted terrorist plot at the

Ritz-Carlton, with Senator DeWayne Winston as the target. Had Edwards been caught? How? Even if he'd been taken, he wouldn't talk. So, how could they have known unless Sayer had woken up and informed them? Why would he have done that? Besides, he was believed to be brain dead. He continued pacing in a quandary. What should they do now? Retreat to the security of the lab? Leave the country?

He glanced out the window and saw several dark sedans pull up in front of the house and into the driveway. Half a dozen men in dark suits emerged from the cars and approached his front door. Several wore vests with "FBI" emblazoned on them, front and back.

He had but one option left to him.

The pounding on the front door and the voice announcing, "FBI! Doctor Hudson, open the door!" was greeted by a single shotgun blast from the second floor and a spray of blood and glass onto the well worn, brick walkway in front of the stately Tudor home.

CHAPTER 44

"So, how's everyone's favorite hero?" Sarah asked as she entered the hospital room where Seamus had remained quarantined for the previous week. She had been visiting twice a day and the space seemed more cluttered with each visit. She glanced around the room one more time to see it festooned with balloons, flowers and drawings from elementary school children all across the metropolitan area. The newspapers, Internet news sites, and television news reports had all built Seamus into a hero extraordinaire, complete with photos of him in formal attire, battered face and all. Donatello's had the good sense to forgive him the cost of replacing the tux.

Seamus looked up at Sarah. "Hey, I thought you were bringing me frozen custard." As she shook her head, he realized she wasn't wearing protective gear. "Hey, what are you doing? Where's your mask? You aren't supposed to come in here without personal protective gear."

"I can when the quarantine has been lifted. Must be that Irish luck. You've been released ... so I'm taking you to Ted Drewes for a firsthand custard experience instead."

Seamus clapped his hands and started to pump his fist in the air for a silent "Yes!" when he realized Sarah seemed distant, her mood positive but strained.

"How're the others?"

Sarah's façade of strength crumbled. Tears welled up in her eyes, and Seamus had to reach out to steady her. She sat down in the chair next to the bed.

"Critical. Th-they're not sure Della will make it." She grabbed a tissue and wiped her face. After taking a deep breath, she continued, "The CDC's been working overtime to figure this one out. All the markers point to a modified H5N1 flu."

Seamus was baffled, unfamiliar with the nomenclature.

"Same group as the Spanish flu from 1918 and the bird flu that caused such a scare a few years ago. It's a really bad one and how Hudson got it has not been determined. But why it hit Della and DeWayne so hard is puzzling. It's like their immune systems were overwhelmed. Their CD4 and T-cell counts are near zero and that let the flu virus ravage their bodies. Only life support is keeping them going right now."

Sarah leaned forward and buried her face in her hands.

Seamus sat on the edge of the bed. "Hey, they couldn't be in a better place. If anyone can pull them through this, it's the doctors and staff here. They'll make it, just watch."

Sarah lifted her head and wiped her face yet again. "They have to. Th-they're family."

"I know, Sarah."

"No, I mean really family. I-I've been holding onto a secret since right before Dad Winston died. Oh God ... I ..."

Seamus leaned forward to listen.

"Shortly after DeWayne was born, Dad Winston and his wife, Lois, had a falling out. He turned to my mom for help and, well, one thing led to another. They had a brief affair and I'm the result. They both felt so guilty about it, they swore they'd never tell anyone ... anyone! But, I think he knew his heart was bad and he knew how inquisitive I was about my father. Right before he died, he told me, gave me the paternity tests as proof, and made me swear never to embarrass my mother by revealing this. He supported us all that time because I'm his flesh and blood." She started to sob again. "They have to survive, Shay. They're my half-brother and sister. They just have to."

After a minute of silence, Seamus replied, "No one will hear it from me, but don't you think ..."

Sarah nodded. "If they make it, yeah, they deserve to know. But not until my mom passes. I made a promise."

Seamus nodded.

He rose from the bed and walked to the small closet where he grabbed his shoes and a fresh shirt. He peeled off the T-shirt, pulled on the polo, and then sat back down to put on his shoes. As he finished tying the laces of his cross-trainers, he looked up to find Sarah standing right in front of him. He stood up to face her and she grabbed him in a tight, sensual hug.

"Thank you for being here for me. For saving my life. For putting up with my, um, moods. I've been waiting all week to do this," she murmured in his ear.

He returned the hug, no blush rising to his cheeks. "Me, too."

"Do you think it might work?" she whispered.

"No, but …"

She stepped back and punched him in the shoulder.

"Hey, you didn't let me finish. I was about to add, we'll only know by trying." He moved up to her, raised one hand, and caressed her cheek. Gazing into her eyes, he leaned into her and kissed her on the lips, a long, lingering, satisfying kiss.

Ten minutes later, they left the room. Seamus turned left as Sarah turned right.

"This way," she said.

"No, I've got one other thing I need to do." As she joined him, he led the way toward John Doe's room. "I heard he fell back into a coma after telling us about the plot. Have you heard anything new?"

"Nada," she replied. "Last I heard they still think he's brain dead."

Seamus felt a quiver and gooseflesh prickled his skin. If that was indeed the case, it was truly a miracle of God that brought him to consciousness long enough to thwart the white supremacists' plan.

"I heard about Hudson just before you arrived. Wife dead in a makeshift hospital room. Single shotgun blast to the head. Nasty way to go. The fibbies have been working through his house and office, but so far, nothing … and no traces of their work in the university lab."

"Guess we still need John Doe for more information, huh?"

Seamus nodded.

As they reached John Doe's room, the uniformed officer at the door acknowledged them, but put up a hand as they started to enter the room.

"He's got company."

Seamus raised his eyebrows. "Is he …?"

"Oh, sorry. No change. Just wanted you to know there's

someone in there."

Seamus opened the door just enough to gaze into the room. A stocky middle-aged man with shaved head and a white polo shirt embroidered with "Destiny Church" in dark blue sat at the bedside reading scripture verses on healing from the Bible. He turned his head at the sound of the door opening. Seamus smiled and nodded. He had asked Delaney to honor the man's request for a pastor from that church. Whether or not it would do any good, he felt glad that Delaney had followed through.

The officer added, "He's been coming here daily for an hour or so." He cocked his head subtly to the side. "For what it's worth."

Seamus listened as the pastor spoke softly to John Doe. Sarah craned her head around him to see what was going on.

"I'm trusting God that you can hear me. And I'm believing He has another miracle for you. No matter what you've done, it's never too late to be forgiven. The only way to heaven is through Jesus Christ. You might have to pay for your mistakes and crimes in this existence, but you can have faith that a better eternity is coming … if you trust in the Lord."

Without prompting, Sarah and Seamus both made the sign of the cross over their hearts and turned to each other. They had seen God's miracles. It had taken until now, though, to recognize them. Would He have yet another one for the Winstons?

CHAPTER 45

Seamus awoke the next morning, sluggish and more than a bit hung over. And somewhat embarrassed by his notoriety. After all, he was just one member of a team, doing his job, nothing he saw as particularly heroic. For dinner, they joined the back of the line of people waiting for a table at Favazza's on The Hill, St. Louis' version of Little Italy. But not for long. Recognized within minutes, handshakes propelled them through the front door and up to the hostess' stand. A standing ovation greeted him in the main dining room. Dinner was on the house, but after the fifth or sixth complimentary beer, he had to stop accepting the freebies. By the end of the meal, he was in no shape to drive and Sarah had taken him home, plopped him on the bed and taken his shoes off. He remembered nothing after that until waking.

He took a little longer shower than usual, and dressed a wee bit more slowly. Breakfast held no appeal but he forced down some juice and whole grain toast and arrived at work only fifteen minutes later than habit.

As he walked into the BOI, everyone he saw wore a surgical mask and latex gloves. A couple of his mates held up their palms and shook their heads as if saying, "don't come any closer." Had there been some biologic threat against the BOI and no one warned him? It wasn't until he got to his desk that he realized <u>he</u> was the "biologic threat."

He saw a "cage" of plastic sheeting from floor to ceiling surrounding his desk. Biohazard stickers emblazoned the plastic at random intervals. A small fan blew fresh air into the enclosure. Through the plastic, he noted the obscure outline of a water cooler in one corner of his corral and of a box of Krispy Kreme donuts on his desk. Near the entrance a slit had been cut into the plastic parallel to the floor with the words, "Mail Drop" stuck onto the sheeting above the slot, while a full mail tray lay inside on the floor below it.

With a smirk on his face, he pulled open the overlapping flaps of plastic that formed the doorway and entered his domain.

Once inside he noticed two tin cans on his desk with strings extending through the plastic toward Stick's desk and toward the Lieutenant's office. Each can was labeled "Intercom." He chuckled. These guys had way too much time on their hands and way too much fun at his expense while he was in quarantine.

He opened the box and pulled out a still-warm glazed donut. *At least they're fresh,* he thought. *Could be worse.* He sat down, leaned back in his chair, and placed his feet on his desk, accidentally knocking over the stack of mail he'd put there a week earlier. He removed his feet and bent down to pick up the envelopes with his free hand, tossing them onto the top of the mountain of mail in the mail tray. As he collected the top envelope, he noticed the return address.

Where do I know that name from? he pondered as he chewed.

A buzzing from one of the cans interrupted his thoughts. He tossed the envelope onto the pile and picked up the can, holding it to his ear.

"Can you hear me now?"

Seamus started laughing and almost choked on donut. "Yeah, partner. I <u>can</u> hear you now, better than my cell service at home."

Seamus heard Stick through the plastic, not the can. "Hey, it actually works." Then, through the can came, "Welcome back, Shay. You feelin' okay? Can we take the masks off?" Stick sounded serious through the can, but Seamus heard numerous snickers through the plastic.

"Not too bad. They told me you guys would be safe as long as I don't get to coughing too much." At that, he forced a coughing fit.

Through the plastic came, "Nice try. But you aren't getting out of work that easy." It was the Lieutenant. He pulled at the plastic doorway and nearly tore down the ceiling tiles where the plastic was duct taped. As he entered the plastic cubicle, Seamus held up the Krispy Kreme box, but the Lt. refused.

"You know a Dillon Watts, from a company called Jessup Genetics?"

Seamus shook his head as he continued chewing.

"Well, he called here three times today asking for you. Call center finally routed the call to me. Seems a friend of his is missing. He's been trying to track him down and can't find him. The name Roger Coulter mean anything to you?"

Seamus gulped as he swallowed the nearly whole piece of donut he'd just bitten off and jumped up from his seat. The first name had jogged his memory. He nudged past the Lieutenant and grabbed the large envelope from the top of his pile.

"Shit," said his superior as he saw the name on the return address.

"Got this right before Delaney called me to the hospital. What's up?"

"Like I said, the guy seems to have disappeared. He worked for Mitchell Hudson at the university. We sent a car out to the address he gave us but no one was home. Here's the guy's phone number."

Seamus sliced open the end of the package and pulled out the contents. He read the letter detailing Roger Coulter's suspicions, suspicions that had already proven true. In it, he named three other individuals.

"Crap. Lieutenant, we still have three perps and some kind of lab unaccounted for."

He finished reading and felt a chill. Coulter had taken his suspicions to Hudson first, before realizing his possible involvement. Seamus handed the letter to his boss, picked up the phone, and speed-dialed dispatch.

"Dispatch."

Seamus recognized the voice. "Ruby, it's O'Connor. Send a car out to …" He gave her the address and what he wanted the officers to check.

"Shay, we've got a unit heading there already. Neighbors reported a bad smell, like something's dead in the house."

Seamus' shoulders sagged as he lowered the phone. *Not something … someone.*

CHAPTER 46

Eric glanced at Heinz to find him with his head on his arms on the lab counter. He felt the same way, utterly exhausted. Following local news reports on the critical condition of Della and DeWayne Winston and using guidelines left behind by Mitchell, they had been working non-stop to replicate more influenza virus and the retrovirus that turned the lymphocytes against the body's own melanin pigment. The darker the skin, the more overwhelmed the immune system became. It had worked. And once they released these two viruses together, the sheer number of critical cases would crush the medical system to a point where they could treat no more cases.

Time was now critical. Somehow, the authorities had learned of their initial plan and stopped it. Edwards was gone. Sayer, from what he could ascertain, remained in a coma. There were just the three of them. How soon would the police learn of their identities and start searching for them?

He stood up slowly from the stool and moved to the entryway of the level-three lab. He donned his protective gear and entered the lab. He had one last task to complete and then he, too, could afford the luxury of a nap. Cautiously, he moved from incubator to incubator. The replication process moved along smoothly. Soon they would have enough material to load a dozen dispersal canisters. Soon they would avenge the deaths of their comrades.

CHAPTER 47

Sarah sat on her lab stool gazing out the window toward the St. Louis Science Center. Whatever had possessed her to take this toxicology lab rotation? It was supposed to be a sanity break from the hectic life in the E.D., but her first five days there had been a deadly mixture of boredom, long hours made longer by the monotony, and a PhD preceptor straight from Geeksville who favored anything and everything made with garlic and onion.

The one good thing about the week so far was that the lab was just one floor above the Department of Molecular Biology and Pharmacology and one of the PhD candidates made it a point to pass on every bit of scuttlebutt coming from Doctor Hudson's old lab. The current gossip raged about the remaining lab personnel who were now missing. She wanted badly to call Seamus and get an update from him but the Geek frowned upon personal phone calls.

She turned her attention to the text she had been preparing for use in a PowerPoint presentation on accidental poisoning in children that she was to give to the E.D. residency group. The history and development of poison control centers was kind of interesting but she was working on the meat of her talk, the most common forms of accidental poisoning and means of preventing them. The drum of approaching helicopter rotors started her thoughts meandering through the previous week's events yet again.

She realized her discontent was more than simply the boredom she faced now. Something remained unsettled. Hudson couldn't have done all of the work himself. As intelligent as he was, he simply didn't have the breadth of experience and training needed to do it all. Others had to be involved and she'd lay odds that the missing people were Hudson's accomplices. She also knew from the building's gossip mill that a zillion crime scene and computer techs had scoured Hudson's university lab and found nothing but his work on the Alzheimer's drug. So where did they make this virus? In her mind 'where' was a bigger question than 'who.'

She again tried to focus on her presentation by staring out the window and hoping inspiration would strike her from the blue sky above, but noticed a man pacing back and forth on the sidewalk. His walk seemed familiar but she didn't recognize him. She watched for a while and his actions seemed a bit odd. She wouldn't go so far as to say his actions were suspicious, but then again, maybe they were. He stopped pacing as a young woman approached him. Sarah stood up and glanced down through the window for a more vertical view of the street and surrounding area. The direction of her walk meant she'd exited the building where Sarah was currently daydreaming, er, working. Their ensuing conversation became animated, almost heated, and at one point, she turned away from the man. Sarah recognized her as a secretary from Hudson's lab. They'd met the day of Della's interview with the doctor. That definitely qualified the man as suspicious.

Sarah quickly closed down her workstation, grabbed her purse, and ran to the door. Thankfully, the Geek was nowhere to be seen and she had to offer no immediate excuse. As she exited the elevator, the woman stepped aside to let her out and then entered the elevator. She seemed upset and gave no hint of recognition as Sarah passed. Sarah's heart began to race in anxious anticipation. She just hoped she wasn't too late.

Upon exiting the building she first turned in the direction where she had seen them talking. He wasn't there. She hurried south but saw no one, so she doubled back in a jog and spotted him heading north along Euclid Avenue. She hurried to fall in behind him, trying to remain cautious and alert to the need to blend in, to not appear as if she were following him. She again noted something familiar to his stride. What was it? Where had she seen it before?

As the man entered the north parking garage, she panicked. Her own car was there as well, but the crowd would dissipate and she'd become obvious to him. How could she follow and not get noticed? Maybe she should just wait at the exit, get the model and plate number, and phone it in to Seamus. Yes, that seemed the better idea.

With cell phone in hand, she milled around the pedestrian walkway near the garage exit and a few minutes later the man emerged driving a late model, sand-colored Infiniti G35 coupe. She memorized the license plate and dialed Seamus again. His voice mail answered after only one ring. *He's in that briefing*, she thought, quietly frustrated.

As she left Seamus a message, she watched the car turn the corner and come to a halt. With non-stop construction going on around the medical center, she realized a work crew flagged him to stop while they moved a large piece of equipment. This was her chance. She raced into the parking garage and up two ramps to her car. Within two minutes, she was on the street and only four cars behind her quarry. They sat there for another five minutes before the construction crew cleared them to move on. So began her first attempt at tailing someone. How hard could that be?

Eric smiled as he glanced into his rearview mirror. He'd spotted the young doctor as soon as she entered the pedestrian walkway on Euclid. She had been almost as meddlesome as that detective whom the news media had adopted as their newest celebrity. If she wanted to follow, he could accommodate her … at least until he got wind of any police presence focusing on him. And if they made it back to the lab without interference, he'd have a little present for her.

CHAPTER 48

Seamus stood at the head of the conference table as point man in the small task force retained to assess the continued threat of a genocidal disaster. To call the mood around the table 'somber' was an understatement. He glanced at each man in the room. Delaney's pronounced frown lines appeared deeper than usual. The lieutenant drummed the table with his fingers, a trait Seamus had noticed only when the man was under extreme stress. LTC Bill Walker, Commander of the BOI, practically yelled into the phone each time he called for this or that, even when he talked to the Mayor, who had made it clear he wanted the full resources of the department called up to stop these men. The other detectives sat low in their chairs trying to avoid the commander's glare. However one looked at it – morally, socially, politically – none of these men wanted this crisis, but it would happen on their watch if they didn't avert it.

Seamus finished detailing the information left to him by the deceased Roger Coulter and watched his superiors sit there, silent and stupefied by the realization there were at least three men out there still working on their version of the "final solution" in a clandestine lab capable of producing untold biological horrors.

Delaney broke the silence. "We believe we've identified the two women that Della Winston identified as Carly and Sue. The older woman, Carly, is actually Marie Strommer. She's a police widow whose husband was gunned down by some black gang-bangers. Relatives say that event radically changed her. Her son, Michael, was killed at the militant's compound. Sue's real name is Rebecca Hirschel. She's a nurse and get this; her last known employer was Mitchell Hudson. Her boyfriend was also killed at the compound. Both are reported to be supportive of the White Supremacy movement. Both are still on the loose."

Silence engulfed the room yet again, but only briefly as the lieutenant voiced what no one else wanted to hear.

"So, what you're really telling us is that we've only cut off a few heads of the Hydra … that besides three men and a lab, we have an unknown number of unidentified supporters, male and female, who would be willing to act as couriers to release these biologic agents anywhere in the world."

"We have to find that lab ..." barked the commander "... and put it out of commission." He fixed his stare on the handful of detectives in the room whose careers now seemed on the line. "Any ideas how we do that?"

Stick interrupted by entering the room. He had a sheaf of papers in his hand. "Here's the personnel data on these three from the university." He started to hand out stapled packets to each man in the room. "We're already circulating their photos and checking out their homes, neighbors, friends."

Seamus leafed through the packet, seeing for the first time photos of the three men. Having briefly glanced at the pictures of the two techs, something struck him as odd and he returned to the photograph of Marcus Schmid. Perusing the picture, he tried to identify the cause of his concern, but the root of that unease only teetered at the edge of his consciousness. He looked up at Stick.

"Do we have anything else on this tech, Schmid?"

His partner shook his head. "Just what you see on his employment record. Why?"

"I don't know. Something's bothering me about him, but I can't place it yet."

As Seamus fingered the man's personnel record and photo, the commander's secretary poked her head in the door.

"Shay, phone call."

The commander frowned. "Not now, Jeanne. Take a message."

"I tried, Sir. It's a doctor at Barnes. Something about John Doe."

Seamus jumped up from his seat.

"Be right back."

He rushed to the secretary's desk, picked up the receiver, and pressed the flashing button for the call on hold.

"Sergeant O'Connor."

"Hello, Sergeant. This is Doctor Carney. Thought you'd want to know that your John Doe has been opening his eyes.

He's not answering questions but he does seem to follow people as they move around the room. It's a good sign."

"So he hasn't said anything."

"Not so much as a grunt."

"Okay. Doesn't sound like something I need to rush over there for, but I'll stop by later. Let me know if he becomes more alert."

"Sure. Just keeping you updated as you asked."

"Appreciate it. You still have my cell number?"

"Yes. Left you a message there as well."

Seamus signed off with a promise to contact the doctor later and took the opportunity to check his voice mail. As expected, the phone beeped that new messages existed. The first two were inconsequential, but he heard Sarah's anxious voice on the third. Something about following someone she'd seen and remembered from Hudson's lab. She gave a make and model for the car as well as the license plate. Her mention of the car model stirred a new level of excitement in him and he ran back to the conference room where he grabbed the sheaf of materials Stick had provided earlier. The car and its plates were a match.

"Yes! Atta girl!"

He looked up to see everyone in the room staring at him.

"She's done it again. At this moment, Doctor Wade is tailing Eric Deamus in his Infiniti G35."

"Where are they?" asked the commander.

Seamus proceeded to dial Sarah's cell phone and held up his hand to stay the question as it rang.

CHAPTER 49

"Where is that cord?" muttered Sarah as she tried to keep an eye on the Infiniti three cars ahead while rooting through the glove compartment. The low battery alarm on her phone had stopped beeping ten minutes earlier. Randomly, she reached into the cavity of her dash and began to pull out tissues, the owner's manual and an assortment of accoutrements found in any young woman's car. No sign of the charging cord. She looked up in time to see the light flick to yellow and screeched to a halt. Nervously she scanned the road ahead for the Infiniti. It was gone.

"Damn!" She pounded the steering wheel in frustration. *I've lost him!*

With the delay of the traffic signal, she took the time to finish rummaging through the glove compartment. No cord. She leaned down and felt below her car seat. Nothing but the debris of a spilled snack bag of chips, a dime, and two plastic bottle caps. Expecting the light to change, she hurriedly groped the space beneath the passenger's seat and then unbuckled her seat belt and rose up enough to take a quick look onto the floor of the back seat. There it was.

With the car behind her honking repeatedly, she lunged for the charger, grabbed it, dumped it into her lap, and gunned it through the intersection to make up for lost time. Only by pure happenstance did she spot the Infiniti on the parking lot of a convenience store one block beyond the light. Focused on the road and cars ahead, the glare of sunshine from the chrome of a passing truck had forced her to glance away and that's when she saw it.

She crossed herself. "Thank you, God," she whispered.

She veered into another parking lot a hundred feet down the road and pulled into a space that allowed her a clean line of sight to the convenience store lot as well as rapid egress. Five minutes later, she was rewarded with a view of the man emerging from the store with a bag of something in one arm and a large fountain soda in the other hand. He placed the soda on the roof of his car as he unlocked it and placed the bag on the passenger's seat. Retrieving the cup, he looked around slowly as he walked past the trunk of the car and entered the driver's side. With a similar sense of caution, he slowly backed out of the parking spot and returned to the street.

Before pulling into the traffic behind him, she realized she had failed to plug in her phone, so she took a moment to do so and allowed a couple more cars to separate her from her target. Nothing would distract her now.

They had initially meandered through the Central West End near the medical campus and then he headed toward the county seat, Clayton. Now, passing by the Galleria shopping mall and adjacent shopping venues a mile southwest of the county government center, he drove south toward Webster Grove, a charming neighborhood of well-preserved and pricey historic homes. As soon as he reached the business district there, he turned east and started back toward downtown Saint Louis.

Was he onto her? Trying to shake her? *No,* she thought. He'd had plenty of opportunity for that when she lost him at that stop light. *What is he doing?* she wondered. A minute later, she followed him onto I-44, heading east into the city.

As she merged with traffic, trying to stay a comfortable distance behind the Infiniti, her cell phone buzzed. She grabbed it but the power cord came free and dropped to the floor. The phone instantly died, but traffic moved too fast for her to retrieve it safely now. It would have to wait.

Eric glanced into his rear view mirror and smiled as he saw the dark blue Jetta. *She's a tenacious one all right,* he thought. He'd almost lost her at the stop light near Clayton, but he pulled into the convenience store and parked conspicuously in hope she'd be alert enough to spot the car. She had been. Now they were on a tour of sorts. They had already chosen the airport as one dispersal site. He needed to select two more. The Galleria had seemed a likely candidate, but the nearby highway construction would hinder a quick getaway. They would consider another mall, perhaps Chesterfield Mall to the west. It offered the fastest escape to the Interstate system.

At the last minute, he changed lanes and exited at South Jefferson Avenue. Turning north, he worked his way to Market Street and then south to Clark Avenue where he drove east past the Savvis Center, Union Station, and finally Busch Stadium. He crossed off the stadium since the Cardinals were away on a long road trip and the outdoor venue made dispersal of their aerosol difficult to control. Union Station, with its unique shops and restaurants, remained a possibility. Dispersal would be easy and with the right timing, he could disappear into the crowd and onto the Metro. Still, as he considered all three potential sites, the Savvis Center, as an indoor arena, topped his list due to the size of its crowds. He made a mental note to check the Center's schedule to see when they might be entertaining a large crowd again.

He continued slowly onto Broadway. His tour had taken long enough. He checked the mirror again. She remained several cars behind him. With no police evident, it was time to return to the warehouse and lab.

Seamus cursed quietly under his breath. Sarah's phone had seemed to pick up his call but then dropped it. Subsequent calls only transferred to her voicemail. He had no need to leave another message. "C'mon, pick up," he muttered as he dialed yet one more time. Still no answer.

CHAPTER 50

Sarah narrowed the gap between their cars. She was in unfamiliar territory as they swept past the new ballpark and drove south on Broadway. She hoped for another red light to give her time to plug in her phone but they hit the timed lights in perfect sequence to keep moving. She realized from the signs that they were heading toward the Soulard neighborhood, but her only experience with the Soulard came from treating drunks in the E.D. during Mardi Gras. She had never been to the farmer's market there and the street names meant nothing to her. She doubted that any of the small, century-old homes could hold the type of lab she expected to find. However, the vast complex of warehouses and light industrial buildings between there and the Mississippi River certainly could.

Sure enough, the Infiniti turned left into the parking area of a moderate-sized warehouse. She saw no street numbers on the building and it was one of several on the block. She needed a landmark, something to help her lead Seamus to the right building. Just above the lot was a large billboard. Its message took her back. "Eternity! Are you prepared? – Destiny Church." John Doe had asked for a pastor from Destiny Church. It couldn't be simple coincidence.

She drove past the building and turned around a short distance further down the street. The Anheuser-Busch brewery and one-time world headquarters loomed above her and the pleasant smell of brewer's yeast permeated her car. Why couldn't she just play tourist and go pet the Clydesdales? No, she had to be on the trail of mass murderers.

She parked along the street a hundred feet in front of the billboard. She couldn't see into the parking lot and there were no windows visible on the small section of building she could see, so she felt safely out of view. Now to get her phone working.

She plugged the power cord into her phone and waited for the screen to confirm that the phone was charging. Holding the cord tightly into the phone she flipped it open and speed dialed the last number called, Seamus. As she heard him answer, the opening of her rear door startled her and she felt cold metal at the base of her neck. She eased the phone between the seat and center console, hoping her action went unnoticed.

"Drive into the parking lot. Right up to the main doors," a gruff voice said.

She glanced into the rearview mirror. She did not recognize the man but saw malevolence in his eyes. She doubted she could flee the car without being shot. She placed the car in gear and eased forward.

"How –"

"You were spotted as soon as you walked onto Euclid. He made sure you could follow him, but we needed some time to set up here for your arrival."

She parked just outside the large warehouse doors and noticed the motorized gate closing. She had no way out now.

"Get out of the car. Slowly. Walk to the doors and go inside."

She heard the rear door open and noted movement in her peripheral vision. She followed suit, taking care to leave her phone behind, continuing to charge, open and tucked away. Apprehension enveloped her as she approached the door and slowly entered the dark warehouse. Before her eyes could adjust to the dim light, she felt a jab in her left upper arm. Everything began to swirl as she became lightheaded and collapsed.

Seamus teetered on the brink of rage with fear preparing to catapult him over the edge. He'd never been afraid for someone else, someone he felt close to, and this new emotion overpowered him. He had answered his phone in gleeful anticipation that Sarah would direct him to the perps and their lab. Upon answering, there was dead air for over a minute and then a rough, ominous male voice ordered Sarah to leave the car and enter a door. What door? Where? He'd heard two car doors slam closed and then dead air again.

"Shay?" A hand gently shook his shoulder. "You okay? What's up?" Stick looked concerned.

Seamus found the control he needed and informed his partner and the others in the room what he'd just heard. He started to flip his phone closed when Stick grabbed it from his hand and put it up to his ear.

"The line's still open. Someone start a trace on this call." Another detective raced from the room as Stick continued to listen. "I hear a train in the background. No, maybe more than one train. Bells! Church bells! Hey, I think I know those bells. Shay, listen."

Seamus attended St. Margaret of Scotland Catholic Church in his own neighborhood, but he'd attended so many weddings at the beautiful Saints Peter and Paul Catholic Church that he knew those bells, too. Five bells, five tones. Each bell named for a saint.

"Soulard. She has a dark blue Jetta. Get every available unit to start looking for it. Focus on the area within two, three blocks of the church, then branch out," barked Seamus, as if he was in charge in a room full of superiors.

Colonel Walker and the Lieutenant each simply looked at each other, cocked their heads, and nodded.

"Do it," said the Colonel. "It's our best play right now. Our only play."

Sarah awoke with a dull headache and stirred slightly. She'd had a dream where she awoke in shackles while Della baked bread with Aunt Beatrice in a small house with no windows. As she became aware of her surroundings, she knew she wasn't captive in some remote place. But just where she was, she had no idea. She recalled the needle stick in her arm, but had they then carried her someplace within that warehouse or moved her to some new location miles away? Would her cell phone lead the police right to them or on a wild goose chase?

As her eyes regained focus, she saw that she was sitting on a floor, propped into a corner adjacent to what looked like a large chemical analyzer, in a brightly lit room filled with an assortment of lab equipment. She could see another room through some windows and some kind of air lock connected the two rooms.

Inside the second room were three men in bio-protective suits and full helmets attached to clean air supply hoses suspended from the ceiling. *What are they doing?* Peering around the analyzer, she scanned the room where she sat and saw a second door leading to a third room. She could see stacks of boxes and shelves of supplies and lab glassware through the windows to that room. *Maybe that's my way out,* she thought. *Has to be.*

She tried to move, but her muscles moved like rubber cement. And exertion worsened the headache. Even if she managed to get to the door and open it, how far would she get?

She noticed movement from inside the other room and slumped back, feigning unconsciousness while trying to continue to watch through nearly closed eyelids. It wasn't as easy as she'd imagined. She could see only blurry images that way, so she gave up and opened her eyes. One of the three men had moved to the airlock and proceeded to decontaminate his suit and some kind of larger canister that looked to be the size of a home fire extinguisher. The de-con process complete, he took off his suit and walked into the room. The analyzer blocked her view of his face, but her rough estimate of his size told her that he wasn't the man she had followed.

As he emerged from behind the boxes, he wore a gray, hooded sweatshirt with the screen-printed logo and name of a commercial cleaning company on the front. He carried the canister in his left hand while his right carried some kind of papers. She still couldn't see his face, but the papers she recognized immediately as airline tickets. He walked right past her, silently, seemingly unconcerned that she was awake. He walked into the far room and approached a distant wall where a large opening appeared, like a door to an elevator sliding sideways. She couldn't see how he activated it. She inched forward and rose up onto her knees for a better view. She wasn't successful, but at least her muscles were starting to work again.

A hiss of air from behind startled her. She turned and saw another man emerging from the airlock. This was the man she had followed.

"Good afternoon, Doctor Wade. I'm sorry we've not been

formally introduced but that doesn't matter any longer." He gestured around the room. "Impressed? Feel free to poke around, although I doubt you'd recognize half of what you see here."

"Where are we?"

"Oh ... that you'll have to discover on your own." He stopped and donned a gray, hooded sweatshirt like the previous man, while his colleague moved through the airlock and decontamination process. "I'm sorry we don't have time to chat, but the police scanner has suddenly gotten quite busy regarding the Soulard neighborhood. We have business to attend to while they're distracted there."

She watched him move toward the other door as the third man donned a gray sweatshirt. Each carried a small box holding six spray cans. Before leaving the room, the man turned back to Sarah and said, "By the way, you're free to leave any time you feel strong enough." He smiled. "In fact, we're counting on it." Sarah felt a shiver as the smile evolved into a sardonic grin. "Please see as many friends and co-workers as possible ... while you're able." He paused. "Oh, by the way, should you get altruistic and try to use one of the bio suits to isolate yourself as you leave, you'll deactivate the only way out of here. Sensors in the suits turn off the exit route if they're moved into this first room. It was a safeguard Doctor Hudson insisted upon. Have a great day."

The two men left the room, exiting the same way as the first man. Sarah struggled to her feet, but did not yet have the strength to follow them. As she crumpled to the floor, she realized exactly what he was telling her. She had already been infected.

CHAPTER 51

Seamus raced from BOI headquarters toward the stadium to pick up 7th Street to get to the Soulard neighborhood. With lights flashing, he moved through the intersection at the old Stadium Plaza and was nearly struck by a gray van from a cleaning company. The van's failure to yield irritated him but he had other priorities. As he passed the new ballpark, the intercom crackled.

"Attention District 4 officers. The target vehicle has been …"

Seamus smiled. Sarah would be safe in no time.

The dispatcher continued, "Two gray panel vans from Janssen Janitorial were spotted leaving the parking lot where the target vehicle was discovered."

"Damn!" Seamus glanced into the rearview mirror and saw the van he'd almost hit, speeding along 7th Street, north of the old plaza. He turned on his siren and as the traffic pulled to the sides of the street he executed a perfect St. Louis "U-turn" and sped past the stadium in the opposite direction. Up ahead the van turned onto Market Street, heading west.

"D3566 to dispatch. Suspect van heading west on Market. Following closely at Kaufman Park. Need backup and road block on Market at Union Station."

Following a series of high profile, high-speed accidents involving vehicles in police chases, a policy had developed against such pursuits. They couldn't even use the term "pursuit" any more. Seamus chose to ignore the policy. More was at stake here than a stolen car or catching a few gang bangers on a joyride.

Seamus watched the van blow through the intersections at 10th and 11th Streets and followed, matching the van's speed despite the dangers. Passing City Hall and then 14th Street, Seamus saw additional police units converging on the area. As they neared Union Station, he saw that police cars, lights flashing, had blocked the road as it passed the old railway station. In horror, he watched the van attempt to bypass the roadblock by veering into the park on the north side of the street and flip as it hit the curb at high speed. Rolling onto its side and sliding across the grass, the van came to a stop just yards before reaching Aloe Plaza, with its restored fountains and dozens of people enjoying the sunny spring day.

A man emerged from the van's back doors and stumbled. He wore a gray, hooded sweatshirt and dark slacks. As he reached back into the van, the hood came down and Seamus recognized Eric Deamus. Deamus retrieved a box and started running toward Union Station, the main doors to the Hyatt Regency Hotel and dozens of shops and restaurants a scant hundred yards away.

Seamus screeched to a halt before the roadblock and jumped from his car.

"Don't let him into the building!" he yelled to nearby officers. As he closed in on the militant biochemist, he pulled his service weapon. Deamus was less than twenty yards from the doors. "Deamus, stop! Don't try it!"

Deamus didn't break stride. The hotel doorman, performing his duties by opening the door, took one look at the police presence, dove back inside the door, and scurried away from view. Pedestrians began to run. As Deamus hit the broad sidewalk in front of the historic main doors, Seamus knew he had no choice. He stopped short, assumed a firing stance and shot three times. Stone on the building's façade splintered with the first two bullets. But with the third, Deamus arched to the right, dropping the box with his right arm going limp. He stumbled on the concrete and fell. A moment later, he reached into the box with his left hand and pulled out a canister that Seamus couldn't identify. With effort, he regained his footing and started toward the doors.

"Deamus, stop!"

As Deamus reached for the brass handles of the door, Seamus fired again, one round. The man arced as if the force of the bullet had lifted him off his feet and he fell backward onto the sidewalk. When Seamus reached him, he saw the man make one final vain effort to flip open the can, go limp, and his eyes glaze over. Seamus checked for a carotid pulse. Nothing. No effort to breath. He was gone.

This was not the first man Seamus had killed in the line of duty, even discounting the raid on the militant's compound, but that made this no easier for him. He fought to control the nausea.

Standing up, he reached into an inner coat pocket, pulled out a plastic evidence bag, and dropped his weapon inside. He knew the drill. Internal Affairs would investigate the shooting. After sealing the bag, he handed it to a nearby uniformed officer and noted the man's name and badge number.

"Sorry, know this is a little out of line but it's your chain-of-custody now. I can't stick around for IA."

CHAPTER 52

After several minutes of rest, Sarah stood again and ventured to take a few steps. Her strength was returning. She took several more steps, gained confidence in her body, and started to investigate the room. The man had been correct. Although she suspected the equipment in the room had their roles in genetic sequencing and other aspects of such research, she had no idea what did what. Feeling stronger, she walked almost normally to the air lock. Beyond the windows was another lab, a highly specialized and tightly contained lab most likely used for viral production, the added security and precautions needed to avoid the accidental release of a dangerous virus.

She opened the first door to the air lock. Its latch released easily. No alarms. The bio suits hung there lifelessly. The acrid odor of bleach and other chemicals assaulted her nose and brought tears to her eyes. She stepped in and inspected the second suit. It looked as if it would fit her, but there was the matter of air supply. The suit design required connection to an air supply line in the lab. She looked around and inside the single cabinet she discovered a portable air supply unit, which she pulled out to make sure it worked. It did. She took that and the suit and lugged them into the room outside the air lock.

She hoped he'd been lying to her. She first carried the air supply unit into the anteroom and once there saw that there was an additional lab to explore if needed ... and a small lavatory, definitely needed. She returned and grabbed the suit. As soon as she entered the anteroom, the lights dimmed and a warning beacon began to flash. He hadn't lied.

Her shoulders sagged and she carried the bio suit back to air lock. It would serve her no purpose.

Going back to the anteroom, she walked up to the door where the men had exited the lab. On the adjacent wall was a single button ... like one for an elevator. Could it be that simple? Would she be going up or down? Maybe it just opened into another room or a hallway.

But not knowing where it opened presented a dilemma.

Would she be playing into their hands and delivering the virus to people on the other side?

Sarah's mind was still a bit too cloudy to wrestle with that one. She sat on the floor next to the door pondering her next move. She knew nothing about the virus other than the previous attack showed that it was airborne and had an incubation period of two to three days. Had she been there for an hour or for a day? She could be contagious now and dead in a day. She refused to leave and risk exposing even a single person to the infection.

Yet, she obviously couldn't stay put. The presence of sinks and a restroom indicated adequate water supply, but she doubted she could make it through a self-imposed quarantine on just water. And what if she did get sick? How would she get help? Did anyone even know where she was? She didn't.

Sarah stood up and began to inspect the room in earnest. She found no phone or other means of contacting the outside world. She attempted to log onto a computer. Password controlled. "So much for Internet access," she muttered. She discovered a stash of candy bars and a small fridge with three sodas. She moved throughout all three rooms outside the air lock, checking every cabinet, every drawer, every cubbyhole, and found no surgical masks or personal protective gear of any kind, no additional foodstuffs, intravenous fluids, or IV sets to administer fluids … nothing else to aid her. She was no closer to solving the impasse.

As Seamus retraced his route back toward the ballpark and Soulard, he heard that Joseph Heintzleman, AKA "Heinz" had been captured alive but critically injured following a high-speed chase down I-64. The State Highway Patrol had spotted him just west of the I-270 interchange nearing Chesterfield Mall. He was unconscious and in route to St. Johns Mercy Medical Center, the nearest Level 1 trauma center. His apprehension accounted for two of the three men at large. Did the other man still hold Sarah captive?

Minutes later Seamus pulled through the police cordon

surrounding a warehouse on South Broadway. Parking on the street, he walked into the fenced parking lot and saw Stick and two crime scene techs inspecting Sarah's blue Jetta.

"What's up? Where's Sarah?"

Stick grimaced and shrugged his shoulders. "So far, all we got is her car and cell phone. She musta managed to wedge the open phone next to the seat without it being seen. Kept the line open so we could trace it, but we haven't found her, or any lab, yet."

Seamus felt ready to explode and his face flushed in anger as the reality of Stick's words intruded into his personal life and emotions. Had they now kidnapped Sarah? He wasn't sure he could go through another hunt.

"Whadaya mean, you haven't found her, yet? Where could they have gone in the time it took us to get here?"

"C'mon, Shay. They coulda moved her to another car and gotten halfway out of the city in that time. You know that."

Seamus jerked his head toward the warehouse. "What's in there?"

"So far, just a warehouse. No lab. We're waiting on a search warrant so we can bust open some locked doors and get a better look, but those doors sure don't hide any space big enough for the kind of lab setup we suspect they'd need."

Seamus stared at the building as Stick said those words. His gut told him she was there. "Screw the search warrant."

"Go ahead, take a look. They left the outer doors wide open. Got two locked areas inside. Look like offices. We should have the warrant in a few minutes."

Seamus barged through the nearby door and entered the building. He walked down a central corridor, off which a dozen bays opened to three-tiered storage areas. At the far end of the main passage, he found four rooms opening into the central strip. The doors to three of these rooms lay open and a quick glance through each portal revealed they were no more than storage areas that required individual climate control. At the fourth door, he found it secured with a keyed deadbolt.

Adjacent to the door was a three-by-four foot window of wire mesh glass but he could see nothing through it. The window was shuttered from the inside.

Stick joined him outside the closed door.

"You said there were two locked areas. Where's the other one?"

Stick pointed off to their right. "Third aisle back leads to an extension of the building. Has bays for four vehicles, two of them gone. Probably the two we got. There's a smaller locked area. Looks like a tool bay. If we find anything, my money's on what's behind this door."

As he spoke, a uniformed officer approached them down the main strip, waving some paper.

"Ahh, time for some action." Stick took the paper and perused it. "Thank you, Judge Turnbaugh." He looked at Seamus. "Gave us full carte blanche." Turning back to the officer, he added, "Bill, let's take this door down."

Less than five minutes later the battering ram left behind a splintered door and easy access to what was obviously a luxurious office. Seamus scanned the area to his left and saw leather furniture and a sleek glass-topped coffee table set off as a small seating area facing the wall and a fifty-inch plasma television along with three small monitors and other electronics. To his right, he noted a finely crafted, black walnut desk with a leather desk chair, matching credenza and bookcases. The back wall held two standard, wood paneled doors, which he quickly discovered led to a closet and a private bath. A third door opened to reveal a steel door like those to a vault.

Seamus walked straight to the vault door, while Stick scanned the desk and nearby walls.

"Looks like John Doe's no longer anonymous. Name's Chad Sayer," said Stick. He leafed through the papers on top of the desk and opened two of the desk drawers. "Looks like typical business stuff, but we'll have to check it all out."

"Not your worry anymore, fellas," said a voice from the door. "We'll take it from here."

Seamus looked away from the vault door to see Bill Delaney

and two junior FBI agents standing in the doorway.

Stick held up both hands and smiled. "Gladly. Have at it. I wanted to see the wife and kids tonight anyway." He walked around from behind the desk. "And then tomorrow I can go back to being a plain old homicide detective and leave this mess behind."

Seamus ignored his partner and addressed the FBI A-I-C. "Bill, you familiar with these systems?" He pointed to the vault door and then the numeric pad adjacent to it.

"Not at all, but we'll get someone here within the hour who is," replied Delaney.

"I've seen three of these systems before. Those electronic locking systems required an eight-digit access code followed by a four-digit code. Attempted removal of the access panel without a specific tool will produce an automatic lock-down for twenty-four hours. Hope your guy knows his stuff."

Delaney scratched his head. "Yeah. Me, too."

Seamus was about to walk away, when he felt an intense need to open the vault. Mentally, he knew from the dimensions of the building that nothing more than a walk-in space could lie beyond the door. There could be no lab there, no Sarah. Or was she there? Was she locked in the vault? He knew that four or five failed attempts would also lock down the vault for twenty-four hours, but he felt an unexplainable urgency to try.

"What's the address here? Seventeen what?" he asked.

"Seventeen sixty," replied Stick.

"That might work for the second code, but thinking about it, it's too obvious," Seamus said. He began to walk around the office. On one wall hung a variety of awards, photos, and other mementos. He scanned these decorations and a framed photo of a man who appeared to be Sayer's father, along with a newspaper article about the man and his obituary, drew his attention. Obviously, the father and his death held importance to Sayer. The man's date of death would qualify as an eight-digit number, but what would the four-digit code be? Sayer's birth date would be too obvious. He scanned the wall for more information, but found nothing useful numerically.

Seamus decided to try the date. He would know right away if the code was correct. If not, he'd have only a few more tries.

He entered 11231973 into the keypad and a blinking red light answered him.

Seamus pulled his cell phone from his pocket, scanned his recent calls, and hit redial on the number for Doctor Carney. The doctor answered on the second ring.

"Seamus O'Connor here, doc. We got a name for our John Doe. Chad Sayer, S-A-Y-E-R. Anything new?"

"Sorry, detective. Pretty much status quo. I'll keep you posted."

"Thanks." Seamus hung up. To expect the man to suddenly wake up and give them his combination was more than a long shot, but no more so than trying to guess at the numbers. Seamus felt drawn back to the photo and article. Returning to the framed piece, he looked at the nametag beneath the photo and the man's first name seemed to glow. *Where is this coming from?* Seamus wondered. He'd had good instincts in the past, but this was novel. He blinked his eyes, but upon returning his gaze to the nametag, the name still appeared highlighted somehow.

He thought about the name, Aaron. Only five letters, but if he took the numeric values of the letters, he came up with 11181514 – an eight-digit number. What about the four-digit number. The phase "father and son" came to mind. What would Chad give him? 'C' would be three. 'H' yielded eight. Then 'A' and 'D.' He had 3814, a four-digit number. That was it; he was sure of it.

He returned to the keypad and extended his hand toward it. Delaney stayed his hand.

"You sure you want to do that? There must be limits to the number of attempts. We don't want to restrict our safe expert tomorrow."

Seamus looked at him. The FBI now had jurisdiction over the site, but Seamus was confident he had the right numbers.

"Bill, don't ask me how, or where this insight came from, but I'm sure I have it. One more try. That's all."

The FBI agent shook his head. "Nope. We'll wait for the

expert."

"And what if Doctor Wade's locked in there? You willing to take responsibility for her death if she suffocates before your expert arrives?"

Seamus felt he was already behind the eight ball in shooting Deamus and abandoning the scene. What more could alienating the FBI cost him?

"Are you prepared to take that responsibility if you cause a lockdown," replied Delaney.

Seamus stared at the agent for a few seconds, and then on impulse punched in the eight digits. The light flashed green. He entered '3814' and the bolt mechanism slid open. With a gentle tug, he opened the door … almost as wide as Delaney's and Stick's mouths hanging open.

"How in the …"

"Told you, don't ask 'cause I don't really know. After you," Seamus said to Delaney.

Seamus followed Delaney into the vault. Empty. There were at least a hundred drawers of various sizes similar to safety deposit boxes except that they, too, appeared controlled by a separate keypad on the wall, not keys. Seamus had never seen this setup before.

The sense that Sarah was present surged through Seamus, even though the room held nothing more than secure, fireproof boxes. Frustrated, Seamus stared at his feet. *Sarah, Sarah, come out, come out, wherever you are.*

CHAPTER 53

Sarah felt the full impact of the moral conundrum she faced. She had chosen medicine as a means to save lives and help people. Yet, realizing she might now carry a deadly virus that could result in mass genocide, she battled between her oath to "do no harm" and self-preservation. If she simply stayed put, isolating herself in a lab that no one had located, she would avoid becoming a modern Typhoid Mary ... and die. Starvation was a miserable way to go.

Would hunger force her out? Would she be found so that her isolation could be maintained as she received medical care? Would she be found in time? Would they find her at all? Or would this lab be her tomb?

She eased down onto the floor next to the exit door, wondering what lay on the other side. She glanced at her wrist to realize they had removed her watch. Again she wondered, had she been there an hour, a day? Two days? Her clothes were dry and her bladder showed no strain. That alone argued for the brevity of her captivity. Still, she had no idea how long she had been unconscious after being drugged. She now appreciated the time disorientation that Della had described.

The blended hum of lab equipment, buzzing fluorescent lights, and blowing of the air supply system serenaded her. She would have no music or radio. No news of the outside world. Without a password, the state-of-the-art computers across the room would provide nothing but the annoying reminder that her multiple attempted logins had failed. She couldn't even double check the time and date.

Sarah closed her eyes, willing her mind to go blank. Wrestling with her dilemma had taken its toll, delivering a level of fatigue she'd never known. She drifted off into a restless sleep.

Sarah found herself in a hospital room gazing at John Doe who startled her by sitting up abruptly and grinning at her. His face began to change and evolved into the face of a black male she'd never seen before. He was there to tow her car from the parking lot. With a crooked smile, he looked at her.

"Yessiree, Doctor Sarah, the Good Lord's smiling on you. He's got a plan for your life. Don't be 'fraid of it. Let Him guide you."

Next, the face peered at her from a computer monitor. Just a disembodied head, floating randomly around the screen, smiling and talking.

"Hudson's the name ... he's still in the game. Hudson's got game, his name is the same. Go for it, girlfriend." The face seemed to distort as the words became gibberish.

Suddenly the face rushed at her. With a start, Sarah awoke just as the man's eyes seemed to merge with her own.

Sarah shook her head. "What a weird dream," she muttered aloud. But rather than dismiss it, she worked to remember every tidbit of it. John Doe. The face. God has a plan for her, would guide her. Hudson. Go for it.

An idea came to her. *It's worth a try*, she answered in thought. She stood and walked to the nearest computer. When prompted for a username, she typed in 'Hudson.' But what about the password? *His name is the same*, she recalled, so she typed in 'Hudson' again.

"Yes!" she exclaimed as the screen displayed the Windows desktop. With a quick move of the mouse, she checked the date and time. She'd only been there an hour and half. She had time. Even with a massive exposure, she couldn't be contagious this soon. At least, she didn't believe so.

She ran across the room and stood facing the large sliding doorway. Taking a deep breath, she pressed the button.

Seamus insisted on staying while the FBI took control of the warehouse and began the tedious process of removing documents, computers, and any other items it deemed pertinent to its case. He examined every door of every box inside the vault. And when his eyes seemed to cross from fatigue, he'd walk around the office, perusing items on the wall and occasionally removing one to look for anything that might be hidden or written on the back. Then, when he could see straight again, he'd resume his inspection of the vault.

After his visual inspection, he decided to try dusting for prints and coordinated his plan with the crime scene techs who were more than happy to have his help. The great majority of boxes were clean. Others showed minimal use with one set of prints found on each – prints that would no doubt take him to Chad Sayer. But one box was curiously clean of prints. Located near the door, it remained pristine while boxes all around it had prints and other signs of use. That struck Seamus as odd.

He stepped back to view the box from a different perspective and noted smudges on the flat, metal wall nearby. When he applied print dust to the area, an array of prints and partials emerged, from more than one individual it appeared. He used tape to lift those prints and with the chief technician's approval, began a closer look at the area with different lights and sprays. Nothing else emerged, but he noted that the prints seemed concentrated in one area. The idea of a pressure panel came to him and he pressed his thumb against the wall on top of a remaining print. With a slight click, the suspect box opened and slid out from the wall. It possessed no lid.

"Bill, Walt, check this out!" he shouted toward the office.

Delaney and his chief crime scene investigator entered the vault to look.

"I'll be damned, a biometric pad."

"For what purpose?" asked Delaney. "I mean, there is no other door. There's no space for any hidden rooms."

"Far as we know," replied Seamus.

"Not likely," countered the FBI agent. "We can account for the space behind each wall and above the vault. Nothing. Building plans show no basement, and even if they dug one secretly, how do they get there? There's no room for stairs or ramps here … or anywhere else in the building. The space is all accounted for." He paused. "Maybe it opens more of these boxes."

Seamus applied print dust to the pad revealing a blend of prints, none of which seemed dominant.

"That's worthless," stated the tech as he gazed at the results of the dusting. "Looks like a bunch of people have been using it."

"Yeah, which is curious since most of the used boxes show only one set of prints," said Seamus. "There's a blur of prints on the wall, and a similar blur here. Why? And why only here?"

Seamus knew he was on the right track. What did the pad trigger? The answer was there. All he needed was Sayer's thumbprint, but that wasn't going to happen real soon. Did he dare to try his luck again? He doubted his thumbprint would do anything, but he'd gotten this far. Still, he could cause an automatic lock-down that might trap them in the vault. His gut said 'go for it.' Taking a deep breath, he pressed his thumb against the pad. The door began to close.

CHAPTER 54

"What the f –" yelled a surprised Delaney.

"Crap, O'Connor. What'd you do now?" The chief tech tried unsuccessfully to stop the heavy door from closing. After it latched tight, he began to pound on the inside, as if someone outside might actually hear it through the layers of metal and reinforced concrete.

Seamus berated himself mentally. He had ignored his own thoughts about triggering a lock-down. Now, they were stuck in there. For how long?

Delaney's glare soon changed to a look of bewilderment. The whole floor slowly began to drop. "I'll be damned, O'Connor. How'd you figure this one out?"

Seamus shrugged his shoulders. "I didn't. I-I don't think I had anything to do with this."

The floor came to a stop and Seamus looked up. They had descended roughly fifteen feet. In front of him stood another doorway, which now began to slide open. Delaney pulled his gun, while all three men prepared for the worst, and then stood there, amazed, as Sarah stared back at him. Seamus started to rush toward her, but she backed away.

"I think they infected me. Don't touch me. Don't come near."

Seamus didn't stop. He'd already been down that road once. He grabbed her and squeezed. She pushed away.

"I knew you'd find me," she lied.

"I think you found us. We had no clue about this place." He turned and gazed at the surroundings. By pure serendipity, they'd stumbled onto the lab ... without Sayer's input. Or maybe it wasn't chance after all. He thought about the strange urgings and the other unusual events of the past week.

He turned to Delaney. "Looks like we found your secret lab. Now ... can we go back up and get out?"

All four entered the space and the chief tech started to reach for the obvious 'up' button when Seamus stayed his hand.

"If this works, we might not be able to get back down here

without demolishing this elevator. And that could risk releasing a major biological threat. Since it seems that no security measures were thought to be necessary down here, it seems reasonable that this thing can be operated from below without requiring a fingerprint scan. Someone should stay here at all times, at least until you can bypass the security above."

Delaney and his chief tech both nodded, and Delaney stared at his man and cleared his throat. "Walt?"

The tech reddened. "Yeah, yeah. I get the picture. I'm staying … but don't you leave me down here."

"Give us five minutes, then press the button. I'll send two of your people down to join you."

Walt stepped out and Delaney pressed the button. The technician waved as the doors closed. "Don't forget."

Seamus looked at Sarah. "We'd never have found this place if it weren't for you."

Delaney nodded in agreement. "That's right. That was quick thinking to leave your cell on for us to trace."

Sarah gave them a subtle smile.

The agent continued, "The timing was also good. One of the patrol cars saw the two vans leaving this lot just before spotting your car."

The floor came to a stop and the vault door automatically opened.

The two men exited the vault, but Sarah remained inside. Seamus saw the look of worry on her face and her alarm became his.

"Shay? There was a third man."

CHAPTER 55

Sarah slowly emerged into the office, a room she'd never seen. She gazed around the room and saw the photos and mementos on the walls. She recognized John Doe, but saw no one else she could identify. She sat down on a leather chair.

"I knew there were at least two men involved. One was in the car with me and one injected me as I entered the building. When I awoke in the lab, I saw three men in bio suits. One left the building about ten, fifteen minutes before the other two. He was carrying –" The memory hit her. "Airport. He's heading for the airport. He wore a grey hooded sweatshirt like the other two and carried a tank … like a fire extinguisher … but I watched them load it inside the containment lab. It must have the virus. He also had airline tickets. Not e-tickets, old-fashioned paper tickets. I saw them clearly. More than one. They must have planned on meeting at the airport."

She jumped up and breezed past Seamus toward the door.

"C'mon. We have to get to Lambert."

She turned back toward him, grabbed his arm, and started to tug. He resisted.

"Hold your horses. What did this guy look like? We can't just go into the airport and expect to see this guy. He's probably ditched the sweatshirt, and he didn't take a van like the other two."

"I-I don't know exactly. The hood covered his face as he left."

"Great. So we're going to go to Lambert International and try to find a guy carrying a fire extinguisher … or something like one. Sarah, think about the odds here."

"Look, Shay. Maybe it's not too late. Wouldn't he be highly suspicious walking into the terminal with a fire extinguisher? And the other ways onto airport property must have some tight security, too. Right? Maybe he hasn't gotten there yet. Maybe if airport security knows about him they can stop him before he gets lost in the crowds."

Delaney nodded. "She's right, O'Connor. Be easier to spot

him coming in than after he's loose on the concourses or inside the secure areas of the place." The agent retrieved his cell phone and placed a call, sending agents to the airport.

Seamus contacted dispatch, which patched him through to Airport Police headquarters. As he finished explaining the situation, Sarah heard him end with "... we hope to fax you a photo and identity ASAP."

Seamus turned to the others. "Don't want to be the party pooper here, but what if he has a fire department uniform? He could waltz right in with a dozen fire extinguishers and probably never be questioned. Or they could have people inside, someone able to pass them through security."

Delaney started to say something but stopped.

"What else do we have to go on, Shay?" asked Sarah.

Seamus looked blank for a moment and shrugged. "Guess it's the best we have. Let's go."

Delaney walked out to the warehouse giving instructions to another agent as Seamus and Sarah rushed past him toward Seamus' car. Racing out of the parking lot, full lights and siren, Seamus notified dispatch. "D3566 on route to Lambert." He then used his cell phone to call the BOI Commander and update him.

Sarah, lost in thought, tried to dredge up her memory of the man so she could provide something, some descriptive item that might help them identify him. As she struggled to recall her fleeting glimpse of the man, she instead recalled her dream. The face had said, "Hudson's still in the game."

"It's Hudson," she blurted out. "We're looking for Hudson."

Seamus eyed her curiously. "Doubt it. He's dead." He pointed to some files on the back seat. "Grab those. There are three men from Hudson's university lab in there. Deamus is dead. Heintzleman's in surgery at St. John's. We're missing Marcus Schmid. Got to be him."

Sarah obliged him and retrieved the files. She perused the folders to find Schmid's photo and studied it briefly before holding it up for Seamus to see.

"Kinda looks like Hudson, doesn't he?"

Seamus glanced at the photo. "Damn. I knew there was something about him that bugged me." He fiddled with his Bluetooth® headset and pressed the button on its side. A second later, he said "M.E." to voice-dial the medical examiner's office.

"This is Detective O'Connor. I need to talk to the doctor who did the Mitchell Hudson autopsy … Right away, please … Thanks. I'll hold." He zigzagged through traffic as he merged onto I-70 heading west toward the airport. "Hey, Doc. Seamus O'Connor. What do you have on the Mitchell Hudson case?" He listened. "Do we have a positive ID?" There was a longer pause. "Thanks, Doc. I might know who it is. I'll get back to you." He ended the call and looked at Sarah as long as he could safely.

"Looks like you might be right. The shotgun blast obliterated the face and the ME's speculating he threw his hands up to his face at the last minute because the fingers were pretty much gone as well. But he got a partial print on the right index finger and the CSI's found a tooth out in the yard. They don't match anything on file for Mitchell Hudson."

"I know I'm right." Sarah went on to explain the dream.

Seamus shook his head. "We're there." He showed his police identification, his left foot giving way to an impatient tapping as he waited for clearance. With a wave, they passed through the security gate, and drove to the police parking area on the west side of the lower main terminal. He took the files from Sarah and together they rushed into the police offices where Colonel Meriwether greeted them.

Sarah zoned out as Seamus re-explained the situation to the Chief of Airport Police. Anxiety pushed her to get onto the concourses and start looking, but she forced herself to remain calm and watched as Seamus provided a photo of Mitchell Hudson to the secretary for copying and dispersal.

"Can we start looking for him now?" she asked.

"Sure," replied Colonel Meriwether. "We'll need every set of eyes we can get. We'll pass this on to TSA as well."

The Colonel handed them security passes that allowed them

full access to all areas of the airport.

"What about evacuating the terminals?" asked Seamus.

"Not sure that would help," answered Sarah. "That might end up concentrating people in an even smaller area than they're in now and that would make it easier to expose them. Unless you can take 'em out onto the tarmac and spread 'em out."

Colonel Meriwether shook his head. "Already started the evacuation. Our protocols call for a thousand foot perimeter. Can't do the tarmac. Too dangerous. We're moving folks out past the parking garages and onto the access roads."

Sarah nodded. "Any wind at all will make it harder to disperse an airborne agent. Where can we help look?"

Seamus interrupted. "What about the aircraft? Could he hook a tank into the emergency oxygen system of one of the large planes?"

The chief looked pensive for a moment, and then replied, "Most of the planes here use an oxygen generating system. No tanks. The only ones to use the old tank and manifold setup wouldn't be likely to reach altitudes that would trigger the system during a decompression emergency." He paused and looked at Sarah. "Look, if he was carrying a tank the size of a fire extinguisher, there's no way he'd get in through the front doors. He'd have to come through a service gate and I've not heard of anything from those entryways. Let me team you each up with one of my guys and get you started in the service areas."

"Colonel, if it's okay, we both know who we're looking for. Let me start on the service areas and let Sarah start working the public areas. That way we can help cover both areas."

Colonel Meriwether cocked his head and said, "Fair enough."

Minutes later, Seamus and Sarah started out in different directions, each with an officer, and the tedious process of scanning faces and looking for suspicious activity began. As Sarah and her escort moved past the Post Office and USO lounge into the baggage claim area, Sarah realized just how long the odds were that Seamus had referred to earlier. There were hundreds of faces, milling around, being herded briskly to the ground transportation exits. Each was a potential target. Many of the men looked vaguely enough like Hudson, the right build or the right hair color and cut. Rapid identification was going to be difficult.

As they cleared the baggage claim area, Sarah noted no one attempting to drift back into the terminal. The faces around her showed determination and fear. They had to know something big was happening. She glanced up at the monitors displaying arrivals and hoped the arriving planes would be kept in a holding pattern. The officer with her continued through the lower level of the main terminal to the chapel and back through the baggage area one more time. They passed by the USO lounge again and then the Airport Authority Offices. When they approached the first set of public lavatories, the officer ducked into the men's side. Sarah did likewise in the women's restroom. The man, or the canister, could be anywhere.

Nearing the escalators and elevators next to Concourse B, Sarah noticed a surge of people heading for the exit doors. This group appeared more disorderly, panicky. The swell of bodies increased as they neared the escalators ascending to the upper level of the airport near Concourses C and D. Security staff and other airport personnel headed up the evacuation from the concourses, directing people to the multiple levels of the nearby parking garage. Sarah followed her escort against the tide.

They passed under the replica of the "Spirit of Saint Louis," Lindbergh's plane, and neared the security checkpoint. A scream penetrated the noise of the crowd and people began pushing and running from the area. Sarah scanned the surrounding area for the cause of the commotion while trying to stay on her feet as people pushed and shoved to pass her. To her left she saw it, smoke.

"Over there!" she yelled to the officer with her.

The officer was already on the move. A man in a maintenance uniform prepared a fire extinguisher and began to lift and point it toward the offending trash receptacle. Sarah ignored him. He was too short and blond. Not Hudson. And the tank had different markings. She searched the area again and saw smoke coming from the upper level as well. Above them,

Hudson appeared on the balcony overlooking the scene.

"Not him! Upstairs!" she screamed to the officer but he had already tackled the unsuspecting maintenance guy.

She raced for the nearest escalator but panicked people jammed the ascending stairway. She moved to the descending escalator and raced up against the movement of the mechanical steps. Keeping an eye on Hudson, she noticed that he, too, was being jostled by the crowd and having difficulty manipulating the tank he carried. She reached the top of the escalator as he began to lift the tank. He hadn't seen her yet.

The crowd pushed him against the railing. It almost seemed that he would be lifted up and over the railing but at the last minute he regained his footing. In the process, however, he lost the tank. Sarah watched and prayed as the tank fell to the floor. She could do little more than that. If it hit nozzle first and broke open, the tank itself could injure those around it as it flew out of control like an inflated balloon let loose. But that would also release its potentially deadly contents on the unsuspecting crowd and the consequences of that could prove far more disastrous. Sarah took a deep sigh of relief as it hit the floor on the bottom side of the tank.

Then he saw her.

She noticed the surprised look of recognition in his eyes, as if she wasn't supposed to be there. But she was there. And she was going to nail that sucker for what he'd done to her family … and for what he was attempting to do right then.

He reached for the tank, but the crowd pushed him back. He lunged a second time, but his reach was a few inches too short. As a gap in the fleeing throng allowed him to stand, he merged with the group and ran with the flow. Sarah kept her eyes on him. He diverted away from the exit doors and ran along the upper level of the main terminal, past the ticket counters, dodging people as they emerged from the ascending escalators near Concourse B.

Sarah fought the urge to follow. She needed to secure the tank first and foremost. She fought against the flow of people and managed to grab the handle of the tank. A man tried to take it away from her. She pulled back. He pointed to the smoke from a nearby trash receptacle, but Sarah shook her head.

"Not with this. It's not an extinguisher," she tried to explain as the man started to fight for it. She kicked him in the shins.

He leered at her and backed away into the crowd.

With tank in hand, she sped toward the ticketing area. She saw Hudson moving onto the last set of descending escalators at the end of the terminal, but stopped long enough to reach through a set of scales and set the deadly tank behind a vacant ticket counter. Then she took off at full speed for the final pair of escalators. Once there, she took no time to wait on the preset timing of the moving stairs. She took the steps two at time, nearly losing her balance twice as the stairs moved beyond her anticipated jump. At the bottom of the staircase, she stopped and turned her head in all directions, searching for her target. She saw him pushing through the security checkpoint to Concourse A, fighting past TSA agents intent on evacuating people and securing the airport.

Flashing her security pass, she ran through the checkpoint.

"Stop that man! Stop him!" Two TSA agents joined the chase.

Sarah was out of breath. She watched as he passed the tenth gate and rounded the corner toward the final gates of that concourse. She pushed through the tightness in her chest and continued after Hudson.

Suddenly from the right, the doors from the lower level burst open and Seamus and two officers lurched through a seating area toward the main corridor. Seamus led the charge and tackled Hudson. There was a brief skirmish on the floor and Hudson broke loose and started to regain his footing, but Sarah had caught up to them at that point and leapt on top of the geneticist. A minute later, two airport police officers dragged a handcuffed Mitchell Hudson away.

CHAPTER 56

"So, how's my favorite hero?" Seamus asked as he entered the hospital room where the CDC had quarantined Sarah for the previous ten days. He had been visiting as frequently as possible, but bureau debriefings, their continued work in tracking down MWA sympathizers, and press interviews had taken their toll on his schedule. He glanced around the hallway outside the room, surprised to see it emptied of the balloons, flowers, and children's drawings that had filled it less than a day earlier.

Seamus looked at Sarah sitting by the window gazing out toward the park. "Hey, this room looks desolate. What happened?"

She looked up at him. "I had the nurses take the balloons and flowers to patients who didn't have any. The drawings are packed up in that bag over there." She pointed toward the single small open closet where a paper grocery sack filled with paper sat on the floor.

Seamus held out a pint of Häagen-Dazs Mocha Almond Fudge and a spoon. She smiled fleetingly and turned back toward the window.

"Hey, this is your favorite. And you're going home this morning. Why the dour look?"

"Worried about Della and DeWayne."

"Why? Looks like they've turned the corner and will recover."

"I know. But at what expense?"

Seamus had no answer to that question.

"What about Sayer?"

"He's still not talking, but he continues to follow people around the room with his eyes and seems to understand simple commands. His doctors are encouraged."

Sarah nodded as she continued to gaze out the window.

"Hey, c'mon. What's eating you? It's certainly not Sayer's condition."

She turned back toward him and pulled her knees up to her chest, wrapping them in her arms.

"I can't help but think of what might have happened." She paused. "I received the CDC report a little while ago about their method. Using an anticancer therapy to overwhelm the immune system while introducing a virulent flu strain at the same time. It was truly capable of hundreds of thousands, maybe millions of deaths. I ..." She choked up.

"They didn't actually expose you." Seamus paused and smiled. "I mean, look at you, no effects at all." He walked over to her, picked up her hand, and urged her to her feet.

"Yeah, I've been wondering about that, too."

"The flu is the flu. Maybe they couldn't risk exposing you without a chance of exposing themselves."

She looked at him quizzically and shook her head.

"But I was infected. They had the bio-suits for protection. Besides, Hudson has been inquiring about me from jail. I heard he's bewildered that I'm not sick."

"Then, there's only one other option ... divine protection. And after all we've been through, and understanding the nature of these people, that's my choice. After all, if He could heal my leg, He could certainly protect you from that infection."

Sarah's grim mood turned reflective.

"Do you think?"

"I think. So does me priest, me saintly mother, and all me uncles. We men discussed it over a pint at O'Malley's ... and for once, six Irishmen agreed."

She smiled and chuckled at his flawless Irish brogue. Where had he been hiding that? Still, she had no such simple answer to her question, and realized she would never get one.

"Okay, then. I guess it's settled," she replied as she ripped the ice cream from Seamus' hands. "Won't stay frozen much longer. Want some?"

Her smile brightened as he handed her the spoon and produced a second from his pocket.

ABOUT THE AUTHOR

Braxton can't lay claim to wanting to be a writer all his life, although his mother and seventh grade English teacher were convinced he had what it would take. He went to Duke University, earned a Bachelor's Degree of Science in Engineering with a major in Bio-Medical Engineering, and found his way into medical school at the University of Cincinnati. Following a residency in Emergency Medicine at Madigan Army Medical Center, he served tours as the Chief, Emergency Medical Services at Fort Campbell, KY and as a research Flight Surgeon at Fort Rucker, AL. Who had time to write?

By the late 1990's, his professional and family life had settled down, somewhat, and his mother once again took up her mantra, "Write a book. You're a good writer." Yet, with no experience in writing anything other than technical articles, he hesitated to try his hand at fiction. That changed in 1997 when the local newspaper held a writing contest for Valentine's Day. Out of 1100 entries, he made it to the top five finalists and realized that maybe he could write fiction after all.

The next ten years saw him learning the craft of writing through local writers' groups, seminars, critique groups and more. His first three completed novels, tucked safely away in their digital prison, are unlikely to ever grace a page of e-ink - mostly because the stories are dated. "The Militant Genome" (©July 2012) marks his first formal publication.

Following the growing trend toward electronic publishing, the book is being released in the e-book formats first. Soon to follow are two additional novels, "Indebted" and "Identity." He is busy writing the sequel to "Identity" now (July 2012).

Fifteen years after that first hesitant start, he can't find enough time to write as much as he'd like. He now lives in Missouri with his wife, Paula. Their two children are grown and with three grandchildren nearby, "Papa" wears a number of hats.

16794966R10168

Made in the USA
Charleston, SC
11 January 2013